The Secrets of Sainte Madeleine

Tilly Bagshawe is an internationally bestselling author. A
mother of four, Tilly and her family divide their time between
their homes in Los Angeles and London. Educated in France
as a child, and a hopeless romantic at heart, Tilly was
inspired to write an epic family saga set in Burgundy during
a time when we were all dreaming of wine, wonder and
escape more than ever before.

Also by Tilly Bagshawe

Adored
Showdown
Do Not Disturb
Flawless
Scandalous
Fame
Friends & Rivals

The Swell Valley Series
The Inheritance
The Show
The Bachelor

The
SECRETS
of SAINTE
MADELEINE

Tilly Bagshawe

HarperCollins*Publishers*

HarperCollins*Publishers* Ltd
1 London Bridge Street,
London SE1 9GF
www.harpercollins.co.uk

HarperCollins*Publishers*
1st Floor, Watermarque Building, Ringsend Road
Dublin 4, Ireland

First published by HarperCollins*Publishers* 2022
1

A catalogue record for this book is available from the British Library

ISBN: 978-000-852182-0 (HB)
ISBN: 978-000-852183-7 (TPB)

Typeset in Sabon LT Std by
Palimpsest Book Production Ltd, Falkirk, Stirlingshire

Printed and bound in the UK using 100% renewable electricity
at CPI Group (UK) Ltd

For Leander and Etta.
Welcome, new guys.

'Where there is no wine, there is no love.'
(Euripides 480–406 BC)

PROLOGUE

The Legend of the Butterfly

Once upon a time, in a France now lost in dreams, when Louis of Orléans was king and all Europe trembled before him, a young man from Burgundy committed a terrible crime.

Some say that, maddened with drink, the man sold his wife and infant daughter to gypsies at a fair outside Flavigny. Others that he killed the child in a drunken rage and that her mother was so deranged with grief, she drowned herself in the Serein River. Whatever the truth, the young man was forced to flee his home in the beautiful village of Noyers. And from then on he carried with him the burden of a sin so great, he knew it could never be forgiven.

For many months he wandered, quite alone, seeking solace in nature and the rich, varied beauty of the Burgundy landscape. From the foot of the Morvan hills, he followed the River Yonne as it flowed through Chinon, Clamecy, Auxerre and Joigny, avoiding the townsfolk and keeping as much as he could to the unbeaten paths and trails. He hunted rabbits in the Forêt de Lancy and foraged for berries in the Forêt du Saulieu, sleeping on a bed of pine needles beneath

1

a blanket of pitiless stars. He made a solemn vow never to drink again, and never, ever to speak of the terrible thing he had done. Each night he cried out to God for forgiveness, for mercy. But, despite his penance, it seemed as if nothing would end his torment.

Until one morning, in a remote coppice outside Vézelay, the young man awoke to find an enchanting, pale yellow butterfly fluttering just inches above his face. When he sat up, the butterfly moved backwards slightly, then continued hovering in place. No flower or nectar seemed to be attracting it. It was there, he felt sure, for him. It was a sign from God, the miracle he'd been praying for.

Getting to his feet, the young man followed the butterfly out of the coppice into a meadow. For four miles he trailed doggedly in its wake until eventually it led him to a tiny hamlet of humble cottages, nestled in a hidden valley. Above the hamlet, at the top of the rise, the young man glimpsed a simple stone building. Framed with graceful arches, it was surrounded on all sides by fields full of vines, more green and verdant than any he had seen before. Figures in robes could be seen moving between the building and the vineyards, gliding back and forth as silent as ghosts. No sooner had the young man laid eyes on this vision than the butterfly disappeared.

'What is the name of this place?' the young man asked a passing villager, a fellow around his own age.

'Sainte Madeleine,' the villager replied.

'And the building on the hill?'

'That's the abbey.'

Certain that God had called him here, the young man climbed the hill. Close up, the abbey was even more beautiful than it had looked from the valley. Climbing roses covered much of its soft grey Burgundy stone, and on the upper floors, turrets and mullioned windows added to the general air of magic, like a fairy-tale castle.

Approaching one of the robed monks, the young man asked to see the abbot.

The abbot was an old man and a wise one. He listened to the young man's story, about the terrible sin he had committed, and his long journey, and the butterfly that had led him to Sainte Madeleine. But when the abbot asked him what the nature of his crime was, the young man refused to answer.

'My sin is too great, Father Abbot. I vowed never to speak of it. Not even to you.'

'No sin is too great for God to forgive,' the abbot told him. But he acknowledged the young man's vow, and agreed to let him stay and work in the abbey vineyards. 'The wines we produce here are the finest in all Burgundy. They feed not only ourselves but the entire village. The Lord has blessed Sainte Madeleine with fertile soil and clement weather. Our part is to repay his blessings with our labour.'

For three years, the young man worked diligently in the vineyards, planting and trimming vines, tilling the soil, picking the ripened grapes at harvest time. The work was hard, but the young man relished it, believing it was his penance and his path to salvation and that the butterfly that brought him here had been God's messenger.

But as the years passed, the harvests began to decline. Heavy rains came, and swarms of beetles, never before seen in this part of the Yonne. Summers became so scorchingly hot they cracked the earth and shrivelled the once plump fruit into useless, blackened raisins that fell from the vines before they could be plucked. Winters grew so cold they froze the ground solid.

Some of the monks started to whisper that it was the

young man's arrival at Sainte Madeleine that had triggered these catastrophes. They complained to the abbot. 'Ever since he came, the Lord has cursed us. We are all suffering for *his* sin. Soon the whole village will starve.'

At first the abbot dismissed their complaints. But after the fourth failed harvest, he called the young man in to see him.

'My child,' he said. 'You must confess your sin. Our Lord already knows all things. But he requires us to speak our offences aloud. Only then can we truly be redeemed.'

'I understand,' the young man said. He returned to his cell.

The next morning, the monks awoke to a miracle. Before their astonished eyes, a yellow cloud descended from the heavens and settled over the ruined vines. As the monks drew closer, they saw that the 'cloud' was actually butterflies, hundreds and hundreds of butterflies, but of a variety they had never encountered before, their wings as pale and delicate as spun gold. After a few minutes, the butterflies disappeared as one back into the blue, leaving behind them grapes as ripe and fleshy as any the monks had ever seen.

Overjoyed, they ran to tell the abbot. 'The harvest is saved! The Lord's favour is once again upon us.'

The abbot hurried to tell the young man the good news. But when he reached his cell, he found it empty. The young man had gone.

The monks of Sainte Madeleine gave thanks to God, and carved beautiful butterflies into the stone walls of their abbey, in remembrance of the miracle he had granted. From that day forward, the vineyards of Sainte Madeleine began to produce the finest vintage Bourgogne Rouge in all of Burgundy, year after year after year. The harvest never failed again.

* * *

A few days after the butterflies came, the young man's body was found hanging from a tree in the woods above Vézelay.

His sin had died with him, unspoken.

He never did break his vow.

PART ONE: ELISE

1923–1930

CHAPTER ONE

Christmas Eve, 1923

'Hey, that's not fair!' seven-year-old Elise Salignac squealed as the snowball hit the back of her head, breaking into a plume of icy crystals. Spinning around, she shook out her blond curls furiously, puckering her pretty lips into an almighty pout. 'I wasn't ready.'

'Then get ready, *pleurnicheuse*,' her brother Alex taunted her. 'It's a snowball fight! There aren't any rules.'

The three Salignac children, twelve-year-old Didier, eleven-year-old Alexandre and little Elise, were playing on the main lawn at Sainte Madeleine, the enchanting Burgundy estate that had been their family's home for generations. Originally planted by Benedictine monks in the fourteenth century, back when Sainte Madeleine was a remote and unknown abbey, the Salignacs' vineyard had long produced some of the region's finest Grand Cru wines. But it was the house, the chateau itself, that was the beating heart of the estate, and that the Salignac children loved with a fierce, consuming passion.

The original medieval structure had been added to over the years, making the present chateau a ravishing medley of different architectural styles and periods. But it retained a certain, simple, ecclesiastical beauty, a peacefulness that lingered everywhere from the arched windows along the *grand couloir*, to the flagstone floors, worn smooth from centuries of use, to the enormous baronial fireplaces, cavernous enough for a man to stand upright in without bowing his head. With its turrets and mullioned windows and its ancient oak doors, studded with iron rivets, the house felt like the children's own private fortress. Even more so today, enveloped on all sides by a thick carpet of freshly fallen snow, muffling the peal of the Christmas bells from the village church in the valley below.

'Duck, Elise!' Didier called out in warning, as another of Alex's icy missiles came flying through the air. But it was too late. This one went straight down Elise's back beneath the collar of her favourite red winter coat, painfully scraping her skin before it melted into freezing water.

Narrowing her eyes in anger, Elise squatted down and scooped up the soft flakes in her hands, trying to pat them into a solid ball the same way the boys did. But somehow whenever she tried it, it never worked properly. The snow remained resolutely loose and fluffy, soaking her knitted woollen gloves and freezing the tips of her frustrated fingers, leaving her with nothing to throw but a shapeless, soggy lump.

'Go easy on her,' Didier whispered to Alex, watching their little sister frantically scooping and patting to no avail. 'She's only seven.'

'She wanted to play,' said Alex defensively, effortlessly perfecting his own next ball.

'Only because she wanted to be with *you*,' Didier chided. 'You don't always have to be so competitive, you know.'

Seeing the two Salignac boys standing side by side, a stranger would never have taken them for brothers. Alex was strong and athletic, and took after his mother with his straw blond hair and cornflower blue eyes. Didier, although taller and older, was often mistaken for the junior of the two. Naturally skinny, with a pale, sickly complexion offset by very dark eyes, there was a certain skittish fragility about him that was at once endearing and unnerving, like a newborn foal.

Chastened by Dids's reproach, Alex set down his snowball and walked over to Elise.

'Not like that,' he told her gently, brushing the half-melted snow out of her hands and drying her gloves as best he could with his scarf. 'You have to press it together quickly. Like this.'

Forgetting her frustration, Elise paid close attention. She was determined to get it right, not only for herself but to please Alex. At this point in her life Elise Salignac lived for two things and two things only: learning about the ways of the vineyard – she was determined to take over at Sainte Madeleine one day, and wasn't going to let the small matter of her gender come between her and her destiny – and making her brother Alex proud.

It wasn't that she didn't love Didier too. Darling Dids was so gentle and shy and good-hearted, how could she not? But it was Alex she hero-worshipped. Confident, handsome, charming Alex, who Elise followed around slavishly like a puppy and did everything in her power to try to impress.

'I think I've got it.'

Delighted, she held up her first genuinely spherical snowball for his approval.

'Yup. That's it!' Alex smiled. 'Now go and chuck it at Didier.'

Elise joyfully hurled the snowball across the frosted lawn. As far as she was concerned, Christmas had already come early. A smile from Alex was all it took.

* * *

Watching her children from the warmth of the chateau's grand salon, Thérèse Salignac felt a rush of affection, followed by a familiar pang of anxiety. Didier really shouldn't be out there in this cold. Not for so long and with the light fading. His chest wasn't up to it.

She rang the nursery bell. It took about a minute for Brolio, the family's elderly and increasingly arthritic nanny, to appear at the door.

'Madame?'

With her stooped bony shoulders and craggy face, her thin skin as wrinkled as a pickled walnut and her eyes as dark and deeply set as two currants pressed into gingerbread, Brolio was as much a part of Sainte Madeleine as the chateau's walls and floor. Her real name was Madame Aubriau, but she'd been 'Brolio' to the Salignacs for as long as anyone could remember. Louis Salignac, Thérèse's husband, liked to say that the nanny's roots at Sainte Madeleine ran as deep as the vines. Although perhaps that was true for all of them, in a way.

'Oh, Brolio, there you are.' Thérèse turned to her with relief. 'Would you fetch all the children inside, please? And make sure Monsieur Didier takes a warm bath, right away.'

'*Bien sûr*, madame.'

'You can have Alissa light the fires upstairs as well, if she hasn't already.'

Brolio shuffled off. Moving away from the window, Thérèse resumed her own lonely place on the chaise longue, close to the fire. Picking up her book, a devotional text by the poet Marie de France, she tried to recapture the sense of calm she'd felt earlier, but it was no good. She couldn't focus.

Louis wasn't home. Still. And it was Christmas Eve.

The prospect of having to attend midnight Mass in the village tonight without him filled Thérèse with mortification and dread. Having to walk into that tiny church with the children, alone. Taking their seats in the front pew reserved for the Salignac family, in full view of all the tenants and estate workers and *their* families, knowing what people would be saying. Knowing, too, that they would be right. She couldn't bear the humiliation.

And yet, thought Thérèse, glancing around the elegant, vaulted drawing room in which she spent so many of the long winter days, *I must bear it*. Gazing up at walls hung with exquisite gilt-framed family portraits and priceless Belgian tapestries, surrounded on all sides by heirlooms and antiques and an eclectic array of objets d'art, Thérèse's heart sank, despite the loveliness of it all. The Christmas tree in the corner, gaudily decorated by Elise and the boys with enamel butterflies of every shape and colour, only served to deepen her depression.

I'm trapped, she thought. *Trapped, trapped, trapped, like a butterfly in a net.*

And I've only myself to blame.

The nursery at Sainte Madeleine was up in the eaves of the house, in what had once been the servants' quarters, back when the estate supported twenty or more staff.

Midnight Mass was over, a solemn affair without Papa, and Elise was tucked up in bed, too excited to sleep. Usually Didier and Alex slept in their own rooms. Only Elise was young enough still to be in the nursery. But it was a tradition at Sainte Madeleine for all the children to sleep in their old, infant beds on Christmas Eve and open their stockings together in the morning. So tonight both Elise's brothers were snoring just a few feet away when she heard it.

A creak on the stairs. Quiet at first, but then it grew louder, more rhythmic and familiar. Ecstatic, Elise sat bolt upright. She would have recognized that heavy footstep anywhere.

'Papa!'

Louis Salignac switched on the fringed standard lamp by the nursery door, bathing the long, beamed attic room in a low, orange light.

'Happy Christmas, *princesse*.' Taking a seat on the end of Elise's bed, he bent low, showering his only daughter with kisses while he waited for his sons to groggily come to.

'Oh, Papa, I knew you'd come,' Elise sighed.

'Knew I'd come? Well of course I've *come*. Where else would I be at Christmas, besides Sainte Madeleine?'

In a rocking chair in the corner of the room, her knees covered by a blanket, Brolio cleared her throat, making her presence known.

'Brolio!' Louis threw out his arms wide in a welcoming gesture. '*Joyeux Noël*.'

The old woman shot him a look that he understood perfectly. Brolio had been his nanny too, as a little boy, and her tolerance for the worst excesses of Louis's behaviour had not increased with age.

'Sorry to wake you,' he mumbled apologetically.

'Hm,' said Brolio. They both knew that disturbing his old nanny's sleep was the very least of what Louis had to be sorry for this evening.

'It's late,' the old woman observed pithily. 'The children need their sleep.'

'I won't keep them long, I promise,' he insisted. Turning back to Elise, he asked innocently, 'I just wondered, as I *am* back, if anyone here would like a story?'

'Me! Me! Me!' squealed Elise, wide awake now and looking deceptively angelic in her white muslin nightgown. 'I want the butterfly story!'

'*The butterfly story?*' Louis rubbed his chin theatrically, pretending to look confused. 'Hm. Now, which one would that be, I wonder?'

'You *know*, Papa! The legend. Our legend.'

'Just get it over with, Papa,' said Alex, also awake now, with a roll of his eyes. Secretly, he too was delighted their father had returned home, but was determined not to forgive him as instantly and completely as Elise had. 'None of us will get a wink's sleep till you do.'

'"*Get it over with*"?' thundered Louis, only half joking. 'Is that any way to talk about the legend of our ancestors?'

'We'd all like to hear the story, Papa,' Didier, ever the peacemaker, chimed in. Of all the children, he was the least happy to see Louis. But he couldn't deny Elise her joy.

'In that case . . .' Louis began, rubbing his hands together as he launched into the familiar tale about the sinful young man and the wise old abbot and the magical butterflies with the golden wings. He was a good storyteller, warm and engaging, and with a keen eye to his audience's reactions, always ready to tweak a yarn this way or that to make sure his listeners were satisfied.

By the time he reached the part about the yellow cloud descending from heaven, and the monks carving butterflies into the chateau's stone walls, all three children were rapt.

'Did you remember to touch the butterflies today?' Louis asked Elise, once he finally drew his tale to a close. 'You know that if you rub them with your fingers on Christmas Eve, that's when their magic is at its strongest.'

'Yes, Papa,' Elise nodded, gazing up at him adoringly. 'I remembered.'

'What about you, boys?'

Louis turned to Didier and Alex, also in their nightshirts, their long adolescent limbs tucked uncomfortably into the wooden beds they used to sleep in when they were little.

'Papa,' Alex groaned. 'I'm *eleven*.'

'And?' Louis shrugged, amused at his younger son's embarrassment. 'Didier, what about you? Are you too old for the magic of the butterflies?'

15

'No, Papa,' Didier mumbled awkwardly. 'Of course not.'

Louis seemed in a gentle enough mood this evening. But Didier had learned the hard way that the smallest thing could rouse his father's temper. Admitting that he'd forgotten to pay lip service to the old Salignac superstition might not be wise.

'The butterflies only work if you're a Salignac, right, Papa?' Elise asked, yawning loudly. 'It's *our* magic, isn't it? Nobody else's?'

'Well. It works best for us, Elise. Let's put it that way.'

Leaning forward, Louis tucked his daughter back in, kissing the top of her head indulgently. 'We're a very lucky family.'

The luckiest, thought Elise, wiggling her toes in contentment beneath the blankets. How wonderful that Papa had come home! She loved the way he smelled when he brought his face close to hers, of cigar smoke and patchouli aftershave and something else that she couldn't name, but that always made her feel safe and loved. She loved his warm, smooth hands, so different to Maman's cold ones, and the scratch of his stubbled cheek as it met her own.

'Right then,' Brolio said firmly. 'Time for bed.'

Elise watched as Louis walked over to each of her brothers' beds, tucking them in too and kissing them the way he used to when they were small. He was even kind with Didier, pretending not to notice his wheezing, and ruffling his hair the same way he did with her and Alex. Everything about tonight was perfect, Elise decided. Perfect, perfect, perfect. The nursery, the house, the butterflies. And now Papa returning from Paris, just in time for Christmas.

You could rely on Papa, in the end. And on the magic of Sainte Madeleine, always.

Once Louis had gone, the nursery was once again plunged

16

into darkness. Brolio returned to her own room, and everything was soon silent save for the sound of Didier's breathing as he slept, shallow and fractured after his latest chest infection.

'Alex?' Elise whispered in the darkness. 'Are you awake?'

'Mmmm,' he replied drowsily. Propping himself up on his elbow, he peered at her through the gloom. 'Are you excited?'

'*So!*' Elise gasped. 'Do you think Papa will have brought us big presents back from Paris? Like he did last time?'

'I expect so,' said Alex, trying to quash the anxious feeling making its way up from his stomach to his chest. He loved their father too, and was happy Louis was home for Christmas, no doubt laden with expensive, elaborately wrapped packages as Elise hoped. But over the course of the last year, Alex had begun to fear that perhaps Louis's bouts of unexpected 'generosity' might signify things other than just love for his children. Unhappy things. Complicated, adult things that Alex guessed at but chose not fully to understand. Holding on to the last vestiges of one's child-hood was a difficult business. One of the things Alex loved most about Elise was her complete and utter innocence.

'Do you think you might fall asleep more easily in my bed?' he asked her.

'Oh Alex, really? Could I?'

'Only if you promise to go to sleep and not wriggle.'

'I promise.'

Throwing back his blankets, Alex patted the sheet beside him. Bounding out of her own bed, Elise slid into the space he'd created for her, radiating excitement like a puppy. *If she had a tail, she'd be wagging it,* thought Alex lovingly.

'Merry Christmas, Alex,' Elise sighed dreamily.

'Merry Christmas Elise.'

'And don't worry about forgetting the butterflies,' she yawned. 'I touched them all three times, for you and Dids too. So Sainte Madeleine's magic will work for all of us now. You'll see.'

Thérèse Salignac stiffened as she felt her husband pull back the heavy brocade covers and climb into bed beside her. In a starched linen nightgown with the collar buttoned right to the chin, and with her long hair fastened in a tight topknot, Thérèse looked more like a nun, or perhaps an alabaster effigy of a saint, than a flesh-and-blood woman in the prime of her life. And a beautiful woman at that, with her high cheekbones, slender figure and mesmerizing almond-shaped eyes fringed with long, dark lashes.

At other times, Louis would have complained about the nightgown, or at least offered up a sarcastic remark. But not even he would dare to cross Thérèse tonight. Not after his latest disgrace and waiting until Christmas Eve to come crawling back to Burgundy in the small hours with his tail between his legs.

I must not succumb to anger, Thérèse told herself firmly. Not only was it unchristian – marriage was a holy sacrament, after all, and Our Lord enjoined all his children to forgive – but to lose one's temper over something as trivial and tawdry as an affair would be beneath her dignity, not to mention *deeply* bourgeois. If there was one thing Thérèse Salignac feared even more than eternal damnation, it was being perceived as middle class.

True, she had married beneath her, and she had only herself to blame for that. The Salignacs were an established Burgundy family, whose domaine produced perhaps the finest wines in the entire Yonne region. To the south and east of Paris, and the south and west of Aube, the Yonne was generally known for producing white Pinots – Bourgogne Blanc. But Sainte Madeleine had stood apart for centuries, producing world-class Bourgogne Rouge, unique and robust

18

red wines that had since become synonymous with the Salignac name.

Yet Louis's family were still winemakers. Not quite the dreaded *trade*, perhaps, but they nonetheless continued to work for a living and had nowhere near the pedigree and lineage of Thérèse's own family, the aristocratic Senards. Thérèse had made her choice however, marrying Louis for love, or so she'd believed at the time, joining her own substantial private fortune to his before dutifully settling down at Sainte Madeleine and bearing him three children.

Lovely children, she reminded herself now. *I have much to be thankful for.* Thérèse might not have Louis's warmth or easy manner, but she loved Didier, Alex and Elise every bit as much as he did. She'd grown to love Sainte Madeleine too over the years. Not just the chateau that had become her home, with all its romance and history: the timeless beauty of its medieval monastic archways, and the whimsical magic of the butterflies, lovingly etched into its thick stone walls. But the vineyard as well – stunning, serried rows of dark green Pinot Noir vines that cascaded from the rise at the top of the estate, like soldiers in some great, benevolent army, all the way down to the valley floor.

When Louis was sober, Thérèse found him charming and witty and handsome, albeit a trifle vain. He could be kind and generous too when the mood took him. Not a model husband perhaps, but a good one: the man Thérèse had fallen in love with. But a very different Louis Salignac emerged once the drink took hold. A man for whom duty, honour, decency and restraint had no meaning. When this Louis had a desire, be it for a new racehorse, a high stakes game of poker or a Parisian whore, he indulged it first, and dealt with the consequences later. Or failed to deal with them, as the case may be.

'Thérèse? Are you asleep?' Reaching tentatively over, Louis placed a warm hand on his wife's stony shoulder.

'No, Louis. I'm not asleep.'

Thérèse's voice was even, calm, like the still waters of a cold lake. Louis's heart sank. If only she could get angry at him, just once. Turned around and slapped him, or screamed or lost her temper; accused him to his face of being a philanderer and a coward. Anything to take the edge off his own guilt, his own inadequacy. Anything to give him hope that, despite his recent relapse, she still loved him. But she never did. All the self-control that Louis lacked, his wife possessed in spades. With her quiet superiority, she destroyed him.

'I'm sorry, Thérèse,' he mumbled, chastened. 'I didn't mean to stay away for so long. I got . . . caught up.'

'Really? Caught up with what?' she asked waspishly. 'Shopping? No doubt the children will awaken tomorrow morning to a mountain of presents.'

Louis winced. He had, indeed, gone overboard on the gift buying, not only for the children but for Thérèse as well, splashing out on an exquisite gold-and-ruby butterfly brooch from a famous jeweller in St Germain. A mistake, he realized now. The riot of boxes, bows and ribbons he'd left under the tree as a peace offering would only add fuel to his wife's fire when she saw them in the morning.

'Thérèse, listen—'

But Thérèse was in no mood to listen.

'Because of course that's exactly what our children need,' she steamrollered on, 'More material things. *Far* better than a father that sets them a good example. You spoil them, Louis.'

She looked at him with the resigned, maternal, pitying expression he so hated. It was designed to provoke, and it worked.

20

'It's Christmas, Thérèse,' Louis snapped. 'They're children. I may be to blame for many things—'

'May you, indeed?' Thérèse laughed.

'But I'm damned if I'm going to apologize for buying presents for my own children and my own wife. That's what Christmas is supposed to be about.'

'Is that so?' replied Thérèse, unperturbed by this outburst. 'And here was I thinking it was about the birth of Christ.'

An unhappy silence descended. To Louis's surprise, Thérèse was the first to break it.

'I heard you go up to the nursery earlier. How was Didier?'

The abrupt change of subject threw Louis off guard.

'He was fine. Why do you ask?'

'His breathing, of course,' said Thérèse. 'He's still getting over a ghastly chest infection. He's been really quite ill for the last three weeks.'

The accusation hung in the air, silent yet deafening: *which you'd know if you'd been here, instead of whoring your way around Pigalle.*

'He seemed fine,' said Louis guiltily. He hoped Thérèse was exaggerating. She'd always mollycoddled their eldest son, which was part of the problem, in his opinion. It didn't help that Thérèse refused to acknowledge there *was* a problem with Didier, insisting that he was merely 'sensitive' and that Louis's 'bullying' only made things worse.

'I'll check on him in the morning,' said Thérèse, rolling back over to signify that the conversation was over. 'Goodnight, Louis.'

'Goodnight, Thérèse.'

Louis heard his own voice echo off the vaulted walls of their bedroom and felt a dreadful loneliness descend. Stupidly, shamefully, tears pricked the backs of his eyes, but he blinked them away. Grown men did not cry.

Thérèse was angry because he'd strayed, and because he'd

stayed away too long. She had a right to be angry. But he hoped she'd soon forgive him. All men strayed, after all. Or at least all Frenchmen. He would stay off the brandy, knuckle down to work at the vineyard again, and repair the breach between them. All would be well.

Having thus successfully stuffed his conscience back in its box, Louis Salignac closed his eyes and fell immediately into a deep and dreamless sleep.

CHAPTER TWO

The summer of 1924 was one of the hottest anyone could remember in Burgundy. While wine growers complained about over-ripened grapes and an 'unbalanced' vintage, children enjoyed themselves paddling in streams and playing in the long grass, building tree houses and generally delighting in the permanent sunshine.

The Salignac children were no exception. Elise, in particular, immersed herself in all that Sainte Madeleine had to offer in the summer: the sights, sounds, smells and sensations of her secret kingdom. Throughout the house itself, doors and windows were left permanently open, allowing what little breeze there was to flow through and cool the chateau's grand rooms, carrying with it the scents of the garden. And what scents there were! Gardenia, freesia and wild-growing honeysuckle, closest to the house. Lavender and sweet rose from the formal gardens further down the hill. And beyond them, from the banks of the stream that coursed through the valley floor, the tangy reek of white garlic flowers. All of these competed with the delicious smells coming from Sainte Madeleine's kitchens, where the two cooks spent long, hot days producing feast after feast for the family and their guests. Heavy, pungent winter smells of roast lamb, onion and garlic were replaced with lighter, but equally enticing, summer scents: elderflower and lemon, lightly poached white fish, home-grown tomatoes as firm and juicy as plums, and a whole array of herbs from tarragon to coriander, basil to dill.

But a summer at Sainte Madeleine was a delight for all the senses. From the stone floors, worn smooth from centur-ies of use, that felt so deliciously cool beneath Elise's bare feet, to the warm grass of the formal lawns, as soft as any feather bed when you lay back and gazed up at the butterflies and bees, dancing across the bright blue canvas of the sky, the entire estate was like something ripped from the pages of a fairy tale.

And yet this summer had been far from a fairy tale for Elise. More of a nightmare, in fact. The blame for that lay squarely with Elise's cousins, the Senards.

Senard. Even the name had come to irritate her, like something horrible stuck in the back of her throat. Distant cousins of Maman's, Roger and Camille Senard and their boys, Thierry and Laurent, had stayed at Sainte Madeleine before, apparently, although Elise had no memory of them.

They'd arrived three weeks ago, on an even hotter day than this one. To her delight, Elise had seen a rare butterfly settle among the lavender, a yellow and black Scarce Swallowtail, and had been following it down the hilly gardens with her net when she suddenly careened head first into a pair of skinny legs. By the time she'd recovered sufficiently to look up and see that the legs belonged to a very tall, very pale boy she'd never met before, with curly dark hair and dark brown, playful eyes, the butterfly had gone.

'I've lost it!' she said furiously, retrieving her net and glaring at the boy.

'Lost what?'

'My Scarce Swallowtail,' Elise snapped. 'I was just about to catch it and you tripped me up.'

24

'How did I trip you up?' the boy protested, amused. 'I was just standing here, minding my own business, and you ran directly into me. I'm Laurent, by the way.'

'That butterfly was going to bring me good luck and you ruined it,' seethed Elise, who was not in the mood for introductions. To her immense irritation, the boy burst into laughter.

'If it's better luck you're hoping for, try looking where you're going!'

After this inauspicious start, the Senards' visit only got worse. Roger and Camille seemed nice enough for grown-ups, as did the older son Thierry who, at eighteen, was fully a man in Elise's eyes. But fourteen-year-old Laurent Senard was a royal pain in the neck, acting all worldly and mature, and completely dazzling both of Elise's brothers, but especially Alex, whom he'd effectively 'stolen', to Elise's dismay.

I hate him, she thought now, glaring through the wire fencing that surrounded the tennis court like a prisoner peering miserably through their cell bars as she retrieved yet another of Didier's mis-hit balls, watching Laurent's long, skinny arms swaying like branches in the wind as he leapt around the court. *I hate him, and I hope he falls in a well and drowns.*

The tennis tournament had been Papa's idea.

There was an old, grass court at Sainte Madeleine, right at the bottom of the gardens close to the chateau gates. Jacques, the groundsman, was responsible for mowing the grass and then rolling it flat with the heavy stone roller that Arnaud Berger had unearthed from the back of one of the old barns up at the winery. Sometimes Alex and Elise would help with rigging up the net and painting the white lines carefully along the edges of the court, although they rarely actually played. But this summer Louis was determined that the court should see some use, and the Senards' visit was the perfect excuse.

The four boys would play doubles and Elise could be ball girl. At first Elise had been happy with the idea, especially as being ball girl meant that she got to wear her new, frilly white tennis dress without the bore of actually having to play. But as the match wore on, and she found herself being sent scrambling after balls hit into bushes and flowerbeds and even patches of stinging nettles, mostly by poor Didier, the whole experience began to wear thin. Add to that the fact that Alex had spent the entire afternoon laughing and sharing in-jokes with Laurent, whom he obviously hero-worshipped, and completely ignoring Elise, and her misery and resentment became complete.

'Game!' Roger Senard, the self-appointed umpire, shouted cheerfully from his courtside perch as his eldest son served yet another exquisitely executed smash. 'Thierry and Didier lead two games to one in the second set, and one set to love.'

Elise sat sulkily in the shade while the boys took a break to get water. It was painfully hot. Even Alex, who was very fit, had sweat pouring off him and was panting like a dog, and Laurent was in a similar state. Poor Didier looked like he might be about to faint, as red in the face as one of Maman's hothouse tomatoes and with his chest heaving in and out like a set of fireplace bellows as he slumped down at the side of the court. Only Thierry Senard looked relaxed, sauntering over to his water bottle and towel, apparently without a care in the world. But then everybody knew that Thierry was special: academically brilliant, classically handsome, terrific at all sport and, supposedly, one of the finest shots in all France. Papa never stopped wittering on about how marvellous he was.

'Is Didier all right?' Camille, the Comtesse Senard, said, leaning over confidentially towards Thérèse. The two women had been close friends since girlhood, even before

Camille had married Roger, who happened to be Thérèse's third cousin. 'He looks like he's struggling a bit.'

Thérèse's upper body stiffened, her eyes fixed on her elder son. Poor Dids! He was, indeed, struggling, and the maternal lioness within Thérèse longed to run onto the court and yank him out of there. Let him lie down in a cool, dark room and read, which was all the poor boy had wanted to do this afternoon. But she knew that if she did it risked precipitating a full-blown row with Louis, which was the one thing Didier dreaded most of all. Louis had always been intolerant of their eldest son's sensitivity – or 'weakness' as he saw it – and had consistently favoured Alexandre over Dids.

'He can't even bloody hunt,' Louis had complained a few years ago when, at a Boxing Day meet, Didier had collapsed from an asthma attack, his entire face swollen, his eyes red and streaming – a 'virulent' allergic reaction to horses, as Dr Villars later explained. 'What earthly use is a son who can't hunt?'

Thérèse wondered whether some of her husband's anger might be born from jealousy. Because Didier was their firstborn, and *she* had loved him so much from the beginning, perhaps Louis had felt pushed out? Whatever the reason for it, Louis's discomfort not only with Didier's physical limitations but with his interests and personality, seemed to be getting worse as the boy grew older and failed magically to transform into the manly, physical, outdoorsy son that his father would have preferred.

Every now and then Louis made an effort to be kinder to Dids. Last Christmas, Thérèse remembered, he had really tried, and for a short while Thérèse had secretly hoped that the father–son relationship might have turned a corner. It was one of the things that had helped her to forgive Louis for his last, disastrous affair, with the dreadful dancer from Folies Bergère. But by the spring, everything had deteriorated again. Consumed with work up at the vineyard – spring meant vine replanting, bud break and flowering, and was always one of the busiest times at Sainte Madeleine – Louis would come home from the vineyard tired and irritable, and it was inevitably Didier who bore the brunt of his moods. The whole situation pained Thérèse greatly, but she was at a loss as to how to improve things.

'I think Didier will be all right,' she told Camille hesitantly. 'Once he's had a rest and a drink. He's not a natural sportsman like your boys.'

'Oh, they're all different,' Camille said kindly, laying a comforting hand over her friend's. 'Laurent's not nearly as sporty or competitive as Thierry. Alex has been making all the points for their team, if you hadn't noticed.'

A year older than Thérèse and much physically plainer, with a solid, square-shaped head, a blunt nose and the sort of wiry, springy hair that refused to be tamed and that she therefore always wore pulled back, lending her a severe look entirely at odds with her character, Camille Senard was a kind woman and a good friend. Like everybody else, Camille had been surprised when Thérèse chose to marry the handsome and dashing Louis Salignac, rather than some quiet, cerebral aristocrat, as they'd all expected. Not that Camille disliked Louis. He could be great fun, when he wasn't drinking. It was simply unfortunate that he and Thérèse had so little in common. And that he was so hard on his eldest boy.

Glancing over at him now, as the match resumed, Camille noticed that Louis had refilled his rosé glass for at least the third time since lunch, and that a dark, brooding look had come over him, which rarely boded well.

Camille's own husband, Roger, wasn't much to look at, despite having fathered two remarkably good-looking sons. Short and round with ruddy cheeks and a hairline that had started to recede in his twenties and never stopped, he wasn't handsome like Louis Salignac. But he was kind, without a trace of his cousin Thérèse's snobbery, despite having inherited one of the grandest estates in all Burgundy, the magnificent Chateau Brancion. He was funny too, and thoughtful and utterly reliable. Privately, Camille had no doubts that she'd made the better marriage of the two.

Elise watched through narrowed eyes as Laurent Senard prepared to serve, willing him to make a mistake. What was it that Alex found so compelling about him?

Since the butterfly incident, Elise had had plenty of time to consider her nemesis objectively. Dark-haired, tall and skinny, with a long nose that did sort of suit him, Laurent seemed to Elise neither ugly nor handsome. Unlike his older brother Thierry, who even Elise had to admit was jolly good-looking for an old person and who all the girls apparently swooned over. Not that Elise gave two hoots about the way either of the Senard boys looked. All that mattered to her was the mysterious hold that Laurent had developed over Alex. *Her* Alex. It made no sense, that was the infuriating part. Laurent was so much less fun than Alex, so serious and boring, always joining in with the grown-ups' conversations about things like politics, which Elise knew for a fact Alex found as tedious as she did. So why was he suddenly pretending to like them, pretending to care, just to please this gangly dark-haired imposter?

Tossing the ball in the air, Laurent cartwheeled forward, his long arm arcing down so that his racquet connected with the ball at exactly the right angle, sending it flying low and fast over the net. *Not a bad serve*, Elise thought grudgingly.

Didier, intensely focused, staggered backwards, reaching behind him to attempt a return. But the ball only connected with the wood at the top of his racquet, and at a speed that sent it flying out of the court yet again, this time in the direction of the kitchen garden.

'Fifteen-love!' called Roger Senard cheerfully as Elise scrambled off after the ball.

But Louis could take no more. Storming onto the court, wine glass in one hand and the other clenched in a furious fist, he marched up to Didier and began screaming at him, hurling insults like a schoolyard bully.

'What in Christ's name is wrong with you?' he erupted. 'Elise could have made that shot!'

Too far away to hear what was being said, Elise registered her father's raised voice and turned to see him looming over a cringing Didier. For a moment her anger at Laurent was forgotten, replaced by a familiar, unpleasant churning in her stomach. She loved Papa, but she loved Dids too, and she wished Papa wouldn't be so terribly hard on him.

Back on the court, an uncomfortable silence had fallen, broken only by Louis's intermittent ranting.

'Do you know how embarrassing it is to have to stand here and watch you letting Thierry down, game after game, point after point?' he seethed. 'You're not even *trying*.'

'I am trying, Papa,' Didier stammered, doing his best to keep his cool in the face of Louis's rage, his red face and threatening gestures and his yelling, so close that balls of angry spittle landed on Didier's face with each spiteful word.

Returning reluctantly with the retrieved tennis ball, Elise could see that her brother's hands were shaking.

'You're useless! You're a bloody donkey,' Louis slurred, losing his footing for a moment in his fury and sloshing a good half of his wine down his shirt. 'Now look what you made me do.'

'Come along now, Louis,' said Roger, stepping down from his umpire's chair to intervene while the other three boys stood awkwardly around, unsure what to do. 'It's only a game. And Laurent does have a very strong serve.'

Muttering something about it not mattering what sort of serve Laurent had, Didier would still have swiped at it like a little girl, Louis left the court in high dudgeon and began weaving his way unsteadily back up the hill to the house. Elise watched him go, heartsick for Dids, and for Papa, and for everyone. Maman looked white as a ghost, sitting with Camille Senard by the side of the court.

Why did these things have to happen? Why couldn't stupid Laurent have sent Didier an easier serve?

The match resumed, but although everybody felt calmer without Louis's angry presence, it was clear that the fun had gone out of it like air from a popped balloon. Ironically, Thierry and Didier won in the end, but only because Thierry could have outplayed all three of the others with one hand tied behind his back. Afterwards, Alex and Thierry helped carry the deckchairs, plates and glasses back up to the summerhouse while Elise scurried around the court, gathering up any remaining balls. Laurent stayed behind, walking over to where Didier was miserably zipping his racquet back into its canvas case, trying to catch his breath.

'You did very well,' Elise heard Laurent telling him.

Didier smiled. 'Thanks. But we both know I played dreadfully.'

'I'm not talking about the tennis,' said Laurent, with a forcefulness to his tone that Elise hadn't heard from him before. 'Who could care less about tennis? I'm talking about the way you handled your father.'

Didier's eyes welled with tears. 'I was so humiliated. So ashamed,' Elise heard him admitting. She watched as Laurent wrapped an arm around her brother's shoulders and squeezed.

'You've no reason to be,' he said supportively. 'I mean it, Didier. You were brave, you stood your ground.'

'Do you really think so?' Didier asked hopefully.

'I do,' said Laurent. 'The only person who should be feeling ashamed is Uncle Louis.'

He left after that to help the others with the clean-up. But Elise saw the effect his kindness had had on her brother, and it stayed with her.

She still hated him, of course. For monopolizing Alex, and ruining her summer. But a small, grudging part of her had to admit that perhaps her distant cousin Laurent wasn't *all* bad.

On the last day of the Senards' visit, Elise was up in the vineyards, watching the men work. At this time of year both the winery and the vineyards were a hive of activity, with final preparations being made before the all-important September harvest. As usual, Louis had brought in seasonal workers to help with the mammoth task of trimming back the vines to the height of the three-foot trellis. While many Burgundy vineyards were modernizing, using tractors for their trimming and only pinching out the surplus grapes by hand, at Sainte Madeleine things were still done in the old way, by men as sun-weathered and rooted to the soil as the vines themselves. In a domaine the size of the Salignacs' this was truly a gargantuan effort, and one that Elise had watched, entranced, every summer since she was born.

Arnaud Berger, Louis's vigneron and one of the estate's longest-standing and most senior employees, eyed the little girl affectionately as he ran his gnarled hands over each plant, considering which leaves if any to trim. The wine they produced – Sainte Madeleine Grand Cru – was the lifeblood not only of the Salignac family but of an entire community. Every cottage in the village, every family, depended on the success of the vineyard. Even the school-teacher and the priest relied for their livings on continued good harvests, and the reliable delivery of top-flight vintage Burgundy. It was a responsibility that Arnaud took seriously, and he knew his master, Louis, did too – even if his enthusiasm for the family business was not as consistent as some might have wished.

At his best Louis could be innovative, visionary and genuinely inspiring, and his passion for the family wines and knowledge of viniculture ran deep. But at his worst, and particularly when he succumbed to the demons that led him to drink, he could be a dreadful bully. Even worse, in Arnaud's opinion, he became closed to advice and spent too much time in Paris, investing in all sorts of businesses and ventures that he didn't really understand. To produce top-flight Grand Cru Burgundy, in Arnaud's opinion, one needed to live and breathe the grapes. Modern technology was all very well, and it had its place in a twentieth-century winery. But there could be no substitute for the intimate connection between man and vine, that divine intermingling of roots, both physical and spiritual, that had been at the core of Sainte Madeleine's since the monks first settled here all those centuries ago.

Arnaud looked at Elise again as she walked through the corridor of vines. He was fond of all the Salignac children but Elise was his favourite, with her fat, baby cheeks framed by plaited pigtails, and her playful eyes the colour of violets. It was sad in a way that she wouldn't grow up to take over the winery, as she had such a fierce interest in the family business. She spent untold hours in the vineyard, eagerly soaking up the magic, mystery and alchemy that went into producing world-class Bourgogne Rouge. But the running of Sainte Madeleine would pass to her brothers eventually. Most likely to Alexandre, who was also captivated by the vineyard, although Arnaud liked to think that there was still hope for Didier to discover his own passion for the family wines.

Louis had made financial provision for Elise in his will. But her destiny involved marriage and children and domestic concerns. Hopefully on another grand French estate, but certainly not here.

It hadn't escaped Arnaud's notice that this summer Elise been coming up to the vineyard more and more by herself, with only her tatty rag doll Sandrine for company.

'Shouldn't you be getting back, *princesse*?' he asked, snapping off a single, wayward leaf before moving up the row to the next vine. 'Tea's at five thirty, isn't it? It's almost six o'clock now.'

Elise shrugged, rearranging her doll's soft limbs in the seat she'd made of her long skirt, stretched over crossed legs. Arnaud loved the fact that she was perfectly happy sitting in the dirt, watching him work and chatting for hours. Elise appreciated a pretty frock as much as the next girl, but she also had a tomboy side. There were no airs and graces about her. Arnaud hoped she stayed that way.

'It's only me for nursery tea today,' she told him. 'The boys are to stay downstairs for grown-ups' dinner because it's the Senards' last night.' The word 'Senard' dripped with bitterness, like a grape crushed too early. 'So I don't think it really matters when I get back.'

'I dare say it matters to Brolio,' the old man muttered, his eyes fixed beadily on the plant beneath his fingers. 'If she's gone to the trouble of making you a *croque* and a *lait chaud*, she won't want it going cold.'

Elise shrugged again sullenly. 'She won't mind.'

This earned a pause, head turn and eye-roll from Arnaud, a rare enough event to make the little girl giggle.

'Oh all right, she *will* mind. But do I really have to go? Can't Sandrine and I stay here with you, Arnaud?'

Reaching out, the old man rested his calloused palm on Elise's blond head.

'Is it really so bad back at the chateau?' he teased her gently.

Elise nodded. 'It is with *them* here.'

'Don't your cousins leave tomorrow?' Arnaud asked.

She nodded again.

'Well then. It will soon be over.'

'So will the summer,' Elise observed miserably. 'And I've missed it.'

'Come now. How have you missed it?' Arnaud frowned.

'I haven't had *any* fun with Alex.'

'Really? Not *any*?'

She shook her head.

Arnaud squatted down on his haunches so that his lined, rheumy old eyes met hers.

'Listen, *princesse*, I know the boys have been leaving you out a bit recently.'

'A *bit*?' Elise's eyes widened indignantly.

'But you shouldn't blame Alex for wanting a lad his own age to play with. He sees your cousins once a year at most. You and he see each other all the time.'

Elise pouted, the famous Salignac stubbornness flashing in her eyes.

'I don't blame Alex. I blame him. Laurent.' She spat out the name like a rotten plum. 'He's not even interesting.'

'Is that so?' Arnaud asked archly. For someone who wasn't interesting, Elise certainly talked about the younger Senard boy a great deal.

'Yes, it is,' she insisted. 'He doesn't like any of the things that Alex and I like: making camps or swinging over the river, or helping you in the vineyard. All he likes is *talking*.' She frowned disdainfully. 'Talk, talk, talk. Blah, blah, blah. He thinks he's a grown-up and he's *not*.'

'He's kind though, isn't he?' Arnaud reminded her. 'Alex told me that he stuck up for Didier when Papa was being hard on him, more than once. Is that true?'

'Well, yes,' Elise admitted grudgingly. 'But I don't care about kind.'

This last declaration was made fiercely and not entirely

convincingly. Balling her little fingers into a fist, Elise pounded it furiously against the cracked, dry earth, not entirely sure what it was she felt so cross about.

'Well,' Arnaud smiled. He loved her best when she was angry. It suited her pugnacious spirit. 'Tomorrow he'll be gone. Poof. You can survive for one more night, can't you, *ma princesse?* All good winemakers need to have patience, after all. And I know you're a good winemaker.'

Standing up suddenly, Elise flung her arms around Arnaud's waist and hugged him tightly. She didn't say anything. She didn't need to. The love and understanding between them went beyond words.

At that moment the figure of the Salignacs' ancient nanny appeared at the crest of the hill where the chateau's grounds met the vineyard, *bâton de marche* clutched determinedly in her hand.

'Uh-oh.' Arnaud nudged Elise. 'Here comes Brolio. I think she means business.'

Elise shot up, brushing the worst of the dust from her skirts. Brolio hated it when she came back from the vineyards looking like a *va-nu-pied*, a ragamuffin. Clutching her doll tightly in one hand, Elise reached the other around Arnaud's neck and kissed him, before flying down the hill towards her nanny, a stream of '*pardon*'s and '*j'ai perdu la notion du temps!*' flowing from her grape-stained lips.

Arnaud watched her go wistfully. The world was changing. France was changing, permanently, he suspected, and not for the better. The old, class-driven order and traditional, rural way of life in which Arnaud had grown up would not return. The Great War had seen to that. Here in Burgundy, with so many young men off at the front, vineyards had been left in the hands of women, children and old men like Arnaud. And when so many of the young men failed to return, the fabric of the old, pre-war society had been torn beyond repair.

Elise had been born in the midst of war, at a time of seismic and profound change. And yet, in Arnaud's eyes, her innocence and wild spirit were reminders of an earlier time, and of all that was still good in the world. It made him sad to think that they, too, would be gone one day. He hoped he wouldn't live to see it.

CHAPTER THREE

Formal dinners at Sainte Madeleine were always impressive affairs, and the farewell to the Senards was no exception. The chateau boasted two dining rooms, a cavernous medieval hall, built originally as a refectory for the abbey's monks, and a smaller but more luxuriously appointed *salle à manger*, where this evening's feast had been laid. No fewer than six of the famous butterflies had been carved into the stone walls of this room, most of them beneath the mullioned windows, and a series of rare and lovely hunting tapestries hung from the high stone walls.

Thérèse, in particular, loved the small dining room with its perfect melding of warmth and grandeur. Conscious as ever of putting her best foot forward in front of Roger and Camille, she'd had a selection of the finest Salignac silver brought out for tonight's farewell dinner, as well as some valuable crystalware that she'd brought with her when she and Louis married. Louis had generously filled the glasses with one of the domaine's best bottles of 1900, a legendary year across Burgundy, famed for its soft, light reds, although he pointedly stuck to water himself. Ever since the tennis match incident he'd made a point of entering one of his intermittent periods of abstinence, to prove to Thérèse and to himself that his drinking was a choice rather than a compulsion. He tended to be more subdued during these interludes, quieter and occasionally even depressed. But this evening, thankfully, he was on excellent form, chatting amiably with Thierry Senard about his plans for next year.

'I did think about university,' said Thierry, elegantly spearing a sliver of roast duck with his fork. 'But when the opportunity came up for a commission in the Second Dragoons, I knew it was the right choice.'

'I should say so,' Louis leaned forward enthusiastically. 'Isn't that the oldest regiment in the country?'

'It certainly is,' chimed in Roger. 'Thierry will make a fine officer.'

The Senards' oldest son was unquestionably one of the most eligible bachelors in Burgundy, if not in all of France, with his classic good looks, easy charm, athleticism and keen intelligence, all on top of the magnificent estate and private fortune he stood to inherit. But despite these advantages, Thierry Senard was humble, sometimes to a fault.

'You know, I envy you Thierry,' said Louis. 'I'd have loved to have taken a commission myself as a young man. But my father died young, you see, and there was no one else to take over at Sainte Madeleine.'

'Yes of course, sir. I can see that,' Thierry nodded dutifully.

Camille Senard glanced over at Thérèse, who stiffened but said nothing. If Louis had ever wanted to be a career soldier, it was only because he would have looked dashing in regimental colours. It was an unspoken but widely known point of shame within the family that Louis Salignac had shirked his military service as a young man, actively avoiding his duty in order to carry on with his party life in Paris. He'd barely set foot on Sainte Madeleine during those years; although he had striven to make up for it later, committing himself to both married life and the estate in his thirties as best as his nature would allow, and fighting bravely, if briefly, at the second Battle of Albert.

'But you'll be an asset to the dragoons, I'm sure.' He smiled at Thierry. 'And France may yet need all the good men she can get, now that Monsieur Doumergue's at the helm.'

Thérèse's heart sank. Why must Louis *insist* on bringing up politics in the middle of a perfectly convivial dinner?

'President Doumergue's not as good as President Millerand was, is he, Papa?' said Alex, who had as little interest in politics as his mother, but wanted to sound grown-up in front of Laurent.

'He's not as good as the shit on my shoe,' muttered Louis.

'Louis, really!' Thérèse frowned disapprovingly.

'What your father means is that Monsieur Domergue is a socialist,' Roger explained to Alex. 'I'm afraid socialists don't think very highly of families like ours.'

'Why not?' asked Didier. He rarely risked asking a question in public in front of his father, but his uncle Roger's kind tone emboldened him.

'Because they're jealous, corrupt, self-serving upstarts,' Louis responded, warming to his theme. 'You can never trust a socialist, boys. Never. Remember that.'

Setting down his knife and fork, Laurent Senard fixed his uncle with a level gaze. 'I'm not sure that's fair,' he announced boldly. 'After all, the president's job is to represent all of France, is it not? Not just wealthy families like ours.'

'Well, that's true, of course,' admitted Louis, wrongfooted.

'Thanks to Millerand, inflation's out of control,' Laurent continued, with a quiet confidence that Louis found unnerving, and not a little irritating, coming from a fourteen-year-old boy. 'Many families can't even afford to buy bread. Shouldn't they be Monsieur Domergue's priority, not us?'

'Maybe, Laurent,' Thierry piped up from the other end of the table. 'But those families won't be helped by another war with Germany. The socialists insist on provoking our enemies, fanning the flames of division.'

'And *we* won't be helped if we're marched to the bloody guillotine,' muttered Roger, earning eye-rolls from both his sons and a giggle from Alex. The way the older generation talked, you'd think the revolution had been yesterday.

'You boys laugh, but it could happen,' Camille chided gently. 'Just look at Russia. It's only six years since the poor Romanovs were murdered. We must never forget that.'

To Thérèse's relief, Sainte Madeleine's two maids, Alissa and Angelique, bustled in at that moment and began clearing away the duck in preparation for dessert. Cook had prepared her pièce de résistance tonight, a towering pavlova made with raspberries picked fresh from the kitchen garden this afternoon. Seizing her chance to steer the conversation back into safer waters, Thérèse turned to Camille.

'What are your plans for the autumn at Chateau Brancion?' she asked. 'Socially, I mean.'

'Nothing terribly exciting, I'm afraid,' Camille reported, a touch ruefully. 'There's the hunt ball of course, in November. You'll both come to that?'

'Of course,' Thérèse assured her.

'Wouldn't miss it,' Louis concurred, risking a smile at his wife.

For once, Thérèse returned it. He was still so handsome, she reflected, and so charming, when he was sober and made an effort.

'I say, look at that!' Roger Senard said as an enormous bowl of berries and meringue was set down in front of him. 'What a treat, eh boys? I must say, Thérèse, your cook knocks the socks off ours.'

The rest of the dinner passed uneventfully, with most of the talk about Thierry's exciting new regiment and Alex and Didier's complaints about having to go back to school in a week's time.

Slipping out for a pee after coffee and cognacs were served, Louis spotted Elise, 'hiding' at the top of the stairs with her face pressed between the bannister rails.

'What are you doing up, miss?' he asked indulgently, creeping up to join her. Adorable in her white muslin night-gown, she smelled of baby powder and soap, and succeeded in instantly banishing his earlier feelings of irritation. 'If Brolio caught you out of bed she'd have your guts for garters.'

'Brolio's snoring like *Amelie*,' Elise pouted, earning a loud laugh from her father. Amelie was the fat sow down at the home farm.

'Cheeky monkey.' Grinning, Louis wrapped an arm around his daughter. 'What's the matter, *princesse*? Can't sleep?'

Elise shook her head miserably. 'I'll sleep when they're gone. Gone, gone, gone,' she scowled.

'Now, now,' Louis grinned. 'They are going tomorrow. And besides, that's no way to talk about your cousins.'

'They're not even real cousins.' Elise's bow-shaped upper lip curled in disdain, giving her a distinct look of her maman. 'They're about a billion times removed.'

'Ah, yes, but that's a good thing,' Louis teased her with a gentle nudge to the ribs. 'It means you can marry Thierry when you're older.'

'*Thierry?*' Elise pulled a face as if she'd just been force-fed a handful of worms.

'What's wrong with Thierry?'

'He's so *old*.'

'Is he?' Louis chuckled.

'Yes.' Elise nodded seriously, not getting the joke. 'At least Laurent's not old,' she added, under her breath.

Her father gave her a puzzled look. 'I thought you hated Laurent?'

'Who told you that?'

'A little bird,' said Louis. 'I heard you've been hopping mad about Laurent monopolizing Alex these last few weeks.'

Elise blushed but said nothing. She didn't know what 'monopolize' meant, but she suspected it was grown-up for 'steal'.

'So it's not true, then?' asked Louis. 'You *don't* hate him?'

'I *do* hate him,' Elise said quickly. And it was the truth, in a way. Just not the whole truth. She told Louis about the butterfly she'd been chasing on the day Laurent arrived, the Scarce Swallowtail. 'It was bringing me Salignac magic, Papa, I'm sure it was, and then *he* came along and made me miss my chance to catch it. He's bad luck.'

'Well,' Louis squeezed her tighter. 'I'm delighted you think so. Because it's Thierry you should be setting your cap at, not his know-it-all little brother. Just think, if you married Thierry, you could be the next Comtesse Senard,' he teased her. 'What do you say to that?'

'I say *non merci*,' said Elise, wrinkling her little nose in disgust.

'You could live in a castle, five times the size of this old shack,' Louis carried on with the joke.

'*Shack*? Sainte Madeleine is not a *shack*,' Elise gasped, wide-eyed with indignation. 'There's no house, or castle, on earth that compares with her! You know that, Papa.'

'I do know it.' Louis kissed the top of his daughter's head. 'I'm only teasing, my Elise.'

He loved how much this house meant to her, how deeply she felt its magic. He'd felt the same way himself as a small boy. Elise's innocence reminded him of his own, in a way that nothing else could any more. It was maudlin, perhaps, to allow himself to travel back to those days, the happy, easy days of his childhood. But it was part of what bonded him so closely with his daughter, and he loved her for it; for knowing that better, truer side of his nature and reaching for it, as if it were still there.

'Come along now, *princesse*. Back to bed before your mother catches both of us.'

Extending her arms and coiling them around her father's neck, Elise closed her eyes and revelled in the scent and feel of him as he lifted her up and carried her back to the nursery.

She would never get married, she decided. Not to Thierry, nor to Laurent, not to anyone. Papa was the only man she would ever love. She would stay here with him and Maman and her brothers, safe at Sainte Madeleine forever, happy among the butterflies and the vines. Nothing would ever change.

CHAPTER FOUR

Elise Salignac's first communion took place on Sunday, 18 April 1926 at the magnificent Basilique Sainte Marie Madeleine in Vézelay.

The Benedictine abbey church dated back to Roman times, and had been a site of pilgrimage for over a thousand years, thanks to the relics of Mary Magdalene that were believed to lie beneath its famous altar. Each year, around thirty local children, girls and boys, processed through the town in their communion finery to take their sacrament here, one of the most important and exciting days of the Burgundy calendar.

Elise awoke that morning in a frenzy of excitement, flinging open the shutters in the spacious, first-floor bedroom she'd moved into since graduating from the nursery. (At ten, she was too old for her little carved wooden bed beneath Maman's painted stars.)

It wasn't raining, thankfully. This had been one of the wettest springs for a generation, slowing down work on the vineyard and generally putting everybody into a foul and grumpy mood. After the poor showing for Sainte Madeleine's 1924 vintage, largely owing to Louis's ill-fated refusal to bring the harvest forward, 1925 had seen things stabilize at the chateau, with a decent enough output of

Grand Cru. But a lot rested on this year's crop if Sainte Madeleine was to retain her reputation as one of Burgundy's most prestigious domaines, so the unexpected rains were a serious blow. Only in the last few days had the first buds begun to make their tentative appearance on the vines, tiny nubby flashes of green emerging from a sea of brown mud, beneath a relentlessly grey sky.

Today, though, the sun was shining, and all was right in Elise's world. Too excited to eat much of a breakfast, she toyed with her bread and *chocolat chaud* before racing back upstairs to Maman's dressing room to get ready, while Papa drove the boys into town.

'Do stand still, Elise,' Brolio instructed tetchily, her wizened fingers fiddling arthritically with the hook-and-eye clasp at the back of Elise's communion dress. 'I shan't be able to do it if you will keep squirming.'

Knee-length Belgian lace, with a delicate line of pearl beading around the neckline and pretty capped sleeves, Elise's communion dress was the most lovely thing she had ever seen, never mind owned. It had been made specially for today's ceremony, much to Maman's disapproval. (Thérèse considered it *far* too extravagant.)

'I'll just pop on your veil,' the old nanny wheezed, before standing back and admiring her charge with proprietorial satisfaction. 'My, my. Well now. Don't you look *lovely*.'

Elise sighed happily, adjusting her veil in the mirror. She couldn't wait for everyone to see her, tall and willowy and graceful in her spectacular dress, outshining all the other girls in the church, and at the procession. Even Dominique Lefèvre, who many people in the Vézelay congregation considered the prettiest of this year's communicants. *Not any more*, Elise thought smugly, gazing at her own reflection. Today was going to be all about her.

Excitingly, but at the same time slightly worryingly, the Senards were coming to today's ceremony and would be seated in the front row pew, alongside Maman and Papa. Thierry was off doing boring army things, but Laurent would be there with his parents. In her more confident moments, Elise fondly imagined him being amazed by how much she'd blossomed since he saw her last, more than eighteen months ago now. Roger and Camille had taken a cruise along the Danube last summer (*so* boring), missing their usual stay at Sainte Madeleine, and a planned Christmas visit had been cancelled at the last minute because of something to do with Papa. Elise didn't quite understand what, although she had begun to surmise that all was not completely well between her parents.

Papa was spending more and more time in their Paris apartment. Arnaud had told her and Alex that he was busy in the city raising money to reinvest in the vineyard, upgrading their machinery and systems to keep up with the rapidly changing times. But when Papa did return to Sainte Madeleine, it was often to screaming rows with Maman that one really couldn't help but overhear, and that never seemed to have anything to do with the vineyard at all. To be fair, it was Papa who did most of the screaming, about the terrible pressures he was under and how Maman didn't understand. Maman just seemed to get quieter and sadder, but in that aloof way of hers that only ever seemed to make things worse in their marriage.

Instinctively, Elise felt sorry for Papa, but she'd learned not to say so to Alex or Dids, who were both very firmly on Maman's side, and insisted that there were all sorts of things Elise didn't understand, without offering to explain any of them. The whole thing was troubling and mysterious, and Elise made a conscious effort to think about it as little as she possibly could.

Appearing suddenly, as if Elise had conjured her, Thérèse caught her only daughter admiring her reflection in the dressing-room mirror.

'Thank you, Brolio,' she said softly. 'You may leave us now.'

Elise spun around, failing to notice her mother's look of disapproval and twirling proudly for her benefit.

'What do you think, Maman? Isn't this dress simply the most glorious thing you've ever seen?'

'What I think, Elise, is that vanity is one of the mortal sins,' Thérèse observed caustically. 'You do realize that today's service is a holy sacrament, not a fashion show?'

'Yes, Maman.' The smile died on Elise's lips, her happiness escaping like water from a leaky bucket, replaced by a familiar, unpleasant churning of guilt in the pit of her stomach.

'Let us pray, then,' said Thérèse, dropping to her knees and signalling to Elise to do the same. 'Heavenly Father . . .'

Closing her eyes as her mother's words rang out, Elise couldn't entirely extinguish the ignoble thought that it was Maman's fault that Papa kept leaving. Piety and goodness was all very well. But really, who wanted to live with a person who was incapable of having fun? Of appreciating a beautiful dress? Of being happy? Someone who saw every pleasure, no matter how innocent, as a sin, and tried to make *you* see it that way too?

'In the name of the Father, and of the Son, and of the Holy Spirit. Amen.'

Alex Salignac stifled a yawn as the double doors to the abbey church swung open and the communion procession began to make its way down the wide nave towards the Magdalen altar. He turned his attention to Elise, towering over the village boy she'd been paired with, her long blond hair plaited and coiled around the crown of her head like a halo. Everybody said that his little sister was becoming very pretty. Alex supposed she was, although to him Elise was just Elise, the same funny, adoring tomboy she'd always been, and his shadow since she was old enough to walk. He had to admit though that this morning she *did* look different: older, and sort of luminous, as if a chink of light from her future womanhood had decided to cast itself back in time and give the world a sneak preview of the beauty Elise Salignac would one day become.

In the front pew, Roger Senard leaned over and whispered in Louis's ear. 'She's a vision,' he said approvingly. 'So tall and grown-up. What a change. Time flies, eh?'

'Yes, it does,' said Louis, his chest swelling with pride as Elise reached the front of the church, dropping to her knees in front of the altar like the other children.

'And that's an exquisite dress,' Roger added. 'Not that I'm much of a fashion critic.'

'Thank you.' Louis smiled. 'I had it made for her specially in Paris. Thérèse thinks it's too much,' he added, a familiar note of bitterness creeping in. 'But just look how happy she is.'

Elise, in fact, *wasn't* happy, although she was doing the best job she could of pretending to be, smiling and hanging her head demurely, while subtly shifting her profile from left to right, ensuring that her audience could observe her prettiness from every angle. The problem was that the one person she wanted to be looking at her, and noticing how sophisticated she looked in her spectacular dress, had barely looked up from his missal since the service began. *Damn him.*

Laurent, taller and skinnier than when Elise had last seen him, sat beside his mother Camille, occasionally exchanging comments with her, but otherwise glued to his stupid prayer book as if Elise didn't even exist. And she knew for a fact that Laurent didn't give a fig about religion. She'd noticed him lock eyes with Alex once or twice, up on the altar. But she might as well have been invisible.

It's not fair, she thought furiously. Just for once, she had wanted to be the centre of attention. But even on her first communion, it seemed, the boys cared only about themselves. Despite Louis's favouritism towards her, Elise was well aware that it was the males who really mattered in Burgundy society. Her role – every upper-class French girl's role – was to look pretty and to marry well. The problem was that however well one performed it, one could only ever hope to be a bit player in the grand drama of life. Which was just plain wrong in Elise's opinion. At ten, she already knew as much as Alex, and a good deal more than Didier, about the mechanics of winemaking and what it took to produce a top-quality Grand Cru Burgundy. But she also knew that the job of running Sainte Madeleine would never be hers.

Today, however, *was* hers, and Laurent's insouciance was really too maddening! All the boys in the procession had admired her, as had the ones watching the procession. Hardly anyone had said a word about oh-so-perfect Dominique Lefèvre, *aka yesterday's news*, Elise thought triumphantly. Even Charles Papin, who was *fifteen* and who all the girls at St Angelique's swooned over, had whistled admiringly as Elise passed by. But of course, Monsieur know-it-all, stuck-up, 'I'm so mature' Laurent Senard would rather die than pay Elise so much as a shred of attention.

Well, two could play at that game.

Holding out her cupped hands to receive her first host, Elise decided that she would ignore Laurent completely after the service. *Completely.* She would look through him as if he were a ghost.

Closing her eyes back at her pew, Elise offered up a fervent prayer, just as Maman had told her to. But it wasn't a prayer of thanks for the grace she had just received.

Please, Lord, Elise begged. *Please let Laurent fall in love with me.*

* * *

Unfortunately, by the time Elise and the other communicants emerged from the church into the dappled sunlight of the square, the Senards had already headed back to Sainte Madeleine in Roger's new motorcar, a gleaming black TD Charronette. Even worse, Alex, who'd recently become obsessed with cars, had begged a lift with them, which meant that Elise had no option but to return to the house with Maman, Papa and Didier. Not the triumphant exit she'd been hoping for.

As Louis drove into the hamlet of Sainte Madeleine itself, little more than a handful of estate cottages, a one-room school and a tiny church, Elise noticed some children playing by the well on the village green. She knew some of them from her early childhood, back in the days when the village was still her playground, before she'd started at St Angelique's.

'Can I get out here?' she asked, leaning forward and wrapping her arms around Louis's neck while he drove, as she always did when she wanted something from him. 'I can walk the rest of the way.'

'Don't be silly,' Thérèse's voice was clipped and peremptory. 'It's about to be luncheon in your honour, Elise. I don't want you disappearing off.'

'I know, but luncheon won't be served till one thirty, and I won't be late, Maman,' Elise pleaded. 'It's only half a mile to the house. I'd like to say hello to Marie and the others. Oh, please?'

Thérèse sighed. 'You're too old to be hanging around with the village children. Besides, you only want to go so that you can show off in that dress.'

'That's not true!' Elise blushed, embarrassed because she knew it was.

'Oh, let her go, Thérèse,' Louis said tetchily, slowing down and pulling over beside the village green. 'Let the child enjoy herself for once. It's only for an hour. What's the worst that could happen?'

'Thank you, Papa!' said Elise, kissing him before scrambling over Didier and out of the car before her mother could stop her.

Veronique Caron, the prettiest of the village girls, watched through narrowed eyes as Elise Salignac climbed out of her family's expensive motorcar and sashayed her way smugly along the lane, puffing out the skirts of her fancy dress like the wings of a newly hatched butterfly.

Stuck-up cow.

At thirteen, Veronique was three years Elise's senior, too old for the two of them ever to have been close friends, even when Elise was young and used to play with the other village girls. Veronique's father, Michel, worked as a picker up at Sainte Madeleine during the season, although most of the year he tended to his own small plot, as well as doing odd jobs locally as a mechanic. Through Michel and his friends, Veronique knew all the latest gossip about Louis Salignac's scandalous 'double-life' in Paris: the gambling, drinking and whoring that had made the local lord of the manor part laughing stock and part envied anti-hero to his impoverished estate workers.

'Well, well, well,' Veronique sneered, her pretty lips curling with envy and dislike as Elise approached. 'If it isn't Lady Muck, come to condescend to the peasants.'

'Oh, lay off, V,' Marie Huppert chimed in, unusually for such a shy, self-conscious girl. 'She's only a kid.'

'So?' said Veronique.

Hubert Ginot, new to the village and Veronique's latest chosen beau, sat up and stared openly at the good-looking blonde girl heading in their direction. With her porcelain skin, delicate features and wildly expensive clothes, Elise looked like a creature from another planet. A better planet, one full of luxury, comfort and ease, things that Hubert had heard of but never experienced.

'She looks like a bit more than a kid to me,' he observed archly.

'She's *ten*,' Veronique practically spat.

Hubert raised an eyebrow, making no effort to hide his surprise. 'Only ten? Are you sure?'

Pascal, a slight, dark-haired boy recently rejected by Veronique in favour of Hubert, saw his chance to win back his beloved's heart.

'Of course she's sure,' he told Hubert disdainfully. 'That's Elise Salignac.'

'Well, she looks thirteen at least,' insisted Hubert.

'Doesn't matter how old she is,' Pascal mocked him. 'She ain't never going to give the likes of *you* the time of day, Ginot.'

'Says who?' Hubert bristled.

'Says me.' Pascal jutted out his spotty chin defiantly.

'He's right,' one of the girls piped up, another minor member of Veronique's entourage. 'All the Salignacs think their shit doesn't stink. Elise is no different to the rest of them.'

'Well, let's see, shall we?' said Hubert, picking up the thrown gauntlet. Scrambling to his feet he approached Elise. 'Hello there, miss!'

'Hello,' said Elise, smiling broadly at him and the group in general.

'That's a beautiful dress you're wearing,' said Hubert, introducing himself.

'Thank you,' Elise preened. 'My father had it made specially.'

It felt nice to be admired by this older boy, and to have stolen some of the limelight from the proud and superior Veronique. Hubert was handsome too in a blond, freckly, solid sort of way. The exact opposite way to Laurent, Elise thought, before reminding herself that she wasn't supposed to be thinking about Laurent.

Even so, it would have been nice if he could have been here, to see her being so admired.

'Must have cost a franc or two,' one of the girls observed, staring enviously at the beading on Elise's lace collar and cuffs.

'It *was* rather expensive,' Elise said blithely, her long dark lashes fluttering over her violet eyes. 'Maman wanted me to wear the grotty old family dress, but Papa felt I deserved something new. It's from Paris,' she couldn't help adding.

Pascal shot Hubert a '*told you so*' look.

Abandoning her position against the wall, Veronique began walking towards Elise, her gait slow and regal like the queen that she was.

'Paris, eh?' Veronique whistled slowly through crooked teeth, the one great flaw in her otherwise much-feted beauty. 'So how much was it? Exactly?'

'I don't know,' said Elise, beginning to feel a touch uncomfortable. 'Around two thousand francs, I believe.'

'That's a lot of money,' Veronique whistled. 'It's probably *almost* as much as your father spends on whores in a night.'

Elise blushed vermilion. Although she'd picked up snatches of information at home from half-heard, whispered conversations between her brothers or reading between the lines of Maman's disappointed looks, this was the first time she had ever heard her father accused outright of doing something wicked. And by a horrid, dirty stranger! Unprepared, she had no idea how to react.

The other children sniggered, huddling around Veronique and drawing closer to Elise, like sharks smelling blood.

'You must feel *very* special,' mocked Veronique.

Elise froze like a hunted deer, her breath quickening. A dreadful churning feeling began in the pit of her stomach. She wanted to say something, to defend Papa, to hit back at this vicious girl and her leering friends. But the words wouldn't come.

A little dark-haired boy with spiteful eyes and a face like a shrew stepped forward until he stood level with Veronique.

'You know what a whore is, don't you, Mademoiselle Salignac?' he leered at Elise. 'Or perhaps you're too young?'

'I know what a whore is,' Elise replied bravely, her voice hoarse and her throat dry as dust suddenly.

'So does *Papa*,' Veronique laughed.

Darting round behind Elise, she suddenly grabbed her, pulling her backwards and pinning her against her own body, pawing at her bodice.

'Whores are girls who wear fancy dresses, like yours.'

'Get off me!' Elise squealed.

What was she doing here? Why, oh why had she asked Papa to stop the car?

Maman was right. I only wanted to show off. Oh, if only I'd listened!

'Only theirs are just a bit lower cut,' giggled Veronique. At the word 'cut', she took hold of Elise's beaded collar and pulled hard in opposite directions. The beautiful Belgian lace dress tore wide open right down the front, making a satisfying ripping sound that had all the girls gasping and the boys whistling and making lewd catcalls. Hundreds of tiny cultured seed pearls ripped from their stitches flew into the air before falling like raindrops into the grass around the well. While some of the younger girls, and even Marie Huppert, scrambled to retrieve them, Elise's hands flew to her chest to cover herself. But Hubert was too quick for her, grabbing both her hands in his and pulling her slender arms forward while Veronique gripped her at the waist so she couldn't move.

'Don't be shy,' Hubert taunted, deciding belatedly that it would be a mistake to allow the rat-faced Pascal to oust him from Veronique's affections for the sake of a girl he stood no chance of ever courting, and whom Veronique clearly loathed. 'It looks *much* better like that. Just how *Papa* likes it.'

Lunging forward, he attempted to thrust a dirty hand beneath the torn lace bodice of Elise's dress. Elise, who'd been frozen with fear and mortification until now, suddenly awoke as if from a trance. Bringing up her knee lightning quick, she rammed it hard into Hubert's groin, eliciting a yelp of pain that could have been heard at the other end of the village.

'You bitch!' he seethed.

Aiming a second kick at his ribs, Elise succeeded in sending him flying backwards, before somehow managing to break free of Veronique's grip and run. But she'd barely got a few yards before her tormentors caught up with her, what felt like a whole pack of village children tackling her to the ground like hounds on a fox. Blinded by tears, her heart pounding, Elise felt the weight of them, pulling and tearing at her clothes and hair and veil in a frenzy of envy and loathing.

She didn't remember much after that. The smell of grass and soil in her nostrils. A knee pressed painfully into the small of her back. Sharp, spiteful fingernails clawing her skin. She heard laughs and a few shouted insults, mostly from Veronique. *Salope! Putain!* Slut. And then a voice. His voice.

'What the hell do you think you're playing at?' Clear and authoritative, Laurent's words rang out like a cymbal. 'Get out! Get out of here the lot of you, before I call the police.'

And just like that, everything stopped. The weight lifted, and the blows ceased raining down, and the shouts and catcalls fell silent. Elise could hear nothing but the pounding of feet as her tormentors ran away, dispersing to their cottages. By the time she rolled over, pulling the grass and leaves out of her hair and spitting mud from her bruised lips, she was alone. Alone with Laurent.

'Are you all right?' Squatting down on his haunches, Laurent placed a tentative hand on her head, gently pushing a matted lock of hair to one side so he could see more of her battered face. Poor kid.

'I'm fine,' Elise insisted proudly. 'What are you doing here?'

'Lunch was ready earlier than expected so your mother sent me down to fetch you. I was halfway through the lower field when I heard a scream. What happened, Elise?'

He reached out to touch her face but she turned away from him.

'Nothing happened,' she said defiantly. But she couldn't seem to stop her eyes from welling up again.

Why, *why* did Laurent have to see her like this? All muddied and torn, with her lip swollen and who knew how many cuts and bruises? It was so humiliating. And yet at the same time, she was so grateful to have been rescued, and so overwhelmed with relief that he was here, that she found herself flinging her arms around him anyway, pressing her face into his familiar, skinny chest and bursting into sobs, just as she would have done with Alex or Dids or Papa.

'It didn't look like nothing to me,' Laurent muttered angrily. 'Who was the ringleader? The sandy-haired boy?'

Elise shook her head.

'He joined in – Hubert. But Veronique started it,' she gasped, between sobs.

'Why did she attack you, Elise? What was this whole thing about?'

A panicked look crossed Elise's tear-stained face. If she told him what happened, she would have to get to the part about Papa, and the things Veronique and the others had said about him. She could *not* tell Laurent those things.

She simply couldn't bring herself to say them out loud, not to him. Whether they were true or not didn't matter.

Misinterpreting her expression, Laurent took her hands in his reassuringly. 'It doesn't matter what you did or said, Elise. Even if you provoked them in some way, what these children did to you was absolutely wrong. Inexcusable. Please don't think I'm not on your side.'

'I don't think that, Laurent.' She looked up at him gratefully.

'It's just that this girl, Veronique, well, she comes from a very different background to you. To us.'

Elise nodded seriously, not understanding but wanting to, and very much liking the way he said 'us'.

'That's probably why she turned on you, in your beautiful dress. Because you have so much, and she has so little.'

Elise nodded again. Probably best not to mention that she'd boasted about how much the dress cost, or that she'd had it made specially in Paris. Laurent didn't need to know all the details.

'The pressure that your father's been under recently, with Sainte Madeleine's last two years' vintages both being so disappointing and now a third year under threat; you have to remember that the village families feel that too,' Laurent went on. He wasn't sure how much Elise really understood, at ten, but he sensed that when it came to the family business she was probably wise beyond her years. 'They're already starting from a position of poverty, you see. And they rely completely on the vineyard's success for their livelihoods.'

'I understand,' said Elise.

'Good,' said Laurent. 'Because if we tell Uncle Louis what really happened to you just now, Veronique's father will probably lose his job. And without his income her family would be destitute. We wouldn't want that, would we?'

Wouldn't we? thought Elise, frowning, and wishing that

Laurent didn't always feel the need to talk down to her quite so condescendingly. Frankly, she couldn't give two hoots if horrible Veronique's horrible father lost his job. After the things Veronique had said about *Elise*'s father, and then destroying her gorgeous communion dress, by far the nicest thing she'd ever owned?

'Don't worry, Laurent,' she said seriously, big doe eyes looking up at him from beneath long, dark lashes, doing her very best to sound grown-up and on his level. 'We won't tell Papa.'

The family were just sitting down to a spectacular first communion lunch when Laurent appeared in the large dining room, his arm around a torn and dirty Elise.

'Dear God!' Louis shot to his feet. 'What in God's name happened?'

'Are you all right, Elise?' Alex echoed, running over to his bloodied little sister, his handsome face a picture of concern.

'I'm fine,' Elise said bravely. 'I was playing with the village children by the river when I slipped and fell down the bank.'

'Your dress!' Thérèse gasped, belatedly noticing the filthy, shredded remnants of Louis's extravagance.

'Never mind the damned dress. Are you hurt, *princesse*?' Louis asked, his voice full of tenderness. 'Really hurt, I mean?'

Elise shook her head. 'Only bruised, Papa. Laurent heard me shout and he came and pulled me out of the gully,' she added, looking up at her cousin with the adoring, puppyish expression that she usually reserved exclusively for Alex.

'What about the other children?' Louis demanded. 'Didn't they help you?'

'They tried, Uncle,' Laurent interjected. 'But her leg was wedged between two nasty-looking rocks. I think they were afraid to move her.'

'Bloody urchins,' Louis muttered furiously. 'I should think they were afraid. That's the last time you're to play with the village children, Elise, do you hear me? The last damned time.'

'Yes, Papa,' said Elise dutifully. *Fine by me.*

'She shouldn't have been playing with them in the first place,' said Thérèse, shooting an accusing look at Louis before turning to one of the maids. 'Tell Brolio to come at once,' she instructed. 'Elise needs a hot bath and to have those wounds dressed.'

'Yes, madame.'

The nanny arrived, tut-tutting through puckered, elderly lips, and Elise was bundled off to the safety of the nursery to be cleaned up. But not before Laurent had squeezed her hand and given her a warm, *thank you* look with his beautiful brown eyes.

I'm going to marry him, Elise decided, with a child's unwavering certainty, reluctantly relinquishing his hand. It didn't matter that he hadn't noticed her yet. He would, one day. Elise would make sure of it.

The next time I wear a beautiful white dress from Paris, I'll be walking down the aisle, about to become Madame Laurent Senard.

CHAPTER FIVE

As fate would have it, it would be over three years until Elise saw Laurent again – not until the Christmas of 1929, when the Salignacs were invited to spend the holiday at Chateau Brancion, the Senard family seat. It was three years during which much changed, for Elise, for the Salignac family, and for France.

At Sainte Madeleine, the downward slide of the vineyard's fortunes had been faster and steeper than anyone might have predicted. Both Louis and Arnaud Berger had watched in anguish as one setback after another blighted vintage after vintage. Some were precipitated by Mother Nature: the excessive heat of 1924, the rains of '26, the blight of grey mould that ravaged much of the Yonne region in '28. But others could have been avoided, or at least mitigated, had Louis been a better businessman. Investment in new equipment and chemical treatments for the vines would have saved them last year, if only Louis had had the fore-sight – or the cash – to make them. Unfortunately, not content with the modest income provided by Sainte Madeleine's smattering of tenant farmers, he'd attempted to bolster their cash flow with various ill-advised forays into the stock market. As a result, the estate was now closer to the brink than ever, although only Louis, Arnaud and

Alexandre, now almost eighteen and increasingly active in the day-to-day running of the vineyard, knew how grave things had become.

'Promise me you won't drink too much at Chateau Brancion,' Thérèse implored Louis the night before they left Sainte Madeleine for the holidays. 'I don't think I could bear a drunken scene in front of Roger and Camille.'

'And you won't have one, my love,' Louis assured her, carelessly tossing exquisitely wrapped presents into an open suitcase on the bed. Despite another difficult year, he remained upbeat and hopeful that Sainte Madeleine's fortunes could still be turned around. He was beginning to feel the same way about his marriage, with himself and Thérèse currently enjoying one of their rare periods of *rapprochement*. He'd made an effort to tone down the past excesses of his life in Paris, and was actually quite looking forward to spending a peaceful Christmas with his family, away from the pressures of home.

'All will be well, my darling, trust me,' he promised Thérèse. 'I'll be a model of restraint and decorum.'

They arrived the night before Christmas Eve, the three children squashed together in the back seat of Louis's new Rolls-Royce Phantom II, a car that he rightly described as a work of art and that Thérèse, equally rightly, called an appalling extravagance. Elise, now a teenager and already considered a great society beauty in both Burgundy and Paris, sat between a moody Alex and a predictably anxious nineteen-year-old Dids. Didier had too many unhappy memories of his father's bullying when in company to feel anything other than fearful at the prospect of a Christmas away from home. And Alex, although relieved that things seemed calmer between his parents, was still angry with Louis for what he saw as wanton mismanagement of the family finances. Just a few days ago, they'd been warned that unless next year's crop produced some really stellar wines, there was a risk that they might be stripped of their Grand Cru status entirely, a catastrophe that hardly bore thinking about.

'It won't happen,' Louis announced breezily, tossing the letter from the Institut National des Appellations d'Origine to one side. 'They're all talk, these boffins.'

'Papa, you can't just ignore this,' said Alex, picking up the letter and angrily waving it in Louis's face. 'These people have power. Real power.'

'I'd advise you to remember who you're talking to,' Louis snapped, glaring viciously at Alex. 'I don't need a lecture from a teenage boy on how to handle the INAO. You forget that Arnaud and I have been doing this since before you were born.'

Arnaud's been doing it, you mean, thought Alex, but he didn't say anything. On this occasion he'd stood down, cowed by Louis's visceral anger. But this was no longer always the case. With a teenager's blind self-confidence, Alex had no doubt that if he were in charge at Sainte Madeleine, he'd be making a better fist of things, and he'd begun to challenge some of his father's decisions more openly. Arnaud did his best to act as peacemaker between the two of them, but the arguments between father and son could be bitter and brutal, and though Louis tended to bounce back quickly, Alex remained bruised for days afterwards.

Even he, however, couldn't fail to feel his spirits lift as Chateau Brancion finally loomed into view. The long, winding driveway to the house was lined with a fresh covering of snow, like icing on a Christmas cake, and the mansion itself sparkled in the twilight, festive and inviting.

'Wow,' gasped Alex as they pulled up in the gravelled forecourt. 'I'd forgotten how massive it is.'

'It is magnificent,' agreed Thérèse, with a longing sigh. 'Architecturally, it has to be the finest house in Bourgogne. Don't you think so, Didier?'

Didier managed a barely audible 'hm' before turning and gazing out of the window with the same, blank disengaged stare he'd been wearing for months.

Thérèse's heart sank. Usually architecture was one of Dids's passions. He'd always been deeply affected by beauty in all its forms and had adored Chateau Brancion as a little boy. But recently Thérèse felt as if nothing could reach her oldest child, no pleasure or interest could pierce his armour of loneliness and withdrawal. It didn't help that Louis got so angry about it. As if poor Didier were being depressed on purpose.

'It's all right, I suppose,' Elise announced insouciantly. 'Not as beautiful as Sainte Madeleine though.'

'Quite right, my darling,' said Louis, flashing her an adoring smile.

Privately Elise was every bit as impressed as Maman and Alex with the Senards' truly spectacular estate. She had been to Chateau Brancion before, but not for many years and her memories were hazy and mostly focused on the nursery, and being allowed to feed carrots to Uncle Roger's hunters. She'd quite forgotten the awe-inspiring scale of the place, with its feet-thick crenellated walls, its moat and drawbridge, its scores upon scores of bedrooms, and of course its grand park, studded with deer like children's toys, that in daylight stretched further than the eye could see, almost to the border with Auvergne.

Uncle Roger barrelled out to meet them, his usual cheerful self, as round and red as a billiard ball. What was left of his hair had turned fully white, Elise noticed, and he seemed to have grown both fatter and shorter since she'd seen him last. No less jolly, though. Everybody loved Uncle Roger.

'Well hello, hello! You're here at last!' he roared, rubbing his hands together enthusiastically. He was soon flanked by the solid, kindly Camille and a veritable army of servants, who set to work taking coats and carrying cases like a colony of liveried ants.

'Are you exhausted?' Roger asked. 'You must be.'

'We're a little tired,' admitted Thérèse, kissing Camille warmly on both cheeks.

'Speak for yourself!' Louis laughed, clapping Roger on the back affectionately and bounding up the steps and into the chateau with the energy of a much younger man. 'I'm raring to go. I could murder a cognac though, Roger, if one's on offer?'

'Of course, old man. Follow me.'

Thérèse looked at him in disbelief. 'Louis!' she whispered, tapping him on the shoulder as he followed Roger towards one of the salons.

'What?' he turned to her guilelessly.

'You *promised*,' she muttered, embarrassed. 'Your drinking?'

'I promised not to overdo it,' Louis responded gruffly, shrugging her off. 'One lousy cognac's hardly going to kill me.'

While Louis disappeared with Roger, a butler showed an anxious Thérèse and the children upstairs to their respective guest rooms.

'Aren't you coming?' Alex called over his shoulder to Elise, who was lingering beneath the vast, elaborately trimmed Christmas tree in the hall.

'In a minute,' she said absently.

The truth was, she couldn't tear herself away. The tree was utterly mesmerizing, like something from a dream. Baubles of every colour and type hung from its thick, needled branches: shiny red orbs, delicate crystal snowflakes, multicoloured tin nutcracker soldiers and elaborately feathered birds, their feet twisted onto the branches with hidden loops of dark green metal wire. The cloying, resinous scent of the needles mingled with woodsmoke from an enormous fire, crackling away in the baronial hearth at the far end of the hall, so that the room smelled like Christmas too; like Elise's childhood. Closing her eyes for a moment, she allowed herself to get lost in the magic, aware that adulthood was already almost upon her, like a thief that had snuck up behind her faster than she'd ever expected.

Soon she would see Laurent.

Hugging the anticipation to her chest, she felt a warm sensation suffuse her entire body. It wasn't as if she'd pined for him these last three years. There'd been too much going on at her school, St Angelique's, and on her occasional thrilling sojourns in Paris, for her to waste her time moping, and plenty of young men around eager to flirt with her and take her mind off her distant cousin. But now that she was actually *here* – now that she and Laurent would be spending the entire Christmas holidays together, getting to know one another all over again in this beautiful, magical chateau – Elise couldn't help but enjoy the rekindling of her old crush, and allowing the old feelings to flood back into her heart.

'It's a good tree, isn't it?'

A male voice from behind her made her jump a mile.

'I'm sorry.' Thierry Senard laughed good-naturedly at her shocked reaction. 'I didn't mean to startle you.'

In a pair of rather old-fashioned, baggy slacks and a dark green cashmere sweater, with his thick blond hair pushed back from his face and smiling broadly, there could be no denying how preposterously handsome Thierry was. Even better looking than the last time Elise had seen him. For some reason she'd never swooned over him the way other girls did though, notwithstanding his film-star good looks. Perhaps it was because Papa never stopped banging on about how perfect Thierry was at everything, using his many accomplishments as a stick with which to beat poor Didier, and even sometimes Alexandre.

'That's all right,' Elise smiled back at him, exchanging

greetings by kissing him on both cheeks. 'My fault. I was miles away. I'm afraid your tree rather put me under a spell.'

'It's a good one, isn't it?' Thierry agreed, cocking his head to one side curiously while he took in Elise's appearance. 'You know, I almost wouldn't have recognized you. I'm sure everybody says this, but I can't believe how much you've grown. How old are you now – fifteen?'

'Thirteen,' replied Elise, pleased. 'I'm very tall for my age.'

'I'll say,' said Thierry. 'Laurent's going to fall off his perch when he sees you.'

Elise felt a little flutter at the mention of Laurent's name, but did her best to hide it.

'Where are your brothers?' asked Thierry.

'Upstairs, unpacking,' said Elise. 'I probably ought to join them, actually.'

'Why don't you come through to the drawing room with me first, and meet everyone?'

Wondering vaguely who 'everyone' might be, and anxious to see Laurent, Elise allowed herself to be persuaded, following Thierry down a long stone corridor hung with gloomy family portraits. At the far end a low doorway opened into a large, richly furnished room. Kilim rugs and silk fringed cushions, as well as a rather spectacular lion's skin spread on the floor, lent the space an exotic, Indian air, but there were plenty of traditional French touches as well, from the ornately carved Louis XV card table to the Parisian standard lamps standing like sentries beside every armchair and *canapé*.

'Elise, may I present Albert Lanceau and Guillaume Duval, two of my great friends from the regiment.' Two sluggish, chinless young men heaved themselves off the couch. 'Albert, Guillame, this is *ma jeune cousine*, Mademoiselle Elise Salignac.'

Elise dutifully shook the two proffered, clammy hands.

'And of course, this fellow needs no introduction,' said Thierry, standing to one side. Turning around from where he'd been standing by the fire, Laurent walked directly towards Elise, smiling broadly.

'Hello stranger.'

Oh God, she thought in panic, taking in his face, his walk, his Parisian manner of dress, with the straighter cut trousers and open-necked shirt, as he came closer. *There he is! He looks so much older.* She knew that Laurent was nineteen now, and away at university in Paris, so she'd expected some sort of change. But not this. Nothing like this. At seventeen, her brother Alex was still a boy in so many ways, and even Dids at eighteen was too shy and nervous to be considered an adult. But in the years Elise and Laurent had been apart, Laurent had managed to turn into a fully grown man, just like Thierry.

Taking a step back, he grabbed hold of both of her shoulders so that he could study her at arm's length, the way an uncle might, before kissing her hello on both cheeks.

'Aunt Thérèse told Maman you'd been growing like a weed, but I didn't know she meant it literally.'

It was meant as a compliment. But Elise felt as if someone had thrown a medicine ball at her stomach. The pain! The disappointment! That day of her first communion, when Laurent had ridden to her rescue, and she'd lied to Papa for him, and then he'd squeezed her hand, she'd convinced herself that there had been something between them. Something secret and special, even if she had been just a child back then. But now she could see quite plainly that she'd been fooling herself. In Laurent's eyes Elise was still just a girl.

Pulling away, she looked up at him in what she hoped was a detached, sophisticated manner.

'*Joyeux Noël*, Laurent,' she said coolly. 'It's been a long time.'

'It has,' he agreed, mollifying her just a little. 'Too long.'

But the brief flicker of hope didn't last long. To Elise's dismay, a dark-haired woman she hadn't noticed before suddenly wandered over from the far side of the room and wrapped a casually possessive arm around Laurent's waist.

'And who is this young beauty?' the woman asked, employing a tone that managed to be simultaneously flattering and patronizing as she greeted Elise. She wore a long, flowy, kaftan-style dress, spoke French with a heavy Spanish accent, and had a deep, resonant voice with a smoker's rasp that clung to the ends of her words. Elise hated her instantly.

'This is my cousin, Elise Salignac,' Laurent explained, leaning into the dark woman in a way that made Elise want to punch her in her bushy-eyebrowed face. 'Elise, this is Ines Colomar. My girlfriend.'

'Must you?' Ines frowned, punching him playfully on the arm. 'You can introduce me as a person in my own right, you know, not just an appendage of yours. How about, "This is Ines, she's an artist"? Or "This is Ines, we met at a rally in Paris"?'

Or how about, this is Ines, she's a stumpy, beetle-browed Spanish witch old enough to be my mother? thought an appalled Elise. All right, perhaps not Laurent's mother, exactly. But she must be pushing thirty if she were a day. The idea that Laurent could be with someone that old was ridiculous. Revolting. The idea that Laurent could be with anyone at all was an offence against Elise's nature. But if this . . . *person* . . . was his type, what hope could there ever be for the two of them, even in the distant future of Elise's womanhood?

Shaking Ines's hand stiffly, she felt the last dregs of her happiness drain away like used bathwater. 'A pleasure to meet you.'

Then, pointedly ignoring Laurent, for her own self-preservation as much as anything, she turned back to Thierry

'If it's all right with you, Cousin, I think I'd better go up to Maman and the others now. I'll need to unpack and change before dinner, and I dare say they'll be wondering where I've got to.'

'Of course,' said Thierry. He gestured to one of the maids. 'Manon? Would you show Mademoiselle Salignac to her room, please.'

Miserably, Elise followed the servant back along the corridor, past the giant Christmas tree that had lost all its magic now, like a snuffed-out candle.

CHAPTER SIX

The Senard family were guests of honour every year at the Christmas Eve carol service held in their village church. Although by no means as grand as the abbey church at Vézelay, or as pretty as the tiny medieval chapel in Sainte Madeleine village, St Hubert's was still a fine example of late medieval Bourgogne architecture and boasted some well-preserved frescoes of which the locals were justly proud.

Thérèse particularly looked forward to the carol service. She loved the thrill of arriving by *carosse*, the traditional horse-drawn carriage emblazoned with the Senard family coat of arms, and of walking down the nave to the front pew like royalty, knowing that all eyes were on her. It was a small, treasured reminder of her own noble heritage, of the part of herself that she'd lost, or at least compromised, when she married Louis. Pride, of course, was a sin. But Thérèse couldn't help but believe that the Lord made an exception for the warm feelings of belonging and happiness that came from being reunited with one's true social equals, the dear and trusted companions of one's youth.

'Is everything all right, my dear?' Camille asked solicitously as their carriage bumped and rolled down Chateau Brancion's long drive towards the village. 'You look troubled.'

71

'I'm fine,' Thérèse replied, not entirely convincingly.

The two women settled themselves in the creaking leather seats that had cushioned generations of Senard bottoms since the early 1800s, with heavy, fox-fur blankets thrown over their knees. Thérèse sat ramrod straight and severely beautiful in a high-necked, charcoal-grey gown and with her hair swept up beneath a black lace mantilla. Beside her sat Camille, square-faced and plain but altogether more festive in a long skirt and bright red woollen jacket that did nothing to mitigate her ruddy complexion, with diamonds casually sparkling at her wrists, neck and ears. Roger, Louis, Didier and Laurent were travelling in a separate carriage a few yards ahead of them, while Thierry, Alex and Elise were in the third *carosse* at the rear. Thierry's friends had driven themselves to the church, and Laurent's paramour Ines had stayed home at the chateau, pleading a headache.

'I suppose I'm still a little worried about Didier,' Thérèse admitted. 'He's been so low recently. I'd hoped the holidays, coming here, might bring him out of himself a little bit. He's always been fond of your boys.'

'And they of him,' said Camille.

'It doesn't seem to have helped, though.' Tears welled in Thérèse's eyes.

'Do you know what's troubling him?' Camille probed cautiously.

Thérèse shook her head. 'I only wish I did. None of us can get through to him. I try, but it's like shouting from one mountaintop to another. He's so far away, Camille. The chasm between us . . .' she broke off, not sure how to finish the sentence, and not wanting to put too much of a dampener on what was supposed to be a special evening.

'Your boys look well,' she observed brightly, attempting to shift gears. 'It was awfully kind of Thierry to take Alex out shooting today. I'm sure he and his chums from the regiment didn't want a teenager tagging along, but I know Alex was thrilled to be invited. He spends so much time up at the winery these days, he almost never gets to spend time with other young people.'

'Not at all,' said Camille. 'I'm sure they were delighted to have Alex with them. I'd hoped Laurent might have joined the party too, knowing his cousin was going,' she added, wistfully. 'He and Alex were so close when they were younger, do you remember?'

'Indeed I do.' Thérèse smiled. Those had been happy days overall, although she remembered how badly poor Elise's nose used to be put out of joint whenever Laurent came to stay, because you couldn't get a cigarette paper between him and Alex.

'I do know what you mean about "chasms" between oneself and one's sons,' Camille sighed. 'Laurent's changed so much since he left for Paris.'

'Has he?' Thérèse sounded surprised.

'Don't you notice it?' said Camille.

'Well,' Thérèse considered. 'He certainly seems much more grown-up these days, if that's what you mean.'

'Grown-up? Hm. That's one way of putting it.' Camille fiddled uncomfortably with the clasp of her evening bag. 'Between you and me, Thérèse, sometimes I feel I hardly know him anymore.'

'I'm sure that's not true.'

'It is,' Camille insisted. 'Laurent's always been very political. He and Roger have never seen eye to eye, as you know. But since he got to Paris and fell in with this crowd of . . . oh, I don't know what you'd call them. Bohemians? It's been all marches and protests. Honestly, Thérèse, some of the things that come out of his mouth! It feels as if he's ashamed of us. Of the family, who we are, everything we stand for. It's heartbreaking.'

'It's probably just a phase,' Thérèse tried to comfort her.

'I hope so,' Camille said miserably, as the horses clattered to a halt outside the church. 'But you met his "friend", Ines? I only found out after she arrived to stay with us, but she's *divorced*.' She dropped her voice to an appalled whisper as the driver helped them out of the carriage. 'Divorced at twenty-three! Can you credit it? And just dropped it into conversation over dinner as if it were nothing at all.'

The Christmas table at Chateau Brancion had to be seen to be believed. A throwback to the grand old days of Napoleon, an army of footmen in full livery scurried back and forth beneath a spectacular Venetian glass chandelier, carrying gleaming, solid silver platters piled high with every culinary delight imaginable. First came the meats: beef, cured ham, goose and smoked duck, with enormous porcelain side bowls of pâté de foie gras. Then the vegetables: powdery roast potatoes, home-grown salsify, haricots verts and courgettes with mint, pungent artichokes poached in warm butter. Entire cheeses arrived, still in their thick rinds, some wrapped in muslin cloths: Camembert, Brie, Roquefort and the local Époisses du Bourgogne that smelled like dirty socks but tasted as creamily delicious as anything on earth. And finally for pudding there were wine-soaked pears with Chantilly cream, candied fruits including Roger's favourite sugared plums imported from Carlsbad, marzipan fruits, crystal bowls of pink and white almonds, and cakes and choux pastries of every conceivable variety.

It was a feast fit not for a king but for an emperor, in a room quite grand enough to compete with any banqueting hall in any castle in Europe. Everybody's eyes were on stalks. But for Thérèse Salignac at least, things began badly when Louis staggered in late and then proceeded to sit down to the table visibly drunk. He'd spent much of the night before, after the carols, bemoaning his strained finances to Roger Senard and drinking into the small hours.

Evidently when he woke up this morning he'd decided to keep going, and it was a ruddy-faced, distinctly unsteady Louis who staggered into the family feast.

Registering his mother's shock and embarrassment, Alex had attempted to smooth things over and distract everyone by entering into a spirited conversation with Roger and Thierry about the wine business. After praising his uncle's spectacular Châteauneuf-du-Pape, he launched into a passionate speech about all the new technological developments in the industry and changes in both supply and demand at the fine wine end of the market.

'Some of the New World wines are really top-flight these days,' he informed Roger. 'Napa might end up giving Burgundy a run for her money in the future.'

'Where?' Roger looked confused.

'Napa. It's in California, Uncle.' Alex smiled. 'Old estates like Sainte Madeleine can't just rest on our laurels and assume we'll have a monopoly on the top end of the market forever. This has been a good year for Burgundy generally, touch wood. But if we don't invest and modernize, we may not see many more.'

'Well, I must say, I'm impressed by how well informed you've become on all this, Alexandre,' said Roger. 'I had no idea about all of these developments. You must be a great asset to your father.'

'Asset my arse,' muttered Louis, under his breath but still audible to those closest to him, including Alex, who blushed vermilion.

'What was that, Louis?' an unwitting Camille asked.

'Nothing, my dear,' Louis attempted an ingratiating smile. 'I merely observed that my younger son is talking complete rubbish.'

An awkward silence fell around the table.

'It's not rubbish, Papa,' said Alex with dignity. 'Times are changing and we need to change with them.'

'Change with them,' Louis slurred, mimicking what he considered to be his son's preachy tone. 'It's change for change's sake, that's what it is. And it all costs money, Alexandre. That's the part you don't seem to understand.'

'On the contrary, Papa . . .' Alex began.

But Louis cut him off, banging his fist down furiously on the table. 'Don't interrupt me, boy! Who the hell do you think you are?'

'Papa, please,' Elise interjected despairingly. She couldn't bear an embarrassing scene in front of Laurent, not on top of everything else. And poor Maman looked like she was about to faint.

'Our last few years may have been difficult, but what about before that, eh?' Louis looked from Alex to the other mortified faces around the table, as if challenging each of them to defy him. 'We had a bloody good run, that's what. I've been running that vineyard since before you were born!' He turned back to Alex, jabbing an accusatory finger in his direction.

'Running it into the ground, more like,' Alex shot back, too appalled at his father's behaviour to bite his own tongue any more.

'*What* did you say?'

Thérèse's cold hand shot out, covering Louis's warm one as it lay, palm down on the table. '*Arrête*,' she whispered in his ear. '*Je t'en supplie. Pas maintenant. Pas ici.*'

There was a final moment's tension, like a crackle of electricity in the air. But when Louis Salignac belatedly registered the pain in his wife's eyes, he did as she asked. Sitting back in his chair like a chastened schoolboy, he let the matter drop.

'Well, well,' Roger Senard said lightly, in a transparent attempt to steer the conversation back onto safer ground. 'You're right on one count, young Alex, which is that things are changing everywhere. Guillaume,' he turned to address

Thierry's friend, 'weren't you telling us just the other night about a shake-up at the regiment?'

'Yes, sir,' the young man nodded.

'Something about learning guerrilla tactics to beat the damned communists,' Roger explained to the table at large, 'if, God forbid, it should ever come to another war.'

Ines opened her mouth to say something, but a pleading look from Laurent made her think better of it. In a demure, buttermilk yellow dress and matching shawl, and with her hair pulled back into an old-fashioned braid, she'd clearly made an effort to dress conservatively for today's festivities.

'For heaven's sake let's not even *think* about war,' said Camille with feeling. 'Especially not at Christmas.'

The rest of the meal continued in relative calm, much to everybody's relief, and after lunch the party decamped into the drawing room for present-opening around the fire. Louis mercifully fell asleep in one of Roger's overstuffed armchairs, and for the first time all day, Elise allowed herself to relax. She was given all sorts of lovely things, including a jewelled hair comb from Didier, a beautiful watercolour painting of Sainte Madeleine from Alex and an exquisite Chinese silk evening bag from Aunt Camille. Laurent had inexplicably given her a book about revolutionary history. Since when had she *ever* expressed the remotest interest in politics? But her disappointment was short-lived when she watched him open his present from her – a pottery coffee mug with his initials on it that she'd both made and glazed herself.

'For when you're in Paris, studying,' she explained shyly. 'If you need coffee to stay awake.'

'Thank you,' he smiled at her, utterly charmed. 'And you really made this yourself?'

Elise nodded.

'I love it. I'll think of you every time I drink from it.'

His delight was genuine. The mug, homemade and imperfect, felt like a bridge back to happy childhood summers.

A bridge that, perhaps, Elise was searching for too? Opening it, he felt a wave of deep affection for the proud, brave little girl who he'd rescued from the village bullies on the day of her first communion, and who'd lied to her father about what had happened solely to please him. To his own surprise, he realized that he'd missed her.

'Look what Elise made for me.' He turned to show the mug to Ines, who was sitting beside him on the sofa. 'Isn't it great?'

Ines turned the mug over in her hands, running her fingers over every bump in its surface in what struck Elise as a deliberately critical fashion.

'It's very sweet,' she pronounced, handing it back with a patronizing smile. 'I remember making cups and bowls for my parents when I was a child. I used to love messing around with clay. How clever you are, Elise.'

'Thank you.' Smiling thinly, Elise made a point of picking up her wine glass and taking a slow, considered sip. Stupid cow, trying to belittle her in front of Laurent. She'd show her.

Walking over to the sideboard, she picked up the decanter and topped up her own glass, before approaching Laurent. 'Some more?'

He raised his glass, smiling. 'Thank you, yes. I'll have a little.'

'And you?' Turning to Ines, Elise 'tripped' on the fringed edge of the rug and lurched forward, sloshing red wine all down the front of Ines's beautiful buttermilk yellow dress.

A look of shock flashed over Ines's features, followed by one of fury as she jumped to her feet. 'What the . . . ?'

'Oh my goodness!' Elise gasped. 'I am *so* sorry! How clumsy of me. Here, let me help.' Grabbing a napkin from the pile on the coffee table, she dabbed ineffectually at the enormous, spreading stain.

'Get off me!' Ines snapped, batting away Elise's hand.

'There's no need to shout,' said Laurent, his eyes darting between his furious girlfriend and a stricken Elise, while Camille sent the maid to the kitchen for towels and a sponge, and Roger yelled after her to bring salt ('best thing for red wine on a carpet').

'No need to shout?' Ines turned on him. 'Can't you see she did this on purpose?'

'Don't be ridiculous,' replied Laurent, embarrassed. 'She tripped.'

All the present-opening had stopped and the entire room was glued to the unfolding drama.

'She didn't *trip*,' Ines looked witheringly at Elise. 'She deliberately ruined my dress because she's jealous.'

'Jealous? Of what?' demanded Laurent.

'Of me, you idiot. Of *us*,' hissed Ines. 'You can't really be that blind, can you? She's been mooning after you like a little lost calf since the day she arrived. I've never seen a more obvious crush.'

'All right, that's enough,' Laurent said sternly. 'You're being ridiculous.'

Elise's heart pounded. The adrenaline rushing through her veins had the helpful side effect of making her eyes well up with tears. To her delight, Laurent wrapped a protective arm around her shoulders.

Then, less delightfully, he turned to Ines and said, 'She's only a kid.'

'Tell that to her,' snapped Ines, and with a last, contemptuous look at both of them, swept out of the room.

'You'd better go after her,' Thierry told Laurent, drawing Elise to one side. 'You know she'll mope for the rest of the night if you don't.'

Reluctantly, Laurent took his brother's advice and followed Ines upstairs, with the briefest of apologetic glances in Elise's direction.

'I'm sorry,' Elise mumbled to the room in general, as the maid began to clean up the wine stains on the carpet and sofa cushions. The stuff really had gone everywhere.

She was met by a general chorus of reassurance and 'don't worry about it, accidents happen' as the present-opening resumed. Only Alex refrained from joining in, shooting his sister a look that plainly meant 'we'll talk later'.

And much later, right before bed, they did.

'Laurent never even came back down for supper,' Elise sighed miserably. She was brushing her long hair in front of the dressing-table mirror in her guest bedroom when Alex came in to say goodnight. 'Can you believe that? That vile woman Ines ruined everything.'

'*She* ruined everything?' Alex raised an eyebrow, not without love. 'Give over, Elise. Why did you do it?'

'It was an accident.' Elise kept brushing.

'Rubbish,' said Alex. 'Complete rubbish. To quote Papa,' he added with a grin.

'Oh Lord, Papa,' Elise groaned. All the drama with the spilled wine had temporarily pushed Louis's embarrassing behaviour out of her mind. 'He was awful today. But you shouldn't have baited him about the vineyard. You know how hard he's been trying to fix things.'

'Never mind that,' said Alex briskly. 'Why did you chuck that wine all over Ines?'

'Because I hate her,' Elise said simply, turning around to face him. There was no point denying it. Alex knew her too well. 'And because she was poisonous about my mug. Laurent loved it until she got all bitchy. And then to have the nerve to call me jealous. *She's* jealous! I don't know what Laurent sees in her.'

Alex came over and perched on the end of the bed, close enough to reach for Elise's hand.

'I don't either, to be honest with you. No one likes her. Not even Thierry, and he likes everyone.'

'Really?' Elise brightened.

'You still shouldn't have done it though,' said Alex. 'Aunt Camille's probably going to have to re-cover that sofa. And the rug's destroyed.'

'She can afford it,' said Elise dismissively, earning herself a reproving look from Alex. 'What? She can! The Senards are rolling in money.'

'That's not the point and you know it,' said Alex.

A brief silence fell. Then Elise asked, 'Do you think Laurent believed me? That it was an accident?'

'Yes,' said Alex. 'As a matter of fact, I do. But only because he's a moron.'

'He is *not*,' protested Elise.

'He is about some things,' said Alex. Then, seemingly out of nowhere, he added, 'I don't think he's right for you, you know Elise.'

'What do you mean?' Elise's eyes narrowed.

'It's obvious you've had a crush on him for ever,' Alex replied bluntly. 'I'm just saying, I hope you grow out of it. It's nothing against Laurent. You're just very, very different people, that's all.'

Elise shrugged. 'I can't help that. I love him.'

'You love him now,' said Alex. 'That doesn't mean you will forever.'

'I will,' Elise insisted with feeling. 'Anyway, everybody knows that opposites attract.'

'Like Maman and Papa, you mean?' observed Alex, with a knowing look. Standing up, he yawned, then stooped down to kiss his sister on the head. 'It's late. We should turn in. Merry Christmas, Elise.'

'Merry Christmas, Alex.'

She watched him go, her heart swelling with love, the

deep, uncomplicated love between a sister and a brother that never hurt or disappointed one the way that other loves could do. Afterwards, she climbed into bed and tried to calm her troubled, anxious spirits, but it was no use.

Had Laurent really believed her? Or had that horrible girl sown seeds of doubt in his mind? He had loved the mug she made him when he opened it, she felt sure of that much at least. '*I'll think of you every time I drink from it.*' Oh, the joy of those words! But the misery of the ones that came afterwards: '*She's only a kid.*'

Only a kid today, perhaps. But not forever.

One day I will *be a woman. And then I'll make him love me, as much as I love him. And I'll marry him, and we'll be blissfully happy together, no matter what Alex thinks.*

Just as long as he didn't marry Ines or some other awful imposter in the meantime.

Please God, Elise prayed. *Let me grow up faster. And let him not fall in love with anyone else. Please, please God, if I never ask for anything else . . . save Laurent for me.*

She was awakened a few hours later by the sound of shouting outside. Pressing her face to the window by her bed, she tried to make out what was happening. But Alex's voice ringing out through the still night air soon made things painfully clear.

'You're a disgrace. Not just to Maman, but to yourself. How could you?'

In a heavy woollen overcoat and boots, Alex stood beneath the bare branches of a sycamore tree berating their father.

Louis, doubled over and staggering around in the snow, mumbled something incoherent in reply. He was obviously blind drunk.

'I've tried to hold my tongue. To be patient. To wait for things to get better. For *you* to get better. But you never do! You just get worse, and worse. You tell me to respect you, as my father. But how can anyone respect you when you don't respect yourself? I won't just sit by and let you take Maman and Sainte Madeleine down with you, do you hear me? I—'

The slap rang out like a thunderclap. Out of nowhere, Louis sprang at his son like a wounded bear, swiping its paw at a rival. His open palm made contact with Alex's cheek, sending him reeling backwards.

Elise gasped, recoiling from the window in horror. She couldn't see Alex's face. Or Papa's, for that matter. But from the still, shocked body language of both, it was clear that something profound had changed between them. A line had been crossed, a step taken that could not be taken back.

Frightened, Elise retreated under her blankets. But their warmth did nothing to lessen the chill in her heart.

PART TWO: ALEX

1932–1938

CHAPTER SEVEN

'I don't see why I can't go.'

Ruth Ballard thrust her eighteen-year-old chin out as far as it would go and pouted across the dinner table at her father.

'Yes you do,' Bob Ballard replied patiently. 'You just don't like it is all.'

'Everybody else is going.'

Bob shrugged, slowly raising a forkful of his wife's delicious grits into his mouth. 'We ain't everybody else.'

'Mama?' Ruth turned plaintively to her mother Jean, usually her staunch defender in battles with her dad. But on this occasion, the Ballard parents were as one.

'I know it's hard, honey,' said Jean, reaching across the table for her daughter's hand. 'And I get why you want to go to the dance. We both do. But times are really tough for so many folks in Winsome right now. It's just . . . it's insensitive.'

Ruth slumped back in her chair and folded her arms across her chest, her mouth resetting itself into a thin, angry line of defeat. There would be no reasoning with her parents now. She couldn't go to the town dance, the one and only exciting, fun event to have been organized in Winsome in well over a year, and that was that. Because of the stupid

Depression – because everyone was so damn poor and miserable, all the time – she was to be denied music and dancing and flirting with young men and all the things that made life worth living when you were eighteen, lived in a sleepy Napa town, and spent your days doing nothing but work.

It wasn't fair.

This evening's disagreement was actually a fairly rare occurrence in the Ballard household. An only child, Ruth generally got along really well with both her parents, who loved and were proud of her and who relied on her heavily to help in the family business. Bob Ballard had built up his small wine merchant's operation from nothing before Prohibition, literally from dust and sweat, to the point where Ballard Wines were supplying half of Napa County and a good number of San Francisco restaurants to boot. But the infamous 1920 law changed all that, effectively wiping out the US wine industry with the stroke of a pen. Wine had always been Bob Ballard's passion, and still was. But he'd had the good sense to pivot immediately and diversify, transforming 'Ballard Wines' into 'Ballard Food and Drink'. Through a combination of hard work, natural salesmanship and thriftiness – ever since Ruth was a small child, every penny the family earned had been ploughed back religiously into the business – Bob had not only survived but succeeded in clawing his and his family's way into the middle class. They now lived in a well-furnished, cosy apartment above the store in town and had money in the bank at a time when many of the men Bob grew up with were literally on the bread line.

It was this disparity in circumstances, this 'luck' as Bob saw it, that he and his family were enjoying at a time when so many others were sinking beneath the waves of economic catastrophe that had crippled America, that made the idea of something as frivolous as a dance distasteful at best, if not outright wrong. He knew it was tough on Ruth. But things would get better eventually, in California and everywhere else. Especially if, as expected, the hated Prohibition laws were finally repealed in the new year. Once that happened there'd be plenty of dances. Plenty of parties and young men and opportunities for the sort of fun and nonsense his daughter craved.

'May I be excused?' Ruth placed her knife and fork neatly in the centre of her empty plate. She'd had no appetite for the meal her mom had made her, but angry as she was, she knew better than to waste food. 'I need to get some air.'

'Sure, honey,' said Bob. 'You go on out for a walk. Clear your head.'

Clear my head, Ruth thought bitterly, scuffing her way along Winsome's dusty Main Street a few minutes later. *Clear it of what? Of all my hopes and dreams? Of anything that isn't work, and deliveries and invoices and stupid stocktakes?*

Everyone in town knew Ruth Ballard – everyone knew everyone in Winsome, a two-horse town just a short buggy ride from nearby St Helena – and a few familiar faces waved in greeting as she passed by. Pretty in a capable, womanly sort of way; with her round, rosy cheeks, full breasts and strong tanned forearms, the product of endless deliveries of heavy wine crates in the California sun, there was nothing delicate about Bob Ballard's daughter. Redheaded and striking, Ruth was also well liked for her intelligence, her ready laugh and her kindness.

Despite her resentment at not being allowed to go to this weekend's dance, she shared her parents' sympathy for the plight of local families devastated by the Depression. Just walking through town this evening, past the rows of run-down wooden houses, their white paint peeling and neglected in the fading light, she'd glimpsed a number of hungry women and children and clocked the haunted faces of their menfolk, sunken and defeated, unable to find any sort of work. After the ravages of Prohibition, which had hit California harder than other places, to be hit with a second economic catastrophe seemed unusually cruel. Of course, everyone was talking about the law being repealed and the prospect of better times to come. Local vineyards were replanting and harvesting again for the first time in over a decade, and the authorities were making no effort to stop them. But those wines would be for tomorrow's tables. Today's cupboards were bare, and the Ballards' neighbours were starving.

Ruth knew she was lucky. But still. It wasn't fair. This was the 1930s, after all, the modern era of emancipation and freedom, of jazz and talking movies and all sorts of thrilling new dances like the Charleston and the Lindy Hop. And she was missing it all.

Popping into the gas station, she spent five cents on a bottle of Coke, a luxury that her dad would not have approved of, but that was partly why she did it. Heading back down towards the river, ignoring the envious glances of groups of kids as she passed, she sat down by the water's edge, opened the bottle with her teeth, and drank it all in one long, angry swig, so quickly that rivers of black bubbles came shooting out of her nose and ran wastefully down the front of her smock. Ruth didn't care. She was over being the good girl, over always doing the right thing. It never got her anywhere. Afterwards, as if to emphasize the point, she leaned back and let out a loud, deeply satisfying and distinctly unladylike belch.

'Bravo!' a man's voice boomed out from the opposite bank, accompanied by loud clapping and laughter.

Startled, Ruth scrambled to her feet. 'Who's there?'

'Oh, don't mind me, please,' the man continued. 'That

was very impressive.' Emerging from the bushes, Ruth saw that he was tall, blond and distinctly attractive. He was also laughing at her. 'If I hadn't seen you with my own eyes, I would have guessed you were a three-hundred-pound farmhand with a beer gut and a bald patch. You're quite the pleasant surprise.'

'What do you mean, sneaking up like that, hiding in the bushes?' she demanded pompously, her embarrassment translating into a priggishness that wasn't like her.

'I wasn't hiding,' said the man, still chuckling as he made his way over the low stone footbridge towards her. He had an accent, Ruth noticed. Not Spanish, but something European, definitely not American. 'I was minding my own business, walking along the river, when I was rudely disturbed by a burp so loud I thought it might have been an earthquake.'

Ruth's blush deepened. He really was horribly handsome. He knew it though, with that smug smile of his. More of a sneer really. And he *had* snuck up on her.

'What's your name?'

He was standing right beside her now, oblivious to her hostility.

'None of your business,' she said haughtily, taking a step back and smoothing down her stained smock in an attempt to restore her dignity. But everything she did only seemed to amuse him more.

'I see,' he grinned. 'Well in that case, I think I will call you "Hank".'

'You will *not*,' seethed Ruth.

'Why not?' teased the infuriating man. 'You belch like a Hank. And as you won't tell me your name, you're leaving me no choice but to guess.'

Lost for words for once in her life, and too mortified to be able to make a joke of it, Ruth turned on her heel and stalked off, back up the hill towards home.

'Oh, come on!' the handsome man called after her. 'Don't be like that. I'm only joking with you.'

Ruth kept walking.

'Hank!' the man yelled, still laughing. 'Come back!'

By the time she reached home, Ruth's cheeks were bright red, from a combination of shame and exertion. She'd run the last half mile, panicked that the smiling, mocking stranger might be following her.

'Good walk?' Bob Ballard asked, without looking up from his paper.

'Oh, just leave me alone!' Ruth sobbed, slamming her bedroom door.

The wine merchant and his wife exchanged glances, then returned to their reading. Ruth was a good girl, really. She'd be over it in the morning.

Two weeks later, on a glorious, cloudless early September morning, Ruth pulled her battered red Model A Roadster pickup into the forecourt of Danson's vineyard. The disappointment of missing the Winsome dance now forgotten, Ruth was once again back to her normal, cheerful self and had thoroughly enjoyed this morning's drive, speeding her way through the narrow lanes that led to Danson's, high up in the hills above St Helena.

Back in the days of Ballard Wines, Grady Danson had been one of Ruth's father's earliest and most reliable suppliers of mid-priced Cabernet Sauvignons. Danson's fruit-heavy wines with their strong notes of currant and plum had been consistent sellers, popular with restaurants and domestic clients alike. But Prohibition, and then Grady's death, had put an end to the winery, and for the last five years Danson's had attempted to make ends meet as a fruit and avocado farm. It was only this year, with a new crop of vines and the much talked about hiring of a hot-shot young manager, that Danson's was potentially returning to the wine business. Today was Ruth's first trip out to the vineyard since it had been replanted, and she was excited to see the place again.

Some things were just as she remembered. The iconic winding drive, lined with black oaks, snaking its way up a steep escarpment to the sprawling Victorian farmhouse. The house itself was unchanged too, a study in faded grandeur with its covered wrap-around porch and sweeping steps down to a flat, wide lawn as big as a baseball field. But a lot of things were different, in a way that made Ruth's heart lift. All of the fruit trees had gone, replaced with row after row of young vines. And the commercial buildings of the old winery had been transformed too, the barns and wine presses and the barrel stores that had been derelict for as long as Ruth could remember. Overnight, it seemed, someone had poured money into the business, with everything freshly painted, and gleaming new machinery, and a small fleet of Ford Doodlebugs parked outside the main barn ready to whisk workers and pickers around the property for the promised harvest.

With her clipboard and order sheets tucked under her arm, Ruth hopped out of her pickup feeling grown-up and professional. Her orders from Pa were simple: 'Get the new manager to commit to as much as you can, but not for more than this price per bottle.' He'd underscored it in red. 'We're all taking a risk here, until that damned law's repealed. So don't you let him upsell you.'

'As if I would, Pa,' Ruth frowned. 'I'm a Ballard, remember?'

It was a confident and happy Ruth who sauntered into the Danson's office, asking to speak to the manager. She recognized the boy on the front desk, Tyler Miller. They'd been at high school together in St Helena, although he was a few years ahead of her, in her cousin Michael's grade.

'I know you,' Tyler said, narrowing his eyes as he tried

to place her. Short and wiry, like a terrier, but with the sort of naughty face that made girls fall for him anyway, he did his best not to stare at Ruth's impressively full bosom rising and falling beneath her white, business blouse. 'How do I know you?'

'School, I think.' Ruth smiled. 'You were Mickey's friend?'

'Mickey Ballard. That's right.' He clicked his fingers, pointing at her in belated recognition. 'You're his cousin. Boy, you've sure grown.'

'I work full-time for my dad now,' said Ruth, handing him one of her newly printed business cards that read simply: *Ruth Ballard. Ballard Food & Drink.*

'Nice.' Tyler studied the card, impressed. 'Your dad's getting back into the wine business?'

'We'll see,' Ruth replied cautiously. 'I'm here to see the new manager.'

'Alex? Oh sure. He's out back, checking on the new barrels. You can follow me, if you like.'

Tyler led Ruth through the cramped office and out through the back door into a cobbled courtyard. A short, fat man was standing next to a half-unloaded truck of oak barrels. Judging by his hand gestures, he was engaged in what looked to be an animated conversation with a much taller blond man who stood with his back to them.

'Hey, Alex,' Tyler called to the tall man. 'Someone here to see you. She's from Ballards', he added, with a wink at Ruth, as if to imply that they were both playing at being grown-ups.

The man turned around.

'Hank!' he grinned broadly. 'Fancy seeing you here.'

Ruth felt her stomach liquefy and an unpleasant softening sensation take hold of her knees. 'You!' she gasped.

'Wait, you two know each other?' asked Tyler, confused.

'Not really,' said the man. 'Alex Salignac,' he introduced

himself, holding out his hand for Ruth to shake. 'It's a pleasure to meet you, Miss . . . ?'

'Ballard,' she muttered, blushing furiously as his fingers gripped hers. 'Ruth Ballard.' Clearing her throat, she began her prepared script, adopting her best businesslike tone. 'My father had a close relationship with Danson's back in the old days, Mr Salignac. As you may be aware . . .'

'It's Alex,' he corrected her, his blue eyes boring into hers in a most disconcerting manner.

'As you may be aware,' Ruth pushed on, ignoring him, 'we are . . . we were . . . the premier wine merchant for this part of the Napa Valley. Now, depending on the changes to the law we're all expecting, we could be interested in renewing our relationship with Danson's and pre-ordering a percentage of next year's vintage. For a reasonable price, of course, which we can discuss . . .'

'Over dinner?' Alex interrupted her. 'Excellent idea.'

'Well, I . . .' Ruth stammered.

'Shall we say tonight at seven?'

'Erm . . .'

'I would talk now, but I'm rather tied up, as you can see, so I think dinner might be more productive,' said Alex, gesturing to the impatient-looking fat man with the barrels. 'Just let Tyler here know where I should pick you up.'

And with that he turned his back, resuming his earlier conversation as if the last minute with Ruth had never happened.

'Salignac, you say?'

Bob Ballard paced the store floor distrustfully as Ruth fiddled with her watch strap, trying not to look nervous. He knew the name from somewhere, he just wasn't sure where.

'That was what he said. Alex Salignac. I think he's French.'

'Hmm,' Bob sniffed, unimpressed. 'And he's young, this fella?'

'Young to be the manager at Danson's, definitely,' said Ruth. 'Tyler said he grew up on a vineyard, so maybe he's more experienced than he looks.'

'Hmm,' said Bob again. 'Well just remember, this is business. Whatever his intentions might be, you're there to get the Danson's order. Nothing more.'

'Believe me, Pa, I have no interest whatsoever in Alex Salignac,' said Ruth with feeling. 'He's smug and arrogant and *sooo* very pleased with himself. He's not for me.'

At that very moment, a smartly dressed, blond young man appeared in the store doorway carrying a bunch of hand-picked flowers.

'For Mrs Ballard,' he explained politely in the very faintest of French accents, handing the posy to Bob as he introduced himself and offered Ruth his arm, promising to have her home by nine thirty.

If he's smug and arrogant, he does a good job of hiding it, thought Bob, watching the two young people climb into the boy's freshly cleaned car. He was still trying to remember where he'd heard the name 'Salignac' as they drove off towards St Helena, Ruth stiff and prim in the front passenger seat.

Ah, well, she was a good girl after all, and clever, and the young Danson's manager was clearly smitten. With any luck she'd land them a big order and at a competitive price before the lad knew what had hit him.

Trevoni's in St Helena was a modest Italian establishment, one of only a couple of restaurants that had managed to keep their doors open through the rough years following the 1929 crash. Alex had chosen it because he could afford it – just, and as long as he ate nothing but bread and cheese for the next month up in the rooms he shared with Tyler above the winery. But also because he suspected Ruth Ballard was not a girl one could easily impress with a fancy restaurant and flowery compliments.

Ordering two Cokes – 'I know they're your favourite' – he handed Ruth the menu, wondering how he was going to get her to relax without the help of any alcohol.

He liked her. He knew that immediately, the moment he first saw her stubborn, infuriated face when she sat down on the riverbank and downed her bottle of Coke as if it were whisky. There was something intrinsically *American* about her, something independent and fiery and strong that Alex had never encountered among French girls, at least not the ones of his own class. Of course, it didn't hurt that she was so pretty, with that red hair and womanly figure and the adorable light smattering of freckles across her nose. It was a long time since Alex had kissed a girl, not since he left Burgundy, in fact, which was almost two years ago now.

Good God. Had it really been that long since the final, screaming row with Louis that had at last pushed Alex over the edge? He could remember it like it were yesterday. It was a glorious early summer's evening in 1930, just months after the Christmas at Chateau Brancion when Alex and Louis had come to blows. That ill-fated holiday had marked a turning point for the worse, not just in Alex's own relationship with his father, but in his parents' marriage, and in Louis generally.

Alex and Arnaud had been up at the winery together, working on an order of new barrels for the coming harvest. Elise was there too, mooching around among the presses and equipment. All three of them were in a joyous mood after an afternoon spent among the vines, carefully examining the leaves and fruit of countless plants with their expert eyes and fingers. Finally, *finally*, Sainte Madeleine was about to produce the bumper harvest that they so sorely needed. Alex could still picture Elise's face beneath the setting Burgundy sun, her wide eyes and huge smile as she pointed out one particular cluster of grapes, as ripe and swollen as damsons and with a perfect sheen and patina to their skin.

'We'll keep our Grand Cru appellation now for sure, won't we?' She looked to him and Arnaud for reassurance.

'Yes,' said Alex.

'Nothing is certain when it comes to wine, *princesse*,' Arnaud chipped in cautiously. 'You know that. There is a magic to each vintage that none of us can predict. But it's fair to say these plants are looking very promising. Very promising indeed.'

Louis had walked in just as they were finishing up for the day. In a three-piece suit, bespoke-tailored at extortionate cost like all his clothes, and with his silk tie askew, he'd obviously just returned from Paris and some sort of business meeting. He was sober, which was a plus. But his face was ashen, and when Elise came over and hugged him, he barely registered the gesture, shooing her back to the house with an impatience he usually reserved only for Didier or, increasingly, Alex.

'What's happened?' Arnaud asked, as soon as Elise was gone.

But Louis just shook his head and said nothing, like a shell-shocked soldier.

'Papa,' Alex pressed gently. '*Qu'est-ce qu'il y a?* Whatever it is, you can tell us.'

Louis ran a shaking hand through his hair. 'I've sold the home farm and manor farm.'

Now it was Alex's turn to go white. Those farmhouses were as much a part of Sainte Madeleine as the chateau itself, and had been attached to the estate for generations. To put them up for sale, and without even consulting him or Arnaud? That was quite an admission.

'I had to,' Louis insisted sheepishly. 'The bank were being *chiant* about our damned interest payments. There was no other way.'

'But . . . what about the tenant families?' Alex asked, once he recovered his voice. 'The Troudeaux and old Monsieur Dupont? Where will they go?'

'I don't *know* where they'll go, Alexandre,' Louis snapped, guilt fuelling his anger. 'I dare say we'll work something out. But this isn't a charity. We *had* to raise funds.'

'So you've sold both the houses?' Arnaud clarified.

Louis nodded grimly.

'But not the land?'

Alex let out a joyless laugh. 'Of course he hasn't sold the *land*. That's more than a third of the estate. Without the income from those farms, we'd have nothing to fall back on the next time the grape harvest . . .'

He let the sentence trail off. Louis's stricken, defensive, devastated face said it all.

'No!' Alex gasped.

Even the usually unflappable Arnaud let out a long low groan and sank his head into his hands.

From then on Alex's memories became a bit of a blur. He remembered his father screaming, and himself screaming back. He remembered poor old Arnaud, in terrible distress, turning and leaving to go back to his cottage without a word, leaving the two of them to it. In his more honest moments, Alex remembered himself saying some true, but unbelievably cruel things to his father, just as he had at Chateau Brancion. Calling him an alcoholic and a failure, a womanizer and a cheat, an embarrassment to Maman and all of them. Louis, no doubt, had been equally belittling.

No blows were exchanged this time. But whatever the rights or wrongs of the argument, this was the end for Alex. He loved Sainte Madeleine too much to sit back and watch while his father destroyed her. It was simply more pain than he could bear. So the next morning, without a word to anyone, he cashed in his birthday cheque from his godmother and bought a berth on the French liner SS *Rochambeau* to

New York. He knew if he told Maman, or Elise, or Arnaud, or God forbid poor Dids, the pressure on him to stay would be unbearable. And he also knew he couldn't stay. Not with Louis, and things the way they were.

Three days later, he was gone.

It took him six months to work his way across America from New York to Napa, and another few weeks before he talked himself into the manager's job at Danson's. Only then did he exchange letters with everyone back at Sainte Madeleine. Emotional, painful letters, but the deed was done. The only person Alex didn't write to was Louis. Partly because he was still too angry. And partly because he didn't know what to say. Reading between the lines of his mother's and Elise's letters, it was clear that the feeling was mutual. That relationship, it seemed, had been damaged beyond repair.

And so Alex had moved on, throwing himself into his new life in the New World with all the energy and optimism he could muster, never slowing down enough to allow himself to miss Sainte Madeleine, or his family, or to reflect on the enormity of his decision to leave. The one downside of his frantic work life was that it had left him precious little spare time for romance. Tonight's date was a rare treat.

'So,' Ruth began, tossing the menu to one side without interest. 'Let's talk about wine.'

'Must we?' said Alex. 'I'd much rather talk about you.'

'The new winery up at Danson's looked pretty impressive,' said Ruth, ignoring him. 'The family has clearly made a big investment.'

'Well, everyone knows the Prohibition laws are going to be repealed,' said Alex, deciding that the only way out of the business conversation was going to be through it.

'Everyone *hopes*,' Ruth corrected him.

Alex shrugged. 'The vineyards that are waiting for

certainty will have missed the boat. Mr Danson wanted to steal a march on our competitors. Just like your father,' he added, beckoning the waitress. 'I'd like the lasagne, please.'

'And for the lady?' the girl asked, with a sullen look at Ruth. She wished the handsome young man with an exotic foreign accent were taking *her* out to dinner.

'I'm really not hungry,' lied Ruth. She knew it was silly, but after the embarrassing belching incident she felt nervous about eating in front of Alex, and didn't want to give him any more reasons to make fun of her. She'd made an effort tonight, in a pretty floral shirtwaister dress that her mother had run up for her on her new Singer sewing machine. She told herself that this was purely for business reasons, but it wasn't completely lost on her that the new Danson's manager was a very handsome man, a commodity that was extremely thin on the ground in Winsome.

'She'll have the same,' said Alex, handing both menus back to the waitress. 'I can't send you home to your parents on an empty stomach.'

Ruth considered being affronted, but then decided that might not help her secure the order at the price Pa wanted. Best to get that done first.

'We'd like to take an initial order of twenty cases, at this price.' Reaching into her purse, she pulled out a piece of paper and handed it across the table.

Alex read the number. 'That's fifteen per cent under market.'

'As of today, there is no market,' said Ruth.

'The offer's too low,' said Alex. 'I believe we can do better.'

'Really? Where?' Ruth challenged him, her grey eyes sparkling. 'How about if we were to pay you twenty per cent up front? Our risk.'

Alex cocked his head to one side, considering.

'Has your father agreed to that?'

'You're negotiating with me, Mr Salignac. Not my father.'

Alex leaned back in his chair, gazing at Ruth with renewed admiration. There were no girls in France like this. The girls Alex had met back home had all been pretty, decorative, and in some cases accomplished daughters of other local noble families. But none had Ruth Ballard's confidence, that aura of capability and ambition that seemed unique to American women.

'How old did you say you were?'

'I didn't,' Ruth smiled, sensing she might be edging close to a deal.

'How about this,' said Alex. 'If I agree to sell you my first twenty cases, at this price, with twenty per cent up front . . .'

'Yes?' said Ruth.

'You agree not to mention another word about business for the whole of the rest of this evening. *And* you promise to enjoy your dinner, and to stop treating me like the enemy, and to tell me all about yourself and your life and your family.'

Ruth smiled, despite herself. 'There really isn't very much to tell. But all right, Mr Salignac. You've got yourself a deal.'

She offered him her hand and Alex shook it, holding her rough, working fingers in his for longer than was strictly necessary.

'A pleasure doing business with you.'

It was nine thirty on the dot when Alex's car pulled up outside the Ballards' store, and a different, dreamy-looking Ruth stepped out and waved him goodbye.

'We were worried,' Jean Ballard told her daughter, as Ruth came inside and positively floated upstairs. 'Pa's been watching for you out the window this past half hour.'

'I don't see why,' said Ruth. 'We weren't late.'

'You were nearly late,' said Bob, frowning.

'That's called "being on time", Pa,' Ruth countered. 'I got the order, by the way.'

'You did?' Bob brightened. 'He agreed at that price?'

'Uh-huh.' Ruth sighed wistfully, a slow smile spreading across her face and seeming to suffuse her whole body.

Jean saw the signs before her husband. 'So, how was dinner?'

'It was OK.' Ruth shrugged.

'Just OK?'

A small, slow smile began to spread across Ruth's face. 'It was . . . interesting.'

'Oh Lord.' Jean rolled her eyes. 'You like him, don't you?'

'I didn't say that,' Ruth protested. But it wasn't long before it all tumbled out.

'He's just different. Really different. I mean, his life, the things he's *been* through, you wouldn't believe. So he grew up in France on this incredible vineyard, and his family are like, practically royalty there, but he ran away to the States because his dad's a drunk who sold off half the estate without telling anyone and he won't listen to reason, and Alex just couldn't sit by and watch it happen. He wants to own his own vineyard here one day. He says he's sure Napa's going to be the new Burgundy. He knows so much about it, Ma, it's no wonder the Dansons hired him.'

'Is that so?' Jean asked mildly.

'I mean, obviously he misses his home and his family,' Ruth went on, without drawing breath. 'Just not the dad. His mom's nice but she's a Catholic and crazy religious. Alex is close to his sister, but she lives in Paris now, and his brother has depression, mainly because the dad bullies him so badly, so Alex felt *really* guilty leaving him behind, but you know, what could he do? He has to live his own life.'

'Did you say "Burgundy"?' Bob Ballard interrupted his daughter's unending, stream-of-consciousness monologue.

'Hmm?' Ruth looked up. 'Oh, yes. Burgundy. That's where his family's vineyard is. Only Alex called it a *domaine*. Sainte Something, I think it was. There's some legend about butterflies, that apparently is really famous in France.'

'Sainte Madeleine.' Bob let out a low whistle. 'Well, I'll be blowed. I knew I'd heard that name before. Salignac. Your boy's only one of *the* Burgundy Salignacs. And he's *here*, at Danson's! What are the odds?'

'He's not "my boy", Pa,' said Ruth. But neither of her parents were buying it.

'The Salignac family have been producing Burgundy Grand Crus at Sainte Madeleine for hundreds of years.' Bob Ballard looked at his wife. 'We're talking serious money, Jean.'

'Alex doesn't have any money,' Ruth corrected him. 'He's walked away from all that. He's self-made. Or at least, he's going to be.'

Jean chuckled. '"Going to be" self-made, eh? Well, we shall watch his progress with interest, shan't we, Bob?'

'Mmm hmm,' replied Bob Ballard, lost in thought. 'We sure will.'

Half an hour later, it was Ruth who was lost in thought, staring up at the ceiling of her childhood bedroom.

Something had happened tonight. Something unexpected and sudden and more than a little bit terrifying. But it had happened, and there was nothing Ruth could do to change it, even if she wanted to.

As loath as she was to believe it, Ruth Ballard had a horrible feeling that she may have fallen in love.

CHAPTER EIGHT

Chantelle Delorme returned to her Paris apartment at three in the afternoon and found herself looking at the familiar sight of her goddaughter Elise, slumped on the chaise longue looking sorry for herself.

'Shouldn't you be in class, *chérie*?' she asked, pulling open the floor-length chambray curtains to let the dappled, spring sunlight into the room. On the third floor of a grand, baroque building in the 6th Arondissement, just off Saint-Germain-des-Prés, Chantelle's apartment felt both bohemian and traditional, a testament both to its owner's eclectic good taste and to the generous family trust that funded it. Faded antique Persian rugs lay scattered carelessly over the parquet floors, and modern as well as traditional art jostled for position on the original eighteenth-century plaster walls. But the most striking thing about the apartment were the views. Almost every room offered sweeping, romantic vistas across the rooftops of the city, and from the pretty guest suite where Elise slept you could clearly make out the iconic dome of Notre Dame.

'Madame Sourian's not well today,' said Elise, squinting at the unaccustomed light as it flooded the drawing room. 'Class was cancelled.'

It was a lazy, obvious lie, but one that her godmother

chose to ignore, under the circumstances. For one thing, everybody knew that Elise's so-called 'History of Art' course at the Sorbonne was no more than a flimsy excuse to justify her presence in Paris; the real purpose of which was to flit around town from party to party, enjoying herself and impressing as many eligible young men as possible. (Also, although nobody said as much openly, to escape the cloying, oppressive atmosphere at Sainte Madeleine. Things had been bad before Alex's departure for the States, but they'd become unbearable afterwards.) More importantly, Chantelle happened to know that Elise had met her father Louis for lunch today, and she suspected that the encounter had not gone well.

'Did you see Papa?' she asked, keeping her tone light as she plumped up the pillows around her goddaughter's reclining form, clearing a space for herself to sit beside her.

Elise nodded mutely. When she looked at Chantelle there were tears in her eyes. 'He was so thin. And shaking,' she confided, biting down on her lower lip bravely. 'His skin looked yellow, Chantelle, like paper that's had tea spilled on it. I hardly recognized him.'

Chantelle wrapped a comforting arm around her. She had no children of her own and considered Louis Salignac's only daughter like family. Chantelle and Louis had walked out together once, a million years ago, before he met Thérèse, and they had remained lifelong friends. But Chantelle's affection for Elise ran deeper than that. Her goddaughter reminded her very much of herself at the same age: beautiful, headstrong and wild, but with a volcano of vulnerability bubbling away beneath the confident, party-girl surface. She loved her, and it pained her to see her suffering like this.

'When people stop drinking after many years of abuse, the symptoms can be extreme,' she explained gently. 'The shaking and all of that. Those can actually be signs that the person is getting well.'

'Papa did not look well,' said Elise in a faltering voice. 'And he didn't sound it either. He says Maman won't let him come back to Sainte Madeleine until the doctor signs some sort of paper. She doesn't understand that Sainte Madeleine is what he needs to *get* well. Sainte Madeleine heals everyone who believes in her magic.'

Chantelle nodded sympathetically, and resisted the urge to tell Elise that it was doctors who helped people get better, not mythical Salignac butterflies. She understood that, for all her outward efforts at sophistication, parts of Elise were still very much a child. In particular the parts that were rooted in Sainte Madeleine, the childhood home that she loved so dearly.

Nor was Chantelle a fan of Elise's mother. She had always found Thérèse to be cold and snobbish, with a puritanical hatred of anything that might bring joy into one's life. But she thought on this occasion the woman was right. For everyone's sake, she needed to force Louis to dry out completely before she took him back. Infidelities were one thing, and an accepted part of upper-class French life. But Louis's drinking had become something else over the years, something far more serious. Not only was it ruining his own life, and the lives of his children, but it had come close to precipitating the demise of Sainte Madeleine, a venerable Burgundy domaine, not to mention a historically profitable family business. Such things were not so easily forgiven.

Thankfully, after a banner year in 1930, when Sainte Madeleine's wines had won just about every honour and award imaginable, and even been named Burgundy Grand Cru of the Year by the prestigious *La Revue du vin de France*, the domaine's fortunes were once again on the rise. Which was just as well, as there was a lot of ground to be made up, debts to be paid off, and land to be – slowly – bought back and restored piecemeal to the estate.

After Alex left for America, Thérèse had, with help from

the family lawyers, won temporary control of Sainte Madeleine's finances, freezing Louis out of all the business accounts. It wasn't a step she'd taken lightly. But in effect Louis had forced her hand, disappearing yet again to Paris in a fit of despair, and leaving poor Arnaud Berger to break the news to Thérèse about the disastrous (and as it turned out quite unnecessary) sale of both Sainte Madeleine's large farms.

Thérèse acted quickly and decisively. She hired a local agent to help her restructure Sainte Madeleine's debts, and handed over the day-to-day running of the vineyard entirely to Arnaud. She also deferred to Arnaud's judgement in ways that Louis could never bring himself to do. When Arnaud came to Madame nervously asking to invest a huge portion of their 1930 profits in new technology and equipment for the winery – the same idea that Alex had been pushing for years before he left – Thérèse signed off on it without hesitation.

'I don't understand wine, Arnaud. Nor do I understand business. But I understand people,' she informed him. 'I trust you completely. Please do whatever you feel is best.'

Looking at a devastated Elise now, Chantelle did her best to stick up for Thérèse.

'I know it seems harsh,' she told her goddaughter. 'But I believe your mother is only trying to help Papa recover. She's also doing her best to protect you and your brothers in the meantime.'

But Elise was having none of it. 'Protect us from what? From Papa?'

'Well . . .'

'I don't *want* protecting from Papa, Chantelle. And Alex has run off and abandoned us all anyway, so he hardly needs protecting. As for poor Dids . . .' She swallowed hard. 'That ship has rather sailed, don't you think? The damage is done.'

'I know, my darling,' Chantelle said kindly. No one liked to use the word 'breakdown' openly, but it was no secret that Didier Salignac had spent much of last year in a private sanatorium, his fragile personality shattered after years of intermittent cruelty from his father.

'Come on,' Chantelle said briskly, deciding it was time to break the spell. Taking Elise's hand, she pulled her up to a sitting position. 'We can't waste all day worrying about your father. Go and put some clothes on. And then if you really don't have classes, I suggest a stroll to the Place Vendôme.'

'Really?' Elise squealed, a look of delight spreading instantly across her features at the prospect of a shopping trip with her godmother. 'Could we stop in at Chanel, just to look?'

'I don't see why not,' Chantelle laughed, amused but also pleased at how easily Elise could be distracted from the parlous state of her family's affairs. 'And, I have more good news. I had a lovely card delivered by hand earlier, inviting us both to dinner this evening at Chez Pascal. From one of your cousins, I believe, a young Monsieur Senard?'

Elise's heart began to pound uncomfortably fast against her ribs. 'Laurent's here? In Paris?'

'The name wasn't Laurent,' said Chantelle, drifting over to her Louis XV bureau to retrieve the card. 'At least I don't think it was. Ah, no, here it is. "Thierry Senard requests the pleasure of your company." Perhaps we could pick up a new scarf, or a little pair of earrings for the occasion?'

'Hmm. Perhaps,' said Elise. The disappointment was sharp but only momentary, and followed by an unexpected sense of relief. Elise hadn't seen either of the Senard boys in years. And as curious as she was to see Laurent again, after today's horrid lunch with Papa she wasn't sure she could cope with the stress of that particular reunion. Dinner with Thierry would be an altogether easier and more relaxing prospect.

Better yet, it would give her an opportunity to look divine, and happy, and make dazzling conversation, so that Thierry could report back to his brother – wherever Laurent was these days – that her life in Paris was a glittering success.

Not that it mattered what Laurent Senard thought, of course. Not anymore. Elise had grown out of all that, and at eighteen had more suitors than she could shake a stick at. Not to mention one in particular that not even her godmother Chantelle knew about yet.

Chantelle watched indulgently as her goddaughter skipped off to her bedroom to get changed. What a beauty she was, so full of life and youth and promise. Of course, Louis had been like that once, she reflected with a shudder.

Please God let Elise's path be different to her father's.

Thierry Senard was already at the table when Elise and her godmother arrived at Chez Pascal. As usual the restaurant was crowded with Paris's most fashionable *beau monde*. Beautiful women, free from the boyish constraints of the previous decade's *garçonne* look, preened in their feminine, satin dresses, cinched at the waist and flared flirtatiously at the ankle. Hats had been largely replaced by softly waved short hair, paired with swipes of pillar-box red lipstick in the style of Jean Harlow. Compared to these shimmering goddesses, most of the men looked unremarkable in their broad-shouldered jackets and baggy pleated trousers. But Thierry Senard was the exception. Standing up to greet Elise resplendent in his regimental uniform, his striking good looks took Chantelle by surprise.

'Good grief,' she whispered in Elise's ear. 'You never mentioned he was an Adonis.'

'Oh, shhh.' Elise brushed her off. 'It's only Thierry.'

Kissing him on both cheeks, she introduced Chantelle and the three of them took their seats, easily the most glamorous party in the restaurant.

'I won't give you a big head by telling you how pretty you look,' Thierry teased Elise, jumping straight back into cousin mode. 'But I must say Paris life seems to suit you.'

'Oh it does,' gushed Elise. 'I adore Paris, and living with Chantelle. She's the absolute best.'

After some obligatory small talk, made easier by the fact that Thierry was so innately confident and easy-going and Chantelle was a natural raconteuse, they ordered escargots and oysters, and the conversation inevitably shifted to family matters.

'So how are your brothers?' Thierry took the bull by the horns. 'We heard about Alex's big blow-up with Uncle Louis. He's in America now, I gather?'

Elise's face fell. 'Yes. He was in New York first, but now he's in California I believe.'

'You believe?' Thierry looked puzzled. 'Don't you know?'

She shrugged sadly. 'He's barely been in touch with any of us. Maman had a telegram when he arrived, and a few letters since. He telephoned last Christmas and when Dids came home from the hospital, but apart from that . . .'

'Aunt Thérèse installed a telephone at Sainte Madeleine?' Thierry raised an eyebrow. 'I never thought I'd see the day.'

Elise smiled. 'Actually that was the one "technological innovation" Papa *did* agree to install before Alex left. Although Alex said it was only so that his mistresses could get hold of him.'

'Elise!' Chantelle reproved her half-heartedly.

'Of course, that was back when he could afford mistresses,' Elise went on, enjoying being adult and risqué in front of Thierry. 'Now he doesn't have a pot to piss in.'

Even Thierry winced at this. Elise was more beautiful than ever, but her coarse language and artfully sophisticated manners felt jarring.

'Maman took legal control of the estate, so he has no access to money and can't borrow against it anymore. She and Arnaud have been running things ever since.'

'Well, I'm sorry about Alex,' said Thierry, trying to steer the conversation away from the awkward subject of Louis. 'I know the two of you have always been close.'

'It's been harder for Maman, honestly,' said Elise. 'Stuck on her own at Sainte Madeleine with only Dids and Brolio for company. She misses Alex dreadfully.'

'I expect he's just terribly busy over there, making his mark,' said Thierry kindly. 'Is he working in the wine business?'

'Oh yes,' said Elise, her tone an odd combination of pride and bitterness. 'Alex has wine in his veins. Just not Burgundy, as it turns out. Or at least not at the moment.'

'He'll be back eventually,' said Thierry. 'He loves Sainte Madeleine. You all do.'

To her mortification, Elise found herself tearing up.

'Yes, well, enough about my family,' she said briskly, reaching across Chantelle for the wine decanter and earning herself a warning glance. 'What's going on with you Senards? I assume Chateau Brancion's unchanged?'

'Same as ever,' Thierry confirmed. 'My parents are creatures of habit,' he explained to Chantelle, making an effort to include her in the conversation. 'They live in an old house in deepest, darkest Burgundy.'

'They live in a palace,' Elise corrected. 'He's being modest.'

'The point being, they tend to potter along with their heads in the sand, steering clear of the modern world as much as they possibly can,' said Thierry.

'I can't say I blame them,' said Chantelle, making a point of passing the bread basket to Elise, who was drinking too much. 'These are frightening times. Especially with that appalling little man Hitler, who just seems to get worse and worse.'

'I agree,' said Thierry. 'The fascists are a problem every-where. Mussolini's an idiot.'

'Well, we have them here too, of course,' Chantelle pointed out. 'Elise and I were both here in February, when those thugs swarmed around the Palais Bourbon. It was terrifying.'

'I can imagine.' Thierry began spreading a thin smear of butter across his bread. 'Part of the problem though is that the communists are even worse. Stalin's an absolute fiend. I don't know if you've read about these terrible purges in Russia, but by all accounts he's murdering literally *millions* of his own people.'

'Please.' Elise held up a hand wearily. 'Enough with all the politics. I feel like I'm at dinner with Laurent.'

Thierry chuckled.

'How is he, by the way?' Elise asked, as casually as she could.

'I'm afraid we're in a similar situation to you and Alex,' Thierry replied sadly. 'None of us really know how he is. Last I heard he was in Madrid. Not living there, but going back and forth a lot.'

'To see Ines?' Elise couldn't stop herself asking.

'See who?' Thierry looked puzzled. 'Oh, you mean the girl who came for Christmas, that last year you were there? Eyebrows Girl? Heavens no. Laurent hasn't seen her in years.'

Elise grinned, delighted. *Eyebrows Girl*. She'd always liked Thierry.

'He's still with his louche, liberal crowd though,' Thierry sighed. 'Spain seems to be their Mecca right now. My brother Laurent's very political,' he explained to Chantelle. 'Very passionate.'

'Is that a bad thing?' she asked.

'Not always, I suppose,' Thierry admitted. 'Laurent's heart's in the right place, but he's caused my parents a terrible amount of worry. He refuses to see how dangerous the communists really are, you see. How far removed they are from his ideals of fairness and justice and . . . all of that,' he finished lamely. 'Anyway, Elise is right. Enough about politics, and errant brothers. Let's talk about Paris and all the parties you've been going to.'

The rest of the dinner passed happily enough, although Chantelle was forced to step in with a firm 'no' when Elise attempted to order a third bottle of claret, and she made sure they all had strong coffees at the end of the meal. Despite her protestations, Thierry insisted on picking up the tab for all three of them, and could not have been more of a gentleman throughout. This was exactly the sort of young man that Chantelle hoped Elise might end up with, although she had to admit that Thierry and Elise came off much more like brother and sister than anything else. So perhaps not him *specifically*.

'Let's all go on to Le Bariton,' Elise proposed excitedly once they emerged from the restaurant onto the street.

'Le Bariton?'

'It's the best jazz club in Paris,' she explained to Thierry. 'A lot of my friends will be there tonight. You can meet them.'

He hesitated, looking to Chantelle for guidance. She was Elise's chaperone, after all, although clearly she kept a pretty loose grip on the reins.

'I'm not much of a jazz man, to be honest,' he told Elise.

'And don't you have classes in the morning?' chimed in Chantelle.

'No, I told you. Madame Sourian's off sick,' said Elise, cleverly remembering her lie from earlier. 'Oh, please, Chantelle. I never get to see Thierry. It'll be *such* fun.'

'Oh, all right,' Chantelle relented. Saying no to her goddaughter had never been her forte, and Thierry Senard seemed like an eminently trustworthy fellow. 'But I'm far too old and too tired to come out dancing, so I'll leave the two of you to it. Just don't stay out till all hours,' she kissed Elise on top of her head, as one would a small child. 'And for heaven's sake go easy on the champagne.'

Le Bariton was a large, brick-walled basement, squirrelled away in a nondescript back street near the Jardin du Luxembourg. A stage, dominated by a battered grand piano, occupied the entire far end of the room, in front of which around thirty tables had been pushed back to create an ad hoc dancefloor, really nothing more than an oval of bare boards covered with sawdust. There was a bar in one corner, already heaving by the time Thierry and Elise arrived, and waiters, incongruously formal in their black-and-white uniforms, darted between the tables serving champagne and vodka drinks.

'It looks like a speakeasy,' Thierry shouted through the din into Elise's ear as they pushed their way inside together. It was hard both to hear and to see, thanks to the low lighting and the heavy miasma of tobacco smoke fogging up the air.

'What?'

'I said IT LOOKS LIKE A SPEAKEASY!'

'I KNOW,' Elise bellowed back, her lithe body already swaying to the beat of the Duke Ellington number being belted out from the stage. 'Isn't it a dream?'

Thierry, who privately thought the cramped, smoky room more of a nightmare, did his best to look enthusiastic. He followed Elise as she weaved her way through the dancers and tables towards a group close to the bar, and nodded and smiled through her inaudible introductions. The party was comprised of two other girls, if you could call them that: a redhead who must be at least thirty, squeezed into a sequined flapper-style dress that did nothing to make her look any younger, and a slightly younger woman in very heavy make-up who Thierry would have bet good money was a prostitute. With them were three men. A young, louche sort of fellow who Elise introduced simply as 'Guy' and his more respectable-seeming friend, who wore a suit and glasses and seemed almost as out of place in the throbbing dive bar as Thierry. And a much older man, handsome but heavy-set, who clearly dominated the group and was paying for everybody's drinks.

The moment Elise arrived, the older man unceremoniously ejected the make-up-caked blonde from his lap, where she'd been happily ensconced, and grabbing Elise's hand, pulled her into the vacated position.

'*Mon chou!*' he exclaimed happily, kissing Elise's hair and neck in an elaborately affectionate manner. 'At last. We'd almost given up on you. Who's your friend?' He gestured without enthusiasm towards Thierry.

'This is my cousin, Thierry Senard,' said Elise. 'Thierry, meet my friend Antoine Renceau. Antoine knows everyone who's anyone in Paris, don't you, darling?'

'I'm sure he does,' said Thierry, shaking Antoine's hand stiffly. 'Elise, can I talk to you for a minute?'

'Oh no you don't, soldier boy,' said Antoine, smiling wolfishly and tightening his grip around Elise's waist. 'You're not stealing her away from me already. She's only just got here. Sit down, son. Relax. Have a drink.' Waving down a waiter, he ordered another large bottle of vodka for the table. Thierry could now see that the blowsy redhead and the louche young man were already blind drunk, and the prostitute, if that's what she was, was well on her way.

'No thank you,' he bristled. 'Elise, please.'

Frowning, Elise wriggled free, promising Antoine she would return momentarily, and followed Thierry into a quieter corner.

'What's the matter?' she asked crossly. 'Why are you in such a bad mood all of a sudden?'

'Elise.' Thierry looked at her seriously, placing both his

hands on her shoulders in a way that reminded her painfully of Laurent. 'That man is bad news.'

'What do you mean?' her frown intensified. 'You don't even know him.'

'I know him by reputation,' said Thierry. 'Antoine Renceau's a well-known fraudster. You must have heard about the shocking way he cheated his partner and investors? Everybody knows about it, even me.'

'Those are just rumours,' Elise said dismissively. 'Antoine told me none of that's true. People are jealous, that's all. Because he's so successful.'

'Oh really? And what about his poor wife? Do you think she's "jealous" too?' Thierry looked at her pityingly. 'You do know he's married?'

'Only in name,' Elise pouted. 'They're separated.'

'Rubbish!' Thierry blurted, frustrated by her naivete. If that was what it was.

'Honestly, Thierry, don't be such a stick-in-the-mud,' said Elise coquettishly. 'Do you have any idea how many girls would kill to be with Antoine?'

'No. I don't.'

Thierry tried not to show how shocked he was by her attitude. But it was painful to watch. If Aunt Thérèse could see her daughter right now, in this place, with these people – sitting on Antoine Renceau's lap, for God's sake – she'd have a heart attack on the spot. Not that one needed to be a puritan like Thérèse Salignac to realize that Elise was heading down a dangerous path, one that would ruin her reputation faster than she could imagine if she didn't turn back.

'He's twice your age,' Thierry tried again.

'So?'

'So I'm taking you home to your godmother's.'

'You most certainly are *not.*'

'Is everything all right?' Walking up behind Elise, Antoine pressed an enormous vodka cocktail into her hand.

'Yes.' 'No,' said Elise and Thierry simultaneously.

'I'm leaving,' Thierry announced bluntly.

'You don't like jazz?' Antoine raised a mocking eyebrow.

'It's the company I don't like,' said Thierry. 'Elise, are you coming?'

She shook her head, more upset than angry. Leaning in closer to Antoine, she took a defiant swig of vodka. 'Not yet.'

'Have no fear, my fine, regimental friend,' Renceau sneered. 'I'll make sure the lady gets home safely in an hour or two. Of course, I can't promise how sober she'll be.'

Thierry turned and left. He wasn't Elise's father. And short of physically dragging Elise out of there, there was nothing more he could do.

Back at the apartment, Chantelle was just about to slip into bed with her *lait chaud* and the latest Dior catalogue when the telephone rang.

She glanced at the gilt carriage clock on her bedside table. *Five minutes to midnight*. Who would put through a call at such a late hour, and why? Tendrils of anxiety, cold and clammy, coiled their way around her heart. If something had happened to Elise . . .

'Chantelle?' Thérèse Salignac's distant, echoey voice crackled down the line, all the way from Burgundy.

Oh God. It was Elise.

'I'm sorry to telephone so late. I hope I didn't wake you,' said Thérèse. 'But I know you usually keep very late hours, and I wanted to wait until Elise was tucked up in bed, so I could speak to you privately.'

'That's all right, I wasn't asleep,' said Chantelle, desperately relieved, but also guilty, knowing that if Elise were tucked up in bed, it certainly wasn't in her own.

'I had a long-distance call from Alexandre today,' said Thérèse. 'In America.'

'Oh?'

'He told me he's engaged to be married.'

'I see,' said Chantelle, who wasn't sure what she'd been expecting Thérèse to say, but certainly not this. 'Well, that's good news. Isn't it?'

'I don't know.' Thérèse sighed. 'Is it? I mean, he sounded happy.'

'Well then,' said Chantelle.

'But he's so young.'

'He's twenty-three,' Chantelle observed. 'That's older than you were when you married Louis.'

'I suppose so. But he's so far away,' Thérèse went on. 'They all are.'

Thérèse had never been especially close to Chantelle, but clearly she needed to unburden herself to someone. Chantelle tried to picture her, all alone at Sainte Madeleine, with only the decrepit nanny and crusty old Arnaud Berger for company. How strange and unnatural that must feel, in such a huge house that had always been full of children and house guests, drama and laughter.

'Is the girl nice?' Chantelle asked, hoping to inject a brighter note to the conversation.

'That's precisely it,' said Thérèse. 'I have no idea. I know almost nothing about her. And what little I do know isn't exactly encouraging.'

'Meaning?'

'According to Alex her name is Ruth and she's a *wine merchant's* daughter,' Thérèse confided in an appalled whisper.

'Oh, Thérèse!' Chantelle couldn't help but laugh. 'Really? Is that what you're worried about? That she's middle class?'

'I don't think you quite understand,' Thérèse clarified primly. 'Her parents live *above a shop*. Oh, I know you and Louis both think I'm a terrible snob.'

'Only because you are,' said Chantelle, not unkindly.

'Perhaps. But this is my son, Chantelle. My Alexandre. Marrying an American shopkeeper's daughter? A Protestant, if you please! It feels as if I'm losing him twice. If only Louis were well, and I could talk to him about it. But as things stand . . .' There was a wobble in her voice, a tremor of real anguish that tugged at Chantelle's heartstrings. Perhaps Thérèse Salignac wasn't made of stone after all?

'Alex will come back to you, Thérèse. Eventually,' she assured her. 'At least he telephoned to let you know. He obviously wanted your blessing.'

'I suppose so,' Thérèse sniffed.

'I take it Louis doesn't know about this?'

'No. Not yet.'

'And the two of you?'

A heavy sigh echoed down the line. 'I get a weekly report from his doctors in Paris. And Arnaud and I write to him every Friday with updates on Sainte Madeleine and what's happening at the vineyard. I know he wants to come home, and I think he will soon. But the doctors all say it's important not to rush things. I'm frightened this news about Alex's engagement might set him back.'

'Yes,' Chantelle mused. 'I can see that.'

'And then there's Elise,' said Thérèse. 'Heaven knows how she'll react.'

'Do you think she'll be upset?' asked Chantelle, surprised.

'I don't know,' Thérèse said sadly. 'I know she felt dreadfully abandoned when Alexandre left. Sainte Madeleine just wasn't the same without him. But the truth is I really don't know much about my daughter's feelings these days. You're the one she's closest to.'

'That's not true,' said Chantelle, although they both knew it was. 'But for what it's worth I'm sure Elise will be pleased for Alex. Yes, she's angry, and she misses him. But I know she would want him to be happy. Who knows, maybe this marriage will be the start of a new chapter, for him and for all of you? It might bring you all closer together again.'

'I can't see how,' bemoaned Thérèse. 'Not while Alex is in America. He's made it very clear that he won't return to Sainte Madeleine while his father's running the estate. Which he will be again once he comes home.'

'Yes, but if there are children?' said Chantelle. 'Surely that might help build bridges with Louis?'

Thérèse let out a derisive laugh. 'American *Protestant* grandchildren? I hardly think so.'

'Would you like me to tell Elise about Alex?' Chantelle asked, eager to bring the conversation to an end. She did feel sorry for Thérèse, but sometimes both her and Louis's knee-jerk social snobbery stuck in her craw.

'Would you?' Thérèse said gratefully. 'That's rather why I called.'

'Of course. I'll tell her in the morning and let you know how she reacts. Then perhaps you can telephone yourself later in the day and talk things through.'

'Yes, perhaps.' Thérèse sounded relieved. 'Or I might just write. Thank you, Chantelle.'

'My pleasure. And do try not to worry too much, Thérèse,' said Chantelle. 'Everything will turn out for the best in the end, I'm sure of it.'

By the time she got back to the apartment, at almost four in the morning, Elise was so drunk the taxi driver had to help her to get her key in the lock.

Staggering into the drawing room, she stooped down to take off her high heels and lost her balance, twisting her ankle painfully as she crumpled to the floor.

'*Merde!*'

Rubbing her already swelling joint, she grabbed an armchair for support as the room swayed and heaved around her like a ship on high seas.

'Dear God.'

Chantelle emerged from her bedroom, pale pink silk robe belted chicly around her waist, to see her teenage goddaughter staggering around like a drunken sailor.

'Look at the state of you, Elise. What happened to Thierry?'

'He left,' Elise slurred, sliding slowly down into a heap on the Persian rug. Her make-up was smudged and her pupils dilated. 'He's no fun anymore. Ushed to be fun.' She tried to sit up again but the effort overwhelmed her and she ended up laying her head on the cushion of one of Chantelle's fringed footrests.

'Why did he leave?' Chantelle demanded. She wasn't at all happy with young Monsieur Senard.

'He didn't like my friends.' Elise shrugged.

'I'm not sure I like them much either,' Chantelle said caustically, 'letting you make your own way home so late, and in this state. Stay there while I make some coffee.'

Twenty minutes later, having been force-fed three *tasses* of strong Peruvian roast and the last of yesterday's brioches, Elise was sober enough to be able to sit at the kitchen table while the first pale rays of dawn sunlight filtered in through the blinds.

'Sorry I stayed out so late,' she mumbled guiltily, while Chantelle refreshed her cup for a third time.

'It's not the lateness, Elise. It's the drinking. It has to stop,' Chantelle told her, with unusual firmness. 'I mean it. Unless you want to end up like your father.'

Elise bit her lip and stared straight ahead. She knew her godmother was right. The Salignacs had struggled with addiction for generations. If the butterflies were the family's magic charm, alcoholism was their curse, just as it had been the curse of the young man in the family legend who had first brought the butterflies to Sainte Madeleine. But Elise wasn't ready to admit it to herself yet, not fully.

'Your mother called earlier,' said Chantelle, changing the subject.

'Well I'm not going back home,' Elise announced defensively. 'I hope you told her. I can't live at Sainte Madeleine with only Maman there. We'd kill each other.'

'Calm down,' said Chantelle. 'She wasn't calling about you coming home. She rang about Alex, as a matter of fact.'

'Alex?'

Chantelle nodded. 'He's getting married.'

Elise froze. She heard the words, but they didn't seem real.

Alex. My Alex? Getting married? No. That couldn't be right.

'He's engaged to an American girl named Ruth,' Chantelle went on. 'I think your mother was worried you might be upset about it. But I'd say it's good news, wouldn't you?'

'Mm hmmm.'

Elise forced a smile while her exhausted, drink-addled brain tried to process this news. What did it mean, that Alex was engaged? Did it mean that he would settle down in America permanently? That he would never come home, or at least not until Papa was dead? If so, then she couldn't feel happy about that. Nor about the fact that he hadn't called her himself to tell her the news. There was a time when Alex had told her everything. She understood his being angry with Papa, about selling off the farms and everything. But what had she done, to deserve being abandoned like this?

On the other hand, she loved Alex, and she *did* want him to be happy. Of course she did. Could part of what she was feeling be envy? That Alex's life was moving forward, albeit on another continent, while her own was . . . *what?*

There's nothing wrong with your life, she told herself,

defiantly. *Just because Thierry Senard has got a bee in his bonnet about your friends and Antoine, and Chantelle worries over you like a mother hen, doesn't mean that either of them is right.*

Later, in bed, turning her face into her pillow to block out the growing light of the morning, Elise struggled in vain to snatch a few hours' sleep. Alex's news still troubled her, in ways she couldn't entirely pin down. As did the painful lunch she'd had with her father earlier. And then to have Chantelle imply that she might be headed down the same path? It was all too much for one day.

But it was the thought of Thierry Senard judging her – and worse, potentially badmouthing her to Laurent – that really sent Elise's anxiety levels into overdrive.

It was so unfair. She'd been looking forward to this evening. How had everything gone so wrong?

Of course, Thierry might not say anything. After all, he'd told her and Chantelle at dinner that Laurent was abroad at the moment, and that he'd been estranged from the rest of the family for some time. Maybe the two brothers wouldn't talk at all? Or maybe, by the time they did, Thierry would have forgotten all about Elise and their abortive night out at Le Bariton?

Maybe.

Probably.

Almost certainly, in fact.

You're overtired and making a mountain out of a molehill, Elise told herself.

But still, stubbornly, the sleep she craved refused to come.

CHAPTER NINE

Alex Salignac married Ruth Ballard on 5 December 1934. Tyler Miller, Alex's friend from Danson's, was best man.

The ceremony itself was a modest affair, with only Ruth's parents and a handful of local friends present at St Andrew's Presbyterian church in Winsome. But the atmosphere couldn't have been happier. The dark cloud of Prohibition had finally lifted, and it felt like the perfect time for two fine, ambitious young people to be setting out on life's journey together. Over the past year, Bob and Jean Ballard had come to love Alex almost like a son. Partly because he was a kind, smart, hard-working boy, but mostly because there could be no mistaking his total and utter besotted adoration for their daughter. As for Ruth, she had never been happier, and looked a vision on her wedding day, glowing and joyous in her simple white cotton dress and muslin veil.

After a very brief, very passionate three-day honeymoon spent at a cabin down in Big Sur, the new Mr and Mrs Salignac returned to Napa with big dreams and limitless confidence.

'We're going to own our own vineyard,' Alex announced to his father-in-law the week they returned from the coast. It was a Saturday night, and Alex and Ruth had been invited over for supper at Bob and Jean's over the store.

Bob Ballard looked over at his wife. 'I thought you already did, son? Or at least, you will one day.'

Alex's face clouded over. 'I love Sainte Madeleine. And things do seem to have stabilized at the vineyard since I left. But while my father's at the helm, anything could happen. And that might be for a very long time. Ruth and I can't live our lives in a perpetual state of waiting and hoping. We need something of our own.'

'I see.' Bob Ballard nodded sagely. He didn't want to burst Alex's balloon, even if the kids' plans were obviously castles in the sky.

'I'll manage the actual wine production,' Alex explained. 'We'll start with Pinot, because it's the grape I know best, but I dare say Cabernets will be in our future. Ruth will be in charge of sales and promotion.' He looked at his new wife adoringly.

'You know, good land in these parts doesn't come cheap,' said Bob.

'We know that,' said Alex, earning himself a loving look from Ruth.

She appreciated the way he always said 'we' when he spoke about their plans. He never treated her like an adjunct in business matters, the way that other men did when they spoke about their wives. They were partners.

'And we know it won't happen overnight,' Alex continued. 'But I'm earning good money over at Danson's now. And Ruth's taken on a lot of extra bookkeeping part-time, when she's not needed here.'

'Have you, honey?' asked Jean proudly. She did worry sometimes that her daughter was taking on too much. But Ruth was young and full of energy, and she seemed happy, which was all you could ask for really.

'We're both savers,' said Alex. 'Plus, I'll be keeping my ear to the ground with land agents for any local auctions where there are distressed sellers. Maybe a plot'll come up that's tricky to irrigate. Or too steep or stony for most wine growers to consider. We're not looking for perfection, and we have the drive and the expertise to turn a place like that around. Believe it or not, Sainte Madeleine has all sorts of drawbacks as a domaine, and my family have had to work around those problems for generations.'

Bob Ballard raised a sceptical eyebrow. 'They seem to have done pretty well out of the place, if that's the case.'

'It is, believe me,' Alex insisted. 'The soil's too acidic, for one thing. And we've always had terrible problems with pests. Burgundy's become a paradise for Pinot Noir, but it wasn't always that way. In fact you could make a case that Napa is more naturally suited to growing grapes, although my father would kill me for saying it. The point is that Ruth and I are willing to work around any problems we may encounter. Aren't we, darling?'

'Absolutely,' said Ruth, taking his hand and squeezing it under the table.

She still couldn't quite believe that he was really her husband, this handsome blond Frenchman who could have married anyone he wanted; who should have wound up with some rich, titled Burgundy heiress, but who had miraculously chosen her, plain old Ruth Ballard, instead. And to think, it all started with a burp.

'Well, this all sounds wonderful,' said Jean kindly. 'But don't forget that Ruth won't have nearly so much time on her hands once your babies come.'

Having only ever been able to have one child herself, and that after great difficulty, Jean was beside herself with excitement at the prospect of grandchildren.

Ruth and Alex exchanged glances.

'You're right, Jean,' said Alex. 'Kids certainly demand a lot of time and energy. Which is exactly why we've decided to wait before we think about starting a family.'

Jean and Bob's faces both fell.

'Wait?' Jean repeated plaintively.

'Hold off for a few months, you mean?' Bob clarified.

'No, Pa. For a few years,' Ruth said firmly. 'Or maybe more than a few,' she added, braving the palpable wall of parental disapproval. 'Right now, all Alex and I want is to work, find our vineyard, and get established.'

Now it was Bob and Jean's turn to exchange worried looks. In their day, there'd been no 'waiting'. Not least because babies had a way of coming, whether you planned for them or not.

'We will have children,' Alex assured them, perceiving his mother-in-law's dismay. 'I promise.' Then, like a true Salignac, he added, 'But obviously the vineyard comes first.'

One spring morning, about four months after the wedding, a letter arrived for Alex at Danson's. The French postmark alone was enough to make his stomach lurch, but it was his mother's distinctive, looped handwriting on the envelope that really tugged at his heartstrings. Agitated, he put it in his pocket. He would wait until the end of the day to open it in private.

It was gone five by the time he got back to the quaint, two-room ranch house he and Ruth shared on the edge of the property. The house was really little more than an adobe hut: whitewashed walls, with simple furniture and a few Native American rugs thrown over bare boards. But it was the closest Danson's had to 'married quarters'. And it was free, which was all that really mattered to Alex.

Relieved that Ruth wasn't back from work yet, he sat down at their minuscule kitchen table and opened his letter, slightly crumpled now from its day spent stuffed into the pocket of his trousers.

'*Cher Alexandre*,' Thérèse began formally. That was a

bad sign. His mother never used his full name unless she was mad about something.

> *I hope this letter finds you well. I must be honest and tell you that I was deeply distressed to learn from one of our friends here in Burgundy that your wedding last winter did not take place in a Catholic church.*

Shit, thought Alex. *Shit, shit, shit.* Who could have told her? He'd barely been in touch with anyone back home. The odd note to friends, one letter to Arnaud Berger, and a few stilted exchanges with Elise had been pretty much his only ongoing connections with France. He deliberately hadn't told his sister the details of his wedding, partly because his marriage was still a sore point, and partly because he knew how upset Maman would be about the whole Presbyterian thing. But the fact was, St Andrew's was Ruth's family church, and it meant so much to her to be married there. Plus, the way Alex saw it, *he* was the one marrying into *her* family, not the other way around. And Bob and Jean had been so kind and welcoming. What was he supposed to do?

'*I understand why you have chosen to turn your back on Sainte Madeleine,*' Thérèse continued, each word a tiny stab in Alex's heart.

> *Clearly your father is much to blame for that. But I had trusted, perhaps naively, that not all of the lessons of your upbringing had been completely abandoned. It appears I was mistaken.*

Alex lowered the letter and pinched the bridge of his nose, holding back a barrage of complex emotions: guilt, sadness, and not a little anger at whoever had spilled the beans to Maman about the service at St Andrew's.

I pray that eventually you may return in a spirit of contrition, if not to France then at least into the arms of your faith. Remember, Alexandre, that it is only the Catholic sacrament of marriage that will make you man and wife in the eyes of God.

Great, thought Alex, determining not to show the letter to Ruth. How devastated would she be to learn that, as far as Alex's family were concerned, their marriage was a fraud.

The second page of Thérèse's letter began more auspiciously:

On a happier note, you will already have seen how well our wines have been doing. But even better than that, Didier has made a full recovery and is now back home and stronger than ever.

Alex smiled. How wonderful for Dids. Of all the things he felt guilty about, leaving Didier was perhaps the worst of all, especially with Elise also now living away from home in Paris. The next line of Thérèse's letter did nothing to assuage his guilt.

I also wanted to let you know that the doctors decided your father was well enough to return to Sainte Madeleine, so he too is now back home, and in much better health than when you last saw him.

He could hardly be in worse health, thought Alex, wondering how long it would take for Didier's nerves to get the better of him again now that Louis had been permitted back into the family fold.

'*He's been helping Arnaud with the spring plantings, and seems quite determined to leave his old ways behind him,*' wrote Thérèse, allowing hope to triumph over experience to a degree that baffled and infuriated Alex in equal measure. He had lost count of Louis's 'fresh starts' over the years, or the number of times that his mother had forgiven him and taken him back.

Things got worse in the next line:

> *I know he feels sorry about what happened between the two of you, and I do so wish that you would reach out to him. But I respect this needs to be your decision.*

'Oh God,' Alex groaned aloud.

He couldn't 'reach out' to Louis. He just couldn't. And forgiveness had nothing to do with it. Since coming to America, and particularly since meeting Ruth, who was a deeply compassionate person, Alex had come to realize that 'forgiving' an alcoholic for drinking was like 'forgiving' a volcano for erupting, or lightning for striking. Papa couldn't help the way he was. And despite everything that had happened – selling the farms, almost running the business into the ground, cheating on Maman, driving poor Dids to a nervous breakdown – Alex loved him.

But he loved Sainte Madeleine more. He loved her more than he admitted, even to himself. More than anybody knew, even Ruth. He'd told himself that he'd left Burgundy because of the rift with Louis. And although that might be true on paper, the real reason was that he could no longer take the pain of watching the home he loved sink into what he feared might be a terminal decline. The rallies of the last two years' vintages had lifted his spirits somewhat. But Alex knew that, particularly without the farms to provide a steady back-up income, Sainte Madeleine was still far from secure financially.

In her letter, in her own subtle way, his mother was asking him to raise his hopes again. To believe that, this time, Louis had changed and that Sainte Madeleine might survive and recover after all. But he couldn't. He just couldn't. The truth was, Alex had never had his mother's faith, in either the Catholic Church *or* his father's better nature. The hope-and-despair rollercoaster would end up wrecking his life, just as surely as Papa's bullying and capricious nature had wrecked Didier's. Alex wasn't about to let that happen.

'*Other than that, I don't have much news,*' Thérèse continued.

> *Life here doesn't change very much as you know. Brolio has been crocheting like a madwoman, keeping herself occupied while everyone's been away, and is of course making a huge fuss of Didier now that he's home. Arnaud has been an absolute rock.*

I'll bet, thought Alex, wondering how poor Arnaud would have taken the news of Louis's 'recovery'.

> *And I'm sorry to say I hear very little from Elise, although perhaps you know more than I do? In any event, her godmother Chantelle assures me that she's well and studying hard.*

Alex smiled to himself, trying and failing to picture Elise studying at all, never mind hard. He missed her and the bond they'd shared growing up, and he wished they could have leaned on one another now, in their shared sorrow. Like him, Elise had been unable to stand the sadness at Sainte Madeleine as Papa's drinking got worse and Didier's depression deepened. She might not have run as far as Alex did – perhaps because she'd always been the closest to Papa, she couldn't bear to abandon him completely? – but she'd left nonetheless. She'd had to, to survive.

How strange to think that we both left our home as soon as we turned eighteen, not because we hated it, but because we loved it too much, Alex reflected. And yet despite all that he and Elise had in common, they'd ended up growing further apart instead of closer together.

Turning back to Maman's letter, he pushed the unhappy thought out of his mind.

'*We do have a wonderful new parish priest in the village,*' wrote Thérèse:

> *Père Bercault. Did you know old Père Martin retired? I think I must have told you. He couldn't go on with his arthritis, poor man.*

Or his dementia, thought Alex. Father Martin had been about a hundred and fifty years old when Alex was born. Sainte Madeleine was long overdue a new priest.

> *Père Bercault is young, I would guess no more than forty. He's really taken Didier under his wing, which is frightfully kind of him. They go on long walks together, talking about theology and the meaning of life. He's really managed to bring Dids out of himself. So that's something else to thank Our Lord for.*
>
> *As for politics, that's too depressing to write about, so I won't. Other than to say that I understand from poor Camille Senard that your cousin Laurent's been quite radicalized. Speaking of radicals, you must write and tell me what you think of Mr Roosevelt.*

Alex couldn't help but chuckle at this. Of course Maman considered 'FDR' a radical.

'*In the meantime, take care of yourself, my darling,*' she signed off.

*But do think about what I said, about you and Ruth
having a Catholic ceremony eventually. You'd both need
to take the act of contrition first, of course. But I know
Père Bercault would be delighted to officiate. We all
miss you here at Sainte Madeleine.*
With love, your affectionate
Maman

Alex was still sitting at the table, lost in thought, when
the door flew open and Ruth burst in.

'Look at this!'

She waved a piece of paper excitedly in front of him, too
focused on her own news even to notice Alex's letter, which
he hastily returned to his pocket. With her Titian hair messy
and wild from the wind and her round cheeks flushed with
exertion, she looked more beautiful in Alex's eyes than ever.

'I've found it!' she exclaimed delightedly. 'I've found our
vineyard.'

The eighty-acre property up near Calistoga was priced to
sell, but it was still more than Ruth and Alex could afford.

'Pa might be willing to come in with us,' said Ruth.

'Absolutely not,' said Alex, with a vehemence that
surprised her. 'We do this on our own or not at all. I didn't
move to the other side of the world to get out from under
my own father, only to wind up beholden to yours.'

'That's not fair.' Ruth bit her lower lip, hurt. 'You told
me your father's a drunken bully.'

'He is,' said Alex, although not without a small pang of
guilt that this might be all he'd ever told Ruth about Louis.
He hadn't mentioned the charm or the laughter, the huge
sense of fun that had been a big part of his early, happy
childhood, before it all went wrong.

'Well Pa's nothing like that,' said Ruth fiercely. 'If he
helped us, it would be out of love. Nothing more.'

'I know that,' Alex said, pulling her close. 'And I love both your parents, Ruth, don't get me wrong. But this isn't about love, or trust. It's about independence. You do want us to be independent, don't you?'

'Well, yes . . .' Ruth hesitated. 'I suppose so.'

'And I mean, what if we buy the place and it fails?' said Alex. 'You wouldn't want to drag your folks down with us, would you? After they've worked their whole lives to build Ballard Food and Drink up to where it is now? This is our dream. Our risk.'

'OK,' said Ruth, who hadn't thought about it like that before. 'If you really feel that strongly. But we need more money from somewhere.'

Alex saw five different bank managers in two days. In each case, the outcome was the same.

'I'm sorry, Mr Salignac, but we can't possibly consider a loan of this size.'

'You have no credit history with us, Mr Salignac.'

'Without significant collateral, I'm afraid our policy wouldn't allow . . .'

And all five had concluded:

'Perhaps if you were an American citizen, Mr Salignac?'

'I can't see what your citizenship has to do with it,' a frustrated Ruth complained over supper in their tiny house at Danson's. It had been another long day of rejection, and poor Alex looked haggard and tense.

'They think I might run home to France if things go badly,' said Alex. 'I'm a flight risk.'

'What nonsense!' Ruth said hotly. 'We're married and I'm a citizen. Isn't that enough?'

'Apparently not.' He pushed a pile of mashed potato around his plate dejectedly.

'Because I'm a woman, I suppose?' Ruth observed bitterly.

'Don't feel bad about it,' said Alex. 'You're a woman and I'm a Frenchman. That makes both of us lepers in their eyes.'

'So that's it then?' Ruth asked him angrily. 'We just give up? Walk away?'

She knew better than to suggest approaching her father again. But Alex could see that she wanted to. Could see, too, the bitter disappointment in her sweet, open, naturally optimistic face. He felt awful for being the one to have caused it, but what could he do?

The next morning at work, he unburdened himself to Tyler.

'I'm caught between a rock and hard place,' he complained. 'The banks won't budge, I don't have the money and I can't go to Bob and Jean. But that land is such good value. Someone else is bound to snap it up soon.'

'Can't you just become a citizen?' asked Tyler. 'I mean, you speak English, and you and Ruth are married. Maybe I'm missing something, but I don't quite see the problem.'

'By the time I've finished the paperwork that land'll be gone,' said Alex.

It sounded convincing. But the truth was he was hedging. Deep down he had reservations, fears that he hadn't admitted even to Ruth, about becoming an American. For one thing it meant swearing before God to 'renounce all allegiance and fidelity to any foreign prince, potentate, state, or sovereignty'. He might not have got married in a Catholic church, but Alex still had enough residual Catholic guilt left in him not to feel comfortable lying under oath. More than that though, emotionally he wasn't ready to 'renounce' France. Not yet. It felt like a betrayal – a second betrayal – of his family, his heritage. Him*self*. He was a Salignac, after all. Becoming a US citizen felt so *final*, as if he were setting it in stone that he would never go back to Sainte Madeleine. Never was a long time.

'What if I came in with you? As a partner?' Tyler suggested. 'Would that make a difference?'

Alex looked at his friend steadily.

'It might. But I couldn't ask you to do that.'

'You're not asking me,' said Tyler. 'I'm offering. I don't have as much put by as you and Ruth do, but it might be enough to tip the balance. And I'm as American as apple pie,' he grinned, 'so I have that going for me.'

'Yes, but you don't want to own a vineyard,' said Alex.

'Co-own,' replied Tyler. 'And who says I don't?'

'It's a huge risk, you know,' Alex countered, his mind racing as he tried to keep his own hopes in check. He knew he could never accept Bob Ballard as a partner. Much too close to home. But Tyler was different. He was pretty sure Ruth would agree, or at least understand why he felt that way.

'The risk would be more yours than mine,' Tyler pointed out. 'You'd be the senior partner, not to mention the one quitting your job here to run the place. I'd stay on at Danson's – and hopefully get promoted to your job, which would mean a decent pay rise for me. The more I think about it, the more I think it's an inspired idea. I mean, come on. What's the worst that could happen?'

'I could lose all your money,' said Alex. 'Every cent.'

He knew he was being overly pessimistic. But such was his horror of being like his father, a sponge and a liar, leeching money from anyone who would lend to him, that he couldn't seem to help himself going too far the other way.

Luckily, Tyler seemed unfazed.

'True,' he shrugged. 'But if I *don't* help you buy this vineyard, I'll have to look at your miserable face for the next God knows how many years, whining about the one that got away. And I'm not sure I could stand that, to be honest.'

Alex laughed. 'OK. But seriously . . .'

'I am being serious,' said Tyler. 'I mean it. Talk to Ruth. But then let's do it. Let's buy this damn place.'

Three weeks later, Ruth and Alex moved in. Sitting on the bare porch with Tyler, their bottoms sinking into rotting pine boards, they opened a bottle of 1927 Sauternes, a gift from Ruth's parents, and toasted their new life with tin coffee mugs.

'To you, my friend,' Alex raised a glass to Tyler. 'You made this happen.'

Tyler batted away the compliment shyly. 'No way, man. This is all you and Ruth. I'm just happy to be the third wheel.'

'I like that,' said Ruth, gazing in wonder across the scrubby, overgrown lawn to the rocky slopes that they would start to clear tomorrow. *It's ours. It's all ours.* 'That's what we should call our wines.'

'What, third wheel?' laughed Alex.

'I was thinking "Tricycle",' said Ruth. 'It's a great, simple image to stick on a label, don't you think? Tricycle Pinot.'

The two boys looked at each other and grinned.

'Hank, my darling,' Alex kissed her. 'You may just be a genius.'

'Seconded!' said Tyler, draining his glass.

Ruth frowned, then laughed. 'Gee thanks, guys. I guess all we need now is something to market.'

'That's your hubby's department,' Tyler observed laconically. 'I'm afraid I'll be too busy raking it in at Danson's.' Looking back over his shoulder into the virtually empty house, he added: 'You know, you could also use some furniture. All I can see is a bed.'

'That's all we need,' grinned Alex, with a knowing look at Ruth.

Tyler could take a hint. It was time for the third wheel to make a move.

Later, once Tyler had gone home and all the wine was finished, Ruth waited for Alex to come to bed.

'What are you doing?' she yawned, watching him pry open a packing crate. 'We can do all that tomorrow. Let's get some sleep.'

'I just need a minute,' said Alex.

Lifting out a large oblong object, he peeled off various layers of brown paper to reveal a painting. In a simple, gilt frame, it depicted a grand, romantic house covered in pale pink roses, with light blue shutters and a wild, flower-filled garden that sloped down a hillside. Moments later, Alex had hammered a single nail into the bedroom wall and hung it, directly opposite their bed.

'I haven't seen that before,' Ruth sighed contentedly as he climbed in beside her. 'It's so pretty. Is it French?'

'It certainly is. That's Sainte Madeleine,' said Alex, kissing her on the top of the head. 'I didn't want to hang it until I'd got a place of my own. *Our* own,' he corrected himself.

'Wow. It's stunning,' said Ruth truthfully, snuggling in next to him. 'Imagine growing up in a house like that. I don't know how you could bear to leave.'

Ruth fell asleep quickly. But Alex lay awake, gazing at the painting until the light faded completely, and he could no longer make out the home of his childhood. The first, true love of his life. But not the last.

I will build a home here, he promised himself. *Ruth and I will be happy.*

I won't make any of the mistakes my father made.

But even tonight, in the sublime depths of his joy, a piece of his heart still longed for Sainte Madeleine.

CHAPTER TEN

Didier Salignac strolled along the riverbank, allowing the back of his hand to brush the tops of the long grasses as he moved. Above him, a blue July sky was dotted with little clouds, and all around him the sights, sounds and smells of summer filled his senses like a fondly remembered dream. Warm air, steaming earth, drowsily buzzing bees and the pungent scents of wild garlic and honeysuckle, all set to the soundtrack of the rushing River Cure. A perfect day.

He was walking with Henri – Father Bercault – and the priest's presence soothed and delighted him every bit as much as the natural beauty of the Burgundy countryside. In fact, Didier reflected, it was almost as if Henri had become a part of the landscape. Certainly Sainte Madeleine's new priest was already a part of the backdrop to Didier's own life, as integral to his existence as the sky above or the solid earth below.

Since the day Father Henri Bercault arrived in the village, life for Didier Salignac had changed, and wholly for the better. Henri was funny and wise and kind. He didn't find Didier's tears or silences embarrassing, and he never tried to stop the first or fill the second. Instead, the new priest walked beside Didier Salignac 'just as Our Lord walks beside each of us, always', accepting and supporting the troubled younger man, without words.

The nurses at the sanatorium had been kind and patient. Without them, and an extended period away from home, Didier knew he might never have found his way out from the deep dark well of depression into which he had fallen after Alex and Elise both left Sainte Madeleine. For a long time he was completely mute, lost in a sadness too profound for words. But as the months passed and his black mood at last began to lift, like a blanket of pitch darkness being peeled back at the edges, inch by inch, words slowly started to return to him.

Once he got back to Sainte Madeleine, and particularly after his mother introduced him to Henri, that initial trickle of words quickly became a torrent. Questions, about life, politics and the world, about God and the life of the spirit, poured from Didier like water from a spring. And from Henri, answers, thoughtful but always direct, with nothing dissembled or cloaked in highfalutin language, the way that other priests talked down to members of their flock. Nothing Father Bercault said was designed to obscure or deceive, still less to set himself apart from, or above, anybody else. Least of all Didier Salignac, with whom he had formed a surprising but intense and genuine friendship.

Didier trusted Henri in a way he had never trusted anyone, not even Alex or Maman. In many ways, Henri was the first real friend he had ever had. The joy that that friendship brought him, the deep well of contentment sprung from human connection, was beyond description.

'Where to now?' Henri asked, pausing at a stile to drink some water from his camping flask, before offering it to Didier. 'We could take the long path up towards Vézelay or head back to the hamlet through Monsieur Marceau's fields.'

'The long path. Definitely.'

Didier passed the flask back to Henri, noticing the way that he held it to his thin lips, sucking his cheeks in as he drank to form soft hollows, like thumbs gently pressed into pastry. By now he knew every line on the priest's face, every shape and expression. Ten years older than Didier, and a good three inches shorter, Father Henri Bercault was darker skinned, with delicate features defined by strong, black brows and an unruly mop of curly dark hair. He was fit, in the lean, wiry way that runners were, and he seemed to Didier to move with an ineffable grace, a sort of languid ease that Didier never tired of watching.

'Not because you're afraid of the cows, I hope?' Henri teased, glancing across the river to a meadow where Farmer Marceau's dopey Friesians swished their tails against the flies.

'No!' Didier nudged him in the ribs affectionately. 'I fancy a longer walk, that's all. Or are you too tired already, old man?'

'I'll give you "old man",' said Henri, vaulting the stile and taking off at a run up the hillside, his shirttails coming untucked from his hiking breeches and flying behind him as he ran. 'Last one to the five-bar gate's a rotten egg!'

Didier lost the race comfortably. He was nowhere near as fit as Henri. But he was happy simply to walk and talk as they caught their breath afterwards.

'Any news of your brother or sister?' Henri asked, as the winding path snaked its way over the rise and down the other side towards Vézelay.

'Only the usual letters,' said Didier. 'Elise telephones every now and then from Paris. Maman saw her when she went to town last month and said she looked well and quite grown-up.'

'You didn't want to go?' the priest probed.

'To Paris? No.' Didier shook his head vehemently. 'The city's not for me.'

'Not even to visit your sister?'

Another headshake, more embarrassed this time.

'I wouldn't fit in there. Elise would feel as awkward as I would. I'd rather wait till she comes home to Sainte Madeleine. She'll have to come back eventually,' he added, slightly plaintively in Henri's opinion. 'They both will.'

Didier Salignac was so tall and handsome, Henri reflected, and so bright and accomplished. And yet he lacked utterly the self-belief that would have helped him make something of those gifts. It was a shame. By all accounts it was his brother Alexandre who'd inherited the family share of confidence. But despite being very much the favoured son and heir apparent to the domaine, Alexandre had come to blows with the father and taken off for America. Perhaps for good, notwithstanding Didier's expressions of confidence about his ultimate return.

'What about your brother?' Henri asked, picking his way gingerly through a patch of stinging nettles. 'Your mother mentioned at Mass last week that he and his wife have acquired a vineyard out in California.'

Didier visibly stiffened. 'So I understand.'

'That's exciting, isn't it?' Henri probed. 'Impressive at his age.'

'Yes.' Didier looked pained.

'What is it, my friend?' Henri rested a hand on his shoulder. 'Do you feel anger towards your brother for leaving? Because that's understandable, you know. It isn't easy being left behind.'

'Anger?' Didier looked genuinely surprised. 'Oh no. I'm not angry with Alex. Not in the least.'

Henri gave him a 'then what is it?' look. Didier bit his lip, struggling to find the right words. If he couldn't tell Henri, he couldn't tell anyone. And yet it was still hard, shameful, trying to articulate his feelings. Anything that involved Louis, however tangentially, was painful to explain to others.

'The thing is,' he began tentatively, 'Alex knows about wine. He's ambitious and passionate and talented.'

'OK.' Henri waited.

'That was why Papa and Arnaud always included him in decisions about the vineyard. Papa intended for Alex to take over the business at Sainte Madeleine one day.'

'And that didn't bother you?' Henri asked. 'As the eldest son, wouldn't you normally expect to inherit?'

'It didn't bother me at all,' said Didier truthfully. 'Quite the contrary. I'm still going to inherit a half share of the estate. But I know nothing about running a vineyard, I'd be useless at it.'

'I don't agree,' said Henri. 'You're smart. You're capable. You might not have a natural interest, but you could learn.'

'Thank you for saying so,' Didier blushed. 'It means a lot that you have faith in me. But I assure you, you're wrong. Managing Sainte Madeleine is a huge responsibility and it's a lot harder than it looks. Ask Arnaud Berger, if you don't believe me. He's been teaching Elise and Alex the ropes since they were tiny children. Alex because he was always supposed to take over, and Elise just because she loved it all. I never had that affinity. Unfortunately, it's not something you can just "pick up", like whistling.'

'Well, no,' Henri chuckled. 'I'm not implying it would be easy.'

Didier shook his head. 'Plus I've seen what the pressure of it did to Papa. It crushed him, like a beetle beneath a boot.'

Henri thought privately that it was Louis Salignac's own demons that had crushed him, aided and abetted by about a thousand gallons of brandy and a congenital sense of entitlement that had nothing whatsoever to do with the 'pressure' of running Sainte Madeleine. But he admired Didier's compassion for the father who had bullied him so badly, and he hadn't the heart to correct him.

'No, Alex was always the man for the job,' Didier insisted. 'He still *is* the man. But now that he's married, and has his own vineyard . . .' He looked away, visibly distressed.

'I see. You miss him,' Henri observed simply.

'Very much.' Tears pricked the back of Didier's eyes. 'I'm happy for him, of course I am. But I'm afraid it means he'll never come back. And I'm frightened about where it leaves me, if Alex and Papa don't reconcile. What if Papa wants *me* to take over the domaine?' His breath quickened in panic. 'I mean, I can't. I can't do it. There's no way.'

'Then don't do it,' said Henri. 'Say no.'

Didier laughed bitterly. 'You don't say "no" to Papa.'

'Your brother did,' Henri pointed out.

Didier looked away. 'Alex is braver than I am.'

'I don't believe that for a second,' said Henri, stopping as they reached the lane that would lead them back to the village. 'I think you're very brave, Didier. Battles of the mind and soul can be every bit as frightening as the battles of the external world. More so, in fact. Never forget that. Our Lord sees your battles. He sees your courage.'

Didier swallowed, too moved to speak. The only other person ever to have called him brave was Laurent Senard, and that was aeons ago, in another life. Henri's faith in him meant everything.

Henri meant everything.

'What do *you* want, Didier?' Henri asked.

'No one's ever asked me that,' Didier replied. 'I did consider . . .' He blushed. 'I thought at one time that I might become a priest.'

Henri smiled broadly, surprised but pleased.

'But that's wonderful! You feel you might have a vocation?'

'Felt,' mumbled Didier, embarrassed. 'Past tense. I considered it, but I know now that my faith isn't strong enough.'

'Everybody thinks that at first,' said Henri breezily. 'If you truly felt called . . .'

'No. You don't understand,' Didier blurted. 'I can never be a priest.'

Henri stopped and looked at him. 'Why not?'

'I have so many sins,' Didier said miserably.

'Do you think I don't?' asked Henri.

'No. Not in the same way,' said Didier. 'I have . . . impure thoughts. All the time.' His voice dropped to a tortured whisper, even though there was no one else around them. 'I can't make them stop.'

'Ah,' said Henri.

'I'm not like you.'

There was a moment's pause. Then Henri said quietly, 'Yes, you are, Didier. You're exactly like me.'

The two men looked at one another. Didier swallowed hard. Was Henri saying what he thought he was saying?

'We're all sinners,' Henri told him, choosing his words carefully. 'But it's not our impulses that define us. It's our actions. What we decide to do – or not do – about those impulses. The Lord loves us as we are,' he added, deadly serious all of a sudden. 'Never forget that.'

They walked on in silence. Henri behaved as if nothing momentous had just happened, but for Didier, it was as if he had stepped into an alternate universe. A world in which, for one shining moment, his true self had been allowed to step out of the shadows and into the light.

'For what it's worth,' Henri observed casually as the rooftops of Sainte Madeleine village hove into view, 'I think you'd make a marvellous priest. But of course, that's a conversation for you and God.'

'Thank you,' said Didier.

It was the happiest moment of his life.

* * *

Alex and Ruth sat huddled over their new Clinton radio, waiting for Jack Benny's comedy hour to finish so that they could hear the news. Or rather, Alex was waiting. Ruth privately preferred the comedy hour, or shows like *Amos 'n' Andy*. After gruelling days working in the vineyard or setting up the new winery, all she wanted in the evenings was to relax. But recently Alex had become glued to the news programmes, especially the worrying developments in Europe.

'Here we go,' he said eagerly, twiddling the dial as Benny's crackly signature music faded away and the newscaster's deep, New York baritone burst into the farmhouse living room.

'*Reports today that the Soviet Union has agreed to send aid to the Spanish Republican forces have been greeted with consternation in some quarters,*' the announcer read. '*Most notably in Italy and Germany. Only last month, Herr Hitler supplied aircraft to General Franco's rebel forces in North Africa and in Spain itself, an intervention that had tipped the balance of power against the Republicans in Spain's escalating conflict.*'

'Damn Hitler,' Alex muttered, sipping chilled Coca-Cola from the bottle. Ruth's parents had bought them an icebox as a wedding present, the second most expensive thing they owned after the Clinton and a godsend during the sweltering California summer. 'That man is such an ass.'

'Aren't we on Franco's side?' Ruth asked, confused.

'Kind of,' said Alex, still trying to listen to the report.

'But I thought the Republicans were the bad guys in Spain?'

'It's complicated,' said Alex.

'They're the communists, right?'

'They're not *all* communists,' said Alex, thinking about his cousin Laurent Senard, who he knew passionately opposed Franco. 'But it sounds as if the communists are backing them, yes. Let's listen.'

'If the communists are backing them, they're the bad guys in my book,' muttered Ruth under her breath.

Alex grinned. He loved Ruth's 'black-and-whiteness'. He'd been that way himself until a few years ago, adopting his parents' political beliefs unquestioningly and swallowing their worldview whole. Ironically, it was only since he'd left Europe and been able to watch the affairs in his homeland from afar that his opinions had shifted. All of a sudden, the world felt a lot greyer than it had when he was growing up at Sainte Madeleine. And it wasn't only the privileged, cloistered bubble of life in 1920s Burgundy that had burst. All across Europe, plates that had started spinning in 1934 and '35 were now careening wildly out of control, in Germany, Italy and particularly in poor old Spain, where the old order was coming apart at the seams. 1936 felt like the year of division, the year that battle lines were being firmly and finally drawn between the communist left. Talk of a second Great War, unthinkable a decade ago, was becoming deafening. It troubled him.

At the same time, he reflected, watching his wife help herself to a second bottle of cola, here in Napa Europe's troubles felt very far away. *He* felt far away. His new life revolved around the vineyard, and Ruth, and her family. Which was what he wanted. Except that sometimes it felt as if nothing else existed. As if the American Dream had swallowed him whole, like a great whale, and there was no way back. Alex still hadn't totally decided whether that was a good thing or a bad.

'Penny for your thoughts,' Ruth teased him, climbing into his lap and wrapping her arms around his neck. Like most evenings, she was exhausted. But she was also profoundly happy, and she loved Alex more every day. 'You are pulling the strangest face.'

'You'd wait for me, wouldn't you?' Alex said suddenly. 'If I had to go to war?'

Ruth looked at him sternly. 'Don't joke.'

'I wasn't joking.'

'There won't be a war,' said Ruth.

'No?'

'No. And even if there were, America wouldn't be in it. *You* wouldn't be in it.'

The news was over. Flicking off the radio, he gave her a kiss. 'You're probably right.'

'No, Alex.' Ruth stood up, properly agitated. 'There's no "probably" about it. I want you to promise me.'

'Promise you what?' asked Alex, confused. 'Why are you angry?'

'Promise me you won't go to war.'

He looked at her curiously. 'Well, it's not on my to-do list. At least not until after our first harvest.'

'I mean it, Alex. Promise me.' To his astonishment, he saw that she was crying.

'My darling, what is it? What's the matter?' He pulled her to him. 'I promise, of course I promise. But why are you crying? Has something happened?'

Ruth nodded, but wouldn't meet his eye.

'I went into Winsome today. I saw Doc Richards.'

Alex's stomach lurched. He felt as if someone had thrown a medicine ball at his stomach. One by one the nightmares danced, cruelly through his brain: Ruth had cancer. Tuberculosis. Some unnamed, hideous, inherited condition that would take her away from him.

Ruth was dying. She had months to live. Weeks. Days.

'I'm going to have a baby.'

Alex stared at her, open-mouthed. It took a few moments, more than a few, for her words to register.

'I'm sorry,' she babbled. 'Please don't be upset. I know it wasn't in our plan, and I know we said we'd wait and we've been careful. But I guess something must have gone wrong, because Doc Richards said he was quite sure, and the baby's due next spring and you absolutely *can't* go to war, Alex! You can't go anywhere in fact, because, well, we're having a baby and I can't raise it on my own and—'

He stopped her with a kiss.

'I'm not upset,' he assured her, all thoughts of war and Europe and 'home' flying out of his head like bats from a belfry. 'A baby, Ruth? *Our* baby? I can't think of anything more wonderful.'

Laurent Senard dug his heels into his chestnut mare and galloped after his brother, dust flying everywhere as the two horses sped joyously across the burnt stubble field. It was a glorious day in Burgundy, and the first time that Thierry and Laurent had been home together at Chateau Brancion in more than a year. Laurent had arrived last night, exhausted after his days-long journey from Morocco, and had collapsed into bed after supper before anyone had had a chance to grill him on what, exactly, he'd been up to all spring. But he knew 'the talk' was coming. And he suspected that his father had deputized the job to Thierry, with today's long ride around the estate designed to provide an opportunity for his elder brother to 'get through to him'.

'*Attends!*' he yelled at Thierry, watching his brother effortlessly sail his gelding over the hedge into the next field. 'Slow down, for God's sake!'

Laurent was a competent rider, but no one could match Thierry Senard's grace in the saddle, his legendary horsemanship just another arrow in a vast quiver of accomplishments. If there were such a thing as Renaissance Man, surely Thierry deserved the title? And yet he carried himself with no arrogance, no conscious sense of his superiority to others, Laurent included. Laurent loved his older brother for that, and admired him more than he could express. All of which made the prospect of the coming showdown worse.

'You're not tired already?' Thierry joshed his little brother, stopping at the edge of the woods to allow Laurent to catch up with him.

'It's not the bloody Prix de L'Arc de Triomphe!' panted Laurent, he and his mare both drenched in sweat. 'Give me a chance.'

'I thought we'd ride on to the pond before we took a break?' said Thierry, looking fresh as a daisy as he reached down to open the gate into the woods one-handed. 'Let the horses drink while we sit and talk. Is that all right? I brought some saucisson and a bit of cheese if you're hungry.'

'Fine with me,' said Laurent, his heart sinking. Sausage and cheese meant 'the talk' would probably be a long one. Why did it always have to be like this?

Laurent had long ago given up hope that any of his family would come to share his political views. His parents saw the world differently and that was that. But as sure as he was in his own beliefs, he did regret the pain that they caused his father in particular, and the wedge that they had begun to drive between himself and Thierry, whom he'd always looked up to and adored.

It took about an hour to reach the big lily pond. Hidden deep in an obscure part of the estate woods, it had been one of Laurent and Thierry's 'secret' hangouts as boys, a place to swim and make camps and escape the watchful eyes of nannies and tutors. While the horses drank thirstily and rested in the shade, Thierry pulled an army blanket from his saddlebag and spread the modest picnic beneath the shade of an ancient sycamore.

'So,' he began, slicing off pungent discs of sausage with a hunting knife. 'How have you been?'

'Fine.' Laurent accepted a handful of meat. 'I've been fine. You?'

'You look thin,' said Thierry, refusing to be deflected. 'Those breeches are hanging off you.'

'I dare say Maman's new cook will fix that,' Laurent

replied breezily. He knew there would be no way to deflect the lecture that was coming, but he couldn't help but try. 'Papa says she cooks everything with suet, and even the *haricots verts* are fried in lard.'

'You're staying a while then?' Thierry brightened. 'That's good news. Maman's missed you dreadfully, you know. We all have.'

'I miss you all too,' said Laurent, fiddling unhappily with a blade of grass.

'Then why do you come home so rarely, Laurent?'

'I'm sorry.' He toyed with a piece of cheese. 'It's difficult. I am working, you know.'

'Doing what?' Thierry asked bluntly.

'You know what. Politics,' Laurent said sullenly.

'What does that even *mean*?' Thierry demanded, his tone becoming angrier despite his best intentions. 'Are you working for "the Party" now? Is that it?'

'Let's not,' pleaded Laurent. 'I know I should be in touch more and I'll try. I promise. But I'm here now and I can only stay a week, two at most. So let's not ruin it by—'

'A *week*?' Thierry interrupted, genuinely aghast. 'Please tell me you're joking.'

'I know it's not long, but it can't be helped,' Laurent muttered miserably.

'Why can't it be helped?' Thierry asked bluntly. 'Maman will be heartbroken. Where are you going that's so earth-shatteringly important?'

'Paris.'

Laurent looked away, fixing his attention on his mare so that he wouldn't have to look his brother in the eye. It wasn't a lie. He was going to Paris. But it wasn't the whole truth, and they both knew it.

'Paris,' Thierry repeated, rolling the word over in his mouth like a rotten piece of fruit.

'Yes.'

'And then where?'

Laurent didn't answer. He didn't need to.

'You'll be killed,' Thierry told him bluntly. 'If you go to Spain, you'll come back in a body bag.'

'Thanks for the vote of confidence,' quipped Laurent.

'I mean it,' Thierry snapped, his fear coming out as anger. 'This isn't a joke, Laurent.'

'I know it isn't!' Laurent shot back, equally angry.

'You're not a soldier,' said Thierry. 'You're not trained.'

'Actually, I am,' said Laurent, turning back to face him. 'If you must know I've spent the last two months at a Republican training camp outside Essaouira. That's why I haven't been in contact.'

'You've *what*?' Thierry put his head in his hands. This was worse than he thought. Laurent was a terrorist now?

'All the foreign volunteers are being trained. We've been doing drills, manoeuvres. I know how to use a rifle, and make a bomb, and I'm fitter than I've ever been.'

Thierry's eyes widened. 'Jesus Christ, Laurent. They're teaching you to make bombs?'

'Like you said, this isn't a joke,' Laurent retorted.

'And who's running these bomb-making camps? The Russians? Stalin's goons?'

'Franco's forces are all trained militia.'

'Exactly!' said Thierry.

'So what are you saying?' Laurent asked, exasperated. 'Would you have us face them unprepared?'

'I wouldn't have you face them at all!' Thierry shouted. 'You are so naive.'

An unhappy silence fell, during which both brothers tried to temper their emotions. In the end it was Laurent who spoke first.

'Look, I don't like the idea of making bombs any more than you do,' he said meekly. 'But if we stick to their tactics, to traditional warfare, we'll be crushed.'

Thierry closed his eyes and pinched the bridge of his nose. He loved Laurent, probably more than he loved anyone. But his stubbornness, his bullheadedness – and when the stakes were so high, and he was so utterly out of his depth? It was unbearable.

The last time Thierry had had such a frustratingly circular conversation with someone so unwilling to listen had been with Elise Salignac in Paris three years ago. But the worst thing that Elise risked was damage to her reputation. If Laurent got caught up in Spain's brutal civil war, he might well be killed.

'I thought you were a pacifist?' Thierry tried another tack.

'I was. I am.'

'Then why, Laurent? For God's sake, *why*? Can't you just protest or something? Go on a march like everybody else? It's not even your country,' he pleaded.

'Why is it important whose country it is?' Laurent responded, willing his brother to understand, even though he knew it was hopeless. 'You should see what's happening over there, Thierry. In Madrid, in Seville. People being kidnapped, tortured, "disappeared". And not just men – women and children too. Franco's forces show no mercy. None.'

'Oh, and Stalin's do?'

'We have right on our side,' Laurent muttered stubbornly.

The 'we' brought tears to Thierry's eyes.

Both brothers longed to reach out to the other. But the gulf between them in that moment was unbridgeable.

When Thierry spoke again, his tone was different. Colder. Resigned.

'I assume you want me to keep this a secret from Papa and Maman? At least for now?'

Laurent nodded. 'I don't see the point in worrying them. Not until we have to. Do you?'

'No,' Thierry agreed. 'They'll have time enough to grieve if you're killed. Until then, we should spare them as much pain as we can.'

He said it so matter-of-factly, it made Laurent shiver.

'How long will you be in Paris, before you go?'

'I don't know,' Laurent said miserably. 'Not long, I expect. I'll be awaiting orders.'

Orders! Thierry couldn't hide his derision. Laurent may choose to view his rabble of civilian terrorists as an 'army', but Thierry would never see them as anything other than what they were: foolish, brainwashed children, playing with fire.

'I wanted to ask you,' Laurent cleared his throat nervously, 'for Elise's address in Paris. I thought I should take the opportunity to see her, while I'm there. Given that it may be . . .'

'Your last chance?' Thierry couldn't help himself.

'Don't say that,' Laurent begged him.

Laurent had worried about Elise almost constantly since Thierry's reports of her wild 'party life' in Paris, and though he hoped his brother had been exaggerating back then, he feared that the opposite might be true. He'd lost count of the times he'd thought about writing to her, or telephoning, or paying a visit. But each time he'd chickened out, too afraid of what he might find.

Now, though, although he hated to admit it, Thierry was right. He might die in Spain. This really *could* be his last chance to see Elise. To do whatever little he could to influence her for the better. And to tell her . . .

To tell her what? He sighed and pushed the thought from his mind. Whatever the reason, he felt a powerful need to see her and to say goodbye, or at least au revoir, before he left.

'Well.' Thierry got stiffly to his feet. 'I think I'll head home.'

'I'll come with you,' Laurent said guiltily.

'No,' said Thierry, more curtly than he meant to. 'You stay, finish the food. I'd rather ride by myself.'

'OK,' Laurent said meekly. Watching his brother vault back up onto his horse in one single, fluid movement, he felt an immense sadness, like a millstone pressing down on his chest.

'I'll see you at supper,' Thierry called over his shoulder as he rode away. 'I'll give you Elise's address then.'

CHAPTER ELEVEN

Laurent stood nervously on the cobbled street in Paris's swanky 6th Arondissement, staring up at the apartment building. It had started to rain, a thin, fine mist of drizzle that had already dampened the letter in his hand.

'*Of course you must stay with me while you're in Paris,*' Elise's godmother, Chantelle Delorme, had written in her flamboyantly looped handwriting. '*You're family, I have a comfortable third bedroom, and Elise would murder me with her bare hands if I let you stay at a hotel. She's thrilled to bits that you're coming.*'

Laurent felt a warm glow hearing this. Was Chantelle just being polite, or was Elise really happy he was coming? If it were the latter, the thought that he was almost certain to sour that happiness, by breaking the news that he was off to fight in Spain, filled him with a guilt and anxiety that he hadn't fully expected. Arguing with Thierry was one thing, and distressing enough. But Laurent knew that Elise had always looked up to him. The idea of disappointing her felt worse, somehow.

There's no point trying to guess her feelings, he told himself sternly, putting the letter back in his jacket pocket. *You'll find out soon enough what Elise thinks, just as soon as you stop being such a coward and ring the damn bell.*

Marching up to the entrance he pressed the brass button. As per Chantelle's instructions, a loud buzz was followed a few seconds later by some automated clicking and whirring, all very modern, and the door opened into small, marble-floored entryway. There were stairs, and a lift upholstered in red velvet, with concertinaed metal gates that you needed to pull to one side to enter and then close again afterwards. Laurent hit the button for the fifth floor, and was soon standing outside a door with the word *Delorme* embossed on the front.

He knocked twice, and after what felt like an age, the door opened.

'Laurent!'

There she was. Elise, smiling and throwing her arms wide. 'I can't believe you're really here.'

'Nor can I.' He smiled back shyly, pleased and surprised by her lack of make-up and her simple, unfussy clothes. 'It's been a long time.'

His first impression was that she was *not* so changed after all, for all Thierry's dire warnings. Or rather, she was much changed, but not for the worse in the way his brother had described. She was wearing a calf-length bottle-green skirt that made the most of her narrow waist and a plain white shirt with mother-of-pearl buttons. With her hair pulled back and a delicate gold butterfly pendant at her neck, she bore no resemblance to the wild party girl Thierry had warned him to expect. And it wasn't only Thierry. Laurent had heard the hurtful whispers from so-called friends in Burgundy about Elise's supposed promiscuity since she moved to the city. '*Mademoiselle Salignac's become quite the bicyclette. Half of Paris have ridden her, apparently. Like father like daughter, eh?*'

But looking at the demure young woman in front of him, Laurent found that very hard to believe. To him, Elise simply seemed like a more mature, more radiant version of her old self. She'd retained the same elfin beauty, the same mane of blond curls, the same violet eyes full of laughter and mischief and fun.

'You look lovely,' he said truthfully.

Flinging her arms around his neck, she hugged him tightly, but only for a moment. 'Come in, come in. Don't you have a suitcase?'

'Only this.' He gestured at the battered canvas duffel bag at his feet. 'I try to travel light.'

He followed her into the apartment, an elegant, light-filled room with enormous windows and spectacular views.

'What a stunning place,' he said, setting down his bag and looking around admiringly at Chantelle's art and furniture. 'Is your godmother at home?'

'Oh, no,' Elise said breezily. 'Didn't she tell you? Chantelle's down in Provence. She's staying at her sister's place in Eze. Some family trouble, apparently. She'll be gone at least a week.'

A look of consternation crossed Laurent's face. Should he stay there, without Elise's chaperone present? There were enough false rumours flying around about her reputation, without him unwittingly adding to them. But if he said something, or refused to stay, and Elise were to take it the wrong way . . . The last thing he wanted to do was hurt her feelings any more than he was already going to have to, by telling her about Spain.

'I'm sorry to hear that,' he said awkwardly.

'Yes, me too,' Elise sighed. 'Not the family thing, I'm sure that will be all right. But I did so want Chantelle to meet you. Anyway, your room is this way.'

She led him down the hallway, with no indication that anything might be amiss. Despite himself, Laurent found himself admiring her figure from behind, which not even her conservative clothes could hide completely.

'Why don't you unpack or whatever you need to do and

then we can go out and explore,' she said brightly. 'Notre Dame, the Tuileries Gardens. I'm longing to show you "my" Paris.'

You're being oversensitive, Laurent told himself, following her to a small but pretty guest bedroom complete with crisp white linen bedding and freshly laundered towels. *This is 1936, not 1836, and Elise is an old family friend. No one will say anything. It'll be fine.*

By the time Laurent was ready to go, the rain had intensified. Dark clouds mottled the sky like bruises, and puddles had already started to form in the dips and potholes that dotted Elise's street.

'So much for the Tuileries,' muttered Laurent, opening a large umbrella for the two of them. 'We'll drown.'

'Hmm,' agreed Elise. 'Come on, then.' Grabbing his hand, she ran around the corner to the busy Saint-Germain-des-Prés and hailed a taxi. 'Le Louvre,' she instructed the driver, brushing the raindrops off her skirt before turning to Laurent. 'If we can't do nature, then we might as well start with art.'

So far, Elise congratulated herself, barely able to contain her happiness as they sped through the emptying streets, everything was going perfectly. *Perfectly.* Operation 'Get Laurent to fall madly in love with me' was officially underway. Chantelle, bless her heart, had agreed to do a disappearing act, although not without a lot of persuasiveness on Elise's part.

'Laurent's practically a monk,' she'd assured her godmother. 'I promise you, Chantelle, he's so moral he makes the Pope look shady.'

Chantelle looked sceptical.

'Ask anyone. Ask Maman,' pleaded Elise. 'He's the last person on earth who'd try to take advantage of me, truly.'

'I dare say,' Chantelle countered. 'But what if *you* were to try to take advantage of *him*?'

'Whose chaperone are you, his or mine?' Elise pouted petulantly, scowling as hard as she could. But she couldn't keep it up for long and soon collapsed into giggles. 'Oh, all right,' she admitted. 'The thought had crossed my mind. But I won't misbehave, Chantelle. I swear on Sainte Madeleine I won't. Pleeeaaase?'

In the end, Chantelle had given in. Secretly she was pleased that another Senard brother was coming to pay court to her goddaughter. Chantelle had liked Thierry immensely, and any brother of his had to be preferable to the alternative. Elise's most recent would-be suitor was a very handsome, very rich, much older Greek heir to a shipping fortune; not a bad catch on paper. As nothing has come of the flirtation yet, this was a felicitous moment for the younger Monsieur Senard to make an unexpected entrance stage left.

With Chantelle out of the way, step two for Elise was to make sure Laurent didn't come over all chivalrous and make a bolt for the nearest hotel, once he realized it would be just the two of them at the apartment. He'd definitely thought about it. Elise had seen the look on his face, that same look he'd had as a boy whenever he was wrestling his conscience. But thanks to her carefully chosen, nun-like attire and (if she said so herself) her brilliantly executed air of nonchalance, she'd managed to get him unpacked and out into the city with her before he had the chance to bolt.

All we need now is time, she thought, playing nervously with her butterfly pendant while she watched him lovingly out of the corner of her eye. His dear, kind face, a little thinner but otherwise the same. His dark eyes and camel lashes, and that untamed hair that should have looked a mess but that had always suited him, somehow. Every fibre of her being longed to reach out and touch him. To press her lips to his, and *be* his, to never, ever let him go again.

161

She'd been in love with him for so long, as long as she could remember, and deep down that had never changed.

The truth was that, despite the rumours, Elise was in fact still a virgin. She might talk a good game, and flirt, and play-act the sophisticated city girl. But the embarrassing reality was that she was just as inexperienced sexually now as she had been when she left Burgundy almost three years ago. She'd made a mistake when Thierry visited her, thinking that her knowing, sexy alter-ego would impress him, and by extension Laurent. She couldn't afford to make the same mistake again. Elise might be many things, but she wasn't stupid. This time around she wouldn't try to show off. She would be herself – her old self. No nightclubs. No flashy restaurants or fast friends. With Laurent she would be good Elise, patient Elise, kind Elise. She would be the very best version of herself and wait for him to come to her.

Please, God. Please, please, please.

'Follow me,' she said now, hopping out of the cab at the Place de la Concorde and heading straight for the new Musée National de l'Orangerie des Tuileries, on the western side of the building. 'You're in for a treat.'

'This is really your stomping ground, isn't it?' said Laurent, allowing himself to be led to a booth selling tickets for the latest exhibition, *Rubens et son temps*. 'I'd never have put you down as an art buff when we were younger.'

'People change,' said Elise, buying two tickets and ushering him inside, out of the rain. 'We're lucky it's so quiet today. Normally there are lines around the block to see the Rubens.'

'I can see why,' murmured Laurent, stepping into a high-ceilinged room hung with some of the most astonishing paintings he'd ever seen. The intimate folds of flesh in *Woman Bathing*. The violence and physicality of *Lion Hunt* and *David Slaying Goliath*, all in colours so rich and vivid they looked as if they'd been painted yesterday.

'This is my favourite,' said Elise, walking into the second room of the exhibition, where the entire far wall was given over to *Prometheus Bound*, a horrifying painting of a young man tied to a rock, having the flesh ripped from his chest by an eagle.

'Really?' Laurent grimaced. 'It's a bit gruesome, isn't it?'

'Well of course it is,' Elise agreed, her eyes fixed on the canvas. 'But it's just so exquisitely done. You'll laugh, but do you know what it reminds me of?'

'What?'

'The day of my first communion. When those horrid children from the village attacked me? I remember feeling like I was being pecked at and pulled apart. Until you came along. Do you remember?'

She turned and looked up at him. For a moment all the beauty of the art receded and the only thing Laurent could see was Elise's face.

Christ, she's beautiful, he thought. He'd noticed her beauty before, of course. One couldn't not. But he'd never really felt it, not like this. Up until this moment, Elise had always been a child in Laurent's mind. A little girl. His *petite copine* – his friend. But the feelings coursing through him now were not remotely platonic.

'Of course I remember.' His throat was so dry, the words came out hoarse and strangled. The urge to lean down and kiss her was frighteningly strong. It unnerved him. 'How could I forget?'

For a few seconds that felt like an age, the two of them stood silently, gazing at one another.

'You were so brave that day,' Laurent said eventually, pulling himself together. 'And so compassionate, covering for the girl who attacked you.'

'I wasn't really compassionate,' Elise admitted, blushing. She may as well tell him the truth now. 'I only did it because you asked me to.'

'Really?' Laurent swallowed hard.

Elise nodded, her eyes locked with his.

Oh God. What was happening to him? This was Elise. Little Elise Salignac. He shouldn't want her. He mustn't.

'They were happy times, those summers at Sainte Madeleine,' he said aloud, desperately trying to push aside this new and unsettling attraction, and mentally put Elise back into the box of 'childhood friend'. No good could come of these other feelings, not with him about to leave for Spain.

To his relief, Elise dropped her gaze and began walking on slowly towards the third room. The mention of Sainte Madeleine seemed to have shifted something inside her, broken the spell between them, at least for now.

'They were,' she agreed wistfully. 'I was terribly jealous, though. Of all the time you spent with Alex.'

'I don't remember that,' said Laurent.

'You probably didn't notice,' Elise smiled. 'I was just the annoying little sister in those days.'

'How is Alex, by the way?' Laurent asked, clinging to the change of subject like a drowning man to a piece of driftwood. 'I still find it hard to believe he's married.'

'So do I,' said Elise, with feeling. 'And with a baby on the way. It all feels unreal to me, honestly.'

And so they started to talk about Alex, and Dids, and Thierry. They spent the rest of the afternoon walking the Louvre's endless corridors, admiring the art together and reminiscing about times past. For Elise it was simultaneously torture and bliss. Torture, because she was sure there had been a spark between them earlier, a shift in the way that Laurent looked at her and spoke to her, but she'd somehow failed to keep the tiny flame alive. Nevertheless it was bliss simply to be in his company after all this time. Even when Laurent went off on boring tangents about politics – Thierry's regiment were still deployed building the famous

Maginot Line defences, a subject which led him into a long rant about Germany and fascism) – Elise remained cocooned in a bubble of happiness. If only the day could last forever! If only she had endless time to win him over, to make him see that they were destined to be together. But nothing was ever easy with Laurent.

By the time they emerged from the museum the rain had stopped, and a newly washed city sparkled before them in the gathering twilight. They walked for a while, with Elise playing tour guide, when Laurent stopped suddenly, grabbing her arm.

'Look at that!'

He pointed upwards. A flight of butterflies, perhaps as many as twenty, swooped down directly in front of them. Pale blue and delicate, with inky black tips to their wings, they'd emerged from two extravagantly blossoming buddleia bushes, their purple blooms spilling over the walls of a private garden by the banks of the Seine.

'I've never seen that many all together, have you?' Laurent asked Elise, transfixed by the fluttering cloud that seemed almost to be waiting for them, performing their unexpected aerial display as a sort of private show, for their eyes only.

But Elise had frozen almost statue-still, too astonished to answer him. It was a sign! It had to be! The day she'd first laid eyes on Laurent – more accurately, the day she'd first crashed into him – she'd been following a butterfly at Sainte Madeleine, trying to catch it in her net. She was only a little girl then. But it was Sainte Madeleine's magic, the legend of the butterflies, that had led her to Laurent, and she'd been trying to catch his heart ever since.

'And now they're back . . .' she murmured, gazing up in delight as the pale blue cloud swooped and soared and eventually retreated back behind the crumbling garden walls.

Laurent looked at her curiously. 'Who's back?'

'Oh! Nothing,' Elise blushed, unaware she'd spoken the words out loud. But it didn't matter that she'd made a fool of herself. Nothing mattered now. She might be in Paris, but the magic of Sainte Madeleine was clearly with her still. She and Laurent *would* be together. The butterflies had confirmed it.

A few yards further on they stopped at a modest riverside bistro for supper. Whether it was all the walking that had flushed her cheeks, or the lingering dampness of the rain still on her skin, Laurent didn't know. But incredibly Elise seemed to have become even more radiant this evening. Her long dark lashes fluttered over those incredible violet eyes, eyes that he'd known for most of his life, and yet had never really, truly appreciated until now. But it was more than just her physical beauty that drew him to her. It was something else, something much more profound. Almost as if her soul were shining.

How was he supposed to leave her, after today? How was he supposed to tell her about Spain, for God's sake? All his earlier strength and resolve seemed to have deserted him. What he wanted most of all in this moment was to be able to sit here and look at her forever. To watch her shine, on and on and on.

'I'm paying for dinner,' he insisted, as they settled into a corner table cheerfully laid with a gingham cloth and lit by a fat candle already barnacled with what looked like a week's worth of melted wax. 'You bought the tickets earlier, so it's my turn.'

'Are you sure?' Elise looked worried. She didn't want to risk offending him. But even through the lens of her adoration, it hadn't escaped her notice how thin he was looking, and how ragged and threadbare his clothes were. Not to mention that *frightful* rucksack he'd turned up with instead of a suitcase, that looked as if it might harbour a small army of fleas. Given that Uncle Roger was as rich as Croesus and twice as generous, Elise assumed that Laurent had declined financial support from his family. But whatever the reason, he certainly gave a good impression of a man without two beans to rub together.

'Quite sure,' he assured her, perusing the menu.

Elise made a point of ordering the cheapest thing she could see, a plain croque monsieur. Laurent opted for moules, which arrived at the table in a steaming haze of wine and garlic so delicious-smelling that she ended up stealing from his bowl.

At first, to Elise's dismay, conversation flagged. They'd talked so much all afternoon, but in the intimacy of this new setting, with wine and candlelight and the low hum of conversation, it wasn't so easy simply to pick up where they'd left off. Elise was also conscious of her drinking and determined to pace herself, tonight of all nights. She must *not* let herself get drunk and ruin things. But staying sober wasn't doing anything to help her nerves.

'How are your parents?' she began awkwardly. 'Chantelle said that you wrote to her from Chateau Brancion.'

'They're well. Thank you.'

Laurent felt the awkwardness too, albeit for different reasons. He didn't want to get drawn into a conversation about his recent visit home, and how painful it had been for all concerned. That would lead on to the topic of Spain and he wasn't ready for that. Not yet.

'And your parents?' he asked stiltedly.

'They're better, I believe,' said Elise.

'Good. Marvellous.'

The soft curve of the tops of her breasts, just visible beneath her open-necked shirt, and the way they rose and fell with each breath, wasn't helping Laurent's concentration.

If she weren't still so young, so perfect . . .

If he weren't leaving for Spain . . .

If he hadn't committed his life to a cause that left him so little to offer, to Elise or any woman . . .

Then, maybe, things could have been different. But as things were, what could he possibly say to her about his feelings? About the depth of his affection, the growing strength of his attraction, the longing he felt when he was with her and the anguish when they parted? What did any of that matter? To ask her to wait for him would be grossly unfair, knowing that the wait might be forever.

'When were you last at Sainte Madeleine?' he ploughed on with the small talk.

'It's been more than a year,' Elise admitted guiltily. 'The Christmas before last.'

'Because . . . ?'

She shook her head, as if pushing away something too difficult to talk about.

'It's hard to explain. Things became so *sad* at home. I just . . . I couldn't. But Maman's visited me here. And the doctors all say Papa's much better than he was.'

'I'm pleased,' said Laurent, squeezing her hand with genuine kindness.

'We have your father to thank for that, at least in part,' Elise babbled on nervously, completely thrown by his touch. 'Arnaud and Alex both said that selling off the home farm was the worst mistake Papa ever made at Sainte Madeleine, and I think secretly Papa had come to think so too. Uncle Roger loaning him all that money to buy it back was a real lifeline.' Belatedly Elise noticed Laurent's astonished expression. 'Oh Lord. You didn't know, did you?'

Laurent forced a tight smile. 'No.'

No one had mentioned anything to him about a loan. He wasn't sure why the omission hurt so much. After all, he hadn't exactly shown much of an interest in family news in recent years. But it did hurt.

'When was this, do you know?' he asked Elise.

'The year after Alex left.'

'And I hate to ask, but do you happen to know how much the loan was for?'

Elise screwed up her face in concentration, trying to remember the figure.

'Could it be five hundred thousand francs?'

Laurent nearly choked on his wine. 'Good grief.'

It was a staggeringly large sum, even by Senard standards, an extraordinarily generous act on his father's part.

'I know it's a lot of money,' Elise said awkwardly. She wished to heavens that they'd never got into this. Talking about money tainted things between them, somehow. But still she felt the need to explain to Laurent just how vital Uncle Roger's loan had been. 'Sainte Madeleine needs those farms,' she told him fervently. 'Everything Alex argued with Papa about – modernizing the winery and investing in new technology – all that turned out to be right. The irony is that, since he left, Arnaud's implemented most of those changes, so now our Grand Crus are doing better than ever. But wine is such a fickle business.'

'I understand,' Laurent interrupted her. 'Really, you don't need to explain.'

'But I do,' Elise insisted. 'I need you to know, Papa would never have accepted the money if it weren't life-or-death for us. Those farms have always been Sainte Madeleine's insurance policy. Our cushion. A few years ago we were *this* close to losing everything.'

Pinching her fingers tightly together, to indicate the closeness of the brush with disaster, Laurent saw that she was shaking.

'You love the place, don't you?' he said.

'More than life,' Elise replied.

A wild love blazed in her eyes, fierce and almost maternal, like a lioness protecting her cubs. Laurent found himself wondering whether Elise would ever love another human being with the same fervour she felt for Sainte Madeleine? In that moment, he doubted it.

At the same time, he felt that she'd revealed something to him, something true and profound about herself. And he realized there would never be a better moment for him to show the same openness, the same courage. To break the painful news about Spain.

'Listen, Elise,' he cleared his throat awkwardly. 'There's something I've been meaning to talk to you about.'

Oh God. Elise's stomach lurched. Was he going to bring up Thierry's visit? She prayed not. After today and all their closeness, she couldn't bear for Laurent to launch into one of his disapproving lectures about her social life and her friends, or to accuse her of 'losing her moral compass'. It might have been true before, but it wasn't now. She'd changed. Changed for *him*. Because she loved him. She needed him . . .

'I'm going away.'

His words hung in the air, dissonant and unexpected.

'Soon,' Laurent pressed on, in the face of her silence. 'Very soon. And possibly for a long time. I came to Paris because I wanted to tell you myself.'

In an instant, all Elise's petty worries about Thierry and her own behaviour flew off and scattered like the cloud of butterflies they'd seen earlier. Her skin felt cold and clammy, and an awful tightness took hold of her throat.

'Going away where?' she asked him.

'To Spain.'

'To Spain,' Elise repeated, shell-shocked. She couldn't be less interested in politics, and had only the most rudimentary understanding of what was happening in Spain, never mind whose side one ought to be on. But she did know that young men were dying there.

'But not . . . you don't mean to *fight*. Do you?'

'There's no alternative,' said Laurent, reaching for her

hand across the table. 'You know the famous line: "The only thing necessary for the triumph of evil is for good men to do nothing." That's truer now than it's ever been.'

But Elise didn't give a damn whether evil triumphed or not. She wanted Laurent safe. She wanted him here in Paris, with her.

'No!' She snatched her hand away as if she'd been burned. 'I don't want you to go. Please, Laurent. Don't go.'

Looking at her beautiful, tortured face, Laurent could have wept. Elise's simple 'Don't go' tugged at his heartstrings far more powerfully than any of Thierry's carefully fashioned counter-arguments against him joining the Republican cause. Not even his mother's despair touched him as deeply.

I love you, he thought miserably. *I don't want to leave you. Oh God, Elise. Don't let me go.*

'I have to go,' he said aloud, his voice raspy and hoarse with emotion. 'I couldn't live with myself otherwise.'

Elise turned away, dabbing her eyes with her napkin. But she didn't bother trying to persuade him out of it. There was no point. He'd clearly already made his decision, and once that had happened, she knew Laurent to be as stubborn and unchangeable as she was.

'Let's go home,' she said, desolate. 'I'm not hungry anymore.'

The walk back to Chantelle's apartment was long and silent, the emotions between them too heavy to form themselves into words. Paris was dreamlike beneath a blanket of stars, clearly visible now that the rainclouds of earlier had moved on; a shining, romantic fantasy of a city, mocking the misery in Elise's heart and the terrible guilt in Laurent's. Never had doing the right thing felt so wrong.

When they finally reached Chantelle's building, the first thing they saw was a vast and ostentatious bouquet of flowers, leaning against the front door.

'They're for me,' Elise blushed, genuinely surprised as she reached down to read the card. 'From Costas.'

Laurent felt an unpleasant constriction in his chest.

'Who's Costas?' he demanded, more curtly than he'd intended.

'Just a friend,' said Elise, burying her head in the enormous heads of freesia and roses. 'I was supposed to go to an event he was hosting this evening, but obviously once I knew you were coming I didn't go. The flowers are only to say I was missed.'

'Hmmm,' grunted Laurent sceptically.

He's jealous, Elise realized, a warm rush of happiness shooting through her, temporarily banishing the awfulness of Spain and his leaving.

He's jealous of Costas. That means he must love me, at least a little bit.

Inside the apartment, Laurent stood around uselessly, watching Elise put the flowers in water. He knew he was being unreasonable, ridiculous even. But he felt angry with her. Angry that another man's flowers had made her happy, if only for a moment. Angry that she would stay here in Paris and be courted by this Costas, and God knew whom else. Angry that he would lose her, even though he was the one leaving without telling her how he felt.

He'd told himself that that was the right thing. That admitting his feelings would be selfish and wrong. That it would hamper Elise's own chances of happiness, and blight her life in a way that he had no right to do, given that he might not survive whatever awaited him in Spain. And yet now that he was here, alone with her in Chantelle's flat; now that it was his very last chance to speak up; he wondered if in fact it was cowardice that kept him silent, and not courage at all?

'Is something the matter?'

Her voice jolted him out of his reverie. She'd arranged

the flowers and was standing in front of him with a perplexed look on her face.

'I just asked you twice if you wanted coffee, but you didn't say a word.'

'Sorry,' he growled, not sounding it.

'Are you angry with me?' she asked, biting her lower lip and fighting back tears. 'About the flowers?'

'Of course not,' he snapped guiltily. 'Why would I be angry? I've more to worry about than flowers, Elise. Or your love life, in case you hadn't realized.'

'Of course I "realized",' she retorted, wounded. Why was he being like this? 'And what do you mean, my "love life"? I told you Costas is just a friend.'

'I'm going to bed,' Laurent announced gruffly. 'Goodnight.'

He was furious at himself for being such a fool, furious at Elise for being so unspeakably beautiful, furious at the fates that had decreed he had to leave her, a defenceless doe for wolves like this *Costas* to pursue. *'Friend' my arse*, he thought bitterly. He knew he should apologize, but the words wouldn't come. There was nothing for it but to call it a night.

'Goodnight,' Elise replied stiffly, too proud to let him see how devastated she felt, watching his bedroom door close.

Afterwards she tried to distract herself, pottering about the apartment aimlessly, making a coffee for herself that she didn't drink, and wondering how on earth this wonderful, miraculous, magical day had ended in catastrophe. Then all of a sudden the awful thought occurred to her that Laurent might be planning to leave in the morning. At dinner he'd said that he was leaving for Spain 'soon', but what did that mean? What if tonight was his last night? Not just in Paris, but . . .

No. Don't. You mustn't, Elise chided herself. But later, lying awake in her room, the terrible, catastrophizing thoughts refused to be quietened.

What if tonight had been her last chance to tell Laurent how she felt, and she'd missed it?

Lying naked on his back with just a thin sheet pulled over him, Laurent stared up at the ceiling. There was a chandelier directly above him, cut from finest Venetian glass and surrounded by ornate cornicing, like the piped icing curlicues on a wedding cake.

Weddings. Alex Salignac was married already, with a new life in America and a baby on the way. *Alex is younger than you*, Laurent berated himself. *But both personally and professionally, he's left you behind.*

He tried to reassure himself that what he was doing mattered. Going to fight in Spain. Staying true to his beliefs. But those choices also meant missing so much, losing so much. And in the darkest recesses of his mind, a small voice kept questioning whether, in fact, it was vanity that motivated him, and not noble sentiments at all? Was he being self-indulgent, pursuing some fantasy of honour and glory at the cost of hurting everyone he loved? First his parents and Thierry. And now Elise.

Oh God, Elise! Beneath the sheet, he ran a weary hand down the length of his body, trying to quell the fire that consumed it, a physical yearning like he'd never known. She'd be asleep now, no doubt still hurt by his churlishness earlier. He pictured her lying in bed on the other side of that wall, her perfect, soft, heavenly body literally feet away from him. Soon they would be divided by mountains and oceans, by the barbed wire and checkpoints of war. She would forget about him, helped no doubt by *Costas*, whoever the hell he was, with his flowers and cocktail parties.

At least, he consoled himself, Elise had not turned out to be living the dissolute lifestyle that his brother had described to him. While it was true that men were courting her – how could they not, with her beauty, her indescribable, ravishing loveliness? – Laurent could at least go to the battlefield knowing that Elise remained innocent at heart, as true to her own morals as he was to his.

That's something, he told himself, vowing to apologize to her in the morning. *It will have to be enough.*

He didn't know he was asleep until the dream began. The most wonderful, perfect, erotic dream of his life. Elise, warm, naked, pressing her body against his back. Her hands, snaking around his chest, pulling at his ribs, willing him to turn around and face her. And when he did, her neck stretching upwards so their lips could meet, tentative at first but then more surely. Her back arching. The rock hardness of his erection pressing against her belly, his hands seeking the downy softness below it . . . and then, suddenly, a jerk, a gasp of surprise, a momentary pulling away that made his eyes snap open and . . .

'Elise!' Scrambling for the bedsheet, Laurent pulled it up over his waist, shaking. This was no dream. This was real. Elise, in his bed, in his arms. Elise naked, willing. *Initiating*. 'What are you *doing*?'

Grabbing a pillow, he threw it into her lap. Confused and embarrassed, she covered herself with it.

'What do you think I'm doing?' she looked at him pleadingly. 'I'm loving you, while I still can. I love you, Laurent.'

'No.' He shook his head, screwing his eyes tight shut. 'No, no, no.'

'Yes!' insisted Elise. 'I love you and you love me too, I know you do.'

'Elise . . .' He gave her a tortured look.

'It wasn't just me, Laurent,' she insisted vehemently. 'The way you kissed me just now – you *want* me.'

He let out a groan of frustration and deep, deep misery. She was right, of course. He wanted her so badly, so appallingly badly. But it wasn't to be. He couldn't marry her. It was as simple as that. He couldn't give her his love in the right way, the way she needed and deserved. And anything less than that would be a betrayal of what they were to each other. A defiling of something perfect, something pure and true. No. He couldn't. He wouldn't.

'I was asleep, Elise,' he told her, begging her to believe him. 'I . . . I thought I was dreaming.'

'Dreaming of *me*,' she countered, defiant tears in her eyes.

'Not like that.'

'Liar!' she shouted at him. 'Why won't you admit it, Laurent? You're in love with me. We're in love with each other.'

'So is this what you do, when you like a man?' Laurent demanded, his desperation making him cruel. 'Or when you think a man likes you? You strip off and fling yourself into his bed, no questions asked?'

'Of course not,' Elise gasped, appalled. 'How could you say such a thing?'

'Is this how it was with *Costas*? Or how it will be, once I'm gone?'

The words spewed out like vomit. Laurent hated himself for his spite, but he didn't know another way to make her stop. And he had to make her stop, for both their sakes.

Sobbing, Elise jumped off the bed as if it were on fire. Grabbing a blanket from the floor, she wrapped it protectively around her.

'This isn't you,' she told him. 'Why are you being like this?'

'Because you're a child,' Laurent said coldly. There was no other way now. He had to keep going, had to make her believe that he wasn't the one for her, that she'd made a mistake. 'Thierry was right. You're playing at being a woman, but you don't know what you're doing.'

'I hate you!' Elise screamed at him, losing control and

becoming the child that he seemed to want her to be. 'You've ruined everything!'

Burning with shame and humiliation, she fled back to her room.

The Laurent she had just encountered was a complete stranger. She'd known him to be pompous at times, moralistic and heavy-handed. But never unkind. Never cruel.

What had possessed him?

Mortification pricked at Elise's skin like spilled bleach. *I want to die*, she thought miserably. Opening her bedside cabinet, she pulled out a bottle of Grand Marnier, a treat that she occasionally afforded herself as a nightcap before bed. Unscrewing the top viciously, she drank what was left in the bottle. Minutes later she was out cold.

When she woke, Laurent was gone. He left no note, no message. Just a neatly made bed and his towels folded on the chair in the corner.

If Elise didn't know better, she could have sworn she heard her own heart crack.

CHAPTER TWELVE

William Alexandre Robert Salignac was born on 5 April 1937, at the new hospital in St Helena. Weighing in at a whopping nine and a half pounds, his arrival into the world came close to precipitating his mother's departure from it. Poor Ruth laboured valiantly for eighteen hours and lost a tremendous amount of blood. By the time William was finally delivered, Ruth's face was so pale she looked see-through, and Alex could tell that the doctors were worried. But in the end both mother and baby pulled through, and the love affair between Ruth and William began.

Alex had read about new fathers feeling jealous of their wife's love for their baby. Of feeling pushed out or rejected, no longer the centre of their partner's attention. Such reactions astonished him. Nothing on earth brought him greater happiness than watching the woman he loved breastfeeding their son; Ruth's eyes full of love, and little William's, turned upwards beneath his thatch of downy blond hair, fixed adoringly on his mother's face. Having been raised by a mother who rarely expressed her affection verbally, and never physically, watching Ruth kissing and touching William was a revelation. She was constantly stroking his fat cheeks or chubby little legs in wonder, almost as if she couldn't quite believe he was real, or that something so precious and beautiful and perfect was hers. Love poured out of her like water through a bombed dam, and Alex felt privileged just to be around it.

It probably helped that he was besotted himself, racing home from the vineyard or the winery as often as he could just to catch a glimpse of William feeding, or sitting up, or crawling. With each passed milestone Alex rejoiced, but also mourned that *already* his son's babyhood seemed to be flying by at an unseemly pace, the magical moments slipping through his fingers like dry sand.

On William's first birthday, Alex and Ruth threw a party in the big barn at Tricycle, with a cake and balloons and multiple bottles of their first-ever Pinot. The new labels had just been printed, a simple line drawing of a tricycle (Ruth's pick) that was already proving a big hit with local wine merchants. At long last it felt as if Ruth and Alex were really on their way.

'Hmmm. It's still a bit young,' Bob Ballard observed, swirling the wine around his mouth with a connoisseur's confidence after each sip. 'But it's got tremendous potential: fruity, warm, full of life . . .'

'Sounds like us,' said Alex, wrapping a proud arm around Ruth's shoulders while William looked on from his wooden high chair, a Ballard family heirloom. 'Still a bit young, but with tremendous potential.'

'I don't know about "full of life" though,' Ruth moaned, rolling her eyes as her son plunged both of his fat fists into his bowl and began smearing chocolate birthday cake liberally around his face. 'I'm exhausted.'

'That's because you do everything, my darling,' Alex kissed her.

'Oh, please, pass me the bucket.' Tyler, William's godfather and still a very regular visitor to the ranch house, extracted a large lump of chocolate sponge from his godson's hair and ate it. 'Must you be so appallingly happy all the time? Spare a thought for the rest of us.'

'You could be happy too if you'd just settle down with Mary-Beth,' Ruth pointed out to him archly.

Mary-Beth Rushly, an old schoolfriend of Ruth's, had been walking out with Tyler for almost a year now. But he had yet to propose, and Alex and Ruth saw little signs of that changing, for all his professed envy of their domestic bliss.

'I thought this was a party,' Tyler frowned, holding out his glass to Alex for a refill. 'That means no nagging.'

'I'm not nagging,' said Ruth. 'I'm just sayin'.'

'Da.'

Everyone turned to look at the baby.

'Da!' he said again, more loudly, delighted to have everyone's attention. Vaguely turning towards Alex, he repeated 'Da, da, da!' banging out the sound with his grimy fingers on the tray of his chair.

'Did you hear that?' Alex looked around the little group in astonishment, as if William had just parted the Red Sea. 'He said Dad! Say it again, Will. Say "Dada".'

'Dada!' William beamed, basking in his parents' smiles.

Picking him up out of his high chair, Alex covered his little boy with kisses. 'Imagine that being his first word!' He turned to Ruth.

'Imagine,' said Ruth indulgently.

'I'll have to teach him to say it in French,' said Alex, practically bursting with pride. 'Now that we know he's a genius.'

Ruth caught her mom's eye and giggled. She was happy. Happier than she'd ever believed possible. Marrying Alex had been wonderful enough. But now, with the vineyard, and their darling little ranch house, and William? Now life was just about perfect.

*　　*　　*

180

'Isn't this perfect?'

Costas Goulandris lay back on the deck of his yacht, *Lady Athena*, gazing at the hoi polloi milling around St Tropez harbour. It was a glorious, high summer day on the Côte d'Azur, they'd just moored in a prime spot where everyone could gaze at them in envy, and he was about to sit down to a champagne and langoustines lunch with a beautiful girl. A girl he'd had his eye on for quite some time, as it happened. Although as usual, they weren't alone, much to his regret.

Elise Salignac had joined him on his yacht a week ago with her godmother, the glamorous Chantelle Delorme, and a gaggle of friends from Paris. Already ensconced in one of *Lady Athena*'s many comfortable cabins were two sets of Costas's friends from Athens, as well as his girlfriend of the moment, a moody Italian heiress named Isabella who'd started to make wearisome noises about wanting an engagement ring. He would have to deal with that situation eventually. Perhaps even pay her off, if the father got shirty. But these were problems for another day. Today was to be savoured and appreciated, and who better to savour it with than the delectable Mlle Salignac? Even if Isabella was giving Elise dagger eyes and making snide comments at every opportunity.

'It is lovely,' Elise agreed, sliding onto the lounger next to Costas's that he'd been saving for her. 'Do you know, until this week, I hadn't been to the South since I was a small girl. My parents used to rent a cabin at Ramatuelle and Brolio would take my brothers and me paddling at the beach.'

'What a fascinating life you've led,' Isabella drawled bitchily.

'Who's Brolio?' asked Costas, ignoring his girlfriend and focusing all his attention on Elise, who was looking particularly ravishing this afternoon in a simple white one-piece swimsuit and flowy linen skirt. He already knew the answer to his question. Unbeknownst to Elise, Costas had had people watching and researching her ever since he'd first singled her out as a potential future bride. He already knew all there was to know about her family history, from her mother's aristocratic bloodline, to her father's drinking and gambling problems, to her worryingly close relationship with the Senard brothers, especially the younger boy, Laurent. But he'd become quite the expert at feigning ignorance, and he enjoyed hearing Elise tell her own story. Apart from anything else, it gave him a chance to test her honesty.

'Brolio was my old nanny.' Elise sighed wistfully. 'Madame Aubriau. She still lives at Sainte Madeleine, waiting patiently for one of us to produce a baby she can look after. Which is hilarious really, given that she's about a hundred and ten.'

'Neither of your brothers have children?' Costas asked, helping himself to a chilled flute of Dom Pérignon and handing another to Elise, still pointedly ignoring Isabella. She'd become so easy to bait, it almost wasn't fun anymore.

'Alex does – my younger brother,' said Elise, her face wrinkling adorably as the champagne bubbles flew up her nose. 'He has my nephew, William. But they live in California. Much to Brolio's disappointment, I'm sure.'

From her perch about ten feet further along the deck, under the shade of a monogrammed canvas umbrella, Chantelle watched her goddaughter talking to their host with growing concern. Not that anything untoward had happened, or even looked likely to happen. For all of her distrust of Costas Goulandris, Chantelle had to admit that during the three years he'd been a part of Elise's social circle, he'd been quite the gentleman. Generous, polite, obviously romantically interested, and yet never pushy or inappropriate in his attentions.

Of course, thought Chantelle, *it's easy to be patient when you have a string of pretty girls as long as your arm, happy to keep your bed warm while you wait.* Although perhaps she was being unfair. Costas was in his prime, after all: still relatively young at thirty-four, unmarried, ludicrously rich and extremely handsome, albeit in a brutal sort of way. Stocky and broad-shouldered, with thick chestnut hair, full, sensual lips and laughing, dark eyes that glittered when he spoke to you, it was hardly any wonder that women flocked to him.

And yet, Chantelle worried about Costas and Elise. *His* interest in *her* she took to be a mixture of Elise's beauty and breeding, combined with her relative lack of interest in him as a suitor. Men like Costas Goulandris weren't used to being turned down, or at least kept on the back burner, which was the way that Elise treated him. Chantelle suspected that this 'playing hard to get' was a large part of Elise's appeal to the dangerously charming Greek, whether it was done consciously or not.

But it was Elise's feelings for him that really troubled her godmother. Ever since the weekend when Laurent Senard had visited her in Paris, something had shifted in Elise, and not for the better. Part of that shift had involved an increasing closeness to Costas Goulandris. She obviously enjoyed his attention. But the question was, why? If it were simply that she found him attractive, Chantelle could have accepted that. But she suspected that Elise was using Costas's 'friendship' to fill the void that had been left by others. By her father primarily, but also her brother, and then more recently by Laurent. Costas's flattery and glamorous lifestyle offered a distraction from all her past pain. Holidays on the yacht, being waited on hand and foot, unlimited champagne, expensive gifts. The best tables at every restaurant. People bowing and scraping wherever one went.

Elise had worshipped her father, but Louis had let her down repeatedly over the years, emotionally, financially and in a myriad other ways. With Laurent now apparently out of the picture, did Costas Goulandris, twelve years Elise's senior and 'together' in ways Louis Salignac had never been, represent the security that she had always craved? If so, that worried Chantelle deeply. Because in her experience, men like Costas had a habit of growing tired of their playthings after a while, no matter how compelling or desirable they'd been at first.

'Heavens, is that Belén?' Isabella stood up, peering over her sunglasses at a willowy brunette, strolling along the harbour with a little Pomeranian dog on a leash. 'It *is*! It's Belén Primo de Rivera. How extraordinary. Yoo hoo, Belén!'

She waved excitedly, beckoning her friend onto the *Lady Athena* before Costas had a chance to stop her. The last thing he wanted was another of Isa's snobby, horse-faced girlfriends guzzling his champagne and droning on about some German duke or Spanish prince they'd danced with at some mind-numbing society ball. But it was too late. Moments later, the girl walked onto the yacht in a plume of cloying perfume, air-kissing everybody before helping herself to a mountainous plate of langoustines and plonking herself down next to Elise, her yappy rat of a dog whining plaintively at her feet.

'Costas, you remember Belén,' Isabella said airily, before introducing her friend to the rest of the party, leaving Elise for last.

'Did you say Salignac?' Belén looked at Elise curiously. 'Where have I heard that name before?'

'I don't know,' said Elise. 'My family's from Burgundy. We have a vineyard—'

'No, that's not it.' Belén shook her head, turning back to Isabella. 'Although I *do* know a fabulous-looking man from Burgundy. Thierry Senard. Have you ever come across him?'

'I don't think so,' Isabella yawned.

'You'd remember if you had, believe me,' Belén said

breathlessly. 'He's in the Second Dragoons and he *is to die for*, honestly. The sexiest fellow ever to wear breeches. No offence, Costas.'

Costas smiled icily but said nothing.

'Thierry's my cousin,' Elise piped up, earning herself another death stare from Isabella.

'*No!*' Belén gasped, taking a long swig of champagne.

'Distant cousin,' Elise clarified. 'Third or fourth or something silly like that. But our families are very close.'

'Are they really? What a small world,' said Belén, also sounding a smidgen put out by Elise's claimed connection. 'Well, Thierry's an absolute angel,' she told Isabella, adding conspiratorially, 'although the younger brother's a real black sheep.'

'Oh?' Isa leaned forward, eager for any gossip that might reflect poorly on Elise. 'In what way?'

'He ran off to Spain to fight for the communists.'

'Scandalous!' Isa gasped, looking out of the corner of her eye at Costas. No one hated the communists more than he did.

'Broke his poor parents' hearts, apparently,' Belén blundered on. 'The mother's never recovered.'

'That's not true,' said an ashen-faced Elise. God knew she had no reason to defend Laurent after the way he'd treated her before he left. But listening to Isabella and her horrid friend spread malicious gossip was a bridge too far. 'Aunt Camille was perfectly well, the last I heard.'

'Then perhaps your news is out of date, sweetie,' said Belén acidly. 'I heard that the brother married one of his fellow "revolutionaries" last month, some ghastly scrubber from Seville, and that the whole family were devastated.'

What little colour was left in Elise's face now drained from it completely. This couldn't be true. Could it? Laurent couldn't be *married*. Her Laurent?

No. Someone would have told her.

She shot a panicked look at Chantelle.

'Who told you that?' Chantelle asked Belén sharply. 'About Laurent Senard being married.'

'Multiple people,' Belén shrugged. 'Friends back home.'

She proceeded to launch into a long, boring diatribe about various friends she and Isabella had in common, allowing the rest of the party to tune out.

'Are you all right?' Costas put a hand on Elise's shoulder. 'You've gone awfully pale.'

'I'm fine,' Elise assured him. 'I think maybe one of the langoustines disagreed with me. I might take a short walk on dry land. Settle my stomach.'

'Would you like me to come with you?' he asked solicitously.

'That's all right,' Chantelle jumped in. 'I'll be happy to accompany Elise. We'd hate to drag you away from your guests, wouldn't we, darling?'

'You're both sweet,' said Elise, 'but I'd honestly rather go by myself. I won't be long.'

Standing up, she hopped onto the jetty and disappeared into the harbour crowds, before anyone could follow her.

'I hope you're happy,' Costas turned on Isabella, his manner changing totally the moment Elise had gone. 'All that nonsense about her cousin obviously upset her. Why can't you and your friends keep your stupid traps shut?'

His tone was so breathtakingly rude, Chantelle didn't know where to look. Belén blushed to the roots of her hair, stammering something inaudible about not meaning to cause offence. But Isabella gave as good as she got.

'I *am* happy, since you ask,' she spat back at Costas, her angry eyes boring into his. 'Your little obsession's become dreadfully boring, darling. An hour or two's break from watching you fawn over Elise will be a welcome relief to all of us. Come along, Belén,' she turned to her friend haughtily. 'We may as well shop while he sulks.'

It was an unedifying display on both sides, and Chantelle wasn't the only guest who felt embarrassed by it. But she may have been the only one fully to catch the murderous glint in Costas Goulandris's eye, like a sharpened steel blade turned towards the sun, as he watched his girlfriend leave the yacht.

Elise walked blindly up the hilly streets behind the port, deeper into the labyrinth of the town. Above her, laundry hung flapping in the breeze between houses that seemed to lean together at the top, like two drunks lurching at one another for support. Down on the ground, housewives darted back and forth from the market carrying baskets loaded with corn cobs and bread, fresh mussels and muslin wrapped parcels of cheese, while workmen called to each other in that distinctive, twangy French patois only ever heard in the South.

Life's going on, thought Elise. As it should. As it must. But without her. Or at least, without what was left of the *old* her. The old Elise Salignac who'd been in love with Laurent Senard for as long as she could remember.

Ever since the awful night in Paris when Laurent had rejected her, Elise had continued to cling desperately to tiny fragments of hope. That he hadn't really meant what he said. That he would come back from Spain one day, when the war was over, and take her in his arms, and beg her forgiveness.

But now all that was over. All pretence gone. All shreds of hope lost to the wind.

Laurent was married. Not *getting* married. Actually married.

The deed was done.

He would never come back to her.

Turning a corner, she stumbled into a fish market, wrinkling her nose at the stench. The fishmongers were packing up for the day, with most of their catch sold. Trestle tables were being scrubbed down and there was blood on the cobbles, partly sluiced with buckets of seawater. Baskets of fish heads and scales and other detritus had been shoved, stinking into corners.

'*Puis-je vous aider, mademoiselle?*'

Elise had stopped in front of a moustachioed man in a soiled apron who still had a few sea trout left on his stall to sell.

'I can fillet it for you?' he cajoled her. 'Fresh and delicious . . .'

Pulling out a lethal-looking blade, he deftly flipped the fish over in his hand and slit open its belly, hooking his finger around a mess of intestines and scooping them out in one, seamless motion.

That's how I feel, thought Elise. *Like I've had my guts ripped out.*

And yet strangely, it didn't hurt exactly. Rather it made her feel numb, detached, like someone walking through a dream. Like a ghost.

'No, thank you,' she shook her head at the man.

'Suit yourself.'

Out of nowhere Elise found herself thinking about Sainte Madeleine. And then of Alex, so far away in America. Loss was nothing new to her, after all. In fact, it had been her constant companion these last few years. She'd been so angry with Alex for leaving. But maybe he'd had the right idea all along? To walk away. To start again. To leave behind childish things.

Looking up, on impulse she found herself scanning the sky for butterflies. But there were none to be seen. No signs for her today. No Sainte Madeleine magic to rescue her.

Laurent was gone forever.

Turning around, she began walking back to the boat.

* * *

It was Ruth who first noticed it, watching William toddling around the yard. Usually he was full of beans after his lunchtime nap, hurling himself into flowerbeds or running after his favourite toy, a rubber ball with a train printed on it that Alex had bought him in town that he took with him everywhere. But today he seemed slower, visibly lethargic. After a few, half-hearted runs he stopped dead, like a car out of gas, and sat down on the grass looking bewildered.

'What is it, sweetie?' Scooping him up in her arms, Ruth felt a shiver of fear run through her. His skin was hot to the touch. Not the warmth of exertion on a summer's day, but real, dangerous, feverish heat. Without thinking or stopping she ran to the winery, carrying the rag-doll floppy Will in her arms.

'Alex!'

He heard the shouts before Ruth had even made it into the courtyard.

'What is it?' he asked, hurrying out of his office to meet her.

'It's William. Feel him. His fever's through the roof.'

Ruth wasn't prone to panic or hysteria, but there could be no mistaking the concern in her voice. Laying a hand on his son's head, Alex immediately understood why.

'Call Doc Richards,' he shouted over his shoulder to Tyler, who was standing in the office doorway watching. 'Tell him we need him out here right away.' Lifting William gently out of Ruth's arms, he began peeling off the boy's clothes, lifting his sodden cotton T-shirt over his lolling blond head. 'Run back to the house and draw him a cold bath,' he instructed her. 'Dump all the ice from the icebox into it. We need to bring his temperature down as soon as we can.'

Ruth nodded.

It was a relief, having Alex take charge. He was always so sure and so capable. *Children get fevers all the time*, she

189

reassured herself as she ran back to the ranch house. She was still worried, but not as panicked as she had been five minutes ago. *He'll be OK. Alex and Doc Richards will know what to do.*

Chuck Richards pressed two fingers gently down on William's swollen stomach, before peering into his throat for a second time. The tonsils were enlarged, the throat itself red-raw. But it was the spreading, strawberry rash creeping over the child's abdomen and arms that gave it away.

'OK, kids,' he turned to Alex and Ruth, pulling the thin sheet back up over the sweating boy and clearing his throat. 'William has scarlet fever.'

Ruth let out a little whimper of anguish.

'Now, there's no need to panic,' Chuck assured her. He'd been Ruth Ballard's doctor since she was born – had delivered her, in fact – and it pained him to see her and her young husband so stricken. 'It's a serious infection, so we have to take it seriously. But you've done everything right: cooling him down, calling me, letting him rest. And he looks like a strong little fella. He should get through this.'

The 'should' pierced Alex's heart like a bullet.

'Is there anything you can give him, Doctor?'

'Well, that depends. There's a serum that's shown some good results in more seriously ill patients,' Doc Richards explained.

'Do you have any with you?' asked Ruth.

'Not with me, no.'

Her face fell.

'But I wouldn't recommend that for William at this stage anyway.'

'Why not?' asked Alex, trying for Ruth's sake not to show how frightened he was.

'For one thing, he's very young. All of the antitoxins for

scarlet fever run the risk of damaging the patient's liver, and that risk rises in infants,' Doc Richards explained calmly. 'Right now, the number one thing we need to do is break his fever. So cold baths, just as you are doing. Lots of fluids. And I'll give you some aspirin you can dissolve for him.' Reaching into his battered leather doctor's bag, he pulled out a small glass bottle of powder. 'No more than three times a day, though,' he cautioned, 'and you must stick to the doses religiously.'

Alex and Ruth both nodded, and thanked him. Ruth stayed with Will while Alex walked the doctor to his car.

'He will make it, won't he?' he couldn't help himself from asking, once they were out of Ruth's earshot. 'I just feel so helpless.'

Chuck Richards rested a kindly, paternal hand on his shoulder. For one fleeting, unexpected moment, Alex found himself wishing that his own father were here. That he had someone to lean on, besides himself; or Ruth, who had enough to deal with poor William.

'Scarlet fever's a horrible disease,' said the doctor, choosing his words carefully. 'But children recover from it all the time. Have faith, Mr Salignac.'

Have faith, Alex thought wryly, walking wearily back to the house. His mother would have said exactly the same thing.

'*Dear God*,' he found himself praying. '*Please save him. Please save my darling boy. If you let Will live, I promise to make things right with my father. I'll go back to Burgundy, and get married in the Catholic church. I'll do anything you ask of me, Lord. Just please make him better.*'

CHAPTER THIRTEEN

'What do these butterflies mean?' Father Henri Bercault asked Thérèse Salignac, taking his seat at the family dinner table. 'I've noticed them carved into the walls everywhere. They're quite lovely.'

'It's an old family legend,' Louis Salignac answered gruffly, before his wife had a chance to speak. 'But for God's sake let's eat before we get into all that.'

Didier Salignac looked from his father's morose, impatient face to Henri's placid, kind, infinitely patient one and thanked God for the hundredth time for bringing the young priest into his life. The fact that Henri was here for dinner, family dinner at Sainte Madeleine, felt like a small miracle in itself. His presence made Didier feel, if not invincible, then at least not naked and vulnerable to Louis's moods in the way he always used to. Wherever Henri was, Didier felt at home.

It had been a long and hectic summer at Sainte Madeleine, with the grand old chateau noisier and more alive than it had been at any time since 1930, the year that the great Salignac exodus had begun. And while it was true that, so far, only Louis and Didier had returned home to Burgundy permanently, the frenzied activity up at the vineyards combined with a steady stream of house guests had provided a much-needed shot of adrenaline for the beloved old house.

In the years after reacquiring the manor farm, Louis had generally been in better spirits, much to Thérèse's relief. He had stayed off the booze, allowing the many, many scars of their marriage to begin to heal, and had gradually found the strength to step back into the family business, supported by the steady hand of the ever-loyal Arnaud. But there could be no denying that it was a sadder, smaller, diminished Louis Salignac who had returned to Sainte Madeleine from his long stint at the drying-out clinic. Physically Louis looked older, and weaker. His famously lustrous hair had started to thin, his skin felt dry and papery to the touch, and his once strong, burly physique now looked frail and wasted. Sometimes, when Thérèse saw him walking into a room, she had to make a conscious effort not to catch her breath. He looked so like his late father now, it was frightening.

But the most pronounced changes were the emotional ones. Louis's famous sense of humour, the impishness that at times could spill over into spite, but that had always belied his wit and energy – all that was gone. It was as if the effort of remaining sober had taken every ounce of strength that he had. Worse, Thérèse feared that by removing alcohol from his life, her husband had somehow also removed a large portion of his capacity for joy. The vineyard had just enjoyed another bumper harvest, the fourth in a row, but even this had failed to raise more than an occasional, half-hearted smile from Louis. So his obvious, demonstrative delight about buying back the manor farm had been a huge relief to Thérèse and everyone else at Sainte Madeleine. He appeared to have blocked out the fact that it was he who had sold it in the first place, for a whopping loss, and that he'd only been able to buy it back thanks to Roger Senard's ludicrously generous loan. But Thérèse was certainly never going to point this out to him.

Tonight though, Louis had come back from the vineyard in a palpably gloomy mood. Things had got worse when Thérèse informed him she'd invited the parish priest for dinner.

'Again?' Louis glowered. 'He was only here last week.'

'I don't see what that has to do with anything,' Thérèse bridled. It was true that she invited Henri for supper far more frequently than she had Sainte Madeleine's old priest, Père Martin. But then no one could deny that Yves Martin had been the most dreadful bore, even before he grew old and infirm. Whereas Henri was delightful company. More importantly, he'd been a transformative influence on Didier, and Thérèse intended to do everything in her power to foster their budding friendship.

'It's just a bit much, that's all,' grumbled Louis, who'd never been as enamoured of Father Bercault as Didier and Thérèse seemed to be. He resented the way that young priest always seemed to be hanging around the chateau, ingratiating himself.

Elise would have understood his feelings, Louis felt sure. But Elise wasn't here, and showed no imminent signs of returning to Sainte Madeleine. Not for the first time, Louis felt isolated and lonely without her.

'Is that your grandson?' Henri asked Thérèse, pointing to a silver-framed photograph of a plump, blond baby displayed in pride of place on the Louis XV card table. If he'd hoped to lighten the mood and ease tensions with Louis, he was to be disappointed.

'Of course it is,' Louis snapped. 'Who else would it be?'

Thérèse shot Louis a disappointed look. 'You'll have to excuse my husband's rudeness, Father. Yes, that's William.' Pushing her chair back, she got up and walked over to retrieve the picture, handing it to Henri. 'He looks exactly like Alexandre did as a baby, doesn't he Dids?'

'I expect so, Maman,' said Didier, smiling encouragingly

at Henri as he finished his salad. 'I can't say I really remember.'

'Of course, none of us have had a chance to meet him yet. Or his mother,' added Thérèse, more than a trifle wistfully.

Henri nodded understandingly. 'I dare say it must be hard for you, having family so far away.'

Louis opened his mouth as if about to say something. But he either lost the thought or thought better of it, closing his mouth again and returning to jabbing morosely at the remnants of his salad with a silver fork.

Just then Angelique, one of the maids, ran in looking flustered.

'I'm so sorry to disturb you, madame, but you're needed at once.'

'Needed?' A worried look flashed across Thérèse's face. 'What for?'

'Monsieur Dupont's here, from the post office in Vézelay.'

'Oh?'

'He has a telegram for you. From America.'

At this magic last word Thérèse shot up and practically flew out of the room, her long skirt billowing beneath her like the sails of a ship.

Louis watched her go, feeling a strange, uncomfortable mixture of affection, sadness and guilt. Thérèse's longing for Alex was as acute as his own for Elise, and it pained him to see it. She had never overtly blamed him for Alex's departure. In fact, she'd taken great pains not to take sides in the estrangement between father and son, an effort that meant more to Louis than he could easily express in words. But he knew that Alex's absence was a cause of great sorrow to Thérèse. As it was to him deep down, although he was too proud to admit it.

'You'd better go after her,' he instructed Didier. 'Find out what's going on. It's pretty unusual for Dupont to trek all the way up here in person.'

'All right, Papa.'

Dabbing his mouth with a napkin, Didier dutifully did as he was asked, following his mother out of the room.

'Let's hope it's good news,' said Henri, smiling weakly at Louis, who didn't smile back. Henri felt deeply awkward, left at the table alone with Didier's father, a man whose tough outer shell he had thus far proved utterly unable to crack. Still, it was his duty to keep trying. As Henri saw it, all the souls at Sainte Madeleine had been entrusted to his care, even complicated ones like Louis Salignac's. The Lord had called him to be a shepherd of men, but he'd never said the job would be easy.

A few moments later, the heavy silence at the table was broken by a terrible sound from the hallway. Part gasp, part sigh, part scream.

'No!' Thérèse wailed. 'NO!'

Louis leapt to his feet and staggered towards the door, feeling as if the ground were sinking beneath his feet. Something had clearly happened, something awful, for the unflappable Thérèse to react in such a way. If there had been an accident – if, God forbid, Alex had been killed – Louis knew that the fragile bridges that he and Thérèse had been rebuilding in their marriage would be burned again beyond repair. She would never forgive him.

Please, Louis prayed. *Please let my son be alive.*

Watching his host stumble, Henri instinctively stood up and offered a supportive arm, but Louis shook him off furiously, like an angry bear swatting away a fly.

'No, Father,' he insisted. 'You stay where you are. This is a private family matter.'

By the time Louis reached the hallway, Thérèse was half leaning, half collapsing into Didier's arms while poor Monsieur Dupont from the post office hovered miserably behind them. Thérèse looked white as a sheet, and Dids wasn't much better, pale and teary-eyed with that sensitive, vulnerable look of his that had always been like a red flag to Louis, for reasons he'd never been able fully to explain, even to himself.

'What's happened?' Louis asked, bracing for impact.

No one replied.

'For Christ's sake, Thérèse. What's *happened*?' he demanded, raising his voice more in fear than in anger. 'Is it Alex?'

'It's not Alex, Papa,' said Didier.

Louis gripped the sideboard for support as a relief too profound for words overwhelmed him. *It's not Alex*. In that moment, Louis loved Didier like never before.

'Thank God,' he said aloud. But his happiness was short-lived.

'It's the baby,' Didier continued sombrely. 'It's little Will, Papa. He died.'

Chantelle Delorme carefully folded the last of her silk scarves, laying it on top of the rest of her clothes before closing the suitcase with a satisfying *click*. She adored St Tropez, and in any other circumstances would have felt low at the prospect of heading back home to Paris. But too many things about this holiday on the *Lady Athena* had left a sour taste in her mouth. She would be pleased to get back to her comfortable apartment. To friends she could trust, and a social world that she knew how to navigate. And she'd be even more glad to get Elise back there with her, away from the nefarious influence of Costas Goulandris, as Chantelle had increasingly come to see it.

Chantelle desperately wanted a kind man for Elise. A stable, steady man. Costas Goulandris might be many things, but he was not that. Chantelle would never forget the terrifying, murderous look in Costas's eyes when Isabella had had the nerve to challenge him about his outrageous flirting with Elise. And then there was Isabella's banishment:

less than forty-eight hours after the unfortunate conversation about the Senard brothers, Isabella had left the yacht party without warning or explanation. Even stranger was the way that no one challenged Costas about his girlfriend's sudden disappearance. None of his so-called 'friends' said a peep. Were they afraid?

Chantelle shivered when she thought about it.

'May I help you with your case, madame?'

A uniformed manservant appeared at Chantelle's cabin door at exactly the right moment. Credit where it was due, Chantelle had to admit that Goulandris's staff had all been first-rate: efficient, impeccably mannered, unobtrusive. Money might not buy you a good character, but it certainly helped with a great many other things.

'Thank you,' said Chantelle, stepping back to allow him in. 'I think I'll go up on deck and wait for my goddaughter. I don't suppose she's back yet, is she?'

'I haven't seen her, madame.'

Chantelle glanced at her watch anxiously. Elise had gone into town early this morning with Costas, for a final potter around and to pick up souvenirs and postcards. But Chantelle had expected her back hours ago. Their overnight train from Nice didn't leave till nine, but even so. Elise had yet to pack, and the windy, coast roads between St Tropez and the city were notoriously unreliable.

Thankfully, just as she was coming up the stairs to the main deck, she heard Costas's voice, warm and low, followed by Elise's distinctive laugh, cascading and melodic like someone running their fingers from the high notes to the low on a piano. It was a sound Chantelle had heard far too little of lately.

But her happiness was short-lived. Emerging into the daylight, the first thing Chantelle noticed was that Goulandris's arm was around Elise's waist. The second thing, to her horror, was that Elise was wearing a long, white lace dress. He was in black tie, looking even more pleased with himself than usual.

Oh God. Chantelle's stomach lurched. *Please don't let this mean what I think it means.*

'Surprise!'

Disengaging herself from Costas's grip, Elise ran over to Chantelle. Extending her left hand, she flashed a solitaire diamond ring bigger than anything Chantelle had ever seen. Like an enormous, sparkly grape. Or perhaps a small plum.

'We did it,' Elise said, giving her godmother a sheepish smile. 'We got married!'

'So I see,' said Chantelle. She didn't trust herself to look at Costas, and it was too painful to look at Elise, so she kept her eyes fixed on the diamond.

'It's stunning, isn't it?' said Elise, misconstruing Chantelle's sudden interest in her ring. 'Costas had it made specially.'

'More than a year ago, I might add,' Goulandris added, sliding up beside her. *Like the snake that he is*, thought Chantelle. 'I've wanted to propose to this young lady for a very long time. But it never felt like the right moment. Until now.'

'Indeed?' Chantelle said archly. 'Not until a few *days* after you tired of your last girlfriend?'

She knew she sounded like a prim, maiden aunt, but she couldn't help herself. The subterfuge, the secrecy. It was all wrong. Costas must have realized that Elise was still reeling over the news of Laurent Senard's marriage. He'd seen her vulnerability, and he'd pounced.

'I understand it looks hasty,' Costas replied politely. 'I'm sure I'd react the same way if I were Elise's guardian. But I assure you, Isabella and I were never in love. She was biding her time with me every bit as much as I was with her. It was always Elise I wanted. I just . . . wasn't sure she felt the same way.'

Chantelle wanted to scream. But she did have to admit

Elise looked awfully happy in this moment. Radiant, in fact. Was it possible she'd misjudged the situation?

'Don't be angry,' said Elise gently. 'Please don't. I'm so very happy, we both are, and you're the first person we've told. No one in Costas's family knows, or mine. Our only witness was the priest and a local *avocat* Costas picked out of the telephone book.'

For a split second Costas's eyes met Chantelle's but he quickly glanced away. If Goulandris had had a lawyer at the wedding, it was no accident. '*Picked out of the telephone book*' indeed. This marriage may have been an impetuous decision on Elise's part, but her groom had clearly thought things through very carefully, and protected himself and his fortune legally from any claims Elise may try to make on it in future.

'Please, Chantelle. I need you to help me smooth things over with Maman and Papa,' Elise continued. 'I know they'll be upset that I got married without them, especially after Alex and his American girl. But at least ours was a proper, Catholic wedding. That should mollify Maman a little, don't you think?'

Her sweet little upturned face, so happy and yet so longing for approval, was more than Chantelle could bear.

'I'm sure it will, darling,' she relented. 'And I am happy for you. Of course I am. It's just all rather a shock.'

'Oh, thank you, Chantelle!' Elise flung her arms around her. 'That means so much to me. To both of us. Doesn't it, Costas?'

'Absolutely.'

Chantelle exhaled, willing herself to believe that she was being unfair to Goulandris, and that this marriage would succeed. After all, with his wealth he could have married pretty much anyone he wanted. If he'd chosen Elise, it was hard to see what motive he might have, besides love. She had precious little money of her own, and no helpful connections.

Perhaps, as his wife, she would bring out Costas's kinder, more decent side? Chantelle fervently hoped so. Because the deed was now done.

'I take it this means you're not coming with me back to Paris?' she asked, forcing a smile.

'We'll stay here a couple more days and then set sail for Greece,' said Costas, placing both hands on Elise's shoulders and massaging them lovingly.

'I can't think of a more perfect honeymoon,' Elise sighed. 'Just the two of us, on the yacht?'

'It'll be even better once we get to Athens,' Costas assured her. 'I can't wait to show you the house. Introduce you to all my friends.'

'Yes. And then maybe, once the dust has settled, we could go to Burgundy and I'll introduce you to my family?' gushed Elise. 'I can't wait to show you Sainte Madeleine. You'll love it. I know I'm biased, but it truly is the most romantic house in France, isn't it, Chantelle?'

Not long afterwards, Chantelle left the lovebirds to it. One of the manservants loaded her case into the back of a private car, and with much waving and beeping of the horn, she set off for Nice.

I'll wait till I'm back in Paris to call Thérèse and Louis, she decided, as the red-tiled roofs of St Tropez faded into the distance behind her. After all, it was too late to change anything now.

As fate would have it, Louis Salignac telephoned Chantelle's building the very day she got home, with bad news of his own. Alexandre's baby son William had died suddenly from a fever.

'Thérèse is in pieces about it,' Louis told his old confidante. 'She's been quite inconsolable. She couldn't face letting Elise know, so she asked me to do it. I don't suppose she's at home, is she?'

'I'm afraid not, Louis.' Chantelle swallowed hard. 'I think perhaps you'd better sit down.'

Louis had put as brave a face on it as he could during the call. But Chantelle could tell his heart was breaking at Elise's 'news'. Alex's departure had been a shock and a betrayal, but it had always been Elise who held the keys to her father's heart. Ever since she was born, Louis had fantasized about walking his darling daughter down the aisle one day at Vézelay cathedral, proudly giving her hand to some suitably noble and impressive French husband. It had never for a moment occurred to him that Elise might just run off into the sunset, never mind do so with a virtual stranger. This was *Elise*, after all. Elise who loved Sainte Madeleine more than anyone. Elise, whose heart surely had always been here, inextricably intertwined with the magic of the butterflies and the fecund vines on which all their lives depended.

Back at the chateau, news of Elise's elopement was met with muted disappointment and disapproval rather than outright despair. Coming as it did hot on the heels of little William's tragic death, the scandal was robbed of much of its sting. Didier was too distant from Elise these days to think very much about it either way. Arnaud Berger, who'd always been something of a surrogate grandfather to the Salignacs' only daughter, absorbed the news in dismayed silence, more worried for Elise than anything else. Only Brolio seemed truly shocked.

'Elise, our Elise, married! To a Greek tradesman, of all things!' the old nanny shuddered, appalled, when Louis broke the news.

'I think in fairness, Brolio, this Goulandris chap's more of a shipping magnate than a "tradesman", per se,' Louis chuckled, amused that the seeds of Thérèse's snobbery should have found such fertile roots in his dear old nanny's heart. 'Chantelle gave me to understand that the two of them are on his enormous yacht as we speak, en route to Athens and entirely uncontactable.'

'Hmmm,' Brolio sniffed, unimpressed. 'Just as well she can't be contacted, I dare say, as I should have a few choice words for her if she could be.'

Thérèse was more sanguine about the match than Louis had expected.

'I suppose Elise knows her own feelings,' she sighed, staring out of the window.

Her apparent lack of concern troubled Louis. He put it down to the fact that she was still reeling from the news about William. That there was only so much grief Thérèse could acknowledge and process at one time. Even so, it was unlike her.

'Although I admit it would have been nice to be invited to at least *one* of our children's weddings,' she continued.

Louis put a frail arm around her shoulders. Despite everything, it was nice to feel like a couple again. Like a team.

'There's always Didier, I suppose,' Thérèse went on. 'I suppose he'll marry one day.'

'I suppose so,' Louis said gruffly and without conviction.

'And at least Elise did things properly, in a Catholic church, I mean,' said Thérèse, continuing to try to talk away her doubts. 'Not like Alex and his wife.'

As the days rolled by, and she gleaned more information about her new son-in-law, Thérèse's position seemed to soften even further.

'Various friends have told me that these Goulandrises are a very good family,' she told Louis excitedly. 'Even before the shipping fortune they were Old Money, apparently. So he's not really middle class at all.'

'Good, darling,' Louis said meekly. He no longer had the urge to take Thérèse to task about her snobbery. Whatever helped her cope with the loss of her only grandchild before she'd even had a chance to meet him was a blessing in Louis's eyes. Like him, he sensed, Thérèse was simply doing what she needed to to get through the days.

The summer that had begun so happily, full of reunions and new beginnings and hope, was ending with the bitter aftertaste of a great wine gone sour.

Ruth and Alex stood alone at the graveside.

Once the preacher and mourners had gone, Bob and Jean had tried to convince them to come back to the house. Tyler had offered to wait in the car, convinced that Alex shouldn't be driving after such an emotional day. But Alex had insisted on staying behind.

'We need to say goodbye as a family. Just the three of us.'

Wrapping his arm around Ruth's shoulder, she felt like a statue, cold and stock still, gazing down into the deep pit where the tiny white coffin was still visible beneath the first, thrown handfuls of earth. Later, the men with spades would fill in the grave. There would be a soft earthen mound; then a headstone; and eventually grass and lichen, little vases of flowers neatly and regularly left by loved ones and well-wishers. Later, Will would be gone. But right now he was *there*. Right there. Still close enough to touch.

Alex felt a crazy urge to jump into the pit, lift out the box, rip off the lid and take him in his arms. He wondered if Ruth felt the same. If she was standing so still because she didn't trust herself not to climb down there and grab him.

'I'm so sorry,' Doc Richards had told them, fighting back tears himself. 'I don't understand what happened. His fever had broken. I really thought he'd make it.'

Ruth had reassured the doctor that it wasn't his fault. That nobody blamed him. That he'd done all he could do.

'Alex and I aren't angry,' she explained through her own tears. 'We're just heartbroken.'

Alex had nodded, said all the right things. But what Ruth said was a lie, at least as far as he was concerned. He *was* angry. Angrier than he had ever been, than he had ever imagined possible. There was so much anger, in fact, he seemed to have lost the power to direct it, but instead found it radiating from him in all directions, like heat from a rage-fuelled sun.

He was angry at God. God had let him down. Broken his promise. Reneged on their deal. Alex had sworn to return to Sainte Madeleine and make things right with his father, if God would only save his darling Will. He had prayed so fervently, and he'd truly believed, in that moment, that God heard him. For the first time in his life, Alex Salignac had had faith. Didier's faith. Maman's faith. The faith of his forebears.

But his faith had been misplaced. God had proved himself a fickle father, just like Louis. In that moment, Alex hated them both.

'We'll never forget him,' Ruth whispered softly.

'Never,' said Alex.

'We'll have other children. But they won't replace him in our hearts.'

'Never,' Alex said again, his voice shaking.

He would never forget Will.

He would never forgive God, or Louis.

He would never go back to Sainte Madeleine.

Never.

PART THREE: LAURENT

1939–1945

CHAPTER FOURTEEN

Laurent sat slumped on the deck of the trawler, watching as the beautiful, broken city of Valencia faded into the distance. Tears streamed down his face, stinging a still-raw knife wound on his left cheek and carving streaked rivulets through the deeply ingrained dirt.

He was leaving Spain, a country he had come to love and hate in equal measure, but that would now forever be branded deep in his soul. The war was over. Franco and the fascists had won. The tattered, exhausted remnants of what had once been the Republican forces had no option but to flee. Their sacrifices had been for nothing. All the death – the executions, the terror, the torture, the starvation – had counted for naught in the end. The beautiful idea of freedom for which Laurent had fought so hard and so tirelessly these last three years, and for which so many of his friends had died, was now shattered, crushed beneath the combined boots of Franco, Mussolini and Hitler.

Despite all the talk of 'reconciliation' and 'healing', despite the victorious Nationalists' bloodless entry into Madrid on 28 March, Laurent knew full well that failure to escape now would mean death for vanquished foreign fighters like himself. He'd already lingered longer than was wise, returning to Seville to do what he could to help his friends there, especially Diana and her family who'd been so kind to him. But it was now late April and time was running out. After walking and hitchhiking to Valencia by night, and sleeping rough under hedges and in bombed-out farms by day, he'd been lucky to find a fisherman willing to take him as far as the Azores. There he hoped to rest and rebuild his strength. And afterwards . . . who knew? At the rate Hitler was mobilizing, a return to France might not be wise or even possible this summer. Laurent still had friends in Morocco, which might be an option? Closing his eyes, he leaned back against his pack, too tired to think about it.

When he woke, night had fallen. The sea was mercifully quiet and a dazzling blanket of stars shimmered overhead, as if to try to remind him that all was not lost, that there was still beauty and wonder in the world. The boat's skipper, a grizzled old man named Leon, crouched down beside him with a blanket and a mug of Catalan stew, a delicious concoction of ground pork, white beans and garlic.

'Drink this,' he instructed Laurent, wrapping the blanket over his shivering shoulders. 'You're skin and bone.'

Laurent did as he was told, sipping slowly but gratefully. He tried to remember the last time he had eaten a full meal, but couldn't. Hunger had been his constant companion these last two years, alongside fear. If it hadn't been for Diana's support, he wouldn't have made it.

'Where are you from?' Leon asked, the first question he had put to Laurent since inviting him on board. In Spain, it was safer not to know.

'France,' murmured Laurent, warming his long fingers around the tin mug.

The fisherman nodded. 'Where were you fighting?'

'All over.' Laurent sighed, gazing out into the blackness. 'Córdoba. Badajoz. Lately in Seville.'

Leon winced. 'You've seen some horrors, then.'

'Yes,' said Laurent.

'I heard the Nationalists executed ten thousand in Córdoba.' Leon shook his head at the madness of it all.

'Something like that.'

Laurent rubbed his eyes. He still had dreams about the killings. Schoolteachers, rounded up and shot in the street by fascist militia for the crime of teaching science classes that 'undermined the Catholic Church'. Young men and women, screaming and weeping, begging for their lives. He would never forget it. Almost as bad were the anguished looks of the starving families that he saw in every defeated town or village. Bandy-legged children with distended bellies, their cartoon-huge eyes sunken in skeletal faces. No one had escaped the cruelty.

In Seville, the city he knew best, thousands of civilians had been executed for 'harbouring' enemies of the state like himself, most summarily shot in the squares of parks.

Diana Muñoz knew the risk she was taking when she brought Laurent home. But he would remain forever grateful that she'd taken it. The two of them had met briefly in Madrid at the start of the war, and kept in contact as best they could as the years passed and the tide of the conflict began to turn inexorably in Franco's favour. Like many Spanish intellectuals, Diana and her parents, Pepe and Maria, opposed the fascists on principle. But they'd taken no active role in the conflict, until deciding to provide a safe house for Laurent.

That wasn't the part he felt guilty about. The Muñozes had helped him because they wanted to, because it was the right thing to do. But deep down Laurent knew that Diana was in love with him. That she'd hoped, once all this was over, or even before, that he might marry her and stay to make his life in whatever was left of Spain. He could certainly have done a lot worse. She was a wonderful girl: pretty, kind, brave, ferociously intelligent. And when they'd kissed, and later made love, the night after one of Laurent's

211

closest friends in the unit had been killed, he'd felt excited and grateful and happy. They spent so much time together, many people assumed that he and Diana were already married, or at least engaged. And when Diana didn't correct them, Laurent didn't have the heart to either.

But he should have. And that was where the guilt came in. He should have, because he always knew there was something missing between them. And that something was his heart. That was the one thing Laurent couldn't give Diana, because it was no longer his to give. He'd left it back in Paris, with Elise.

Oh God, Elise! How their last meeting tortured him. It had been bad enough saying goodbye to Thierry on such painful terms. But in that case he'd really had no choice, short of abandoning the cause. With Elise, though, he'd made a conscious decision. Not only to banish her from his bed, but to blame her for being there, to punish her emotionally. *Why? Why had he done it?* At the time he'd convinced himself that it was concern for Elise, for her moral welfare and happiness, that had guided him. But as the weeks and months passed, and the horrible realities of Spain's war unfolded before him in an apparently endless vista of cruelty and death, a more uncomfortable truth dawned. Laurent had also rejected Elise because he was jealous. Jealous and possessive, over a girl he knew he *couldn't* possess, at least not yet. But if he couldn't have her, he couldn't stand the thought of anybody else doing so. So instead of doing the decent thing and walking away, he'd behaved like a resentful child, shaming Elise for having the same sexual feelings he had himself. As if he resented her for having become a woman. Resented her for loving him.

That awful night had been almost three years ago now, and he'd had no contact with Elise since. No contact with anyone back home, in fact. And now, as he sailed away from one war, shattered and defeated, the prospect of another loomed large and ugly. If the news reports were to be believed, Hitler's lust for *Lebensraum* was insatiable, and his confidence seemed to be growing daily.

Most people in France continued to believe that war with Germany could still be avoided, and that, even if it did happen, the famed Maginot Line, the country's great defensive marvel, would protect them. But Laurent wasn't so sure. He'd had first-hand experience of Germany's military might in action in Madrid. People were not as afraid as they ought to be.

'Try to sleep,' said Leon kindly, after Laurent declined a second mug of stew. It was delicious, but his stomach wasn't used to large quantities of food. 'If the weather picks up, I'll wake you.'

Laurent squeezed the fisherman's hand, hoping his gratitude was understood through his exhaustion. Reaching into his pack, he pulled out the worn, dog-eared photograph of Elise that he carried with him everywhere, rubbing it lovingly between his fingers like a talisman. He found it hard to sleep now without first looking at her. Then, carefully replacing the photograph, he extracted a grimy envelope containing a letter to his parents. It had been too painful to write while he was in Spain, impossible to know what to say. It wasn't easy now. But he wanted Roger and Camille at least to know that he was alive. That he'd made it out.

'Send this for me? If you can?' he asked Leon.

'Of course,' the fisherman nodded.

Seconds later, Laurent was out cold once again, in a sleep too deep for dreams.

'We need to move her, Mr Goulandris. We're running out of time. Your wife needs to be in a hospital.'

The young doctor looked imploringly at Costas. But he

continued to shake his head, like a Roman emperor giving a thumbs down at the Colosseum, condemning some poor slave to death. Elise Goulandris was not about to be torn apart by lions. But if she lost much more blood, both she and her baby could die.

'My son will be born at home,' Costas announced imperiously. 'No Goulandris has ever been born in a hospital, and I'm damned if my boy will be the first.'

'But, Mr Goulandris, if your wife needs a blood transfusion . . .'

'I said no,' Costas snapped. 'Now get back in there and do your job.'

Wearily, the doctor opened the master bedroom door and returned to his patient. He did not understand men like Costas Goulandris. From the dogged insistence that his unborn baby would be a boy, as if by repeating it he could make it so, to his wanton lack of concern for his young wife's welfare, the shipping magnate seemed like the worst type of bully, a caricature of Greek machismo. Unfortunately, in this case, he called the shots.

'All right, Mrs Goulandris,' the doctor said briskly, battling to keep the despair out of his voice as he took his patient's hand. Pale and delirious, with her sweat-soaked hair stuck to her face like seaweed on a rock, the poor girl looked so exhausted and weak. 'You're almost there. Now let's get this baby out, shall we?'

Elise groaned as another agonizing contraction swept through her body, pain taking over every one of her senses. She was dimly aware of the doctor's voice. Occasionally other external, 'real' things asserted themselves as well: the dawn sunlight, chinking through the shutters; the rose-shaped cornicing on the ceiling over the marital bed. How many times had Elise stared up at that plaster rose in anguish, wishing she were anywhere else, while Costas brutalized her? Because that's what it had become, his lovemaking. Brutal and angry, an assault, not just on her body but on her spirit, her soul. And now, God help her, she was about to bring a child into that misery, into the hateful sham of her marriage.

Or not. Surely pain this bad must mean that she would die? And the baby too? It would be sinful to wish for it. And yet her longing for release, for it all to be over, was so overwhelming, it was as if her body were making the prayer for her.

She knew she had made a terrible mistake, almost as soon as Chantelle left for Paris. With all the guests gone, and only a skeleton crew, Costas had insisted they set sail for Greece immediately.

'Must we?' Elise had asked, coiling herself around him trustingly. Little did she know then how misplaced that trust would turn out to be. 'I'd like to explore St Tropez a bit more, now it's just the two of us. We can book a table at L'arc en Ciel as Monsieur and Madame Goulandris!'

Costas laughed and pulled her to him, kissing her roughly in a way he never had before. 'I haven't waited three years to have dinner with you, Elise,' he told her. 'We sail tonight.'

That very first night, trembling in front of him in the silk negligee he'd bought her from the little boutique in the harbour, Elise had begged him to be gentle. Still a virgin, despite all her Parisian flirtations, the only naked man she'd ever been close to was Laurent, and then only for a few, mortifying moments. So when Costas emerged from the bathroom stark naked, as hairy as a gorilla and with his cock jutting out obscenely like an enormous pepper grinder, nerves had overwhelmed her. But he cared not a whim for her terror, pulling off her negligee with a grin and gorging himself on her body like a starving man at a feast. Clawing at her back, grabbing and biting at her breasts, he pushed her thighs open roughly with his knees before launching himself inside.

Elise screamed, as much from shock as from pain, although there was plenty of both.

'Relax,' Costas commanded, reaching down for the bottle of olive oil he'd brought with him for the purpose, and using it to mitigate Elise's complete dryness while he forced himself in and out of her.

'Christ,' he laughed, rolling off her once he'd finally climaxed and wrinkling his nose at the blood on the sheets. 'It's so long since I slept with a virgin, I'd forgotten all this. Oh, don't look so miserable,' he added, kissing her perfunctorily on the nose. 'The first time is always the worst. You'll enjoy it eventually.'

Perhaps, with another man, that might have been true. But Elise never did enjoy sex with Costas. Their two-week 'honeymoon' aboard the *Lady Athena* at least taught her what to expect. Her new husband's sex drive was relentless. Two, sometimes three times a day, he would expect her to go to bed with him. Panicked, and in considerable physical pain, Elise quickly learned some tricks to help herself. As foreplay was apparently not in Costas's repertoire, she made sure to use the oil herself, liberally, before she came out of the bathroom. She also figured out that he climaxed more quickly when she feigned a struggle. So she taught herself to scratch and kick and to look him in the eye defiantly whenever he climbed on top of her. That usually got the misery over with more quickly.

She clung to the hope that, once they finally got to Athens, things might calm down. And, to some extent, they did. Costas took great pride in showing her his house for the first time, a magnificent Palladian mansion in the hills above the city, all-white pillars and fountains and spectacular views.

'See what a good match you made, Mrs Goulandris?' he smiled at Elise, nudging her playfully in the ribs as they stepped out of the chauffeur-driven Rolls-Royce that had come to collect them from the yacht. 'You're a rich, married woman now.'

One of the strangest things about Costas was the way that he seemed almost unaware that he was treating Elise badly. Often during the daytime, he would behave quite normally towards her, as if nothing were wrong between them. The charm that he'd evinced so consistently during the long years of their 'friendship' was still there. It was just that he now turned it on and off when it suited him, like a tap. So Elise never knew which version of her husband she was going to get.

What was true was that her new home was beautiful. In terms of material things, Elise now lived a life of luxury beyond anything she'd seen before, or even imagined. Anything she wanted, she could buy, from jewellery to paintings to couture dresses. There were servants at her beck and call twenty-four hours a day, and a fleet of luxury cars permanently at her disposal. Fresh flowers arrived daily for her bedroom and dressing room, and she was never, ever expected to do anything for herself, from picking up a towel to reserving a table at a restaurant.

The quid pro quo for all of these perks was that she provide Costas with sex on demand, look beautiful at all the dinners and functions and yacht parties he dragged her to with his boring Greek friends; and, crucially, accept that her every move would be watched. Not only did the servants all report to her husband regularly, but whenever Elise left the compound, a security detail of at least two armed men would follow her.

'It's for your safety, darling,' Costas insisted, when Elise complained about feeling spied on.

'But why would I be unsafe?' Elise demanded. 'I mean, who would want to hurt me?'

He waved a hand dismissively, to indicate that the matter

was closed. 'This is normal in Greece. Is that a new dress, by the way? Very pretty.'

Too proud to admit how unhappy she was, Elise wrote letters to Chantelle and to her family at Sainte Madeleine proclaiming her bliss, and sending photographs of her new, lavish lifestyle in Athens. The constant ominous rumbles emanating from Hitler's Germany still seemed unreal in Greece, and the idea of full-scale war was widely dismissed, especially in the rarefied circles in which Elise now mingled. So it was easy to paint a picture of comfort and indulgence, however little that equated with Elise's true emotional experience.

Just occasionally, in her letters to Arnaud Berger, she would allow chinks of honesty to pierce the fairy-tale narrative, in a way she couldn't allow herself to do with her parents. She admitted to Arnaud, for example, that she'd been 'relieved' when her honeymoon yacht trip ended, and that her pregnancy had been 'uncomfortable' at times. Was a childish part of her hoping that Arnaud would read between the lines, as he had so often when she was a child? That he would see her unhappiness and rescue her? Or did she just need to tell someone, in some small way, that beneath the facade she was feeling quite desperate? Either way, writing letters home became an important ritual during the first year of her marriage, and the replies she received from Sainte Madeleine, full as they were with 'home news', became a lifeline she couldn't have lived without.

Occasionally in these letters Elise would permit herself to ask for news of Laurent, always in as casual a way as possible. But it seemed no one had heard anything, not even Uncle Roger and Aunt Camille. In her wiser moments, Elise reflected that this might be a blessing. All the doors between them had been closed and locked, after all. What solace could she possibly find, pressing her ear against them?

The nausea began less than a month after they got to

Greece. Awful, sudden bouts of vomiting, that seemed to come on out of nowhere. And then the tiredness, a sort of warm, heavy limbed sluggishness that made even the slightest exertion feel like an appalling effort. For months Elise hid her symptoms. She didn't want to admit what they meant, even to herself. But as her breasts began to swell and grow painfully tender, and her small pot belly finally started to protrude, there could be no more avoiding it.

A baby. Now she was well and truly trapped.

'Push, Mrs Goulandris. Push! I can see your baby's head.'

The young doctor's voice sounded tinny and distant, like a faint radio distress signal crackling over a battlefield. Consumed with the battle, Elise tuned him out. She didn't need to be told to push. Her entire body seemed to have been turned inside out, pulled agonizingly apart in its attempt to expel the life inside her. The pain was indescribable, part cramping ache and part violent stabbing. Certain that she was going to die, with a sort of primal knowledge that lay deeper than reason, Elise closed her eyes as a slide show of memories played out before her:

Sainte Madeleine, as it was in her childhood, full of laughter and light.

Sitting on the nursery rocking horse, listening to Alex talking about the latest camp he'd built out in the woods.

Riding on Papa's shoulders as he ran full pelt down the sloping lawn, roaring like a great bear.

Laurent, in his tennis whites, comforting Didier.

Laurent. Married. Far away. Lost to her forever. And yet, as painful as that was, it was Sainte Madeleine that Elise yearned for the most, as she felt the life force drain from her body. Sainte Madeleine, her soul, her beautiful home. Why, why had she ever left?

And then all of a sudden she was back in her bed in

Athens, back in the now, with a terrible scream ringing in her ears, a warm wet gushing of fluid and blood between her legs. And before she'd realized that *she* was the one screaming, a small, white, vernix-covered body had arrived. It was over.

'Congratulations, Mrs Goulandris!' The doctor's relief was palpable. 'You have a healthy baby boy.'

Elise slumped back against the pillow, too weak to move.

A boy. That would make Costas happy. He'd already chosen the name: Andreas.

Her eyes still closed, Elise listened to her son crying, lusty and furious, and surprised herself by smiling. *He's as unhappy to be here as I am. An angry little Salignac.*

A few moments later, wiped somewhat clean and wrapped in a muslin cloth, the doctor handed the baby to her. Without thinking, Elise held him to her breast. He suckled instantly. Gazing in wonder at this tiny person, his lips moving and his perfect, miniature fingers resting on her skin, she felt the love rise up within her like floodwater.

'Hello, Andreas,' she whispered, gently stroking his thick black hair. 'Hello my darling.'

The next great love affair of Elise's life had begun.

William was dead. And yet, almost obscenely it seemed to Alex, life went on. The sun continued to rise every morning over the Tricycle vineyards, and to set every evening, bleeding beautiful streaks of pink and orange into the skies over Alex and Ruth's farmhouse. Thérèse still sent letters with news from home: Elise's sudden marriage and move to Athens; the birth of her son, Andreas; Thierry Senard's promotion. And while the storm clouds of war gathered in Europe, in Napa another gentle spring gave way to another warm summer, and people went about their business as if nothing were amiss.

At first Alex resented this oppressive normality. But as

the weeks and months passed, and he immersed himself once again into the life of the vineyard, rooted as it was in the soil and the seasons, he came to appreciate the distraction that work provided. From bud break in March, when the bright mustard flowers appeared as ground cover between the vines, to fruit set in May, and the excitement of the first, tiny green grapes appearing, there was a constant stream of tasks to be done. Leafing and canopy management were barely complete by July, when *veraison*, the ripening of the fruit, began in earnest. And though Pinots were always one of the last varieties to be harvested, in mid-August, with such a tiny staff and only himself managing the sales end of the business, Alex frequently found himself working eighteen-hour days.

As his grief slowly began to morph from a searing agony to a constant, dull ache, other worries began to take precedence. Ruth, pregnant again and permanently exhausted, was not herself. Listless and withdrawn, she never cried, and rarely talked about Will. But it didn't take a doctor to see that she was depressed.

'It's probably hormonal,' Doc Richards had assured an anxious Alex, after one of Ruth's regular pregnancy check-ups. 'Roughly a third of mothers experience profound mood changes before birth. She'll come through it.'

Alex hoped he was right. Because short of bringing Will back from the dead, he had no idea how to help Ruth. He'd suggested that she come back to work in the winery. He could certainly use the help, and perhaps the rhythms of the office would help her the way they'd helped him? But she'd simply shaken her head, *no thank you*, and gone back to the bed where she seemed to sleep away most of her days.

So Alex was startled one morning in the middle of the harvest to see Ruth not only up but running, as fast as her legs could carry her, down to the winery.

'Have you heard the news?' she panted, her cheeks flushed, as she walked towards the crushing vats, already full with grapes.

'What news?' asked Alex, grabbing a chair for her to sit down.

'Hitler's invaded Poland,' Ruth said breathlessly. 'Can you believe it? I thought you'd want to know right away.'

For a moment Alex just stood there, stunned. The two men working the wine press stopped what they were doing briefly, but then resumed their work. To them, Alex realized, this was news from far away. Unexpected, perhaps, and not entirely unimportant. But still something to be filed as 'happening to someone else'. It was a story. It wasn't real.

Ruth sat down and turned her face up expectantly towards his, waiting for a reaction.

'Why aren't you saying anything?' she asked.

'Because I don't know what to say,' Alex replied truthfully. 'I know it's been talked about but . . . I suppose I never thought he'd actually do it.'

'Will there be war, do you think?' Ruth asked. 'In Europe?'

'I don't know.' Alex rubbed his eyes. 'I hope not.'

He felt such a strange mixture of emotions. Happiness, that at long last something seemed to have jolted Ruth out of her stupor. Guilt, that he could feel happiness over news as terrible as this. And something else, a sort of longing mixed with fear, almost like a *pulling* sensation deep in his chest. If Britain declared war, Daladier would surely follow suit. What would that mean for France? For his family? For Sainte Madeleine, the home he had abandoned twice: once physically when he sailed for America; and then again, in his heart, after Will died?

'Come back and listen to the news with me,' said Ruth. 'There might be more bulletins on the wireless. We can hear them together.'

She reached up for Alex's hand, a small gesture, but an

important one for both of them. It was the first time Ruth had asked for his company, actually wanted to be with him, in months. In that moment, relief trumped every other feeling.

'I'd like that,' he said, helping her lovingly to her feet.

Tyler and the others could handle things here for a few hours. Right now Alex needed to be with his wife. The world might be about to fall apart. But Alex's world – Ruth and the new baby – were coming back to him. Nothing mattered more than that.

CHAPTER FIFTEEN

Laurent rolled over on his bunk and tried to block out the noise coming from the radio of the fellow next to him. He was sleeping in a dance hall in Casablanca, one of scores converted for the purpose of housing foreign refugees like himself. And while he was grateful for the shelter, he bucked against the living conditions.

Ever since war was officially declared two weeks ago, the Germans had been bombarding Morocco's airwaves with propaganda, most of it directed at the country's Muslims and explicitly anti-Semitic in nature. This particular broadcast was from Radio Stuttgart, and was full of the usual disinformation, mingled with age-old legends and slurs. Abdul, the young man who slept closest to Laurent, was glued to his radio set, lapping up every poisonous word.

'Would you mind turning that down?' Laurent asked, after a few torturous minutes. 'I'm trying to sleep.'

'This is important,' said Abdul. 'The Fuhrer's got the French on the run, and the Brits have done nothing so far except air-drop a few leaflets. I reckon the whole thing'll be over by next year.'

Depressed, Laurent knew better than to get drawn into an argument. It wasn't Abdul's fault that he swallowed the Nazis' lies whole. Like many of his countrymen, he was illiterate and barely educated, beyond the basic, religious indoctrination he'd received as a child. Although it was still a French protectorate, nationalism was on the rise in Morocco, and becoming increasingly entwined with the various fascist movements gaining momentum across Europe. With most of the country's Jews already poor and living in *mellahs*, effectively ghettos, and heavily discriminated against by the French authorities, on a bad day it felt as if there was little standing in the way of the tidal wave of ignorance and hatred flowing through the country like sewage.

But on other days, Laurent felt more hopeful. Like many other defeated Republican fighters fleeing Spain, he'd found a safe haven in Morocco, and was doing his best to repay that hospitality by teaching. A Catholic priest in Essaouira had set him up with a school in Casablanca, providing basic French language and mathematics lessons to some of the city's poorest children. Laurent quickly found that the classroom provided him with an opportunity to educate his pupils in other things as well, including the pernicious effects of propaganda. It might be a drop in the ocean. But it was *his* drop, his chance to do something, however small, until he could figure out a more concrete way to contribute to the war effort.

Turning his face to the wall and wedging a rolled-up blanket behind him to try to shut out Abdul's radio, he pulled out a weeks-old copy of *La Dépêche du Toulouse*, and started rereading the articles for the hundredth time. French newspapers were the closest Laurent could get to home. He still had no idea whether the letter he'd given to the Spanish trawlerman had ever made it to his parents at Chateau Brancion. There was no way for his family to reply to him, even if it had. Laurent had written one more note since then, explaining that he was currently in Morocco, recovered from his ordeal in Spain and with hopes of eventually joining some sort of Allied force in North Africa. But now that war had officially been declared, only a fraction of international mail was getting through. Newspapers, even old ones, were jealously hoarded.

'*Toulouse Battalion in victorious assault on Germany's Western Border!*' the headline announced, setting the tone of relentless optimism that continued throughout the article. Perhaps, in this particular case, it was true. But Laurent knew from friends of friends that the narrow corridor leading to the Western Front, bordered as it was by 'neutral' Luxembourg and Belgium, had been heavily mined by the Germans, and that French casualties in the first few weeks had been appallingly high. Thankfully, Thierry wouldn't have been amongst them. According to the newspapers, the Second Dragoons were still down in Grenoble, preparing for a possible operation against the Italians. No one was yet saying publicly that the supposedly unassailable Maginot Line might, in fact, prove vulnerable. But privately, Laurent understood, politicians were worried.

'Please keep Thierry safe,' Laurent prayed. 'And Maman and Papa, and all my family.' He thought about Elise in Paris with her godmother, and wondered whether their lives had changed at all, or whether the merry-go-round of gallery visits and dinners and parties continued. Did the war feel real in Paris, yet? From what Laurent had read, it didn't seem so. But then perhaps Elise had returned to Burgundy by now? It had been years, after all, since he'd seen or heard from her. If Uncle Louis had managed to stay sober, and used Papa's loan wisely at Sainte Madeleine, then perhaps the childhood idyll Laurent remembered so fondly had been restored, and Elise's happiness with it?

He hoped so. It all felt so very far away.

Slipping the newspaper back under his bed, he closed his eyes and tried to picture Elise's face. Not as it was when he last saw her, wounded and shamed from his rejection in

226

Paris. But as she had been as a young girl: curious, feisty, full of mischief, fun and life. Would that carefree world ever return, for any of them? Or was France destined to go the way of Spain, its old joys and freedoms trampled upon and destroyed, apparently forever?

Father Henri Bercault knelt in front of the cross in the tiny church of Sainte Madeleine. Eschewing the woven cushions, embroidered by generations of Burgundy widows, he allowed his knees to press directly against the cold hard stone; a minuscule penance for his myriad sins. Not that Henri's personal failures and struggles mattered a jot when compared to the magnitude of evil currently facing the world.

How on earth, after the tragedy of the Great War, had things been allowed to come to this?

'Protect me from despair, Lord,' Henri prayed. It would be as dangerous to fall prey to hopelessness as it would be to join the smug ranks of his fellow countrymen who chose to believe either that Hitler would be swiftly defeated, or, worse, that a German victory might not be as catastrophic as 'liberals' like Henri were making out. As parish priest, Henri had overheard far too many casual conversations between his parishioners that seemed to adopt this view. The 'at least they're seeing off the communists' brigade, willing to turn a blind eye to Nazi atrocities on the spurious grounds that they were defending 'law and order' and protecting traditional, European values.

If the letter Henri had just received from his friend Father Pawel showed anything, it was that the Nazi ideology was as devoid of Christian morality as it was of shame. The time to act was now.

'Sorry I'm late.' The church doors creaked open, and Didier Salignac crept inside. In baggy Oxford slacks, with a navy-blue sleeveless sweater pulled over his white shirt, he looked even more handsome than usual, a fact that Father Bercault tried and failed to ignore. 'I got held up at the vineyard,' said Didier, automatically taking a kneeler cushion from the basket beside the altar and joining Henri before the cross. 'Is everything all right? You sounded awfully worried when we spoke yesterday.'

Henri made the sign of the cross and got back to his feet. Taking a seat in the front pew of the empty church, he signalled for Didier to join him.

'I am worried, Didier,' he admitted. Reaching into his pocket, he pulled out Pawel's letter and handed it over. 'I think we should all be worried. Read this. It's from a priest I know in Warsaw.'

Didier scanned the two messily handwritten pages. Written in haste, he suspected, and probably in fear, judging by the contents, Father Pawel described in blunt prose the appalling treatment of the Jews in his parish.

From the very first day, the Germans started pulling young Jewish men out into the streets and shooting them in cold blood. Homes throughout the Jewish quarter were looted and then burned. Many of the elderly burned to death inside them. Others are being taken to labour camps. Grandmothers! What work can they possibly do? One of my parishioners saw a man in his eighties beaten to death trying to join a food queue in Castle Square. And not by the Germans. By Poles! By his neighbours. Christians, or so they claim.

Refolding the letter, Didier handed it back. 'That's terrible,' he said sombrely. 'But you knew things were bad in Poland. It's not as if this is happening here, in France.'

'You don't think this could happen in France?' Henri looked at him, disbelieving.

'The Germans could invade, I suppose,' said Didier. 'Not

that I think they'd succeed,' he added quickly. 'But even if they did, it wouldn't be the same.'

'Wouldn't it?'

'No,' said Didier, more firmly. 'Frenchmen wouldn't turn on their neighbours. They wouldn't set fire to somebody's home just because they were a Jew.'

His sincerity was so endearing. If it weren't so tragic, Henri would have laughed. As it was, he took Didier's hands in his.

'My dear boy. I assure you, they would. I'm fond of your mother, as you know. But have you never heard the way Thérèse speaks about the Jews?'

'Well yes, of course, but that's just snobbery,' said Didier. 'Maman's a terrible snob. All that generation are. But she wouldn't *kill* anyone.'

'She wouldn't have to,' said Henri seriously. 'All she'd need to do is stand by. Let the violence go unchecked. Believe me, Didier, it could happen here and it could happen on day one, just like it did in Warsaw. The time to prepare is now.'

'What do you mean, "prepare"?' Didier pulled his hands away, worried. He certainly didn't support violence, against the Jews or anyone else. But he didn't want Henri to put himself at risk. If anything were to happen to him . . . Didier closed his eyes tight, willing himself not to think about it.

'I mean organize,' said Henri. 'Reach out to the Jewish community here, in Burgundy. Have plans in place if, God forbid, the Germans *do* invade. We'll need safe houses, food banks, an underground network of support, ready to go. Will you help me, Didier?'

Will you help me?

Didier looked up at the stained-glass window, depicting one of the stations of the cross. He wanted to say no. *No, I won't help you get yourself killed. I won't help you seek out trouble before it's even arrived. I won't put at risk the one, wholly good thing that's ever happened to me.* But saying 'no' to Father Bercault was no more within Didier Salignac's power than it was for him to tell his heart to stop beating, or to stop time from passing.

'Of course I'll help you, Henri,' he heard himself promise. 'Just tell me what you need.'

Back in the drawing room at Sainte Madeleine, Thérèse was reading a very different sort of letter aloud to Louis.

> *Last Saturday, Costas and I were invited to a very glamorous reception at the Tatoi Palace. It was the first time I'd been anywhere important socially since Andreas's birth, and I wore a divine new dress from Dior. I danced with King George (twice!) even though his mistress was there, a rather dreary Englishwoman named Joyce. Costas was pleased that he'd singled me out, I think. He bought me a lovely diamond hairpin afterwards. Next time I write I'll send a picture.*

'Our little Elise, dancing with the King of Greece,' Louis sighed contentedly between puffs on his cigarillo. 'Palaces and diamonds and Dior. What a life she's leading, eh?' He tried not to let himself think about how fervently he wished Elise were leading that life closer to home. 'Clearly no one seems worried about the Krauts invading any more. Or the Italians for that matter.'

'No,' Thérèse agreed cautiously.

It wasn't only the war that made her anxious and uncertain. It was Louis too. She knew how keenly he felt Elise's absence, and she sympathized. But to her profound dismay, he had recently started drinking again. 'Modestly,' for the time being, as Thérèse had written to Alex. But she knew from bitter experience that the downward slope from a glass of Sainte Madeleine at lunch to chaotic, drunken misery could be steep and slippery in Louis's case. He'd already taken up smoking, which she suspected was in an effort to help him delay the first drink of the day. It seemed to be working so far. But after everything they'd been through, everything they'd weathered as a couple, it was devastating for Thérèse to find herself back in this state of tension, permanently bracing against an uncertain future.

As for Elise, Thérèse's own feelings about her absent daughter were mixed. On the one hand, the strict Catholic in Thérèse disapproved of the naked materialism she sometimes felt was expressed in some of Elise's letters. Quite apart from the moral aspect, it was vulgar to care about things like diamond hairpins and Dior gowns, and frivolous to mind about fancy balls. Especially now with half the world at war, even if Greece did seem to be insulated from the worst of things. On the other hand, it *was* a relief that Elise had married so well, and that she seemed to be so very happy in Athens with her millionaire husband and new baby son. And dancing with a king – twice! That was certainly not to be sniffed at.

'Does she say anything about Christmas?' asked Louis, hopefully. He'd grieved for his lost relationship with Alex over the last few years, and reached a point of reluctant acceptance that his younger son was effectively no longer in his life. But he could never get used to not seeing Elise. Never.

'No, darling,' said Thérèse. 'You know she's longing to bring Costas and the baby home to meet us. But travel's out of the question now. I'm afraid it will be until this ghastly war's over, whenever that is.'

'Hmmm. I suppose so,' grumbled Louis.

He missed Elise. After the initial joy of being allowed back into the fold at Sainte Madeleine, reaping the benefits that his sobriety had afforded not only in terms of rebuilding the chateau's fortunes, but in repairing his marriage to Thérèse, Louis had once again started to resent the feeling of being isolated in Burgundy, stuck at home with only Thérèse and Didier for company. His yearning for Paris and the diversions of city life was at times almost as strong as his yearning for a drink, although he convinced himself that he had the latter under control. But whereas alcohol was all too readily available, getting to Paris had become a terrible palaver now that war had been declared, and was no longer something one could do on a whim.

'But what do you want to go to the city *for?*' Thérèse would ask, a note of disappointment and criticism creeping back into her tone that Louis had hoped was gone forever. And of course, it was an impossible question to answer. The truth – '*Because I'm bored*' – would understandably offend her. But then he and Thérèse had always been profoundly different people, with profoundly different needs.

His relationships with other people at Sainte Madeleine were shifting too, most noticeably with Arnaud Berger. After a string of good vintages, some considerable reinvestment in the winery, and with the farms now back in the estate's fold thanks to Roger Senard's much-needed injection of cash, Louis considered his work at Sainte Madeleine to be effectively done.

'You're the vigneron,' he informed Arnaud cheerfully. 'I'd say it's high time I got out of your hair and let you run the place again. I have every faith in your ability to keep us ticking over, now that we're back on track.'

'But, monsieur,' Arnaud would reply, respectful as always but at the same time unable to hide his astonishment. 'This war is going to change everything. At a minimum there will be terrible disruption. To our sales, our distribution, our workforce. Sainte Madeleine needs you now more than ever.'

It was an attitude that infuriated Louis. If the war really

was going to ruin their business – something that the naturally optimistic Louis found hard to believe – then surely that was even more of a reason for him to take a back seat? Why break his back to bottle wines that nobody was going to be able to buy?

Louis was too old to fight, of no practical use to Arnaud at the winery, and his constant company at home was once again becoming irksome to his wife. The fact that he'd started to permit himself an occasional glass of red with his lunch had nothing to do with anything. If Elise were here, she'd understand. All work and no play made Jack a dull boy and all that. But heaven only knew when he would be able to see his daughter again.

Thérèse minded more about the babies. William's death had hit her hard, for Alex's sake, but also because she'd never had a chance to meet her grandson or hold him in her arms. It made her all the more desperate to dandle little Andreas on her knee in the nursery at Sainte Madeleine, and for the child to become a part of their lives.

Louis looked forward to meeting his grandson too, eventually. But it was his daughter he pined for. He would have sacrificed just about anything to have Elise join them around the tree at Sainte Madeleine this year, gossiping about parties and dresses and the carefree life that she, alone among the Salignacs now, still seemed to be living.

Angelique came in to clear the coffee tray and to confirm that Thérèse wanted lunch served at one.

'Just something light today,' said Thérèse, sitting down at her bureau to reply to Elise and to begin a new letter to Alex. 'Maybe a salad niçoise, if Cook can spare the tuna? It's only going to be Monsieur and myself.'

'Yes, madame.'

Thérèse dipped her pen in the inkwell thoughtfully. Writing to Elise was a simple enough thing, but she found composing letters to Alexandre increasingly difficult and demanding of her full attention. Will's death had left a crater of loss that had only served to widen the gulf between him and his old life here at Sainte Madeleine. The only words of comfort Thérèse knew how to give were religious ones that did nothing to salve Alex's pain. She agonized about whether to pass on news about Andreas's birth, fearful of offending Alex by rubbing salt in his and Ruth's wounds, but equally loath to exclude them from Elise's joy.

'Where's Didier?' Louis asked, interrupting her train of thought.

'He's down at the church, I believe. Helping Father Bercault,' Thérèse replied, irritated. She did wish Louis would find something to do, and not forever be bothering her. He was becoming so needy lately.

'At the church *again*?' Louis scowled. 'What the hell does he *do* there? He should be up at the winery, helping Arnaud.'

Biting back a '*so should you*', Thérèse said simply, 'I'm sure he's making himself useful.'

Disgruntled suddenly, Louis stubbed out his cigarillo and got to his feet. 'I think I'll take a walk before lunch,' he told Thérèse. 'Leave you to it.'

Outside, a sharp, unexpectedly chill wind signalled the onset of autumn proper, presaging the winter to come. The avenue of sycamore trees lining the long drive waved their bare branches forlornly like starving orphans, stripped of their leaves and shivering in the cold. Above them, heavy clouds gathered in ominous, rain-filled clusters, like dirty sheep huddling in the corner of a sodden field.

Louis shivered. How strange it was to be thinking of frosts and snowfall, he thought, when only weeks ago the evenings had been warm and full of light and the grapes had hung, swollen and sugar-heavy on the vines. Like the sudden onset of war, it felt to Louis as if everything had changed in an instant. But never for the better. Always for the worse, from light to dark.

One minute he'd been young and full of promise. The next he was an old, recovering alcoholic, shuffling around Sainte Madeleine with no vigour, no purpose. The future he'd envisaged for so many years had gone completely now: Alex, running the domaine. Elise, married to a local nobleman's son. Grandchildren scampering around the estate, amusing Thérèse, while Louis continued to live his 'split' life between his mistresses in Paris and his family here.

None of that had happened. Instead, Thérèse had 'saved' him. And now here he was, left with just her and Didier, the child who seemed to reflect all his failures back at him – as a father, and as a man. Didier, who seemed content to follow the local priest around like a poodle, while other young men his age were off fighting the Germans, doing their bit. Louis still couldn't fully articulate what it was that he disliked so much about his oldest son's friendship with Father Henri Bercault, or why it made him so angry.

He just knew in his bones that the priest was bad news.

CHAPTER SIXTEEN

'For you, madame.'

The baker pressed a brown paper bag into Thérèse's hands with a sympathetic smile. The freshly baked madeleines inside were still warm, and Thérèse could smell their sweetness through the bag.

'You're very kind, Monsieur Lefèvre,' she told him, touched by this small act of kindness. 'But I really can't accept. You have other customers in far greater need than we are.'

'Please,' the old man insisted. 'I remember they were always Mademoiselle Elise's favourite. We're all so sorry about what's happening up at Sainte Madeleine,' he added, dropping his voice to a whisper.

'Thank you,' Thérèse whispered back nervously, taking the cakes and hurrying out of the shop, before the baker could engage her in any further, indiscreet conversation. He was referring to the German officers who'd been billeted up at the chateau. Having the enemy swarming the streets of Vézelay like rats was bad enough, swanning in and out of the bars and shops and churches in their hateful grey uniforms as if they owned the place. But being forced to take them into one's home? That was a different order of dreadfulness. For the first time, ordinary townsfolk like

236

Monsieur Lefèvre had reason to pity the likes of the Salignacs. Although in truth, what was happening in France was appalling for everyone.

Over the spring of 1940, German forces conquered Northern Europe with a speed and efficiency that took the whole world by surprise. In just six weeks, beginning on 10 May, the Nazis defeated the Allied forces sufficiently to take France, Belgium, Luxembourg and the Netherlands. After Operation *Fall Gelb* succeeded in pushing British, French and Belgian forces back through the Ardennes all the way to sea, where they were evacuated from Dunkirk by the British in Operation Dynamo, *Fall Rot* had begun in France in June. A devastating air bombardment was swiftly followed by an onslaught of German tanks, sailing through the Maginot Line like a warm knife through butter and pushing deep into the country. In less than ten days, Hitler's army reached Paris, occupying the city unopposed. French humiliation was complete.

And yet, bizarrely it seemed to Thérèse, daily life continued. Under Pétain's Vichy government, the country was split between the Northern 'Occupied Zone', which included Burgundy, and the 'Free' South. But all of France now operated effectively as a German protectorate. Once the initial shock of seeing uniformed Germans in the streets began to wear off, it was remarkable how quickly the wounds of defeat seemed to fade, and a new reality began to assert itself.

The first German officers arrived at Sainte Madeleine in July 1940, just days after Louis had received a letter from Vézelay's mayor, informing him that the estate was to provide 'Essential Housing' for the 5th SS-Sturmbrigade and the 28th SS Volunteer Panzergrenadier Division.

'Naturally, you will only be expected to house a handful of the most senior commanders,' the mayor wrote, although Louis and Thérèse failed to see what was 'natural' about it.

'No one is suggesting that Sainte Madeleine become some sort of barracks,' the mayor assured them. 'You may of course continue living on the estate and operating the domaine and vineyards as you see fit.'

By this point, as Thérèse had predicted, Louis was once again drinking heavily, and Arnaud was managing the vineyards single-handed. Both the volume and quality of last year's vintage had declined significantly as a result. But like the rest of the country, Thérèse had bigger things to worry about. She reminded herself that many, many people had it worse than she did, including her dear friend Camille Senard.

While Thérèse and Louis were being forced to play host to the enemy at Sainte Madeleine, Camille and Roger had been turned out of Chateau Brancion completely. Their beautiful home had been commandeered by the Nazis as an 'administrative centre', whatever that meant, and the Senards had been forced to move into one of the estate's dower houses in the village.

Meanwhile, rumours were rife everywhere that Himmler, in particular, had some nonsensical conviction that Burgundy was in fact an ancient German kingdom. All the local officials were denying it, but it seemed that plans were afoot to transform the region into a new and separate 'model state', some sort of centre for German cultural excellence. Thérèse felt angry and impotent about all of it, but what could one do?

'I don't know why you keep banging on about the Senards,' Louis had complained to her a few nights ago in bed. Since he'd resumed drinking in earnest, he'd gone back to picking unnecessary fights with Thérèse, making a difficult situation even worse. 'At least they don't have to sit down with the bloody Krauts at breakfast, like we do.'

'They've lost their home, Louis,' Thérèse insisted. 'I don't see what could be worse than that. Especially coming on top of everything else they've been through these past few years.'

'Like what?' slurred Louis.

'You know perfectly well,' Thérèse snapped, her own frustration levels rising. 'Laurent, sneaking off to Spain like that and then marrying some girl with no family, no connections of any kind, and who nobody knows from Adam.'

'Alex ran off to America and married some girl *we* don't know from Adam,' Louis reminded her.

'That's completely different,' said Thérèse.

'How?'

'Because Alex isn't a communist, Louis,' Thérèse said angrily, 'and nor is Ruth. Leaving home to make your own way in the world is hardly the same thing as becoming a . . . *guerrilla*. Not to mention the fact that we heard about our son's wedding from him, not through third-party gossip,' she finished with a shudder. 'Why you insist on arguing about this is beyond me.'

Louis grunted and rolled over, falling moments later into a drunken sleep.

The morning the Germans first arrived had been difficult for everybody at Sainte Madeleine. Poor Brolio, now completely deaf and bent double with age like a storybook crone, was beside herself with panic.

'She thinks they're going to storm in and set fire to the place, raping and pillaging as they go,' Thérèse confided in Arnaud in a rare moment of candour. 'The poor thing's swallowed whole all the news reports about devil worshipping and heaven knows what else. Will you have a word with her?'

'I'll try, madame,' Arnaud replied. He was worried too. Having Germans at Sainte Madeleine was an appalling affront. But as ever, he kept his concerns to himself, focusing only on the harvest, the life cycle of the land and the vines that remained constant and unchanging even through the turmoil of war. With Louis 'checked out', Arnaud Berger was the vineyard's last line of defence.

To everyone's relief, in the end only three men arrived, none of whom appeared to be the baby-bayoneting type, at least on the surface. There were two youngish captains, both of whom disappeared immediately to their prepared quarters at a word from their senior officer, and looked, as Louis later observed 'like they wouldn't say boo to a goose'. The only other 'guest' was an older *Generallutnant* (a major general, as Thérèse later came to learn) by the name of Gunther von Hardenberg. Tall and slim, with a strong jaw and rather patrician features, von Hardenberg introduced himself in flawless French, without a trace of an accent, and from the beginning was the very soul of politeness, apologizing for the 'appalling imposition' of his presence at Sainte Madeleine, and assuring both Louis and Thérèse that he would ensure he and his men impacted their lives as little as possible.

'I won't say "forget we're here", as I understand that's impossible,' he told Thérèse, following her into the house and insisting on carrying his own suitcase. 'But if there's anything we can do to lessen the inconvenience to your family, Madame Salignac, I hope you'll let me know. These are difficult times for all of us.'

Thérèse hadn't been expecting such consideration from an enemy soldier. She found herself quite unnerved by it, and by Major General von Hardenberg in general.

That had been a few weeks ago now, and since then the major general – Gunther – had been as good as his word, ensuring that his men stayed out of the family's way as much as possible. As she crossed the square at Vézelay, clutching her bread and Monsieur Lefèvre's warm madeleines, Thérèse reflected guiltily that she no longer felt entirely unhappy about the German soldiers' presence at Sainte Madeleine. Yes, they were the enemy, and she reminded herself that every day. But on a purely human level, there were days when it felt almost like a blessing to have a man in the house besides Louis and Didier (who was technically a man, but in Thérèse's eyes would always be a needy and vulnerable little boy). To share her meals with someone cultured and considerate and capable of holding a civilized conversation.

She would never have admitted it to the baker, or to anyone else for that matter, but privately, in her heart, Thérèse was beginning to think of Gunther as a friend.

The dagger was drawn before Laurent had a chance to react. He'd been in a deep sleep, shattered from the tension of another day's waiting. Endless, awful waiting in the punishing heat for an enemy attack that never seemed to come, staring blindly across featureless dunes that stretched to the horizon. But now suddenly, he was wide awake, every nerve vibrating, every sense alive. Even so, all he saw was a momentary flash of steel in the moonlight, and Maurice's lithe body arcing through the air, before slamming back down in a cloud of dust.

A few seconds later, Laurent's closest friend in the division held up the limp body of a two-foot snake, dangling it in front of him with one hand. 'Horned viper,' he grinned. 'Lethal. A few more seconds and you'd have been a goner, *mon ami*.'

'Fuck!' Laurent recoiled, his heart pounding. 'FUCK.'

'Shhhh!' voices hissed along the sand dugout. 'Are you morons trying to get us all killed?'

In Maurice's other hand was the snake's head, devilish hornlike scales above both eyes giving it a positively demonic appearance.

'Welcome to Egypt,' he whispered, tossing the gruesome trophy at Laurent's feet.

Unlike Laurent, Maurice was a born soldier. Strikingly

fit, and blessed with lightning reactions, he was also well trained and used to desert conditions. Algerian born to French parents, Maurice had joined L'Armée d'Afrique in his teens, and served as a camel-mounted *Méhariste Saharienne* before the start of the war. Rumour had it that he'd even trained some of the Foreign Legion recruits in Libya, although Maurice denied it.

Since the fall of France, a rag-tag alliance of volunteer fighters like Laurent had joined forces with General Maxime Weygand's now heavily depleted professional soldiers in North Africa, supporting the British as they attempted to keep control of the region. Initial successes, such as the capture of the Italian Fort Capuzzo in Libya by the British 7th Hussars, had been followed by a brutal Italian counter-offensive into Egypt throughout June and July. Reports of 'heavy losses' in newspapers back home did little to convey the horror of what these desert battles were truly like. Although, like most of the men, Laurent preferred the combat, brutal as it was, to the waiting.

He'd barely had time to kick away the viper's head and thank Maurice for saving his life when the deafening boom of thousands of exploding shells sent a column of fire soaring into the sky.

'This is it!' the sergeant yelled, unnecessarily, as all along the trench men leapt into life, grabbing bayonets and rifles and fumbling for helmets and ammunition clips. Laurent followed suit, retying the laces on his boots with shaking fingers.

'You'll be fine,' Maurice roared in his ear as the sergeant's whistle blew. 'Just look for the machine guns. The Brits' howitzers should have taken out the S-mines, but there'll still be Eyeties manning the outposts.'

Men began to scramble over the side of the trench, scuttling into the dunes like sand crabs. Laurent was among them, bayonet drawn, running blindly just a few feet behind

Maurice. The terror and adrenaline he remembered from Spain, but the *scale* of battle here was different. Apocalyptic in a way that Seville and Barcelona had never been. North Africa was just so vast, with its blazing skies and boundless dunes. The roar of artillery here was indescribable, so loud that it shook the bones long after it had destroyed the eardrums. Afterwards, Laurent would remember only sensations. His teeth rattling in his jaw like loose coppers in a tin mug as mines exploded just yards from his feet. The gentle flutter of his eyelids as shrapnel flew past his face, so close that he felt the breeze of their passing. He was dimly aware of the dying. Men running alongside him one minute and dropping to the ground the next, the lucky ones felled cleanly with a bullet, versus being blown quite literally to pieces by an Italian mine. But there was so much noise and light, movement and dust, these things passed swiftly and with no time for reflection, like shadows in some awful dream.

'Down!' Laurent dropped to the ground, spitting sand as fine as flour from his parched lips. His small company of infantrymen had advanced about a hundred yards, no more. Now it was the sappers' turn to move forward, clearing a path for the tanks through whatever was left of the Italian mines.

'OK?' Maurice was at his shoulder, offering a drink of water from his billycan. 'Take it,' he urged, when Laurent shook his head. 'You need it more than I do.'

Laurent drank. He wasn't thirsty, not consciously anyway, but it was comforting to follow Maurice's lead. Maurice was a real soldier, who knew what he was doing. All of a sudden his brother Thierry's words came back to him, from that awful day in the woods back home. *'You're not a soldier, Laurent. Don't be so naive! You're not trained. If you go to Spain, you'll come back in a body bag.'*

He was right, thought Laurent, a wave of love unexpectedly overwhelming him for the brother who'd tried to save him. *I was naive*. But then how could one not be? How could someone who hadn't actually experienced battle ever expect to understand what it was like? Laurent couldn't have known that one year of fighting would turn into two, and three and four. That one war would turn into another, with no respite in between. That his home, his family and his darling Elise might end up being lost to him, not just for a while, but forever.

Would he have done things differently, if he had his time over? With Elise, certainly. But with everything else? It was a question he couldn't answer.

'Ready?' asked Maurice, reaching over to take back his water bottle and taking a sip himself.

Laurent nodded. 'I think so.'

'They'll give the signal soon. Just keep an eye out to our right. There's at least one machine-gunner out there who . . .'

It all happened in an instant. The ground, exploding beneath their feet. Maurice, his entire left side blown off, shooting through the air like a rag doll. Laurent falling backwards, aware of nothing but the whistling in his ears and a strange lightness in his body.

It was too late, after all.

'Elise!' he heard his own voice cry out.

Then nothing.

Elise looked on lovingly as Andreas toddled around the sandpit, snatching up handfuls of sand and watching, fascinated, as the grains rained down between his fat fingers.

'They're so lovely at that age, aren't they?' her friend Belinda observed in that clipped, British voice of hers that always made Elise want to sit up straighter. 'I wish Jonas were one again.'

Both women glanced across to the big grass playing field, where Belinda's seven-year-old son Jonas was squabbling loudly with his older sister about something or other.

'I've nothing to compare it to,' said Elise, sipping her coffee. 'But I must say Andreas seems pretty perfect to me.'

It was a warm September afternoon in Athens' Royal Garden, a vast public park directly behind the palace. Elise often brought Andreas to play here, accompanied by his nanny Athena, who went with them everywhere at Costas's insistence. Whenever she could she met up with Belinda, another 'foreign' wife forging a life for herself in the city. Like Costas, Belinda's husband Dimi came from a wealthy, upper-class family, and had rigid ideas about a woman's place in the world, and how things should be done. He was controlling, openly unfaithful, and a completely absent father. Unlike Costas, however, Dimi was never physically threatening, and was content for the most part to let Belinda come and go as she pleased with the children.

'How are things?' Belinda asked, alarmed by the bruises she could see peeking out from the sleeves of Elise's expensive silk blouse. She had a pretty good idea how Elise might have come by them, but she wanted Elise to confirm her suspicions of her own accord. 'With you and Costas?'

'Things are the same,' said Elise, smiling bravely.

'You had an accident, did you?' Belinda gestured to the bruises. Elise, who hadn't realized they were showing, blushed deeply and tugged at her sleeves, but it was too late. Her eyes welled up.

'He's only done it once. Since I've been pregnant, I mean,' she admitted.

Bastard, thought Belinda. What kind of man beat a pregnant woman? But outrage wasn't going to help poor Elise. Practical advice was what she needed.

'Can't you just . . . keep out of his way?' she suggested awkwardly. 'In that huge house?'

'I can,' Elise nodded, 'And for the most part I do. I asked for my own bedroom this time around,' she said, absentmindedly patting her still-flat stomach. 'I was so sick with Andreas and up and down to the bathroom half the night, which used to drive Costas mad, so he agreed right away. That's been a big help.'

'Well, that's something I suppose,' said Belinda, trying not to show how appalled she was by Elise's injuries.

'But we still do have to see one another. Dinners and events are the worst.' Elise shuddered. 'He's fine while the guests are there, but once everyone's gone . . . let's just say drink brings out the worst in him,' she finished, with devastating understatement.

'I'm so sorry.' Belinda put her hand over Elise's and squeezed supportively. But Elise pulled away, looking nervously over her shoulder to where two men in dark suits stood like sentries, watching their table.

'Costas's spies,' she hissed in a whisper through a forced smile.

'No!' Belinda whispered back. 'Really?'

'He says they're for my and Andreas's protection, but really they just report back to him. If he thinks I've been complaining about him to you, or anyone, there'll be hell to pay.'

Belinda nodded and they changed the subject. It wasn't long before their conversation turned to the war. Both what might happen in Greece, and the latest news from their respective countries. Britain had suffered some significant losses, but nothing compared to the ignominy of what had happened in France.

'My godmother's last letter from Paris was heartbreaking,' said Elise. 'She said the spirit of the city's been completely broken. People are just accepting the German occupation. As if it's nothing.'

'Not all people, I'm sure,' said Belinda. 'Perhaps they feel there's nothing they can do about it, so they may as well, I don't know, get on with it?'

'Perhaps.' Elise's eyes glazed over. It was clear she was miles away.

'It's hard, being so far from home while all this is happening,' said Belinda. 'I feel the same way, believe me. But we have our own war to fight, Elise, as mothers.'

'What do you mean?' Elise frowned.

'That we must fight for our sons,' Belinda said simply. 'Costas and Dimi are bound to get one of their mistresses pregnant at some stage, if they haven't already. And illegitimacy is no bar to inheritance here. We must stay to fight for our boys' interests.'

'What about *our* interests?' Elise asked quietly.

'Well I'm not as badly off as you, obviously,' Belinda admitted sheepishly. 'But one must be realistic, Elise. Divorce isn't an option here. You'll never see your children again.'

'I know that,' said Elise, watching Andreas's nanny brush sand off his white-and-blue sailor suit. She loved him so much, it was painful. She would die rather than leave him. 'But maybe . . . don't you ever think about escaping?'

Belinda looked alarmed. 'Escape where? How?'

'I'm not sure how,' Elise admitted. 'As for where, my dream would be to get back home.'

'To Paris?'

'No, not Paris. *Home* home,' said Elise. 'To Sainte Madeleine. Burgundy, where I grew up.'

The last letter she'd received from Arnaud Berger had worried her, not so much for what it said as for what it didn't. Ever the soul of discretion, Arnaud would never write to Elise openly about her father's drinking, or Didier's increasing anxiety with German soldiers in the house. Even problems at the vineyard were downplayed. But Elise had known Arnaud all her life, and reading between the lines she was deeply concerned. All was not well, in her parents' marriage or at the winery. The picture Arnaud painted of her mother's growing closeness to one of the German officers worried Elise most of all. But somehow it only served to make her longing for Sainte Madeleine more intense.

'I'd love to raise Andreas there,' she told Belinda with a sigh. 'But obviously that's not possible right now.'

It won't be possible ever, thought Belinda. *Unless Costas dies.*

'But maybe, once the new baby's born, I might find a way to get to London?' Elise was thinking aloud. 'If I can persuade Costas somehow that it was his idea . . . that the children would be safer. He has a townhouse there.'

'Safer? In London?' Belinda's eyes widened. 'You do realize London's being bombed to smithereens? The German raids started ten days ago.'

Elise sighed. 'It was just a thought. A daydream, really.'

Perhaps Belinda was right. Perhaps her role now, her duty, was to stay here and 'fight' for Andreas, trapped forever in a miserable, violent marriage for his sake? And yet, *surely* that couldn't be the only option? She had already lost Laurent. She tried to picture him right at this very moment, somewhere in Spain, presumably, with his wife and maybe children by now? The pain of that was indescribable. But was she to lose Sainte Madeleine too? Was she to turn her back forever on everything and everyone she loved, apart from her children?

If she had to choose between Andreas and escape, then of course she would choose her son. But she wasn't ready to accept that outcome yet. She wasn't ready to roll over, like all those people in Paris Chantelle had written about.

I'm a Salignac, for God's sake, she reminded herself. *We're smart, and we're fighters. Fighters to the end.*

Reaching up to the chain around her neck, she pressed the tiny gold butterfly between her fingers for courage.

One day she would do it. Fly away. *Comme un papillon.*

CHAPTER SEVENTEEN

Laurent carefully peeled back the paper and pulled out his feast: a small roll of bread, two slices of dried mutton and slab of local goat's cheese. The scorching sun had already softened the meat and melted the edges of the cheese into a soft gooey paste that smelled delicious. Food in Chad was better than in most of French Equatorial Africa, but meals in the Free French barracks were still usually miserable affairs involving a lot of chickpeas and canned haricots. Today's picnic was a rare treat, not just because it involved cheese and meat, but because Laurent had an entire afternoon to himself to walk down to the river and eat it.

Looking up, he watched a pair of butterflies perform a brief, aerial mating dance before fluttering off downstream, and found his thoughts turning once again to Elise. Where was she right now, at this moment? What was she doing, saying, thinking? Sometimes looking at the photograph of her that he carried with him was a comfort. But at other times, like now, he knew instinctively that looking at her face would only intensify his pain, reminding him of what was out of reach. Resisting the urge to pull the disintegrating snapshot out of his pack, he instead made a conscious effort to pull himself back into the present.

He looked around him. Fort Lamy wasn't a particularly

beautiful city. But despite the punishing heat, and the flies, and the ugly concrete buildings, Laurent determinedly found the good in the place. In the sluggish waters of the Chari River, where he cooled his feet now, sitting on the scrubby bank. In each savoured bite of his mutton and cheese, an unexpected gift from a local farmer. In the friendships, such as they were, that he'd made with the other fellows in the barracks. He was alive, after all. He was alive, and Maurice was not. Every breath he took now, he must take for both of them.

How it had happened, Laurent still didn't really know. The awful, last image of Maurice would be with him forever: his body effectively split down the middle, flying through the air like a marionette in some grotesque puppet show. But apart from that, the battle in Egypt was vague. Laurent had no memory of his own injuries, or of physical pain. No memory of being stretchered to safety, or the journey that followed by jeep across the border into Libya, to the field hospital where they saved his life. Even though, so they told him afterwards, he'd remained conscious throughout.

Perhaps the brain blocked out what it couldn't handle, remembering only what it needed to? Maurice. The longing for France and for Elise that he'd felt, right before the blast. Those were the things that stayed with him. And then later, more tangible, consistent memories. Whiteness, whiteness everywhere, like fresh fallen snow. The nurses' uniforms. The dazzling sunlight that stung the eyes. The bright white-washed walls of the 'hospital', really a converted farm building a few miles outside Al Bayda. And other things. Smells, like the sharp tang of disinfectant, mixed with the sickly iron stench of blood. Or sounds, some calming, like the song of the desert lark or the trumpeter finch outside his window; some plaintive or visceral, like the moans and screams of his fellow patients.

Hours became days became weeks became months. Laurent recovered. Slowly, it seemed to him, step by step, breath by breath, swallow by swallow. Miraculously, the doctors said, with barely a scar to show for the grenade attack that had killed almost all the men around him and permanently maimed the rest.

'You've been spared, my son,' the chaplain told Laurent, the day he left Libya to join his new unit in Free French controlled Chad. 'God saved you for a reason.'

Did he? thought Laurent. His faith, once rock-solid, had been sorely shaken over the last four years. But with or without God, he had his own reason for living now. His own sense of gratitude, and of purpose. When he fought, he fought for Maurice. But every other breath he took was for Elise. He could push away thoughts of her in the moment if he needed to. But only because he knew they would return. They would always return. Somehow, he must make his way back to her and confess his love. He must marry her.

That was his purpose. *She* was his purpose. He just wished it hadn't taken so much suffering and death to make him see it.

'Can I help you?'

Major General Gunther von Hardenberg walked up behind Thérèse and put a steadying hand on her waist as she teetered on the ladder, with a heavy wine crate in her hands.

'Please,' he reached up, relieving her of the crate. 'Let me take that for you.'

Turning around, Thérèse blushed. She hadn't heard him come into the pantry, and wasn't sure how to react.

'You really shouldn't be lifting heavy boxes you know, madame. Not with so many able-bodied men in the house.'

'Oh, that's all right,' said Thérèse. 'I wanted a particular bottle for tomorrow's dinner, so I came in here to dig around for it. You and your men have better things to do than to fetch and carry for me.'

'Nonsense.' Gunther smiled. 'It's the very least we can do, after all your and Monsieur Salignac's kindness.'

Setting the case down on the floor, he offered Thérèse his hand as she descended the ladder.

'You're kind to say so,' she told him, aware of the warmth of his palm as it pressed against hers. A pleasant sensation. 'But we both know Monsieur Salignac was unconscionably rude to you yesterday.'

Last night's dinner had provoked a mortifying scene from Louis, the likes of which Thérèse hadn't suffered since before he went away to Paris. Paralytically drunk, he'd suddenly turned on Gunther after an innocuous remark he'd made about the butterflies carved into Sainte Madeleine's walls. Tearing into him for being a 'philistine', Louis had mocked everything from Gunther's accent to his manners to his family before launching into a dangerously seditious rant about the Third Reich in general and its 'filthy, moustachioed turd of a leader'. Not that Thérèse disagreed with him about the last part. But these were the sorts of outbursts that could get one shot, and everybody around the table knew it. Poor Didier had turned completely white and began to tremble uncontrollably, convinced that the whole family would be dragged off by the Gestapo. But Gunther had reacted with amazing forbearance to the whole situation, sending his men back to their rooms before things deteriorated further, and calmly suggesting that Louis might see things differently in the morning.

'Nothing's going to happen, son,' Gunther assured Didier, after Louis stormed off to bed.

'But your men. They heard!' Didier wailed hysterically.

'They heard a drunk man talking nonsense, in the privacy of his own home,' said Gunther, grasping Didier firmly by the shoulders. 'There will be no consequences, Didier. You have my word.'

Thérèse had been too shocked to say anything at the time, but inside she could have wept with gratitude. Perhaps now was the moment to express it?

'It's water under the bridge as far as I'm concerned,' Gunther told her, his kind brown eyes holding her blue ones for just a little longer than they should have as she reached the bottom of the ladder. 'These are stressful times.'

'Even so. I'm very grateful,' Thérèse told him sincerely.

Now it was Gunther's turn to blush. Madame Salignac was a wonderful, beautiful woman, and he was finding it increasingly difficult to hide his attraction to her. But hide it he must, for all their sakes.

'Not at all. We all say things we regret when we've been drinking.'

'Yes.' Aware of his closeness, and the fact that his fingers still held hers, for some reason Thérèse felt unwilling to pull herself away. 'I suppose we do.'

The truth was that Louis didn't regret anything he'd said last night. His hatred, not just of the Germans but of Gunther personally, was growing like a dangerous cancer that added to Thérèse's anxiety exponentially. In private he'd already as good as accused her of having an affair with the major general, simply because the two of them behaved civilly to one another. Which was ridiculous, of course, not to mention laughably hypocritical coming from Louis, who'd had more dalliances over the course of their marriage than there were beads on Thérèse's rosary.

And yet it was hard not to daydream sometimes about what her life would be like had she married a man like Gunther. Not Gunther himself, of course. He was a German. But someone like him, with the same sensibilities, the same innate decency, the same handsome, noble face and gallant, old-fashioned manners. The same . . .

'I'll leave you, madame.'

His voice brought Thérèse back to reality.

With a slight bow, he reluctantly released her hand and walked back towards his office in the east wing of the house.

After he'd gone, Thérèse stayed in the pantry for a long time, thinking. Emotions were stirring within her, unfamiliar and frightening emotions. But with them came a happiness that she couldn't explain, and that she knew instinctively she did not want to let go of.

How strange this war was. How many things were changing.

'A letter for you.' Costas, looking handsome and rested and smelling of lemon cologne, tossed the envelope down on the breakfast table in front of Elise. 'From Paris. I'm surprised it got through.'

'So am I,' said Elise, reaching for it and stroking the paper reverently in her hands. Chantelle's elegantly looped hand-writing looked like a message from another world.

'I suppose now that we're all under the Fuhrer's control, the cursed Germans have less to fear,' Costas observed, reasonably, helping himself to fresh coffee and toast. 'At least not from civilian communications.'

'I suppose so,' agreed Elise.

Now that she was in the late stages of her second pregnancy, Costas seemed to have settled into a more relaxed, less paranoid state of mind about her life and whereabouts. It still rankled that his wife didn't love him – notwithstanding the fact that he certainly didn't love her – but for the last month he'd treated Elise civilly, and even quite tenderly at times. Elise hated that it only served to heighten her suspicion. When would the tide of Costas's cruelty turn again?

And then of course there was the shock of the German

occupation. The Wehrmacht had finally invaded Greece in April, meeting little or no local resistance. Despite sharing many of the Nazis' views, like most Greek men Costas bitterly resented the German presence in Athens, and the arrogant way that their oppressors sauntered publicly around the city. Overnight, Costas's rage and frustration found a new target in Field Marshal Walther von Brauchitsch. It provided a welcome respite for Elise, even if she didn't know how long it would last.

'Aren't you going to open it?' Costas asked her, signalling to the maid to refresh Elise's glass of freshly pressed orange juice.

'After breakfast,' she replied, painting on a smile as she nibbled her own toast and resting a hand on her enormous belly. 'It's such a rare treat to hear from Chantelle. I want to make it last as long as possible.'

She watched as Costas wrestled with his own emotions, weighing up which reaction to have. Should he insist she open the letter now, so that he could hear its contents? Or should he let it go as something trivial, keeping the peace between them? In the course of her short marriage, Elise had become adept at reading her husband's facial expressions. Knowing what Costas was thinking had become a survival skill, and one of the most important weapons in Elise's wifely armoury. On this occasion, once again, the cards fell in her favour.

'As you wish.' He returned her smile. 'You know it'll only be about gossip and fashion, anyway.'

'All the better,' Elise appeased him. 'I *love* gossip and fashion, and heaven knows there's precious little of either here.'

Costas's knee-jerk sexism was another weakness that Elise had learned to use to her advantage. If he chose to believe that all women were foolish, shallow creatures with nothing better to talk about than dresses, Elise wasn't about to disabuse him of the notion. The more he underestimated the enemy, the better.

Breakfast dragged on. It felt like an age to Elise before she could retreat to her private bedroom suite overlooking the Acropolis, and settle down on her Italian silk chaise longue to read Chantelle's letter in peace.

'My darling Elise,' her godmother wrote. '*I can't tell you how happy it makes me to hear you so well and happy. Andreas sounds quite divine, and of course I am longing to meet him. But the main thing is that you feel settled in Greece and in your married life with Costas.*'

Lowering the letter, Elise pinched the bridge of her nose and took a moment to compose herself. *This is good*, she reminded herself sternly. *This is what you wanted.* Her own anguish was bad enough without knowing that she'd also burdened others she loved with the weight of it. Her parents couldn't help her now, and nor could Chantelle. So why worry them with her problems? She had, after all, brought the misery of her marriage to Costas entirely on herself. If she told Chantelle how unhappy she was, her godmother would only blame herself. Elise couldn't allow that.

'*I don't know if this will reach you, or what the situation is in Athens now,*' the letter went on. '*But I suppose we have a better chance of the censors letting it through if I steer clear of politics altogether, so I'm going to stick to my news.*'

Two paragraphs followed that would no doubt have pleased Costas, about Paris friends and what they were up to, who was having an affair with whom, and (Chantelle being Chantelle) an update on how the couturiers were struggling to design new collections, what with all the wartime restrictions on cotton, wool and silk. '*As if people don't still have to dance, and go to dinner!*'

Elise smiled. She could hear her godmother's outraged

voice, as if Chantelle were sitting next to her. But the next paragraph wiped away the smile, along with everything else Elise had been feeling.

'*I heard from your mother last week,*' Chantelle wrote:

> *A lovely long letter, about you and Alex, who had another baby, I gather? How wonderful, after all that they went through. She also had happy news from your cousins, the Senards. Thierry, who I liked so much when he came to Paris, is back home in Burgundy now, having finally been released from a POW camp somewhere in the South. And Laurent, who I know you were close to, is alive and well and somewhere in North Africa supposedly. His poor parents finally received a letter from him, long delayed. He managed to get out of Spain – not married after all, if you can believe it. That turned out to be a case of wartime Chinese whispers. But in any event, he's all right, which I knew you would be delighted to hear.*

Elise's hand flew to her chest. As if she could physically stop her heart from breaking by holding it in place.

'*Not married after all . . . wartime Chinese whispers . . .*'

Chantelle wrote as if it were nothing! An afterthought! *Oh God.*

The room started to spin. Chantelle's letter fluttered out of Elise's shaking hands and she started opening and closing her mouth like a dying fish, gasping for air.

Laurent wasn't married! Laurent had never been married! Which meant that Elise's marriage to Costas – this night-mare she was living, and might have to live for the rest of her life – had all been for nothing? That she'd ruined her life over a rumour? A mistake?

One of the maids heard the thud and came running.

'Kyria? Madame?'

Elise lay on the floor, semi-conscious, her glazed eyes fixed on the ceiling.

'Call Mr Goulandris!' the maid shouted to her colleagues.

'He left for the office an hour ago.'

'Then call an ambulance.'

Elise watched, stricken, as the tiny bundle was handed to the nurses and whisked hurriedly out of the room.

'What's happening?' she asked the doctor, panicked. 'Where are you taking him?'

'It's all right, Mrs Goulandris . . .'

'No, it's not all right!' Elise wailed, struggling to sit upright. Her labour had been sudden but traumatic, a terrible shock to her body. 'Tell me what's happening. Why wasn't he crying?'

Gently but firmly, the doctor eased her back onto her pillow. 'Your son is alive but he's very premature. His lungs may not yet be fully developed, and that can be serious.'

'Bring him back!' Elise sobbed, desperate. 'I want him with me!'

The shock of Chantelle's letter had been awful, over-whelming. To know that she had lost Laurent for nothing – that he was still free, while she was trapped in a loveless marriage – was terrible enough. But now to be told that she might lose her baby over it? That her little boy had been born so early he might die? *No.* She couldn't let it happen. She wouldn't.

'He's being given oxygen, Mrs Goulandris,' the doctor explained, as calmly as he could. 'We need to see how he responds to that first. Whether he can breathe on his own . . .'

Silent tears streamed down Elise's face. The doctor was still talking, but his words washed over her. *Please let him live*, she begged, not knowing whether her prayer was to God or to the universe in general. *Please.*

Just then the door flew open and Costas burst in. Seeing

the empty crib, he ignored Elise and turned on the doctor. 'What the fuck happened? Is it dead?'

'Mr Goulandris.' The doctor stood up. 'I'm afraid your wife went into early labour. She was extremely unwell when she . . .'

'Are you deaf?' Costas bellowed. 'I didn't ask about my wife. I asked about the child.'

'Your son was delivered alive, and is currently receiving oxygen,' the doctor replied stiffly. Even allowing for the shock of what had happened, he found Costas's disdain for his poor wife distasteful. 'As I was explaining to your wife, the next few hours will be critical. If he—'

'Another boy?' Costas smiled, interrupting him. 'That's wonderful. We'll name him Giorgios. Well done, darling.'

He patted Elise on the head, like a dog who'd just performed a trick for its master. It was in that moment that any last vestiges of doubt left her.

I have to leave him.

She didn't yet know how she was going to do it. Despite the bombings, the British were still holding out against Hitler. London was probably her best bet until the war was over. If she could make it there, somehow, with her children, then maybe eventually she could get back to Sainte Madeleine. Raise her boys in France, far away from their father and from Greece, a country she had come to hate with a deep, abiding passion.

Who knows, perhaps when all this madness is over, Laurent and I might even find a way back to each other?

But these were all prayers for another day. Right now all that mattered was that her son should live. *My Giorgios. Born from tragedy. But born to set us free.*

'Oh, Alex! We can't afford it.'

The dark blue paintwork of the brand-new Ford Coupe gleamed in the sunlight like a sapphire ring. Adjusting the baby on her hip, Ruth had to shield her eyes from the dazzle.

'Sure we can,' Alex said confidently. 'Tricycle's had a banner year. Besides, it'll be good for business.'

'How?' Ruth laughed, peering through the windows at the tan leather interior, like something you'd see in a first-class railway carriage. 'You tell me how buying this car is going to help us sell one more bottle of Pinot, Alex Salignac.'

'Why is Mommy such a killjoy, Sarah. Hm?' Alex asked their baby daughter, scooping her up out of Ruth's arms and holding her over his head, kissing her chubby little legs while she screamed with laughter. 'Why can't Mommy just be happy Daddy bought the Super Deluxe Coupe that every other wife in Napa would be *delighted* to drive around in?'

'I am happy,' said Ruth, punching him playfully on the arm. 'And it is gorgeous. I just think it's extravagant, that's all.'

She was right, of course. It was extravagant. And in all likelihood, it probably wouldn't help them shift more wine, although right now they hardly needed any more help in that department. Already this had been their best year for sales, and the 1941 vintage looked set to be even better, as hard to believe as that was. Although still small, Tricycle was fast becoming a Napa label to be reckoned with. If things kept going at this rate, they might soon be up there with Inglenook and Beringer.

Yes, the car was a luxury. But for Alex it was also a symbol. It was something he and Ruth had worked for and earned, not just in the monetary sense, but emotionally too. After losing Will, and Ruth's depression, not to mention all the suffering that had preceded those things, at least for Alex – watching Sainte Madeleine's decline, leaving France, and the breakdown of his relationship with his father – they *deserved* their current happiness. They *deserved* Sarah, their chubby, healthy, happy daughter, whose laugh lit up Ruth's face like a firework. They *deserved* Tricycle's success. They *deserved* their own happy marriage. And, God damn it, they *deserved* this car, whether the rest of the world was on fire or not.

None of which was to say that Alex didn't worry about the war. The speed with which France had fallen to the Germans was shocking enough. But the comfortable ease with which the Vichy government seemed to have 'accommodated' its new masters was almost worse. Not that everyone was complying. The American press reported tales of Resistance bravery, some of which were mind-bendingly heroic: young women risking torture and death to help Jewish children cross the Alps into Switzerland; elderly men sending vital radio signals across the Channel to alert the British to enemy movements, knowing they'd be shot on sight if caught. And of course, the Free French were still fighting in the other theatres of war, most notably North Africa, where Laurent Senard had apparently joined some elite desert battalion. How ironic to think that it was Laurent, the family peacemaker, out on the battlefield, while he, Alex, always the hothead, remained cocooned in peaceful prosperity an ocean away.

As guilty as that made him feel, it wasn't as bad as the stomach-churning letters Maman had started to send from Sainte Madeleine, making repeated reference to the 'charming' German officers billeted there, and what 'lovely' dinners they'd had together. '*Papa's been finding things difficult lately,*' she wrote in her last note, a euphemism presumably for Louis's increased drinking. '*Arnaud's been taking care of things at the vineyard, but Gunther's truly been a godsend around the house.*'

A godsend? Sometimes Alex wondered if his mother was just naive, or if it was worse than that. The wilful blindness that her letters seemed to show, to the atrocities these 'charming' men and their fellows were committing across the globe, pained Alex deeply. The entire world was going to hell in a handbasket, and yet back home at Sainte Madeleine his own mother seemed quite content to put all that to one side.

'Shall we take a drive?' Opening the rear door, he plonked Sarah's fat bottom onto the soft leather seat. 'I'll be the chauffeur and you can sit on Mommy's lap.'

'Where will we go?' asked Ruth excitedly, getting in and letting her daughter climb all over her. As Alex had already gone and bought the thing, she might as well enjoy it.

'How about Danson's?' said Alex, starting the engine. 'Show Uncle Tyler what he's missing? And then we could stop in town if you like, take your parents out for a soda?'

'Sure,' said Ruth. 'Just don't drive too fast.'

She was happy too, for Alex and for herself. She thanked God every day that America was not a part of this terrible war, and that Alex could stay here with her, safe. After Will, she wasn't sure she could survive any more loss.

We're so very lucky.

CHAPTER EIGHTEEN

'Welcome aboard, Mrs Goulandris. Allow me to help you with your case.'

Elise nodded her thanks to the captain, clasping Andreas's hand tightly as she stepped from the gangway onto the creaking, rocking ship. It was three in the morning in Port Said, Egypt, and little Giorgios was fast asleep in his papoose, his breath rising and falling rhythmically against Elise's chest. But Andreas was wide awake and visibly frightened, clinging on to his mother like a barnacle to the keel of a boat.

Elise didn't blame him. She was nervous enough herself, and could only imagine how vast and dark and terrifying everything must seem through a toddler's eyes. The pitch-blackness of the night. The muffled voices, speaking strange languages. The mingled smells of diesel oil, saltwater and the sharp tang of jute mallow leaves being boiled on the dockside to make Molokhia, the traditional Egyptian breakfast stew, all so different to the familiar smells of home. But worst of all must surely be the looming sides of the cargo ship that was to take them to London, a berth secured only after much arm twisting and bribe-paying from Costas. *The ship must look like a monster to him*, Elise thought guiltily, with its rusted iron rivets like a thousand glaring eyes.

Squatting down to his level, she flashed Andreas her most reassuring smile, making sure to keep her voice slow and even, as much to combat her own rising anxiety as to soothe her son. 'Come along, my darling. Let's find our cabin, shall we? I think it's definitely bedtime.'

She knew she would sleep, despite her nerves, and no matter how basic the accommodation. They all would. The last two weeks had been exhausting almost beyond endurance, as Elise and the children made their way by train, boat and on one occasion horse-drawn cart from Athens to Crete, and then eventually on to Egypt. Two days in Cairo to rest and get their papers in order, a process that had involved greasing yet more palms. And then a sudden message, delivered in person just a few hours ago: *The boat leaves from Port Said tonight.* A scramble to pack. Half-eaten food, left on the table. Crying, confused babies bundled into the back of a strange car. And now here they were, on board. If all went well, in five days they would reach London, and safety. *A new life.*

Elise had begun work on Costas the same day she left hospital with Georgios, a tiny, feeble speck of a baby weighing little more than a bag of sugar.

'He looks like a chick that fell out of the nest,' Costas observed, on one of his rare inspections of his younger son. 'Let's hope he toughens up as he gets older.'

'I know,' said Elise. 'We need to build his strength up and be extra vigilant. Luckily Persephone Xanthoudakis has given me the name of the best man in the world for premature babies. Dr Robin Heywood-Bryce. He's at the Lister hospital in London, but I've already telegrammed him about Giorgios.'

'Excellent.' Costas nodded approvingly. Spiros Xanthoudakis was a titan among Athens' social elite. Elise knew that any recommendation from Spiros's wife would appeal to Costas's snobbish side.

As the months passed, Elise made sure that 'Dr Heywood-Bryce' and his advice became a regular topic of conversation, cementing London as an intrinsic part of her and the children's lives. She also made sure to tell Costas about all the times she felt slighted or humiliated by occupying soldiers while out and about in Athens, from time to time opining wistfully about how much better things were in Britain.

'If it were just for myself, I wouldn't mind it so much,' she told Costas after breakfast one morning, while tending to a fussy, mewling Giorgios. 'I just hate the idea of our boys growing up feeling like second-class citizens.'

'Second-class citizens?!' Costas erupted. 'What are you talking about, woman? They're Greeks. More than that, they're Goulandrises.'

'I know, darling,' said Elise, in her meekest, most conciliatory voice. 'Which is why I simply can't *bear* to see them living in a city with German masters. I can only imagine how must worse it must feel for you.'

'Hmmm,' grunted Costas, unsure whether he was being appeased or pitied.

'But the Nazis have got us where they want us, haven't they?' Elise went on, her naive schtick by now down to a fine art.

'What do you mean?'

'Only that there's simply no way to gct one's wife and children out of the country any more. Not without outsmarting the entire Wehrmacht machine. You mustn't blame yourself, Costas.'

After that, things came together rapidly. Costas had taken the bait like a gullible trout, his pride his undoing, as ever. Calls had been made to shipping industry friends in Crete and Cairo, and to contacts in the British Foreign Office. Money had been spent, papers forged and the townhouse on Eaton Terrace made ready. Getting Elise and the boys to London for the remainder of the war was now Costas's idea, a cunning plan to put one over on the arrogant Germans. Not only would his sons be raised free (and Giorgios have the added benefit of being able to receive Dr Heywood-Bryce's world-class ministrations in person), but Costas would be able to resume his bachelor life in Athens free of all constraints. No more broken nights and crying babies. No more irksome small talk at mealtimes with a wife he still liked to control, but no longer actually liked. Yes, London would be better all round, if he could pull it off. And if Elise didn't like it, well, too bad.

'It's not the *Lady Athena*, I'm afraid,' the captain said apologetically, ushering Elise and the boys into their cabin, a spartan room with two bunks and a folding campaign table for the cases. 'I was aboard your husband's yacht once, years ago. What a vessel.'

'It's perfect, thank you,' said Elise. Her own memories of the *Lady Athena* were all unhappy. There was nothing about Costas's yacht that she missed now, apart perhaps from not having to worry about a German U-boat blowing them out of the water.

The captain left, and Elise busied herself settling the boys into bed. Andreas in his own bunk, with the blankets tucked in extra tightly the way he liked them, to form an inescapable cocoon. And little Giorgios with her. *What a good little chap he is*, thought Elise, kissing the top of his lolling head as he slept soundly through the transfer from papoose to bed. With his long nose and mop of dark curls, he reminded her of Laurent. Certainly he looked nothing like his father, unlike Andreas, who was the spitting image of Costas, down to the very last mannerism.

That was one thing she would always be grateful to Costas for: her darling boys. It was her love for them that must sustain her now, Elise told herself, pulling her precious photograph of Sainte Madeleine out of the suitcase and sticking it to the cabin wall beside her pillow. Until this terrible war was over, and she could return to her beloved home. Until the day that she could see France again, and Papa and Maman, and her brothers. Until she and Laurent were together once more, face to face.

It's coming, she told herself. She might not know when, or how, any of these things would happen. But happen they would. She would make sure of it.

She'd got this far after all. She'd made her initial escape. What happened next would be up to her.

Elise fell asleep rocked by the waves and dreaming of London and U-boats and Sainte Madeleine.

Didier pulled his wool coat more tightly around him and blew on the tips of his gloved fingers as he followed the lane into the village. It was only October, but already the first frosts had come to Burgundy, crisping the grass into sharp needles that crunched beneath one's boots, and coating the trees and hedgerows with a glistening film of white.

Today had been a quiet day at the winery, and old Arnaud Berger had let him go early. Most days, if he were honest, Didier felt like a spare part on the domaine, and as much of a hindrance to Arnaud as a help. Even so, he felt a duty to show his face every day, and do what little he could to help rebuild Sainte Madeleine's fortunes, what with Papa drinking again and the war putting an end to their exports, effectively decimating the business. Working at the winery also gave him an excuse to get out of the house, and away from the German officers whom he still feared, despite Gunther's kindness.

'Do you know how much longer they'll be billeted with you?' Henri had asked him casually one evening.

'No,' replied Didier. 'We haven't been told anything. I have no idea what they actually do all day while they're here. The younger ones go off to Vézelay most days, but Gunther – Generallutnant von Hardenberg – he's always hanging around at home, tapping away at the typewriter in his office.'

There was a bitterness to Didier's tone that surprised Henri. 'I thought you didn't mind him? Wasn't he the one who you said had behaved decently to your father?'

Didier looked pained. 'Yes,' he admitted. 'And he's been kind to Maman and me.'

'But?'

'It probably sounds ridiculous, but I almost *want* Gunther to behave like a monster. It makes me angry when he doesn't.'

Henri chuckled. 'Harder to hate him, you mean?'

Didier grimaced. 'I don't know about hate. I don't think hate is ever the answer.'

'I agree,' Henri said seriously. 'In fact, one could argue that hatred is what got the world into this mess in the first place.'

'Even so,' said Didier. 'One can't help but feel guilty, having civil conversations with a man who I know is fighting for such an evil regime.'

'Don't feel guilty,' said Henri. 'You're adapting to your situation, as we all must do. But if this man does have some humanity, you should appeal to it.'

'What do you mean?'

'Try to get him to see the evils of Nazism,' said Henri. 'Try to change his mind.'

'Me?' Didier sounded astonished. 'I can't talk to Gunther about things like that!'

'Why not?' asked Henri. 'The Lord calls all of us to different work, Didier. Perhaps he has given you this opportunity for a reason? Remember St Luke's gospel: "There is more rejoicing in heaven over one sinner who repents than over ninety-nine righteous ones who do not need to repent."'

Didier thought back over this conversation now as he reached the lichened gate to the rectory, really little more than a humble priest's cottage. It was teatime, and he'd decided to drop in on Henri rather than go straight home to a drunk Papa, and Maman playing happy families with Gunther. He wished he could tell Henri that he'd 'converted' von Hardenberg since they'd spoken, and successfully saved a soul. But the shameful truth was, he hadn't challenged Gunther at all. While other young men were out there risking their lives daily on the battlefield, Didier was too much of a coward even to begin an awkward conversation at the dinner table.

I'll ask Henri to hear my confession, he decided on the spur of the moment, letting himself in with the key Henri had given him months ago, so he could come and go at the rectory as he pleased. Once his guilt was out of the way, they'd be able to enjoy a café and brioche together.

'Henri?'

The cosy sitting room and kitchen were both empty. But the lights were on and the fire was lit in the wood burner, so he must be home.

'*Henri, c'est moi. Où es-tu?*' Didier shouted up the stairs. *Nothing.*

A strange sense of trepidation came over him as he climbed the creaky wooden flight and stepped into the narrow upstairs hallway, the hairs on his forearms standing on end like the soft spines on a cactus. A second wave of self-loathing hit him – *must I always be so afraid?* – but he pushed it aside, opening the door to the bedroom.

All the curtains were drawn and the room was in virtual darkness, save for one, flickering church candle propped on the desk. Henri sat with his back to Didier, still in his priestly robes after the noon Mass. He had headphones clamped over his ears, and transistor radio equipment scattered in front of him. In his right hand was a pencil, with which he was transcribing something onto a notepad, painstakingly slowly. Even from behind it was clear from his body language that he was intently focused on what he was doing. Not by a flicker did he register any awareness that someone had entered the room.

Didier stood frozen, processing the magnitude of the scene playing out in front of him. *What if he'd been the Gestapo? Or even just a nosy villager, with a loose tongue?*

'Henri!' His voice came out loud, angry. '*Qu'est-ce que tu fous?*' *What the fuck are you doing?*

Henri spun around, shooting out of his chair as if he'd been electrocuted.

'Didier!' Pulling the headphones off, he clasped both hands to his pounding heart. 'Dear God, you scared me.'

'Scared you? I should hope I scared you!' Didier yelled viciously, appalled at how much he sounded like his father. 'What are you *doing*? Are you mad? If the Germans saw this . . . if anyone saw . . .' Marching over to the desk he began picking up the various components of the radio set and tossing them angrily onto the bed. 'You must get rid of this. Tonight. Burn it. I'll help you.'

'Didier.' Reaching out, Henri rested a hand on his arm, but Didier shrugged him off angrily.

'Didier, you must stop,' Henri said calmly. 'I need that equipment. Lives depend on it.'

'Whose lives?' Didier demanded, shaking.

'British lives. French lives. Brave young men and women, fighting for our freedom, depending on our help.'

'No.' Didier shook his head, tears rolling down his cheeks. 'No. You must stop, Henri. Don't you realize how dangerous this is? What about *your* life?'

'My life belongs to God,' Henri said simply. 'I made that decision long ago.'

'Fuck God!' Didier shouted, grabbing him by the shoulders and shaking him with a force he didn't know he had in him. 'What about me? You're all I have! Don't you care?'

'Of course I care,' Henri's face crumpled. 'You know I care.'

'Liar!'

And then it happened. Didier didn't know whether Henri reached for him, or whether it was the other way around. All he knew was that their lips were together, and then their bodies, clasping, pulling, grasping desperately in the darkness. He felt his cold hands in Henri's hair, and Henri's warm ones clasping his neck as the kiss gripped both of them, drawing them together with a force stronger than reason or will, stronger than faith or guilt, rage or fear.

'I love you,' Didier sobbed, his breath warm in Henri's ear as they finally drew apart. 'Please. Please don't leave me.'

Henri sat down on the edge of the bed and put his head in his hands. While he composed himself, Didier came and sat beside him.

'I'm sorry,' he began.

'Don't be.' Henri shook his head wearily. 'You were being honest.'

'Yes, but—'

'I love you too, Didier,' said Henri, sitting up and looking him in the eye. 'That's the truth, and none of us can hide the truth from God. But . . . I'm a Catholic priest. *This*, between us? It can never be.'

'I know that,' Didier said simply. 'I'm not asking for that. I'm just asking you not to do *this*.' He gestured behind him to the radio parts, and then to the headphones and notepad still on the desk. 'You'll get killed.'

'Only if I get caught,' Henri smiled.

'Don't joke.'

'I'm not, really,' Henri took his hand, holding it with infinite tenderness. 'But I have to do this, Didier. It's my duty. As a priest, as a Frenchman. As a man. I told you when this war started that we needed to do something. To act, to help the Jews.'

'Yes, but I thought you meant giving money or writing letters or . . . or . . . offering prayers,' protested Didier.

'Did you?' Henri asked gently. 'Be honest with yourself, Didier. You knew I was talking about more than that. We both were. It's just that now that it's become a reality.'

'I'm too cowardly to see it through,' Didier cut him off bitterly.

'I didn't say that.'

'You didn't have to. "None of us can hide the truth from God." Right?'

Henri touched Didier's cheek. It broke his heart how little self-esteem he had, how little self-love. That such a sensitive, loving, beautiful spirit could have grown up to have such a low opinion of himself. Of course, it was the father's doing.

'You are lovely in the eyes of God,' said Henri. 'And you are not a coward. We are all called to different work, Didier. For the present moment, this is mine.'

'But you asked me to help you,' said Didier miserably.

'You do help me,' Henri assured him. 'Your love helps me. Your understanding helps me.'

'You know what I mean.'

'Yes, I do,' Henri admitted. 'But it was wrong of me to ask you for that kind of help. You're not suited for it. I am.'

'I don't want you to die,' Didier said plaintively, his bottom lip trembling.

Henri put his arm around him and gave a rallying squeeze. 'And I won't,' he said confidently. 'At least, I'm not planning on it. Just don't mention any of this to your mother.'

Didier rolled his eyes to heaven. 'Don't joke.'

'About Thérèse?' said Henri. 'I wouldn't dare. Now why don't you go downstairs and brew us some coffee, while I finish up here. I won't be long, I promise. And then we can talk about everything, properly.'

Didier did as he was asked, stumbling back downstairs and into the little priest's kitchen like a man in a dream. He felt frightened and shocked, and yet at the same time, preposterously happy.

He loves me. Henri loves me.

When Elise arrived at 64 Eaton Terrace, it felt like she was stepping into a storybook. With its white stucco facade, elegant sash windows and grand porticoed entrance, complete with tall white columns, all set behind black, cast-iron railings, it was exactly what Elise imagined a London townhouse should be. Just a few streets away, however, piles of rubble and bombed-out shops and houses still bore witness to the terrors of the Blitz. The frenetic German bombing campaign had finally ended in London on 11 May, but the scars on the city remained, from Buckingham Palace to the slums of the East End and everywhere in between.

To Elise, though, London was heaven, her first taste of freedom since the day she and Costas married. Of course the staff at Eaton Terrace all reported to him. She had no doubt she was still being watched, to some degree. But it was nothing like the oppressive 'shadowing' she'd grown used to in Athens, with Costas's goons following her everywhere from the park to the hairdresser, and her every move monitored.

'Why have all the bedrooms been opened? And both drawing rooms?' Elise asked the housekeeper, a round, bouncy little woman named Mrs Dalton, the morning after her arrival. 'It's only me and the boys here.'

'Mr Goulandris telegrammed instructions for the whole house to be opened, ma'am,' Mrs Dalton explained nervously.

'I see,' Elise frowned. 'Did he say why?'

'Not to me, ma'am. Although I understand from Mr

273

Thomas that the master was anticipating you might do some entertaining? What with His Majesty King George also being in London.'

Elise smiled to herself. Costas's snobbery really knew no bounds and was second only to her mother's. He was inordinately proud of the fact that he'd managed to smuggle his family to London using the very same route that the Greek king had taken, via Crete and Egypt. Now ensconced in his usual suite at Brown's Hotel, by all accounts King George II was already making a nuisance of himself with the British Foreign Office, demanding much bowing and scraping while running around Belgravia with his latest mistress.

If Costas thought Elise planned on spending her time in London throwing cocktail parties for the king and his entourage of Greek sycophants, he had another think coming.

'I'm sure his majesty will have better things to do than attend parties,' she told the housekeeper diplomatically. 'And we really can't justify the waste of heating and lighting unused rooms, not with a war on. I'll need my bedroom, the nursery and a single spare room for guests,' she explained firmly. 'The smaller drawing room will also be quite sufficient. Everywhere else, you can have the maids put the dust sheets back on. I'll square it all with Mr Goulandris.'

'As you wish, ma'am,' said the housekeeper. 'I assume the young masters' nanny will need her own bedroom as well? Or will she be sleeping with the children in the nursery?'

'I won't be employing a nanny,' Elise announced breezily. 'We have more than enough staff here if I need to run out for some reason. But I plan to take care of Andreas and Giorgios myself.'

Mrs Dalton looked momentarily panicked. Mr Goulandris's instructions had been very clear, on this point in particular.

Three potential nannies were expected for interview that very afternoon.

'Are you sure, ma'am?' she asked Elise nervously, explaining about the interviews. 'Perhaps you should meet the candidates first? See what you think, before you decide.'

'Thank you, Mrs Dalton, but I'm quite decided,' Elise assured her, with the same polite firmness. Costas wouldn't like it. But what could he do, from two thousand miles away? 'I'm the children's mother, after all. I don't imagine any candidate could do a better job looking after them than I can.'

And so things went on throughout October and November. Elise, heady with her own newfound autonomy, pressed ahead with the life she wanted: redecorating the children's bedroom with cheerful butterfly wallpaper that Costas would have *hated* – she couldn't take them to Sainte Madeleine yet, but a life without butterflies was a life without magic, and she couldn't have that; avoiding the ex-pat Greek community like an unpleasant smell; and drinking. More than she should, she admitted. But it wasn't easy to resist temptation.

She would never forget the first time she walked into Costas's wine cellar, an Aladdin's cave of some of the rarest and most valuable bottles to be found anywhere in Europe. But it wasn't only the wines themselves that took her breath away. The whole look and feel of the subterranean room, with its cool, damp brick arches and that musty familiar smell, took her back to her childhood at Sainte Madeleine with painful immediacy. Drinking, for Elise, was about more than simply craving alcohol, although God knew those feelings could be overwhelming on their own. But it was also a link to her past, to everything and everyone she had left behind at Sainte Madeleine. Including, perhaps, herself. Looking after the boys all day long was wonderful but it was much more exhausting than Elise had expected. Her evenings were long and lonely, the cellar was there and, perhaps most importantly of all, there was no one to stop her.

At first Costas bombarded Elise daily with enraged telegrams, demanding that she follow his instructions on running the household to the letter. These she largely ignored, while being careful to avoid outright conflict where she could. In intermittent letters to Athens, she did her best to placate him with one spurious excuse after another:

'London isn't how you imagine it, darling,' she wrote. 'Of course I'd love to be throwing parties. But I assure you nobody would come. And if I opened the whole house up, I'd have the Home Guard at my door, demanding to know why. Everyone's "drawing their horns in", as they say here. Making do and going without. There's a dreadful fear that Britain's losing this war, and that's put a dampener on everything.'

This last part, at least, Costas knew to be true. By September of 1941, the Germans had decisively conquered Western Europe. Rommel was pushing the British back in North Africa and looked set to take the Suez Canal. And the invasion of the Soviet Union had been a stunning success, bringing Hitler's army within striking distance of Moscow. England herself remained free, but without American intervention it was hard to see how Mr Churchill was going to turn the tide.

As for his own marital battles, Costas decided to let these go – at least for now. There would be time enough to bring his errant wife back to heel once the war ended. Then Elise would once again learn her place – lessons Costas would make sure she remembered permanently. But for now, as long as she remained faithful and under his roof in London, he decided to take the path of least resistance. If Elise wanted to play at being a middle-class English housewife who couldn't afford a nanny or a half-decent staff, it was no skin off his nose.

One morning in early December, London awakened to a thick blanket of snow. Drawing back her bedroom curtains in Eaton Terrace, Elise winced at the brightness of the sparkling wonderland in front of her. The gardens of Belgrave Square lay smothered in white, like a frosted cake, millions of individual snowflakes glinting like diamonds beneath a crisp, cloudless blue sky.

Hurriedly downing a glass of Eno's – a miraculous English hangover cure that had become her best friend – Elise put on her dressing gown and slippers and rushed into the boys' room.

'Wake up sleepy-head!' Lifting Andreas out of his bed, she inhaled the sweet, warm, innocent smell of him, all soft skin and clean cotton pyjamas. 'Look outside.'

The little boy pressed his nose against the cold glass windowpane, his dark eyes widening in awe. He had never seen snow, other than in picture books.

'Chrishmash!' he gasped delightedly, looking up at Elise for confirmation.

'It *does* look like Christmas, doesn't it?' she beamed back at him. 'Shall we wake up Giorgios and go and play in it?'

Ten minutes later, while the servants looked on, amused, from the townhouse windows, Elise was racing into the garden square clasping Andreas's mittened hand in hers. Strapped to his mother's chest in his fur-lined papoose, baby Giorgios was completely invisible save for the red bobble on the top of his woolly hat.

'Bless her,' Mrs Dalton observed, watching Elise helping to build a snowman and generally frolicking around in the snow like an over-excited puppy. 'She's as much of a kid as they are.'

Cupping the fresh, soft flakes in her hands, Elise did indeed feel like a child again. It always snowed at Sainte Madeleine in the winter, and more often than not they'd had white Christmases. She found herself thinking about Alex and Didier. About Brolio, nodding off in her rocking chair in the corner, while Papa told them all the story of the butterflies every Christmas Eve. The Legend of the Papillons.

I must tell the story to Andreas, this year, Elise thought happily, watching him tumble about in the snow. Of course, it wouldn't mean much to him yet. He was still too young, and had never set eyes on Sainte Madeleine. But once the war was over . . .

Vague fantasies formed in Elise's mind, each lovelier than the last. Of herself and the boys, living at Sainte Madeleine, happy and free. Of Laurent, back from the war, safe and well, finally declaring his love for her. Of course, Costas was missing from all these scenarios, whited-out of the picture just like the ugly brown winter grass of Belgrave Gardens, blanketed with snow. *If only it weren't for Costas. If only it weren't for this blasted war.*

'Good morning, miss. Morning, boys!' Bert, the paper boy, came bounding along the path with his sack of newspapers over his shoulder, taking Elise by surprise. 'Isn't it fantastic?'

'It really is,' gushed Elise. 'I adore the snow. Do you know Andreas has never seen it before?'

'The snow?' Bert frowned, confused. 'I'm not talking about the *snow*, miss. I'm talking about the news.'

'What news?' asked Elise.

'Haven't you heard?' Reaching into his sack, he pulled out the latest edition of *The Times* and handed it to her.

Elise blinked. Above a picture of an American warship, the USS *Arizona*, in flames and sinking beneath the waves, ran the headline: *JAPAN ATTACKS HAWAII*.

'How awful!' said Elise, her mind turning instantly to all those poor American sailors, burning to death.

'Awful?' Bert frowned. 'No, miss. It's not awful. It's bloody marvellous.'

'How is it marvellous?' Elise asked, confused. 'America's on our side.'

'They are now,' Bert said, ecstatic. 'Don't you realize what this means, miss?'

Elise looked at him blankly. Clearly, she didn't.

'It means the Yanks are finally, officially at war.' He grinned from ear to ear. 'It means we're saved, miss.'

CHAPTER NINETEEN

'Christ, it's beautiful.'

Laurent marvelled in wonder at the Corsican landscape, laid out before him in all its russet autumnal glory. Beech, cork oak and chestnut trees spread out their golden canopies in between the seemingly endless acres of maritime pine, whose needles gave off a sharp, tangy scent that hung deliciously in the September air. Gently sloping meadows dotted with traditional stone barns and the occasional whitewashed farmhouse provided a ludicrously bucolic foreground to the seemingly endless forest, while in the far distance the magnificent Maquis mountains completed the picture with their own rugged beauty.

'We're not here to sightsee, you know,' his comrade reminded him, dropping down to his haunches as they inched deeper into the trees. 'Let's find some cover.'

By the time Laurent's First Free French Division arrived in Corsica as part of Operation Vesuvius, in September 1943, after four long years fighting in Africa, Laurent was not the same person who had left Spain back in 1939. Even back then he had already developed a cynicism, unknown to his younger, idealistic self. The things he'd witnessed in Madrid and Seville, the depths of human cruelty and depravity and the ease with which neighbour had turned on neighbour, had eradicated all traces of the naive, hopeful teenager he'd once been. Of the boy who saw the world in simple terms of black and white, right and wrong.

But *this* war, and in particular the bitter fighting of the North African campaign, had taken Laurent beyond cynicism, into a mental state that was harder to describe in words. A certain numbness had taken hold. A sort of weary calm, rooted in self-preservation, that lessened one's suffering and yet, at the same time, robbed that suffering of all meaning, and all the emotion that made it worthwhile. As the horrors of battle continued to mount, month after month, year after year, it became something that he couldn't sustain. He couldn't both survive and live. It simply wasn't possible. And so living had been postponed for later, for the mythical future of his fretful dreams; a future full of peace, and France, and Elise. And Laurent had set about the pressing business of survival.

In 1942 the tides of war in Africa had finally turned. America's entry into the conflict had helped, as had the arrival of the British First Army and parachute divisions in Tunisia. When Montgomery's Eighth Army captured Tripoli in January 1943, it felt as if all the years of dust, death and defeat might at last be at an end. Laurent tried to feel happy. He did feel happy, as far as the numbness allowed. But, unlike the British and American forces, whose cama-raderie sustained them and helped to make victory all the sweeter, the French troops remained divided. Infighting and distrust was rife between de Gaulle's Free French, the March divisions and the regular French army, many of whom Laurent and his compatriots felt had been tainted by their ties to the Vichy regime.

As a result, when the First Free French deployed to

Corsica to help liberate the island from the Italians, Laurent's emotions were bittersweet. On the one hand it was a blessing to leave Africa, and an honour to be able to fight for Corsica, which as far as Laurent was concerned *was* France. He'd spent two happy summers here as a boy on his cousins' farm outside Sartène and had nothing but fond memories of the island. Memories that today's stunning landscape were already bringing back to him. But on the other hand, the numbness, along with the miserable feeling that it was 'every man for himself' dampened both his enthusiasm and his happiness to be 'home'.

'Did you hear that?'

The young soldier next to him lifted his rifle anxiously, peering into the wooded gloom. The two of them had taken up positions in a partially protected knoll just a few yards into the thick forest.

'I didn't hear anything.'

Unhurriedly, Laurent raised his own rifle. The heavily wooded Maquis mountains were difficult terrain and frighteningly unfamiliar to many of the men. Italian and German snipers could emerge from the trees at any moment, completely unseen until they were right on top of you. But Laurent remembered the drill from his stint in the Atlas Mountains of Morocco, and felt more capable than most.

'There it is again!' the young man hissed, with rising panic, right before a young doe bolted out of the shadows, twigs cracking beneath her feet as she pranced away.

'Fuck!' the soldier exhaled, lowering his gun.

Behind him, other members of the company giggled and made mocking comments, one or two throwing playful stones.

'I hate the fucking mountains.'

'No you don't. You hate the Wops. Big difference.'

Laurent spun around. The voice came from a few feet behind them and he recognized it instantly. 'Bernard?'

'Holy shit.' A short, stocky maquisard, one of the local Corsican Resistance fighters, scrambled up the thorny hillside. 'Is that Laurent? Laurent Senard? What are the fucking chances?'

The two cousins hugged, ignoring the muted wolf whistles and jeers from the other men. 'I can't believe it,' Laurent grinned, shocked, feeling a rising sense of happiness for the first time in forever. The last time he'd seen Bernard had been at Chateau Brancion, the Christmas after Elise and the Salignacs were last there. A lifetime ago, but he hadn't changed, at least not physically.

'How are you?'

'I'm good, man.' Bernard grinned back at him, white teeth flashing in the darkness. 'I mean, I'll be better once we get rid of these bloody Eyeties. But I'm fine.'

'And your family?'

'Still alive,' Bernard replied cheerfully. 'What about yours? How's Thierry? I heard he was back home in Burgundy.'

'You probably know more than I do,' said Laurent. 'Next to nothing got through to North Africa, and I've moved around so much. I—'

A volley of sniper fire from the ridge above them put an abrupt end to the conversation. A few feet to Laurent's left a man fell to the ground screaming. Behind him, two others fell silently, dead.

Dropping to their bellies, rifles raised, the whole company began to snake their way forwards and upwards through the thick brush. Laurent, momentarily robbed of his numbness, felt cold tendrils of fear coiling themselves around him. He and Bernard weren't close but he was *family*, and that meant everything in the shadowy depths of war. If anything were to happen to Bernard . . . if his cousin were killed tonight, moments after they'd found one another, and that precious connection were lost? That thought frightened Laurent more than the enemy snipers.

Be careful, an anxious voice inside warned him. *Focus.* One mistake was all it took.

Back in Vézelay, Didier had bicycled into town from Sainte Madeleine, a beautiful ride on this still-warm September day. Pollarded plane trees lining the country lanes waved their stubby limbs defiantly in the breeze, seeming to presage better days to come. There was a scent of wild garlic in the air, that mingled with the pungent tang of warm earth and mown grass to give a last whiff of summer. *Something ending*, thought Didier as he pedalled, his cheeks flushed red from exertion and fresh air. *But something beginning too.*

Chaining his rickety old Huret to a lamppost at the top of the town, he slung his *sac à dos* over one shoulder and made his way down the cobblestoned hill toward the main town square. Officially he was here to pick up his mother's ration of flour and sugar, and to see if any fresh meat was to be had from Monsieur Dupont's *boucherie*. But he also hoped to run into Henri, who'd taken to riding into Vézelay before dawn most mornings to help officiate at the early cathedral Mass.

'Bonjour, Monsieur Salignac.' Vendors who'd known Didier from a little boy greeted him from shop doorways, forbidden hope shining in their eyes. 'Beautiful day.'

'It certainly is.'

Didier smiled. He felt a tremendous lightness, almost a joy. But it quickly dissipated when he reached the bottom of the hill and turned the corner into the Rue du Cathedrale. Something was different. German soldiers, their faces tense and drawn, gathered in groups of five or six, watching the locals with narrowed eyes. Further along the road, where it widened out into the main town square, Didier could see more soldiers, urging groups of French civilians to move on. A familiar knot of anxiety began to form in the pit of his stomach.

'Has something happened?' he asked a young mother. She was ushering her children back into a small courtyard that gave on to apartments, out of the soldiers' view, and when she looked at Didier, there was fear in her eyes.

'In the square,' she said, and nodded curtly before scurrying away.

Didier walked slowly past the soldiers. Nobody stopped him, although he expected the hand on his shoulder at any moment, demanding to see his papers or what his business was in Vézelay. Instead, like an unhappy magnet, he found himself pulled inexorably towards the Place du Cathedrale, and whatever it was that had caused crowds to gather and faces to fall.

At first he couldn't see anything. A line of German military vehicles had parked across the entrance to the square, blocking his view. There were soldiers everywhere, more SS uniforms than Didier had seen in Vézelay since the occupation began. He noticed Gunther among them, talking earnestly to a small group of officers, but again he slipped past without incident, just one body among the scores pushing forwards into the middle of the square. And then suddenly, there it was.

A gallows, hastily constructed. Little more than plywood and nails.

Eight bodies swinging. Six men, two women, their necks lolling sideways at grotesque angles and their legs hanging, like broken puppets.

Resistance fighters, thought Didier, his eyes welling with tears and his heart swelling with conflicting emotions. Sorrow. Horror. Anger. But also guilt, terrible guilt that these men and women had had the courage to give their lives for France, while he sat and waited for liberation to arrive, as passive as a child.

I wonder if Henri knew any of them? He walked towards the hanging corpses, part of a slow, silent procession of townspeople. Despite being frightened and revolted, he needed to see for himself; to witness the full barbarism of these monstrous men for whom so many in France had become apologists, even Didier's own mother. He and Henri never spoke about Henri's secret work anymore. Silence was safer for both of them. But Henri knew how proud Didier was of his courage and commitment, his devotion to a cause bigger than—

'Oh God! No!' A voice rang out, a scream that echoed through the square.

Didier didn't recognize it as his own. All he knew as he dropped to his knees was that it was Henri's grey, dead face above him.

'NO!'

Instinctively the rest of the onlookers moved away, lowering their eyes and quickening their pace. Didier stayed on his knees, like a disciple at the foot of the cross, sobbing uncontrollably.

How could it be Henri? It couldn't be. It wasn't. He wasn't wearing robes. Henri always wore robes when he was saying Mass.

But it was. It was Henri. His eyes, his lovely eyes, the only eyes that had ever seen Didier as he truly was, were still open, fixed now forever in a sightless gaze. And his blue lips, the same soft lips that had pressed themselves to Didier's, were parted just slightly, as if he'd breathed his last mid-prayer.

'You! Get up.' The SS guard towered over Didier, rifle in hand. 'I said get *up*!' A sharp nudge in the ribs from a polished, black jackboot elicited a yelp of pain. But Didier remained slumped on the ground. He couldn't have got to his feet in that moment, even if he wanted to. 'Get up or I'll shoot you.'

Didier didn't move. He heard the familiar click of a rifle being cocked, then a dreadful pause.

'It's all right, Sturmmann Leitner. You can stand down.' A softer German voice cut through the silence. 'I know this man.'

'But Generallutnant von Hardenberg – the fellow's refusing to comply with my orders. He's obviously an associate of the traitor's.'

'I doubt that. I suspect he's simply in shock. The young man has a nervous disposition,' Gunther explained.

'Yes but, sir! They obviously knew each other,' the guard protested. 'He's been making a spectacle of himself, and the general gave strict orders—'

'Father Bercault was the parish priest in this man's village,' said Gunther tersely. 'I'm billeted there. It's a tiny place. Anyone from Sainte Madeleine would have recognized the priest. I said, stand down.'

The guard looked nonplussed, but didn't dare to argue further. Gunther squatted down on his haunches and, slipping both arms under Didier's armpits, physically hauled him to his feet. 'Come along,' he said briskly, ignoring Didier's awful, keening, animal wail as he dragged him to his waiting jeep and bundled him into the back seat. 'Let's get you home.'

Thérèse was in the garden, picking basil leaves for tonight's salade de tomates when Gunther's jeep roared up the drive. One look at his face told her something terrible had happened, even before she saw Didier tumbling out of the back seat with his arms tied behind his back, running around screaming as if he'd been shot.

'What on earth . . . ?'

'Help me get hold of him,' Gunther instructed. He had a bloody gash across his cheek above which a dark bruise was already beginning to form. Very rarely for him, he sounded panicked. 'We need to get him inside.'

It took Thérèse, the gardener's boy and one of the young German captains to restrain Didier, who was ranting at Gunther now in between his screams, calling him a murderer and threatening to kill him. After five long minutes, they managed to get him inside the house and to hold him down long enough for Gunther to plunge a syringe into his arm.

'What the hellsh going on?' Louis, blind drunk already, staggered into the hallway just in time to witness Didier slump forwards, barely conscious, into the young German captain's arms. 'What've you done to my son?' He looked at Gunther accusingly.

'I've given him a sedative, monsieur,' said Gunther, whose bruised eye was now starting to close up completely. 'A strong one. He needs it.' He turned to the captain. 'Herman, take him to his bedroom and lock the door.'

'Sir.'

'What's *happened?*' Thérèse turned desperately to Gunther. 'I don't understand. Did Didier attack you?' She reached up to touch his injured cheek, but he brushed her hand aside, almost angrily.

'It's just a scratch. This isn't about that.'

'Well what, then?'

Gunther looked at her, stricken. 'I'm sorry to have to tell you . . .' he cleared his throat, 'that Father Henri Bercault was executed this afternoon.'

Blood drained from Thérèse's face. 'Executed?' she whispered.

'Yes.'

'*Why?*'

'For high treason against the Fuhrer,' Gunther said stiffly, as if the formality of his words could somehow lessen the horror of what he was saying.

'High treason?' Thérèse repeated the words numbly. This made no sense. No sense at all.

'Father Bercault was captured along with the rest of his Resistance cell in the woods outside Vézelay this morning. All eight admitted their crimes and were hung at two forty-five in the Place du Cathedrale.'

A dreadful silence fell. A silence in which the gulf that existed between Thérèse and Gunther, the yawning, unbridgeable chasm that had always been there, but that they had both tried to deny, unequivocally asserted itself. In that moment, Gunther became what he had always been: an occupying soldier, just like all the other hated soldiers who had taken over Burgundy. The enemy. And Thérèse became one of the millions of oppressed who had suffered under the Nazi jackboot. It didn't matter anymore who Gunther was as a man, an individual. His personal acts of kindness and gallantry. The company and friendship and support that he'd provided Thérèse at Sainte Madeleine, at a time when Louis had once again abandoned her and the estate on the altar of his addiction. Or rather, it didn't matter enough. Henri was dead. Murdered, as far as Thérèse was concerned, however Gunther might choose to phrase it.

Thérèse and Gunther looked at one another hopelessly. Both knew that Henri's hanging had changed everything. Things would never be the same.

''S good riddance as far as I'm consherned.' Louis's rasping, spiteful voice broke the spell. Swaying unsteadily from foot to foot like a ship in the wind, he looked from Gunther to Thérèse and back again. 'Never liked the fellow.'

'Louis!' Thérèse gasped, appalled. 'How can you say such a thing?'

'How can I say it? Easily, that's how.' Louis jabbed a

finger aggressively in his wife's direction. 'Don't pretend you didn't know whassh been going on with Père Bercault and Didier.'

'Going on? What do you mean "going on"?' Thérèse demanded, too distressed to be embarrassed by Louis's shameful, drunken behaviour.

'The man was a pervert. A bloody deviant.'

'Monsieur Salignac,' Gunther interrupted him loudly. 'For your son's sake, I urge you in the strongest terms never to repeat that accusation.'

'Oh, you do, do you? You *urge* me?' Staggering across the room, Louis stopped just inches from Gunther's face, close enough for Gunther to smell the brandy on his breath. 'Well I *urge* you to stay the hell away from my wife, understand? German pig.'

'*Louis!*' A mortified Thérèse stepped forward, but Gunther held up a hand to stop her.

'It's all right,' he told her. 'He doesn't mean it. He's drunk.'

He does mean it, Thérèse thought desperately. *And he's always drunk.*

In that moment she hated Louis. Hated him for his weakness. Hated him for treating her so badly that she'd had to turn to Gunther, a Nazi officer, for emotional support. Hated him because now Henri was dead, and she couldn't forgive that, and so now she would have no one. No one at all.

Louis's eyes narrowed, as if he were trying to come up with some stinging rejoinder. But unable to do so, he merely muttered an unintelligible insult under his breath and weaved his way pathetically out of the room, clutching the furniture for support.

'I apologize,' Thérèse told Gunther stiffly once he'd gone.

'No need.' Gunther cleared his throat awkwardly. He longed to place a comforting hand on Thérèse's shoulder, as he would have done yesterday. But Father Bercault's hanging had ended that chapter between them, as abruptly and as finally as the breaking of a man's neck. Even so, he owed it to Thérèse to warn her, and to help her as far as he was able. Didier's behaviour today in town had been suicidally dangerous, and Louis's outburst just now wasn't far behind. If something didn't change, Henri Bercault's would not be the last hanging to affect Sainte Madeleine.

'You must understand, madame, this is a dangerous situation.' He forced himself to look Thérèse directly in the eye as he explained exactly what had happened with the guard in the square, and Didier's very vocal and public outpouring of grief. 'If I hadn't been there, your son would have been shot.'

Thérèse let out a muffled cry of anguish. Despite herself, she reached for Gunther's hand, squeezing it briefly before letting it go.

'Consorting with a member of the Resistance is punishable by death,' he told her, as gently as he could. 'So is homosexuality.'

Thérèse opened her mouth to say something, but then shut it again, too devastated to speak.

'I'm sorry to speak so bluntly,' said Gunther. 'But things are changing in France, madame, and the rules will be more strictly enforced from now on. The general has given us strict orders to shoot any suspected collaborators on sight.'

Thérèse sank unsteadily into a chair, taking a moment to compose herself before responding. She knew that he was trying to help her, and she appreciated it. But the pain of what he was saying, of what had happened, was almost more than she could bear.

'What do you suggest I do?' she asked quietly.

'Keep your husband at home if you can't keep him sober. And get Didier out of here.' Gunther's response was unequivocal. 'As far away as you can. Somewhere safe, and ideally isolated, where he can recover.'

'What if he won't go?'

'He must,' Gunther replied grimly. 'If it comes to it, I can sign paperwork to have him certified insane. But we must act quickly. A lot of people saw what happened today.' She nodded in silent misery.

'Do you know of anywhere?' Gunther asked.

'I think so,' said Thérèse. 'There's a convent, near Haut-Folin, up in the mountains. It's a silent order, very remote. I know the Mother Superior there.'

'Perfect,' said Gunther. 'Once he gets there, she must keep him there. Will she understand that?'

'She will.' Thérèse stared bleakly out of the window. There had been so many happy times in this room when the children were little. How on earth had it come to this? Alex, gone, fighting with the American army somewhere in Asia. Elise in London, both of them with children that Thérèse hadn't even yet met. Louis, unravelling before her eyes like a carelessly dropped spool of wool. And now Didier, the last of her children left to her, to be sent to the Morvan massif, locked up like a criminal.

And to think of poor Father Bercault, poor Henri, dead! Thérèse hated the Germans. And yet here was Gunther, one of those Germans, risking his own neck to help poor Didier, and to help *her*. Truly the world had turned upside down, and it felt to Thérèse as if it would never be righted.

'Thank you, Major General.' Reaching up, she offered Gunther her hand for the last time. He pressed it briefly to his lips, the closest he would ever come to admitting his feelings for her, before ending their meeting with a clipped, formal bow.

'Good luck, madame.'

Bernard ladled a generous helping of lentil and sausage stew into a tin bowl and handed it to Laurent. The steaming food smelled delicious, and as the men huddled around the crackling campfire, the sense of warmth and relief was palpable.

'You did good, today,' said Bernard, settling in beside Laurent with his own bowl of stew. 'I saw you take out those two Wops up on the ridge.' He closed one eye and made a shooting motion with his hands. 'Where'd you learn to shoot like that, Cousin?'

'Morocco, mostly,' said Laurent, sighing. 'Too many places.'

'I hear you,' said Bernard cheerfully. 'Sometimes it feels like we've been at war forever. You were in Spain too, weren't you?'

Laurent nodded.

'Bad show, that,' mused Bernard, with admirable under-statement. 'Still, the tide's turning now.'

'You said you'd had news from home,' said Laurent, changing the subject. He'd had enough of battle for one day.

'Right!' Bernard brightened. 'I forgot about that. Yes, my mother's had quite a few letters from your mother. Your parents and Thierry have been living in one of the dower houses, I believe, since the Krauts took over Chateau Brancion.'

'The Germans commandeered the house?' Laurent asked.

'Three years ago,' Bernard said awkwardly. 'Sorry, mate. I assumed you knew that part.'

Laurent shook his head. Not that he was surprised, when he thought about it. A huge estate like his family's was bound to be used for the war effort in some capacity. It was just weird to think that every time he'd pictured Maman or Papa or Thierry together at home, they'd actually been somewhere else the whole time. In unfamiliar rooms, with unfamiliar paintings on the walls.

'The Salignacs have had it worse, though,' Bernard went on.

Laurent's ears pricked up. He'd forgotten that Bernard's family were also distant cousins to the Salignacs, on his mother's side. Upper-class Burgundy society was embarrassingly incestuous.

'They've had SS actually billeted *with* them at Sainte Madeleine. I'm not sure I could handle that.'

'No,' agreed Laurent. 'Me either. Do you happen to know if Elise moved back there?' he asked, as casually as he could. 'The last time I saw her she was living with her godmother in Paris, but I assume she would have gone back home once the Germans invaded.'

'My goodness, you really are out of the loop, aren't you?' said Bernard, draining the dregs of his stew with a loud slurp. 'No man, Elise got married before the war. Some filthy rich Greek fella.'

'Married?' Laurent's throat went dry. He'd been about to take another spoonful of food, but froze now with his spoon in mid-air, like a child playing musical statues.

'Uh huh,' Bernard rattled on, oblivious. 'They have two kids, I think. They were living in Athens, but your mother said that the rich husband managed to wangle a passage to London for Elise and the children. So I think she's living there. And you know Alex is an American now . . .'

He kept talking, but Laurent wasn't listening.

Elise was married. Married with two children.

His Elise.

Except she wasn't his. She had never been his. And he had only himself to blame for that.

'Are you all right, old man?' Bernard asked. He was waving a hand in front of Laurent's face, like a hypnotist trying to break a trance. 'You disappeared on me.'

'Sorry,' muttered Laurent. 'Just, thinking about old times, you know.'

Elise!

He felt the numbness creeping back, but this time he

welcomed it, like a long-lost lover. The thin cloak of protection it provided was all that stood between him and oblivion.

Arnaud Berger flexed his fingers and toes, willing the warmth back into his arthritic joints. Early mornings were getting harder, not just physically, but emotionally too. So many terrible things were happening, it was hard sometimes to find the energy to drag oneself out of bed. The rhythms of the vine still helped, the steady, reliable drum beat of nature and the seasons that had rooted Arnaud to the land since boyhood. And not just any land. *This* land, *this* domaine. Sainte Madeleine with her dry, crumbling soil that Arnaud had rubbed between his fingers so many times, he could feel it in his dreams, along with the sound of the rushing river, and the Salignac children's distant laughter.

All of that was still there, locked tight in the old man's heart. But it was getting harder and harder to live on memories alone. To reconcile the joy of then with the horrors of now. The young priest who'd been so kind to Didier, hung in Vézelay square. Didier, driven off in the middle of the night by the tall, thin German, to God knows where. Madame crying and praying like never before. And as for the master, what could one say? Louis Salignac's tragedy had been unfolding long before the war. But even so, it was painful for Arnaud to watch a man he'd known since boyhood, a man with such promise, disintegrate into such a rotten, embittered, shell. Especially this last time, after he'd returned from Paris so changed, and bought back the farms. For a while everyone had had such high hopes that both Louis and the vineyard had turned a corner. But it was not to be.

Sliding back the heavy cast-iron bolt, Arnaud pulled open the doors to the big barn. Three huge, oak casks containing this year's vintage took up most of the space on the ancient stone floor, each one with bowed sides over ten feet tall. It was a tiny crop compared to the old days, but the quality was once again improving, providing Arnaud with a tiny chink of light in the gloom. He checked these casks first every morning, mounting the little wooden stepladders to peer into the magical, deep purple liquid that was the life-blood of the domaine.

Knees creaking, the old man climbed slowly up the first cask and looked down.

At first it was hard to make out what he was seeing in the half-light. But it soon became clear, even to Arnaud's rheumy old eyes.

Louis Salignac, face down, his wine-soaked jacket billowing on the surface and strands of his thinning black hair fanned out around his head, like the legs of a starfish.

Arnaud waited for the shock to hit him but instead he felt nothing but deep, deep sadness. As awful as it was to see Louis like that, there was a terrible inevitability to it. To the curse of Sainte Madeleine, and the Salignac family – alcoholism, grimly claiming another victim. Slowly, with tenderness, Arnaud reached down and touched the back of his master's head. There was no need to move him, or call for help. He had clearly been dead for some time.

Was it an accident? Arnaud wondered. Had Louis stumbled into the winery drunk last night, slipped and fallen in? It was certainly possible. But it was also possible that he'd taken his own life. That the despair of what he was, and what he might have been, had become too much for him. Either way, Arnaud grieved silently for the boy he'd once known. *Le pauvre.*

Poor Monsieur. And poor Madame! Arnaud's thoughts turned to Thérèse Salignac, who'd already suffered so much.

In a few minutes Arnaud would have to walk down to the house and tell her what had happened. Dear God, could things get any worse? And what on earth was to become of Sainte Madeleine, with the master dead and Monsieur Alex, Mademoiselle Elise and now even Monsieur Didier all gone?

All Arnaud Berger knew was that it was going to take more than the myth and magic of Sainte Madeleine's butterflies to save the Salignacs. And though it pained him to think it, perhaps they, like France, were beyond saving?

CHAPTER TWENTY

Alex watched the butterfly give a last, feeble flutter of its wings and then collapse, lifeless, onto the dusty ground of the tent. He tried not to envy it.

Alex had never believed in hell. Even as a child, when his Catholic faith was strongest, and when Thérèse had done her level best to instil the fear of eternal damnation into all her children, the concept of an 'otherworldly land of misery' had always seemed silly to Alex.

The Philippines hanged that. Hell was real all right, and just like Dante's Inferno it had different levels, each one more agonizing than the last. The jungle fighting had been beyond brutal. Alex and Tyler, who'd joined up together after Pearl Harbor and been shipped out from Salinas barely six weeks later, soon found themselves shoulder to shoulder with poorly trained men from the rag-tag Philippine army, waist-deep in swamp, their toes rotting in sodden boots, trying to spot snipers in zero-visibility monsoon weather. But even those miseries were as nothing compared to the camp.

Bad military miscalculations on the Allies' part, combined with a fatal early prioritizing of the European theatres of war by both Churchill and Roosevelt, resulted in a series of swift and resounding defeats across Asia. Captured by the Japanese less than a month after their arrival, Alex and Tyler witnessed horrors that they knew they would never speak of back home, in the unlikely event they survived. Men, boys in some cases, who'd fought alongside them tortured and beaten to death before their eyes. Others, starved to emaciation, shot for missing quotas, or for working too slowly or even just stumbling when they walked.

The camp at Bataan held a mixture of American forces and local Filipinos. Within the first thirty days of capture, 60 per cent of Alex's division-mates were dead. Those who weren't shot died either from septicaemia (the result of untreated battle wounds) or succumbed to dysentery, exhaustion, hunger and despair. And yet still, another level of hell awaited.

Typhus fever made its first sweep through the camp in June. The Filipinos got the worst of it that time, with scores of good, brave men reduced to shivering, rambling skeletons, screaming at the pain of the light in their eyes. But the second wave of disease, in September, hit the American tents the hardest. Alex watched, helpless, as Tyler succumbed, first to a hacking cough and fever, but eventually to the point where he was too weak to move from his makeshift cot.

'Will he make it?'

Alex looked despairingly at Dr Luke Golton, the New jersey medic who'd done so much to keep hope alive since his arrival at the camp in May. With his white, freckly skin and shock of orange-red hair, the skinny Golton looked as out of place in the sweltering jungle as a parrot in an Alaskan winter. But his wry humour had been as much of a lifesaver to his beleaguered fellow POWs as any of the feeble 'treatments' the Japanese had permitted him to administer.

'Fifty-fifty,' Luke told Alex matter-of-factly.

It was early morning, and only the two of them in Alex and Tyler's tent. The other men had been dispatched to work duties before dawn, but Alex had stayed behind, risking a beating to ensure that the doctor saw Tyler today.

'He should be out of it, though, with the shot I've just given him. So you don't need to worry about leaving him.'

'Thank you,' said Alex. Morphine was more precious than diamonds in the camp, and Alex suspected the tiny dose Luke had just given Tyler had come directly from his own, private supplies.

'You two close?' the pale young doctor asked. He couldn't fail to notice the anguish in Alex's eyes, that seemed to run deeper than the usual misery of the camp.

Alex nodded, his eyes welling with tears. Even if he wanted to, he couldn't find the words to express what Tyler meant to him. He was his brother, as much or more of a brother than Didier had ever been. Without him, Alex would never have founded Tricycle. He would never have survived losing Will, or leaving Ruth and Sarah behind, or the unspeakable suffering they'd witnessed and experienced together since coming to Asia.

'You can keep this too, if he needs it at the end,' the doctor said, pressing a small glass vial into Alex's hand.

Alex bit down hard on his lower lip, willing himself not to cry.

'But if he dies in his sleep, I'd like it back.'

'Of course.' Alex choked up, too grateful to know what else to say.

'Chin up,' said Luke, patting Alex on the shoulder as he packed up his bag. 'Half of them live.'

'It's been three days now.' Mrs Dalton, the housekeeper, cast a worried glance at Elise's bedroom door. 'Do you think we should call a doctor?'

Thomas the butler shrugged. 'I don't see what a doctor

can do. If a person wants to drink themselves to death, they'll do it.'

'Oh, don't say that!' Mrs Dalton's ample bosom began to rise and fall in distress beneath her starched shirt. 'What would become of the children?'

Ever since the news of Louis Salignac's tragic death reached the house on Eaton Terrace, the housekeeper and maids had been caring for Andreas and Giorgios full-time while their mother took to her bed. Or rather, while she took to the brandy bottle next to her bed, occasionally sobering up sufficiently to stagger downstairs for some food, but otherwise remaining locked in grief up in her room.

'I'm going to go in,' the housekeeper said finally. 'See if I can't talk some sense into her.'

'Best of British,' said the butler. 'I'll be downstairs if you need me.'

Hearing the door open, Elise groaned and turned to face the wall. Lying on top of the bed, with a silk, kimono-style dressing gown tied loosely around her tiny body, she looked smaller and more frail than Mrs Dalton had ever seen her, like a baby bird fallen from its nest.

'Good morning, ma'am.' Ignoring Elise's cries of protest, she pulled open the curtains. 'I've brought you up some breakfast and the post. You've had a telegram.'

'A telegram?' A rare flicker of interest crept into Elise's voice. 'From France?

'No ma'am. From Athens.'

The flicker died.

'Mr Goulandris sent his condolences.'

Elise closed her eyes. She didn't care about Costas, or his 'condolences'. Papa was dead. The last thread connecting her to her happy childhood had been broken. First she'd lost Alex. Then Laurent. And now Papa.

Even if she made it back to Sainte Madeleine somehow, once all this was over, it was too late. Her sons would never know their grandfather. There would never be another Christmas like the ones Elise remembered, with Papa in the nursery, telling the story of the butterflies and the young man who never broke his promise and died, broken-hearted, in the Vézelay woods . . . *I can't give my boys any of that*, she thought despairingly. *I can't even go to the funeral.*

'Ma'am, you must get up,' Mrs Dalton asserted bravely, perching on the end of Elise's bed. 'And you must stop *this*.' Reaching for the brandy bottle on the bedside table, she snatched it away before Elise could stop her.

'Give that back!' Elise snarled.

'No, ma'am. I won't. I know it hurts. But your children need you. You came here for them, didn't you? To give them a better life? Well what life can they have without their mother?'

Sitting up, Elise glared at the small, plump Englishwoman. How dare Mrs Dalton scold her like a child. Didn't she know what had just happened? What Elise had lost forever?

'This will kill you, my dear.' The housekeeper held up the brandy bottle defiantly. 'And then who will raise Andreas and Giorgios, hm? Their father?'

'No!' gasped Elise, shuddering. 'No. They can't go back to Costas. Never.'

'Then you must stop this nonsense, ma'am. I'm sorry to speak so bluntly, but you must. Or you stand to lose even more than you have already.'

Tyler died on a Monday.

By Wednesday Alex had a high fever and body aches. On Thursday he collapsed on work detail, and by Friday he was completely delirious, fighting for his life.

Afterwards he would remember very little from that time. Snatched images and sensations, fragments of dreams, were all that stayed with him, the lines between reality and hallucination irretrievably blurred. Past and present, too, melded into one. Dr Golton's voice, willing him to fight, became his father's, cheering him on at a polo match in Dijon. The dirty white tent canvas above his head became the nursery ceiling at Sainte Madeleine. And the soiled blanket, balled up and clutched to his sweat-soaked chest, was baby Will, small and precious, nestled against him.

The worst days were when his fever broke, and the swelling in his brain subsided enough to allow hell back in. Bataan, the camp, the agonizing pain in his head that felt as if his skull were being slowly crushed in a wine compressor. Tyler, dead. Will, dead. He tried to think about Ruth and Sarah. About how much he loved them, and they him, and how they needed him to fight and survive and come home. But it was hard. In a strange way, immersing in the pain was easier. With shame, Alex realized that he was no longer sure whether he wanted to recover. The fetid lunacy of his sickbed felt safer and more familiar than the world outside.

But recover he did, to Dr Luke's delight.

'Welcome back, mate,' the skinny medic grinned, the morning that Alex finally managed to sit up and drink some broth.

'I wish I could say it was good to be here,' Alex croaked back sardonically.

'Man, you're not bitching already?' Luke teased him. 'Well, I for one am delighted you've pulled yourself together. It's about time you Californians stopped hogging all my morphine supplies.'

Alex forced a smile. He was grateful to the New Jersey doctor, of course he was. But he'd changed. The man sipping weak vegetable broth now was not the same man who'd crawled into this camp-bed eleven days before.

That Alex could have told his wife everything. This Alex knew there were things about which he would never speak, not even to Ruth.

That Alex would have been content to return to Tricycle after the war and pick up where he'd left off. This Alex knew that without Tyler, it would never be the same. More than that, he knew that he couldn't run from his past – or his destiny – forever.

And even if he could, he no longer wanted to. France was a part of him, as deep in his soul as anything, or anyone, else ever could be. Sainte Madeleine was a part of him. His family was a part of him, even Papa, who had so enraged him when he was younger and come so close to ruining the estate forever. Alex had made a life in America with Ruth. But he was still a Salignac. And like a sturdy vine, the love he shared with Ruth could take root just as easily in Burgundy as it could in Napa. As long as he took good care of it. As of course he would.

Slumping back onto his sweat-soaked cot, his mind was made up. If he made it through this hell – if – Alex would return to Sainte Madeleine.

Louis Salignac was buried on a cold Sunday in October, in the Salignac family vault at Sainte Madeleine parish church. Thérèse, sombrely magnificent in a full-length, black Edwardian mourning dress, her drawn face covered with a black lace mantilla, stood rigid-backed in the tiny church-yard as the temporary priest from Vézelay recited the familiar words: '*Libera me, Domine . . .*'

Beside her, Camille and Roger Senard shivered beneath their black woollen coats. And a few feet behind, Thierry Senard stood next to Chantelle Delorme, who somehow contrived to look agelessly beautiful and effortlessly glamorous in a mink coat and black felt hat, despite the simplicity and tragedy of the occasion. Other than that, the only mourners in attendance were the estate staff: poor old Arnaud Berger, who'd found Louis's body, and the ancient Brolio, who now needed a wheelchair and had been pushed

to the service by one of the maids. A few of the village field
hands hovered respectfully near the lichened gate, their caps
in their hands. And at the very back, paying his respects as
unobtrusively as possible, the German officer, Gunther von
Hardenberg in his grey SS uniform, clutching a Catholic
missal in his hands.

After the service, the small family group walked back up
to the house for sandwiches and wine, an awkward gathering that was not helped by Thérèse's brittle grief.

'It must be hard for her, with none of the children able
to be here,' Thierry observed quietly to Chantelle as they
sat down together on a corner sofa.

'Yes,' Chantelle agreed. 'It must.'

She tried not to show how shocked she was by Thierry's
appearance, and how very altered he was from the young
man she'd met in Paris before the war. He was still handsome. Really good looks like his never vanished completely.
But by God, he'd aged. His rounded, youthful cheeks of a
few years ago were sunken and hollow now, and dark
shadows hung heavily beneath lined eyes. He was thin too,
unhealthily so in Chantelle's opinion, which was odd given
that he'd spent the last three years living at home with his
parents, presumably doing nothing more stressful than
helping out on the home farm.

'According to my mother,' Thierry told Chantelle, 'Aunt
Thérèse got a telegram the other day from Alex's wife in
America.' Glancing distrustfully across at Generallutnant
von Hardenberg, who was chatting with his fellow German
officers by the fire, Thierry instinctively lowered his voice
to a whisper. 'His regiment had contacted her to say that
Alex is believed captured somewhere out in the Philippines.
I mean, wonderful that he's alive, of course. But how awful
for Aunt Thérèse, not to be able to tell her own son that
his father's died.'

'I don't think Didier knows, either,' Chantelle whispered

back, also eyeing the Germans with suspicion. 'He was completely broken, apparently, when . . . you know.'

'Yes, I know.' Thierry grimaced. 'Henri Bercault was a brave man.'

The way he said it made Chantelle wonder whether Thierry had known the priest personally. Could he be part of the Resistance too? That would certainly explain the physical changes. Nothing aged one like the stress of risking not just your own life, but your elderly parents' too, knowing that you were never more than a hair's breadth away from capture or betrayal.

'Have you heard from Elise?' Thierry asked her. 'I gather she's in London?'

'Yes – and well, as far as I know.' Chantelle sipped her wine. 'I mean, she's devastated about Louis, of course. They were always very close.'

'I remember.'

'But she seems devoted to her little boys, so I assume things are all right there. I hope so anyway. It did seem a little odd that the three of them moved to London without Costas.'

'You know him, don't you? The husband,' Thierry asked casually. 'Goulandris, isn't it?'

'I wouldn't say I know him,' said Chantelle guardedly. 'I've met him.'

'What's he like?'

'Not an easy man to get to know. But what about your brother?' Chantelle asked, eager to change the subject. 'Am I right he was in North Africa, with the Free French?'

'He was at one point.' An awful sadness clouded Thierry's tired features. 'But I don't know where he is now. My parents had hoped to hear from him after Tunis fell to the Allies, but there's been nothing for months.'

'I'm sure he'll be all right.' Chantelle took Thierry's hand and squeezed it. 'He's made it this far.'

'I hope so,' said Thierry. 'I just feel so guilty.'

'Guilty? Whatever for?'

'It should be me out there on the battlefield, not Laurent,' Thierry explained. 'If I'd only stopped him from leaving for Spain, he'd be safe at home now.'

'Oh, come on,' said Chantelle reasonably. 'That was years ago. And he was a grown man when he left. A young one maybe, but old enough to make his own decisions. I don't believe anything anyone could have said would have stopped him. I know Elise tried.'

'You know, it's funny,' said Thierry. 'A part of me always thought that those two might end up together.'

Chantelle had thought the same thing herself, once. It was obvious during her years in Paris that Elise held a torch for Laurent Senard. But they'd seemed to Chantelle to be so different. And really, how often did things work out in the long run with one's childhood crush?

On the other hand, Costas Goulandris hadn't been *at all* the husband she had in mind for her goddaughter. In the rare letters Chantelle had received from Athens, Elise insisted they were happy, and Chantelle tried to take this at face value. But a part of her couldn't help but wonder what might have been.

It was past midnight by the time Thérèse crawled into her bed, as bone-tired as she could ever remember being. Reaching out, she ran her hand over the dip in the mattress that was the last remnant of Louis's presence there. Over thirty years of marriage, much of it deeply troubled. But she had loved him once. For better or worse, Louis Salignac had been the companion of her life. And now he was gone.

Thérèse was not an emotional woman. Not for her the easy release of tears. Instead, she allowed the pain to settle on her chest, to seep into her bones and become a part of her. And then she prayed.

Lord, thou art my strength and my shield.
If it is your will, I ask you to shield me from this suffering.
If it is not your will, I ask for the strength to bear it.
In your son's name, Amen.

Louis was gone – her children too, at least for the present – but Sainte Madeleine remained. With all her heart Thérèse longed to be able to do what Didier had been forced to. To retreat to a religious order, to the peace of the mountains and of Christ. But if there was one thing that Thérèse Salignac did understand, it was duty. Her duty now lay with the estate. With this house, and the vineyard, both of which she must preserve for future generations.

Gunther and his men were still billeted at Sainte Madeleine, but there were no longer any cosy family dinners or civilized chats over *petit dejeuner*. Instead, an unspoken understanding now existed that Thérèse and Brolio would take their meals together at different times to the Germans, with a view to their paths crossing as infrequently as possible. Given how high tensions were in Vézelay between the townsfolk and the occupiers, and the increasing incidents of sedition and retaliation occurring right across Burgundy, there was really no alternative. Thérèse would never again be 'friends' with a German. But for as long as Gunther and his men remained at Sainte Madeleine, so must she.

Once they'd gone, and once her children returned, as Thérèse still believed they eventually would; then she would be free to go. But until then she was as trapped as one of the chateau's carved butterflies, with their flightless wings embedded forever in Sainte Madeleine's stone walls.

CHAPTER TWENTY-ONE

'By golly, it's hot. What wouldn't I give for an ice-cold bath!'

Jenny Martin, one of the British nurses, fanned her beet-red face with her hands, rolling her eyes at her friend, Anne Whitmore.

'Forget the bath,' Anne replied, whipping sweat-sodden sheets off one of the beds with practised efficiency. 'I'd sell my soul for an ice-cold gin and tonic.'

'God, yes!'

The two girls were stationed at a villa outside Rome, a crumbling medieval pile that had been commandeered by the Allies as a makeshift field hospital. It was July 1944, a month after the liberation of Rome, and although spirits were high after that joyous day, so were casualties. Young men, British, French and American, had been pouring into Anne and Jenny's 'ward', many with unspeakable injuries. Faces, half blown off by mortars, legs and arms so shrapnel-ridden there was no option but to amputate. Some poor fellows were beyond help, where gangrene had set in, or advanced sepsis. And then there were the psychological illnesses. People often referred to them as 'scars', but that term had always felt wrong to Anne. A scar was something that had healed. Most of the shaking, screaming, terrified individuals who reached for her hand in the dead of night, squeezing so tightly she feared her fingers might break, were not healed at all, but stuck in a living hell as bad or worse than anything they'd experienced on the battlefield.

'Don't "God yes" me,' said Anne, feigning crossness. 'You might be having that gin and tonic in two weeks' time. While I'll be stuck here, eating horrible leftover spaghetti for supper and sleeping in an oven.'

'They'll give you some leave soon, I'm sure,' said Jenny kindly, before groans from the next room interrupted them. 'I'd better go. That sounds like poor Sergeant Rivers again.'

Anne watched as her friend bustled off to tend to her patient. Officially, all the nurses served all the men, but unofficially most of the girls had specific casualties that they tried to work with consistently. Bonds were formed, human connections that were every bit as important to a successful recovery as the medical treatments the men received.

'Nurse Whitmore!'

The familiar, stern voice of the matron sent a shiver down Anne's spine. *Miserable old battleaxe*. With her heaving, starched bosom and permanent, glowering expression, Matron Albermarle made all the young nurses feel as if they were back at boarding school, about to get the cane.

'Yes, Matron?'

'What on earth are you doing, standing around like a mooncalf?'

'I was just—'

'We have new patients arriving. You're needed in the *sala da ballo* right this instant.'

The villa's grand ballroom, a vast, high-ceilinged affair with marble floors, a Murano glass chandelier and French doors, opening out onto the formal lawn, had been transformed into a sort of emergency room. All new arrivals were brought there first to have their injuries and condition assessed, before heading either to theatre or to one of the various recuperation or treatment wards. Cooler than the rest of the house, thanks to the permanently open doors, many of the nurses nevertheless dreaded working in the *sala da ballo*, which had become a byword for exhaustion, misery and death. But Anne actually liked the fast pace of the intake ward, that feeling of being needed and so rushed off one's feet that there was no time to worry about the heat or the screams of the dying or any of it.

'Nurse! Over here.' One of the doctors, an American, summoned Anne over as soon as she walked in the room. 'I'd like you to stay with this man, please. He's been given some morphine, but I'd like you to try to keep him conscious until we're able to move him into theatre. Legs,' he added, glancing down perfunctorily at the blood-soaked bandages covering the patient's entire lower half before moving on to the next bed.

Taking the doctor's place on the edge of the bed, Anne took the man's hand and looked at his face for the first time. His eyes were open. Lovely eyes, Anne thought, despite the pain she could read in them; dark brown like mahogany and fringed with thick, black lashes.

'What's your name, my love?' she asked him.

Thin lips, tight with pain, twitched slightly in his pale face, but Anne couldn't make out an answer. Belatedly clocking the French uniform, she tried again.

'*Comment tu t'appelles?*'

'Laurent.' He whistled the word through bared teeth, gritted tight. Then, in English managed: 'My name is Laurent Senard. If I die . . .'

'You aren't going to die,' said Anne matter-of-factly.

'Please.' His eyes bored into hers, imploringly. 'It's important. If I die, I need you to—'

'NO!' Anne interjected sternly. 'I don't have time for this

311

maudlin nonsense, I'm afraid, Mr Senard. You're not going to die. There's barely a scratch on you, look.'

They both glanced in the direction of Laurent's mangled legs. And to Anne's delight, he grinned.

'That's better,' she said, grinning back and gently pushing a stray curl back from his clammy brow. 'No one likes a whinger. We've got people here with proper injuries, you know.'

'Sorry,' croaked Laurent. Just as he was about to smile again, his eyes suddenly fluttered and closed and his fingers loosened in Anne's hand.

'Bugger,' she muttered, under her breath. 'Mr Senard. Laurent.' She slapped his cheek and tried prising open his eyelids with her fingers. 'Wake up, please. I said WAKE UP!'

By the time Laurent did wake up, it was the small hours of the morning, and the four-hour operation to save both his legs had been completed. Anne, who'd been on duty since eight that morning with no breaks besides a thirty-minute catnap in the late afternoon and a snatched supper of soup and bread around ten, was delighted to find the Frenchman both alive and in the 'minor injuries' recuperation ward. At a minimum that meant there'd been no amputations.

'Well, well, well. Mr Senard. You've come back to us.'

Laurent gazed woozily upwards at the English nurse's face. He remembered her, and fondly, although the reason for that was lost to him now, along with all sense of time passing. Had she sat by his bed hours ago, or weeks ago? He couldn't say. All he remembered was pain, and then no pain. And that, somewhere between the two, this buxom, blond girl with the freckles and the cut-glass British accent had made him smile.

'I told you you wouldn't die. Lot of fuss about nothing,'

she added, unable to hide her delight that he'd come through what must have been a gruelling operation.

'You did,' he said weakly. He tried to find a smile, to reconjure the tiny, precious flicker of happiness he'd felt before. Instead he felt the familiar numbness begin to settle.

'I'm Anne, by the way. Anne Whitmore.' She grabbed his hand and shook it, relentlessly cheerful and practical in the face of his depression and inertia. 'The good news is the doctors have saved your legs. The bad news is, it's going to take a lot of work to get them working properly again. And the even *worse* news is . . .' she leaned in close, so close that he could smell the soap on her skin and the clean, herbal scent of shampoo in her hair . . . '*I'm* taking charge of your recovery. So, you'd best get some sleep, Mr Senard. Believe me, you're going to need it.'

Laurent gripped the two wooden bars with weary fingers, feeling the strain on his wrists as he inched agonizingly forwards. It didn't help that his palms were sweating like fountains. Nor, of course, that he still couldn't put any serious weight on his feet.

'Very good.' Anne's voice cut through the muggy air cleanly, like an English razorblade through Italian silk. 'Keep going. Just a few more feet.'

It was August, and punishingly hot, but most of the men still preferred to undergo their exercise and recovery sessions outdoors, in the villa's spectacular grounds, rather than in the gloomy stable blocks converted for the purpose. Laurent was supposed to do two hour-long sessions per day, but he rarely made both unless they were outside, under the big laurel tree by the lake, and unless Nurse Whitmore was supervising. The weight of depression still hung heavy in his heart, a permanent, blanket-thick smothering of all that was hopeful or curious or alive inside him. But just occasionally, this young, perennially bubbly Englishwoman was able to break through, especially when they were outside and on their own.

'I can't,' Laurent panted, his sweat-slick palms already beginning to lose their grip.

'Try,' said Anne gently. 'Put your left foot on the ground.'

Laurent winced, his forearms shaking with the strain. 'I . . . I can't. It won't hold me.'

'I promise you it will,' said Anne. 'Try.'

'I am bloody trying!' he yelled back at her, frustration and shame fuelling an anger he hadn't known he felt until that moment. Losing his grip completely, he let go of the bars, collapsing into a crumpled heap on the grass.

'Sorry,' he muttered, once he'd finally manoeuvred his legs around to a position where he could sit up. 'I didn't mean to snap.'

'No,' said Anne, kicking off her shoes and taking a seat beside him. 'It's me who should be apologizing. I know you're trying. That was a stupid thing for me to say.'

They sat for a moment in silence, gazing back up the hill at the villa, shimmering in the heat.

'Beautiful, isn't it?' said Anne at last, with a sigh. 'Hard to imagine as a private house, though. I mean, who'd want to live rattling around in a place that size?'

'Hmmm,' Laurent nodded vaguely. Probably best not to mention that he'd grown up in a house at least twice the size of the villa. 'Where's home for you?'

'Me?' She looked surprised. It was the first personal question he'd asked her. She hoped that was a good sign. 'Well, England, obviously.'

'London?'

'God no.' She pulled a face. 'I'm not a city person at all. I grew up in a little village in Somerset. My father's a vicar. Lots of village fetes and doing the church flowers and . . . that sort of thing.' She blushed, aware that she was rambling. It didn't help that Laurent kept staring at her with those dark, intense eyes, not saying anything. 'I dare say life in France is very different. You probably have no idea what I'm banging on about.'

'Not so different. Church. *Fetes*. We had all that.'

'You must miss it.'

It was a simple enough statement, a truism that applied to everyone caught up in this awful war. But somehow Anne's words brought the darkness crashing back down. Laurent looked away, momentarily overcome with emotion. Yes, he missed it, if 'it' meant France. Chateau Brancion. His family. But the *it* he really missed was something he could never return to, something that was lost to him forever. Elise. But also the man he had been with Elise, the man who hadn't seen all the things he'd seen, done all the things he'd done. The man he could never be again.

'Is there someone special?' Anne asked, reading his mind. 'Someone waiting for you?'

'No.' His answer was instant. 'No. There's no one.'

It was October when the letter arrived. The sweltering summer that had gripped Central Italy since the liberation ended as swiftly as it began, with autumn descending almost overnight.

Hurrying outside to look for Laurent, Anne felt the cold morning air chill her lungs. It made her happy, this change in seasons, the red leaves crunching under her feet as she walked and the smell of woodsmoke in the air. Her friend Jenny had returned home, but strangely Anne herself no longer yearned for Somerset, or at least not as keenly as she once had. Perhaps because Italy felt more like England now that summer had passed, and the days had begun to shorten. But also because she could see her work here bearing fruit.

Many of the men she'd nursed since the spring had been discharged now, some back to their regiments at the front, others returning to their homes and families across Europe. The war wasn't over, but it seemed clearer now than at any time in the last five years that the Germans were going to lose eventually, and perhaps not even in the too distant future. Naturally that lifted everyone's spirits. But perhaps the single most cheering thing to Anne was the change in Laurent Senard.

She'd grown deeply fond of the quiet, brooding Frenchman over the last three months. Thanks to their physiotherapy sessions, his physical recovery had been remarkable. He was walking now and even starting to take short runs, albeit with a visible limp. But it was the psychological changes in Laurent that really warmed Anne's heart. The crippling bouts of depression that had plagued him when he first arrived had steadily grown both less frequent and less severe. And as those clouds receded, a dear, kind and thoughtful young man had been allowed to emerge like light from a long-hidden sun. Anne had come to look forward to their time together, and the rambling, eclectic conversations about everything from art to philosophy to astronomy or books. War and home were both off limits as topics, a tacit, unspoken agreement that had established itself naturally between them as the weeks wore on. But something else had established itself too: a certain closeness, an emotional intimacy that Anne had come to cherish more than was probably wise under the circumstances.

'Monsieur Senard!' Spotting Laurent jogging slowly along the lake path, she ran down the hill towards him, waving the envelope and calling him by his civilian name, a sort of running joke between them.

'Miss Whitmore!' he shouted back, in the low, resonant French accent that Anne had come to love. 'What's that?'

'It's a letter, you cretin. What does it look like?' Anne teased, hitting him playfully over the head with it before handing it over. 'Postmarked from Burgundy, France, and addressed to a Captain Senard. I wondered if you knew him?'

Normally Laurent would have joined in the joke, but this time, he couldn't. A letter! A letter from home. How on earth had they known where to reach him? Different thoughts raced through his head. Perhaps Cousin Bernard had told his parents that he'd been shipped off to Italy after the Corsican campaign?

Other men had got letters, of course. Laurent had looked on in envy countless times as friends and comrades tore open their precious envelopes, both at the front and here, at the field hospital. But after so many years of silence, so long spent constantly on the move and unreachable, the fat, handwritten envelope in his hand now felt unreal. To be touching something that, only weeks ago, his loved ones at home had touched . . .

'It'll probably be more interesting if you open it,' Anne observed archly. 'That's the way letters usually work.'

Nervously, Laurent forced a smile before carefully unsealing the envelope and pulling out the precious folded note inside.

There were three sheets, all in his mother's slanting, spidery hand, and all written on the thick, watermarked Chateau Brancion letter paper that both his parents kept on the desks in their respective studies. The smell of the paper alone moved him almost to tears. But as he read on, joy turned to anguish.

'What is it?' Anne asked, seeing the colour drain from his face. 'Laurent – has something happened?'

With trembling hands, he refolded the letter and slipped it back into the envelope. Then he looked up at her, and in a voice of utter desolation that Anne would never forget, said:

'Yes. It has. My brother Thierry.' He cleared his throat,

desperately trying to contain his emotions. 'He was diagnosed with cancer of the pancreas. The same week they brought me here.'

'Oh, Laurent!' Instinctively, Anne put her arms around him, and Laurent fell into them, sobbing.

'He died, Anne.' Hot tears streamed uncontrollably down his face. 'Thierry's dead.'

CHAPTER TWENTY-TWO

Alex returned home to Napa in June 1945, a month after the war in Europe had ended.

It was an ordinary morning at Tricycle, and Ruth wasn't expecting him, or even thinking about him. She'd trained herself not to ever since word got back to Winsome that Tyler Miller had died in the same Philippines camp where Alex was being held. Trying to imagine life without Tyler was hard enough, but the thought that Alex might not come home to her was more than Ruth could bear. If he was dead, she reasoned, she would hear about it soon enough. If not, there was nothing to be gained by torturing herself, thinking about how he might be suffering. She had a vineyard to run and a daughter to raise, and for the most part, Sarah and Tricycle between them had saved her sanity.

But ever since VE Day, the mental compartmentalizing had become harder. The newsreels were full of footage of celebration across Europe, and of joyful reunions between returning soldiers and their families. Ruth watched the news with her parents, Bob and Jean, and tried to share in the general mood of elation. But it was hard. In America, the torture continued. Fighting limped on in Asia, with the beleaguered Japanese refusing to surrender. Worse than that, Ruth had heard awful rumours flying around about

American POWs being summarily executed, rather than released, as their captors were forced into retreat.

So when the kitchen door opened that June morning and Alex was standing there, looking gaunt but otherwise well and smiling at her sheepishly, the first thing Ruth did was scream. The second thing she did was to drop Sarah's bowl of oatmeal on the floor, sending shards of china and slop flying everywhere and prompting Sarah to burst loudly into tears.

'Nice to see you too, Hank.'

They fell into one another's arms, and for the next few days remained permanently entwined, touching and embracing constantly while Sarah was awake and making love like maniacs as soon as the little girl was asleep.

Ruth felt grateful that, after almost four years apart, their love bond and mutual attraction remained intact and unchanged.

But many things *had* changed. And as the summer wore on, Ruth grappled to come to terms with them. The first, and most significant difference was in Alex himself. Before the war, they'd shared everything. But Alex never spoke about the Philippines, or the camp, or Tyler's death. It wasn't just that he didn't go into detail. He didn't speak about it at all. It was almost as if he believed his silence could erase the past, wipe clean the slate of horrors that he'd witnessed, experienced, or perhaps, Ruth wondered in her darker moments, even perpetrated? War changed all of us, after all. It wasn't impossible that Alex, faced with a life-or-death situation, might have made choices, done things, that he regretted. In as tactful a way as she could, Ruth tried to reassure him that nothing he'd done, nothing he told her about, would change her love for him. But these exchanges only seemed to increase his anxiety and unhappiness.

'It's not that, Ruth,' he tried to explain, when she summoned up the courage to ask him outright if guilt were one of the emotions holding him back. 'I mean, I *do* feel guilty. Guilty that so many died . . . that Tyler died . . . and I lived.'

'But that's not why you won't talk to me?' she prompted, desperate to understand.

'No. I can't talk because I *can't*. It's not "won't" and it's not just to you. I just . . . I can't. I closed the door and that's all there is to it.'

Ruth let it go. She had to. But she grieved for the full, free connection that they'd once had. Their marriage and love were both as strong as ever. But the open, unfettered innocence of their early union was gone, and gone forever.

The next change was Sarah. When Alex left for war she'd been a toddler, sweet and fat and cherubic, the apple of his eye. Now she was five years old, and being asked to love a man who was, at best, an idea conjured through old photographs and her mother's stories, and at worst a complete stranger. Alex, bless him, was superhumanly patient. He never took his daughter's reticence or shy, distrustful glances personally. Or, if he did, he did a heroic job of hiding it in front of both Sarah and Ruth.

'It's all right,' he'd tell Ruth endlessly, as the little girl clung to her skirts in the kitchen or hung back when the three of them were out walking in the vineyard. 'She'll come around in time. We have the rest of our lives to get to know one another. She'll fall in love with me eventually,' he added jokingly. 'All women do.'

Ruth laughed, and teased him for being vain. But in her heart, she was worried. What if Sarah didn't come around? Ruth knew their daughter a lot better than Alex did, and she could tell that, as well as not knowing him, Sarah resented her newly returned father. After all, for as long as she could remember, she'd had Ruth and the ranch and Tricycle all to herself. But now that Alex was home, she was being forced to share all three. Ruth watched her daughter's jealousy building with increasing alarm, and no practical plan in mind for how to fix it.

And then finally, there were the physical losses to contend with, all the people who had died and places that had been usurped or destroyed. Before the war, it hadn't seemed to matter much that all of Alex's close family and friends apart from her were back in France, a country Ruth had never visited and knew little about, beyond what she'd seen in movies or read in romantic novels. There was the picture of Sainte Madeleine, of course, that hung in their bedroom. And Alex's stories, and the letters from his mother that he sometimes used to read aloud to her by the fire. But the people in those letters and stories were like characters in a book to Ruth. She didn't know them, let alone love them, beyond the projected affection she extended to anyone and anything that was a part of her darling Alex. The Salignacs weren't *real*, in the sense that they played no part in Ruth and Alex's life in Napa. Not like Ruth's parents, who had known Will and loved him, who'd been there the night Ruth and Alex met, and the day they married, and the day they bought Tricycle.

But now, suddenly, Alex's family *were* real. His home, his life in France before her, had snuck into his kit bag somehow and come home with him from Asia, making their presence felt on a daily basis, and not in a good way.

'My father died, and I didn't even *know* about it till a year later.' Alex tried to explain his conflicting emotions to Ruth on one of their regular visits to Will's grave. 'None of us were at the funeral. Not one. How must that have felt for poor Maman?'

'I'm sure it felt dreadful,' said Ruth, sympathetically. 'But at the same time, my love, no one blames you. The war separated families everywhere.'

'I know that.' Alex kissed her. 'My family were separated before the war, though. I left.'

'For good reason,' Ruth reminded him.

'Yes,' said Alex. 'At least, I believed so at the time. The thing is, I'm not sure it's even about "blame". It's more, I don't know, responsibility, I suppose. That, and coming to realize that there isn't endless time. My cousin Thierry Senard was at that funeral, and now even *he's* dead. I can't tell you how shocking that is. If you'd known him, you'd understand.'

If I'd known him, thought Ruth, frustratedly. *But I didn't know him. I can't share this with you, Alex. I can't feel it the way you do.*

'I always thought that one day, I would put things right with Papa,' Alex went on. 'Just like I thought that Tyler and I would come back here together and run Tricycle. And that one day, you and I would watch Will go off to high school, and to college. Watch him getting married.'

'I know.' Ruth squeezed his hand tightly. 'Believe me, I know.'

'But those things didn't happen,' Alex went on. 'We ran out of time. They died. We lived.'

Ruth frowned, wanting to understand, but not at all sure what he was driving at.

'Yes,' she said. 'We lived. And so?'

'So now it's up to us not to waste any more time!' he said passionately. 'To meet our responsibilities now, not later. To be true to ourselves. To do what we can for the living. You understand, don't you?'

'I'm not sure,' Ruth replied defensively, removing a weed that had grown up in a crack at the base of Will's headstone. 'I think we are being true to ourselves and meeting our responsibilities. We're raising our daughter, aren't we? And making a go of it at Tricycle? I think Tyler would be proud if he could see the vineyard now.'

'He would be,' Alex agreed, hugging her fiercely. 'Please, don't take any of this as a criticism of you, my love. You're amazing and wonderful and perfect in every way, just as you've always been.'

Ruth rolled her eyes lovingly. 'OK, OK. Enough with the flattery.'

'It's me who needs change,' said Alex. 'Of course Sarah's our first responsibility. But she's not our only one. Not my only one, anyway.' He looked at Ruth pleadingly. 'My mother's all on her own at Sainte Madeleine. By all accounts the vineyard's fallen into a desperate state. Partly the war, partly Papa's mismanagement. Old Arnaud Berger's done his best, and has at least produced a vintage every year, which is quite a feat under the circumstances. But he can't go on forever, and the estate's in danger of sinking if someone doesn't take over soon and stop the rot. My brother Didier's clearly in no fit state to run a bath, never mind a complex estate like ours.'

'What are you saying?' asked Ruth. Although the sinking feeling in the pit of her stomach suggested she already knew the answer.

Alex took both her hands in his. 'I know it's a lot to ask, Hank. And you don't need to answer right away. But how would you feel about selling Tricycle and us moving to France? For good?'

By the time Laurent made it home to Burgundy, Thierry had already been buried in the Senard family vault. There had been no chance to say goodbye, in death or in life, and the pain of that fact tore at Laurent's heart. Memories of their last conversation together, the day they rode to the lake and Thierry tried to convince him not to go to Spain, haunted Laurent's fractured dreams night after night. It was almost a decade ago now, but the despair he'd felt then rose up again inside him now as if it were yesterday. *How could he have done it? How could he have treated his beloved brother so badly?*

It was the same story with Elise. The two people Laurent loved the most in the world, he had hurt unconscionably and then abandoned. It had taken more than a year, and the miracle of Anne Whitmore's friendship, to help him get over the grief of finding out that Elise was married and a mother and lost to him forever. But Thierry's death was even worse. At least Elise was still alive, still on this earth. One day, he would see her face again, touch her hand, hear her laugh, even if all those things now belonged to another. But he would never see his brother again. Never.

The weight might have broken him had it not been for his parents, whose own grief was unfathomable, and who needed him now more than ever.

'You're all we have now, Laurent,' his mother sobbed, falling into his arms the day he came home to the chateau. 'You must stay. Promise us you'll stay.'

He held her, trying to hide his shock at how frail she'd become, and how *old*, like a tiny, malnourished bird. Camille's hair was completely white now, and all the robustness and solidity Laurent had long associated with his mother was gone. If anything, the changes to his father were worse. Roger Senard looked much the same physically as he had the last time Laurent saw him. But the happy twinkle in his eye, the laughing, optimistic spirit that had always been his hallmark and had made him the man that he was, beloved by everyone who knew him; that had gone, snuffed out like a candlewick crushed between two wet fingers.

'Your mother will be all right,' Roger told his son, on one of their sad, slow walks around the chateau grounds. 'She blames herself for not seeing how ill Thierry was. But it wouldn't have made any difference. The sort of cancer he had would have killed him anyway.'

'I'm sorry I wasn't here,' said Laurent, painfully aware how inadequate those words were.

'You're here now,' said Roger, whose kindness at least remained the same. 'The estate will fall to you, obviously,' he went on. 'There's an awful lot to learn. Thierry had a lifetime to prepare for taking on the chateau, but I'm afraid you're going to have to start from scratch.'

'Let's not talk about that now, Papa,' Laurent said awkwardly. The idea of living out the rest of his days as lord of the manor was anathema enough. But the thought of trying to step into Thierry's shoes felt like sacrilege. There was no part of him, not one iota, that had ever coveted his older brother's inheritance. He hadn't wanted Chateau Brancion when Thierry was alive, and he certainly didn't want it now.

'My dear boy, I'm afraid we must talk about it,' Roger said firmly. 'This estate provides a livelihood to countless families. It's our duty as Senards not to let them down. Your mother and I won't live forever, and we're going to need practical help here long before we shuffle off this mortal coil.' Seeing Laurent wince, he put a gentle hand on his son's arm.

'It's not what any of us wanted or expected. But it's what has happened.' Tears welled in his eyes, and at that moment Laurent would have given everything he owned to ease his father's burden. 'We owe it to Thierry to do our very best.'

It wasn't until the spring of 1945 that Laurent saw Anne again.

'*I'm finally going home,*' she wrote to him, at the home farm address he'd given her, where his parents had been living during the occupation. '*Everything's being packed up here, which feels awfully strange. The last of the patients go home this week – I dare say there's an Italian aristocrat somewhere who wants his house back – and then it's our turn.*

'*I'll be coming through Paris for a few days on my way.*'

She gave him the dates. '*If you can get there, it would be lovely to see you and say, "au revoir". (Not goodbye, as you must promise to come to Somerset one of these days, whatever happens . . .)*'

Closing his eyes, Laurent could hear her cheerful, capable, relentlessly upbeat voice as if she were sitting beside him, and realized with a pang how much he missed her.

'I'm going to Paris for a few days,' he told his parents over another subdued breakfast at the chateau. 'An old friend from Italy's going to be there. We went through a lot together.'

'Of course you must see him,' said Roger, refilling his coffee cup with the slow, arthritic movements that it pained Laurent to watch. 'Thierry always stayed close to his friends from the regiment. Very important, loyalty.'

Laurent didn't have the heart to disabuse him, or the inclination to get into a conversation about Anne and her role in his life. But he set off for Paris feeling brighter than he had in months, a feeling that only intensified once he got there and saw her, standing looking rather lost outside the Gare du Nord.

'I hardly recognize you out of your nurse's uniform, Miss Whitmore,' he greeted her, smiling broadly and kissing her on both cheeks. In a tweed skirt and hat, with a green Viyella blouse tucked in at the waist, Anne looked even prettier than he remembered and about a hundred times more British.

'Well I easily recognize you without your uniform, Monsieur Senard,' she shot back. 'You never really suited being a soldier, let's be honest. If you were any good at it, you wouldn't have that limp.'

'That? Oh, no, that's just from the inferior nursing care I received in Italy. The doctors were great but the convalescent facilities were a shambles.'

'I'll give you "shambles"!' she laughed, hitting him with

her handbag. 'What does a girl have to do to get a drink around here?'

They spent that first afternoon downing cocktails at the Hotel Raphael, and the next one on a hungover but raucous tour of all the galleries and museums they could find that hadn't been either bombed, looted or repurposed. It was a far cry from the last time Laurent admired the artwork in Paris, with Elise at the Louvre before the war. Partly because so many of the Old Masters were now under lock and key in bomb-proof basements, but also because, unlike Elise, Anne knew absolutely nothing whatsoever about fine art. Monet she pronounced 'splodgy' and Renoir 'garish'. Picasso was 'all right, I suppose, if you like big noses'. But her main complaint was that there weren't enough paintings of dogs or horses on display. 'I always think a lovely dog painting cheers people up, don't you?' she asked Laurent earnestly. 'Where I'm from, dogs and horses are *very* popular.'

It took Laurent a full forty-eight hours to recognize the strange, unfamiliar, warm feeling that seemed to have invaded his chest since the moment he set eyes on Anne again. It was happiness. Not the burning, intense, almost painful happiness he used to feel around Elise. That was a happiness sprung from longing and passion, the fleeting but treasured flip side of a dangerous coin.

This was something quite different. Something easy and gentle and calm and just . . . happy. Perhaps he didn't recognize it because he'd never actually experienced it before? Even as a little boy, he'd been so intense, his pleasures always tinged with a certain anxiety, a terrible tendency to overthink things. Anne was the exact opposite personality. Practical. Straightforward. Instinctive. Optimistic. Laurent didn't need her or yearn for her the way he had for Elise. She evoked none of the same life-or-death desperation that Elise did, that over the years he'd come to believe was synonymous with love. But for the first time it struck him that perhaps that might be a good thing? That simply spending time with Anne was a good thing. Wholly, unequivocally good.

He extended his stay in Paris by a week, then by two. Anne did the same, much to her parents' consternation.

'I do feel guilty,' she told Laurent as they strolled hand in hand along the banks of the Seine, tearing chunks of bread from opposite ends of a warm, fresh baguette. They were staying in the same guesthouse but in separate rooms, and still hadn't kissed, but an unspoken intimacy was clearly starting to form between them. Anne wondered what was holding Laurent back, but she knew better than to ask him or to push. 'Mummy wrote to say she'd organized a big welcome home tea for me at the vicarage, and Mrs B had practically killed herself making trifles and jellies and whatnot. Apparently, Daddy was mortified to have to call it off and stand down half the village.'

'I'm sorry,' said Laurent, not looking remotely sorry as he watched Anne eat and thought again how pretty she looked in the early mornings with her cheeks flushed and her straw-blond hair blowing in the breeze. 'I know I'm being selfish, wanting you to stay longer.'

He tried to picture the world that she'd grown up in, the solidly middle-class, British world of vicarages and trifles and village intrigue. It sounded nice, but utterly alien. On the one hand, any world that had produced Anne Whitmore was a good world in Laurent's book. But on the other, the idea that it might try to reclaim her and leave him behind, filled him with a dread too appalling to be contemplated.

Something was going to have to give.

It was quite by chance that he ran into Chantelle Delorme, staggering out of an *épicerie* in Montmartre, laden with bags and packages.

'Laurent Senard!' Dropping her treasures on the pavement, Elise's godmother enveloped him in a heartfelt hug.

'I don't believe it. How are you, my dear? And what are you doing in Paris?'

Laurent began to explain, but it wasn't easy getting a word in edgeways.

'I was so dreadfully sorry to hear about your brother,' Chantelle prattled on, accepting his offer of help home with her shopping. 'Just an awful, awful thing. I hope your poor mother is holding up? Although I dare say it's a great comfort to her having you home safe. You're living in Burgundy, you say? The last time I was there was for Louis Salignac's funeral, but I haven't been back since liberation. Is much changed?'

They agreed to meet for dinner that evening to catch up properly. Thankfully Anne had already made plans to see a girlfriend, another nurse from Italy days, so Laurent would be able to talk to Chantelle alone.

The apartment was as he remembered it. Walking into the salon, with its big, picture windows and elegant furniture, felt like walking back into the past. *If only he could walk back into it! If only he could change it. Take back what he'd said, what he'd done.* But he pushed the thoughts aside. He knew now with certainty that that way madness lay. What was done was done.

Even so, this was the last place Laurent had set eyes on Elise, and her presence was everywhere. Clearly Chantelle felt it too.

'It feels strange, doesn't it? Being here without her.'

He nodded. 'I heard she was married.'

'Yes.' Chantelle spoke quietly, watching his reaction.

'With two boys. Is that right?'

'That's right. Andreas and Giorgios. They've been in London for some years now, since 1941, I believe. Just Elise and the children. Costas stayed on in Athens.'

Laurent nodded, not quite sure how to process this last piece of information, or what it might mean.

'Is she happy?'

Chantelle inhaled sharply. The boy deserved the truth, but she wasn't at all sure what the true answer to that question was.

'I don't know,' she admitted eventually. 'Elise and I haven't spoken properly since her wedding. I know she wrote to her mother that she *was* happy in Athens. I think she enjoyed the luxurious life that Costas was able to offer her.' Chantelle chose her words carefully. 'And I know she's devoted to her children. But beyond that,' she shrugged. 'Louis's death hit her hard, I believe. But then none of us are happy all the time, are we?'

'No,' Laurent said thoughtfully. 'No, we aren't.'

'You've met someone, haven't you?' said Chantelle.

The question took Laurent so completely by surprise, he wasn't sure how to react. 'Er, I . . . well, I, er . . .'

'I sensed it as soon as I bumped into you today,' said Chantelle, pouring him a large glass of Sainte Madeleine Burgundy. 'You seemed different. Content. Who is she?'

'Her name's Anne,' said Laurent. And little by little, awkwardly at first but then more freely, he told Chantelle about Italy, and the British nurse who had come to mean so much to him. It was a relief to talk about it. Finally to admit his feelings out loud, not only to someone else, but to himself. The fact that this was Chantelle, Elise's godmother, and that he was having this conversation here, in the last place he'd been with Elise, the *only* place they'd ever shared a bed, made it even more cathartic.

Elise was married. Elise was gone. It was time to move on.

'Will you marry this girl?' Chantelle asked, once he'd finished.

'I think so.' Laurent smiled, surprised himself by how obvious it suddenly was to him. 'If she'll have me.'

'Oh, I expect she will,' Chantelle smiled. Quite apart from

the fact that Laurent obviously loved her, what girl in her right mind was going to turn down the heir to Chateau Brancion? 'For whatever it's worth, Laurent, I know Elise loved you. And I dare say you loved her, too.'

'I did. I do,' Laurent admitted. There seemed no point in denying it, not to Chantelle.

'But great love is not always the foundation of great happiness. Try to remember that.'

After supper, Laurent embraced Chantelle warmly, grateful for much more than her delicious coq au vin. 'I'd like to see you again, before I leave Paris,' he said, slipping on his jacket. 'If I were to leave you a letter for Elise, would you make sure she gets it?'

'Of course,' Chantelle assured him. 'But think carefully before you put pen to paper, Laurent. Some things may be better left unsaid.'

Anne was still awake when he got back to the guesthouse. Still slightly tipsy after her night out with her friend, she answered the door to her room with her hair tied back, her face scrubbed bare of make-up, and wearing a white cotton nightdress embroidered with rosebuds that made her look about twelve years old.

'Oh, hello!' Her face lit up when she saw him. 'How was your supper?'

'Will you marry me?' asked Laurent.

Anne looked at him, frowned, then laughed. 'What brought this on? If you don't mind my asking.'

He shrugged. 'I came to my senses, that's all. You've brought me back to life, Anne, in more ways than you know. I can never repay you for that.'

'I don't need "repaying", you idiot. I love you.'

'So is that a yes, then?' He looked at her shyly from beneath his mop of dark curls, and any faint vestiges of doubt still lurking in Anne's heart blew away like dust in the wind.

'Yes.' Coiling her arms around his neck, she pulled his face to hers and kissed him. 'It is a yes. Yes, I'll marry you, Mr Senard.'

Later, after they made love for the first time, they lay in Anne's single bed, staring up at the ceiling in companionable silence.

'That was very nice,' she told him, squeezing his hand.

'It certainly was,' Laurent agreed, extracting a Gitane from the packet by the side of the bed and lighting it happily.

'Do you think we should live in Paris?' Anne asked, practical as ever. 'At least to begin with? I know neither of us have any money, but one seems to be able to live quite cheaply here, and I expect we can both find work easily enough if we put our minds to it. We could rent a little place, maybe even save enough to buy after a year or two.'

Oh shit. Laurent's heart sank. *I never told her about Chateau Brancion.*

Propping himself up on one elbow, he turned to face her nervously. What was it she'd said to him once about the villa in Italy, and how awful it would be to 'rattle around' in some 'great, big pile'?

'About that . . .' he began.

'Yes?'

'The Paris thing sounds wonderful. It's just that . . . there might be one *teeny* little snag.'

'A letter's come for you, ma'am. From Paris.'

Elise slipped off her silk Dior headscarf and put down her crocodile-skin handbag on the side table in the hall while the boys ran giggling past her towards the kitchen.

'Do keep it down, you two!' she yelled happily after them. They'd just spent a wonderful morning frolicking in Hyde Park and playing hide and seek among the beech trees. London in peacetime was like a city transformed, it delighted Elise to see her boys run free and enjoy themselves without a care in their little worlds.

'A letter, you say?' Elise exhaled, unpinning her blond hair that she'd grown out longer now and shaking it loose around her shoulders. 'Did you put it on my desk?'

Mrs Dalton nodded and smiled, pleased to see the young mistress so happy. She'd been through so much, poor thing, first with Mr Goulandris pretty much abandoning her to raise their boys alone in a foreign country, and then with her father's death, which had hit her so terribly hard. At least she'd started to lay off the sauce at last, a relief to everyone at Eaton Terrace, and a huge step forward in Elise's own happiness.

Sitting down at her desk, Elise kicked off her sandals and picked up the letter. It was indeed postmarked from Paris, but even without that clue she would have recognized her godmother's immaculate, cursive handwriting anywhere.

Dear Chantelle! She smiled to herself, carefully slicing the envelope open with a silver letter opener embossed with the Goulandris family crest. *How good of her still to write to me, after the way I've behaved.*

She knew she'd been distant with her godmother during the war years, and hurtfully so. Ever since she'd married Costas, in fact, and been too proud and embarrassed to admit her terrible mistake, she'd pulled away from everybody that she loved, but Chantelle especially. Elise pulled out the folded pages eagerly and began to read.

The first was a short but typically kind note from Chantelle herself, sending Elise and the boys all her love and promising to write again in the coming weeks with more news; but explaining that the purpose of this letter was to pass on another.

From Laurent.

Just seeing his name on the page sent a jolt through Elise's body that made her catch her breath. She already knew from her mother that he'd survived the war and had returned to Chateau Brancion to comfort a grieving Aunt Camille and Uncle Roger after Thierry's death. But beyond that, Thérèse had said nothing, and Elise hadn't asked, too afraid of her own emotions to probe any more deeply. But now here was Chantelle, writing that she'd seen him! That they'd spoken, and had dinner together, and that he had asked her to pass on the enclosed note to Elise, to be sure that she received it but that nobody else would know that he'd written; which she did now with love.

'*Whatever he writes, my darling, please know I am always here for you should you need or want me,*' Chantelle signed off. '*Your loving godmother, C.*'

With trembling fingers, Elise unfolded the letter from Laurent.

She read it once, then twice, before refolding it and placing it lovingly and with infinite care into her top desk drawer and locking it with a small gold key. Then she got up and calmly informed Mrs Dalton that she wouldn't be joining the children for lunch and that she needed the rest of the afternoon to see to some 'important business' and mustn't under any circumstances be disturbed.

Years later, she would remember the contents of Laurent's note word for word. What he wrote shattered her. And yet at the same time, it was the most precious, most beautiful letter she had ever received.

'*My beloved Elise,*' he began.

Firstly, let me congratulate you on your marriage and the birth of your sons. Although it has been many long years now since we saw one another, I know that you have always been a deeply loving and maternal person. I have no doubt that you are a wonderful mother.

Secondly, I want to apologize, from the bottom of my heart, for the cruel manner in which I behaved that night in Paris, when I left for Spain. I was young, and I was frightened. But that is no excuse. If you knew how my behaviour that night has haunted me these last nine years; how I longed to take back every word and gesture; you would at least have the satisfaction of knowing that my crime did not go unpunished. And that for every moment of pain I caused you, I suffered a hundred such moments in my own heart. I am so sorry, my Elise.

'My Elise.' If only she were his! If only that were true. Elise had broken off at this point and taken a moment to compose herself. She'd tried so hard to forget that night, to block it out. But Laurent's words brought all the old anguish, and all the love, flooding back. The more he wrote, the worse it got.

I must be honest and tell you that when I first learned of your marriage, my reaction was a selfish one. Foolishly, perhaps, I had hoped that if I made it home alive, I might have the chance to right some of the wrongs I did to you. That I might eventually win your heart, as you had long ago won mine.

Tears streamed down Elise's face as she read on. Could he really not have known that he had always had her heart? Always, always, always, since the day of her first communion, or perhaps even before then? Since the day she first saw him, chasing after the rare butterfly at Sainte Madeleine with her net. Didn't he know that the seeds of her love had been planted long ago, somewhere deep in the mists of childhood, in another life?

336

Arrogantly, I imagined your life frozen while mine changed. I pictured you in Paris, or at Sainte Madeleine, still a girl, when all along you were in Athens and then in London, a woman with a life and family of your own. I tell you frankly, Elise, that for a long time my heart was broken. And the worst part of it was that I had no one but myself to blame.

I could not have written to you then, even had I known where to send a letter. I had no noble feeling to offer. No kindness. No generosity of spirit. None of the things that I wanted so badly to give to you.

I am writing to you now because that has changed. I can find comfort now in your happiness, because I have found happiness of my own.

'Happiness.' Elise mumbled the word aloud. When was the last time she had been happy? Truly happy? Not since before Costas, that was for sure. She wanted to trace her happiness back to Laurent, to the last time she was with him. But even then there had been conflict, her love for him interwoven with anxiety and pain. Closing her eyes, she realized that the last time she'd been fully happy was probably in her teens, back at Sainte Madeleine. It was leaving the chateau that had been her biggest mistake, the beginning of all the sadness that had followed.

'*I have met someone, Elise,*' Laurent wrote. '*An English girl named Anne who nursed me in Italy, and who has been the truest of friends to me.*'

Elise swallowed and focused on her breathing, the way she used to after Costas would hit her. *In. Out. In. Out. Let it pass.* She forced herself to read on.

Anne is as good and kind a person as you could hope to meet. I have asked her to marry me, and she has said yes.

In. Out.

Yet after everything that has happened, I find myself in need of your blessing. Elise, I love you. I always have and I always will. I feel no guilt in admitting it, because it's the truth and because it is beyond my power to change. But you are married with children. Your life has moved on, and so must mine. I hope, one day, to have a family of my own, and to let something good spring from all the pain and loss that we have lived through.

I know that you understand. And I hope that you can find it in your heart to give me the blessing that, for too long, I was not man enough to give to you.

God bless you, Elise. And know that if you need me, I am here for you always,

Laurent

Dear God, where to begin?

She must reply. Today. Send a letter back to Chantelle in Paris. But what should she say? How to respond in kind to such an outpouring of love without ruining his present happiness? Because that, Elise determined absolutely, she must not do. Whatever she wrote, she must cause no harm. No harm to Laurent, but no harm also to herself or her boys.

It struck her forcefully in that moment that she was no longer the wilful, free-spirited, stubborn young girl that Laurent had known and loved. Never again could she act wholly and completely for herself. Being a wife mattered not a jot to Elise. Whatever claims to her love or loyalty Costas might have had, he squandered long ago. But being a mother was everything. She had lost Sainte Madeleine. She had lost Laurent. But she still had Andreas and Georgios. They were her life now.

And she *had* lost Laurent, she reminded herself sternly. She must face that reality now. Elise had never met this 'Anne' and was not a good enough person to sacrifice her own life's happiness for a stranger. If this Englishwoman were all that stood between her and being with the love of her life, Elise would have trampled over her rival's heart without a moment's hesitation. But of course, she wasn't.

There was Costas. Living separate lives was one thing. But if Elise attempted to divorce him, he would take their sons back to Greece and she would never see them again. He'd said as much once, explicitly, during one of his rage-fuelled rants about her staying in London, aware perhaps belatedly that he'd been manipulated into letting her go in the first place. Elise had no reason to doubt that he would make good on his threats. Divorce was not, and could never be, an option.

And then there was Laurent himself, who'd always been so much more moral and upstanding than she was, at least in Elise's own eyes. Elise might be willing to take an 'all's fair in love and war' approach to Anne's feelings, but Laurent would never behave dishonourably. It was one of the things she loved most about him.

No. The deed was done. There was nothing for it but to give her blessing, freely and without caveats. To grant him that relief, at least, as he tried to forge a life for himself back home.

To love someone enough to let them go. Wasn't that supposed to be the test? The proof that one's love was real and deep and true?

Let no one ever say that I didn't love him.

Steeling herself, Elise put pen to paper.

PART FOUR: WILLOW

1947–1970

CHAPTER TWENTY-THREE

Alex and Ruth sold up in Napa and moved to Sainte Madeleine in the winter of 1946, with seven-year-old Sarah and their new baby son Tyler in tow. And almost nine months to the day later, in the same bedroom where Alex had made his entry into the world thirty-five years earlier, their daughter, Willow Jean Salignac, was born.

With her fiery red hair, light blue eyes, and pale, porcelain complexion, she had her mother's looks times a thousand.

'No trace of my family there,' Alex joked, as Ruth attempted to put their youngest daughter to her breast. 'Just look at that *hair*! Are you sure she's mine?'

Ruth rolled her eyes. 'Quite sure. And I see plenty of Salignac,' she added, gazing down at Willow's furious, impatient little face and tightly balled fists as she waited impatiently to be fed.

The addition of a third child to their growing family was the last of Ruth's challenges. With nothing to go on apart from Alex's romantic, rose-tinted memories and one idealized painting, Ruth had been profoundly shocked by the real Sainte Madeleine. From the outside, the house was certainly ravishing, all ancient stone walls, overgrown climbing roses and cascading red *laurier* blossoms tumbling down from fairy-tale turrets. But inside, the chateau was positively medieval. Rust-brown water spewed angrily from cast-iron taps in the one and only bathroom, the kitchen was falling apart. Ruth was expected to cook all the family's meals either in the small, decrepit range oven, or on an iron griddle stretched over a constantly burning open fire. There was, thank God, a large, turn-of-the-century icebox that Alex's father Louis had purchased in Paris some thirty years earlier and installed at Sainte Madeleine, despite his wife's protestations that it was an unnecessary extravagance. In the heavy, wet heat of Ruth's first summer in Burgundy, this had enabled her to enjoy an occasional cold drink, not to mention keep meat and fish for longer than a single day. But there was no refrigerator, no gas, no electric toaster like the one Ruth and Alex had had in their kitchen in California.

Upstairs, things were not much better, with sparsely furnished bedrooms (the top-floor rooms were still lit with oil lamps!), many of which had visible mould on the walls and floorboards so bowed with age and damp they looked like the deck of a half-sunk ship. Not that there wasn't a charm to the place, or items of real value and beauty scattered amid the squalor. That was the great irony from Ruth's perspective. Priceless oil paintings hung on the peeling walls, and some fine Persian rugs had been tossed over the rotting bedroom floors, which in turn supported antique walnut beds as well as a number of exquisite Louis XV dressers and *armoires*. At first Ruth couldn't decide whether Alex's mother didn't care that the house had fallen into such an advanced state of disrepair, or whether she simply hadn't noticed. By the time Willow was born, however, she'd realized it was the latter. Her mother-in-law spent so much time at church and in prayer, thanking the Lord for Alex's safe return, that her spiritual life effectively blocked out all physical, practical matters.

'We'll sort things out bit by bit,' Alex had reassured Ruth

breezily, when she tentatively raised some of these issues. 'A lot of estates went backwards during the war.'

'Sure, but from what starting point?' asked Ruth. 'Those gas lamps in the kids' bedrooms are a serious fire risk. And no one should sleep in the east wing until we do something about the mould. God only knows what spores your mom's been inhaling.'

'You worry too much,' a smiling Alex insisted. 'Gas lamps and a bit of damp never did me any harm growing up. The kids will love it here, you'll see.'

He was right about that part. Sarah and baby Tyler did seem happy from the very beginning, roaming the idyllic gardens and spending almost all their days outside, either in the grounds or up at the vineyards, while Alex worked with Arnaud on the great 'Recovery Plan'. Money was tight. The farms that Louis had disastrously sold, and then bought back with Roger Senard's loan, had both been requisitioned by the Nazis and planted with nothing but beet and potatoes for the last three years, two staples for the occupying troops. Replanting them with the region's more traditional wheat and barley was costly and time-consuming, and even though Alex and Ruth brought in some Charolles sheep and Bresse poultry in the meantime, in the beginning it was a struggle just to break even.

As for the vineyards, they were effectively starting from scratch, planting two new, heavy-cropping varieties of Pinot in hopes of immediately boosting production, and enriching the soil with the same nitrogen fertilizers they'd used to great effect in Napa.

Arnaud Berger was not convinced. 'Better a small, quality vintage of traditional Sainte Madeleine Grand Cru than a big harvest of *le picrate*,' he warned Alex.

'I've no intention of churning out cheap plonk, Arnaud,' Alex laughed. 'I just need to get things moving again before the man from the bank turns up and starts seizing the furniture. Or my wife leaves me, whichever comes sooner.'

There was no danger of Ruth leaving. Despite her misgivings, she worked hard to make a go of things, often sitting up late into the night poring over French-language books once the children were in bed.

'No one will take me seriously if I can't speak the language,' she told Alex, whenever he urged her to call it a night. 'And I'm not having you translate for me everywhere we go. If the children can pick it up then so can I, even if my accent is *horrible*.'

'Nothing about you is *horrible*, my darling,' said Alex, planting a kiss on the top of her head. She'd spent the entire afternoon painstakingly 'restoring' the carved butterflies in the salon, gently brushing away decades of accumulated dirt and stains with a horsehair paintbrush and a bottle of white spirit. Like everybody else, Ruth had come to love Sainte Madeleine's butterflies, and her children were enchanted by them and the old family story, so it was a labour of love she was happy to undertake. But it was still hour upon hour of work, and she wanted to finish before the new baby was born.

'I see how hard you try, and I appreciate it,' said Alex, rubbing her shoulders before snaking his hand down over her round, pregnant belly. 'It will all be worth it in the end, Ruth, I promise you. I love you so much.'

Willow's birth was a magical moment for the whole household, and it felt to everyone as if it marked the official 'rebirth' of Sainte Madeleine. From the very beginning, the little girl was a force of nature. Compared to her gentle, sweet-natured older sister Sarah, and rambunctious but straightforward brother Tyler, the youngest of Alex and Ruth's children was quite the handful. Ruth often joked that her daughter 'put the "will" in "willow"', with her stubborn streak and fiery, sometimes uncontrollable temper.

Although she was named in memory of her beloved older brother, in temperament and personality she reminded Alex most closely of his sister Elise. Loving and emotional, passionate and intense, little Willow Salignac did nothing by halves. She was also ruled by the same twin stars that had governed Elise's early childhood: her older brother (Willow worshipped Tyler just as Elise had adored Alex); and Sainte Madeleine.

'Our house is the best, most beautiful, most magical house in the whole wide world!' Willow would proclaim on a regular basis, running her small fingers over the carved butterflies that Ruth had so lovingly restored. 'Don't you just love it here, Sarah? Can you believe how lucky we are?'

'Of course I love it, dearest,' Sarah replied patiently. 'I'm just busy folding these towels right now.'

Kind and naturally maternal, like Ruth, Sarah adored both her younger siblings and was like a second mother to Willow. But she was far more even-tempered than her little sister, and not at all prone to the emotional outbursts that made up so much of Willow's communication with others.

Alex put it perfectly one Christmas. At seven in the evening on Christmas Day, Tyler was playing contentedly with his new radio set by the fire in the grand salon, while twelve-year-old Sarah helped Lysette, the new maid, clear away the coffee cups. Willow, meanwhile, was passed out exhausted on the floor in a sea of crumpled-up wrapping paper, toys clutched tightly in both hands and with chocolate smeared all over her angelic, four-year-old face.

'I see it now,' Alex said to Ruth, lovingly taking her hand in his.

'See what?' yawned Ruth. She was too tired for riddles.

'The difference between our children. Sarah and Tyler are Americans,' said Alex. 'But our little Willow is French. *Cent pour cent. Non?*'

Ruth chuckled. 'Yes. Perhaps.'

But there was no 'perhaps' about it. Willow had been born in Burgundy, and her roots in its rough, acidic soil ran as deep as those of the vines growing on the hillside. The house was her castle, the estate and vineyards her kingdom, and the various characters who lived there her courtiers, an eclectic but marvellous crew.

As soon as Alex and Ruth took over the estate, Thérèse began spending more and more time at a convent-cum-religious retreat just outside Vézelay that provided rooms for paying laity, only returning to Sainte Madeleine for one weekend a month. Willow relished these visits and would happily sit for hours playing with her grandmother's rosary beads and lace mantillas, nattering away in French or learning Latin prayers by rote in return for little boiled sweets from Lourdes that looked like robin's eggs.

'Granny's so boring,' Tyler would complain. He resented losing Willow as a playmate when Thérèse came to visit and failed to see the appeal of prayer beads and a few stupid bits of old lace. 'And those sweets she gives you are *degeulasse*.'

'I like them,' Willow shrugged. 'You're just jealous because I know Latin and you don't. *Pater Noster, qui es in . . .*'

'God, shut *up*!' Tyler snapped. 'You're such a show-off. No one cares about your stupid old Latin.'

Then there was Brolio, the family nanny who'd been an old woman when Alex was born and was now practically fossilized up in the nursery, where she spent most of her days in a bath chair eating fudge and listening to sport on the radio, one of the few modern 'contraptions' that Ruth had introduced at the chateau of which the old woman approved. Willow and Tyler both enjoyed sitting with her, partly for the fudge, but also in hopes she might be in one of her chatty moods and launch into stories about the old days at Sainte Madeleine.

'Your father could be terribly badly behaved, you know,' Brolio would tell them gleefully. 'Although he was never quite as bad as *his* father.' Willow loved hearing about the antics of her dead grandfather Louis, who sounded like tremendous fun to her, despite what Daddy said about him.

But, again like Elise, Willow's most constant childhood companion was Arnaud Berger, who still worked every day up at the vineyard and for whom her father had the utmost affection and respect. Willow followed Arnaud around like a puppy. Fascinated by the vines and the soil and the whole, alchemic mystery of winemaking, she hung on his every word just like Elise used to. Ruth loved to watch the two of them, stooped old man and adoring little girl, hand in hand, strolling through the rows of Pinot Noir, thick as thieves.

'She's so happy here,' said Alex, wrapping an arm around Ruth's shoulders. They were standing in the newly planted herb garden behind the house, with a good view up the hill to the vineyard. The sun was setting and it was past time for Willow to come in for her supper, but Ruth hadn't had the heart to summon her yet.

'She is,' Ruth agreed. 'I think old Arnaud might be her best friend in the world.'

'Are *you* happy?' Alex asked nervously.

'Me?' Ruth looked at him, astonished. 'What a question! Of course I am.'

'I wonder sometimes,' he said honestly, rubbing the back of her neck with his fingers. He loved her more now than he had when they met, something that he once wouldn't have believed possible. 'I know it was hard for you, leaving Bob and Jean. Leaving home. And the state things were in here when we arrived.'

Turning to face him, Ruth stood on tiptoes to plant a kiss on his lips.

'I miss my folks sometimes,' she admitted. 'But home is

where you are, Alex. Where *we* are, no matter what state it's in. You oughtta know that by now.'

'We're going on a trip, team,' Alex announced one morning at breakfast, laying the letter he'd been reading down on the table.

'To London?' Willow asked, hopefully.

Thanks to one of Brolio and Arnaud's stories, she'd recently developed a bit of an obsession with meeting her aunt Elise and 'the Greek boy cousins' as she called the Goulandris boys. She couldn't understand why Daddy had such a cool and interesting sister, yet they never got to meet her. And whenever she asked him about it, he got all weird. Like now, with his crumpled-up face.

'No. Not to London,' Alex said patiently. 'To my cousin's house, here in Burgundy. Think of it as a mini vacation.'

Ruth raised an eyebrow, placing steaming bowls of *chocolat chaud* in front of each of the children along with broken-off hunks of warm baguette, their favourite breakfast.

'A vacation?' she gave Alex a look. 'Since when do we do those? You do realize it's less than two weeks till harvest starts.'

'All the more reason to go now,' said Alex. 'Arnaud and the guys can handle things without us for a week. It'll be fun.'

'Fun?' Ruth sounded puzzled.

'Oh, come on Hank, don't be such a killjoy.' Alex mocked her worried expression.

'I'm not being a killjoy,' Ruth protested. 'I'm just surprised. You're not generally known for your spur-of-the-moment vacation plans, honey, no offence. What brought this on?'

Alex passed her the letter.

'You remember I told you my uncle Roger died last year? I mean, he wasn't really my uncle, more a sort of third cousin. But he was a big part of my childhood, and such a lovely man.'

'I remember,' Ruth nodded. 'The one who helped your father buy back the farms.'

'*Exactement*. Anyway, his wife Camille moved into one of the smaller houses on the estate, and their son Laurent and *his* wife have moved into the big house at Chateau Brancion. They've just had a baby, and Laurent wrote, asking us to stay. It's only about fifty miles away and it's such a beautiful place.' He turned to his children for back-up. 'You'd like a vacation, wouldn't you kids?'

'Definitely!' Sarah smiled broadly. The days when she'd been wary of Alex, after his return from the war, were far behind them now. At almost thirteen, she was extremely close to her father. 'I love babies.'

'What else do they have there?' Tyler asked suspiciously. He didn't like babies.

'Everything,' enthused Alex. 'Stables full of horses. Lots of dogs, if I know Laurent. A big hay barn where you can jump off the bales. A lake with a swing . . .'

'I want to go!' Tyler hopped up and down in his seat, sold.

'What about you, Willow?' Alex asked his unusually reticent youngest child. 'Aren't you excited to meet your new baby cousin?'

'Not really,' Willow pouted. If France had a national junior sulking team, Willow Salignac would unquestionably have qualified. 'I don't see why we have to leave Sainte Madeleine for a whole *week*. Especially if we're not even going to London.'

'Because, my love,' Alex chuckled, 'believe it or not there is more to this world than our home, magical as it is. It's good to change things up every now and then.'

'Daddy's right,' said Ruth, getting excited herself at the unexpected prospect of a trip away.

'Trust me, when you see Chateau Brancion, you'll fall in love with it,' Alex told Willow. 'Everyone does.'

'Not me,' she mumbled sullenly.

A week! A whole week away from Brolio and Arnaud, and her and Tyler's new camp. And in the summer, too? Ridiculous.

'Oh. My. God. Oh my *God*, Alex!' Ruth burst into laughter in the front seat of the family Renault as they drove up the drive at Chateau Brancion. 'You didn't tell me it was Versailles. How rich *are* they?'

'A very American question, if I may say so, my darling,' Alex grinned back at her, 'and one to which I don't have the answer. But it is a rather special house.'

'It's not a house, it's a palace,' gasped Sarah, echoing her mother's astonishment.

'Where's the lake with the swing?' asked Tyler, sticking his head anxiously out of the window. 'I don't see the lake, Dad.'

'It's behind the house,' Alex assured him. 'What do you reckon, Willow? Was it worth the trip?'

'We'll see,' Willow sniffed, determinedly nonplussed. 'I just hope their dogs are nice.'

Alex couldn't help but remember Elise's reaction the first time they'd been driven up this same drive as children, and how she, too, had felt it would be disloyal to Sainte Madeleine to allow herself to be impressed by Brancion. But the Senards' chateau's magic and majesty had won her over in the end. Alex suspected that Willow wouldn't hold out too long.

'Alex Salignac.' Laurent came out to greet them before Alex had turned the engine off, with two lurchers yapping at his heels. 'You look the same, damn you, you bastard. And how long has it been? Twenty years?'

'About that,' admitted Alex sheepishly. 'Too long.'

They hugged, patting each other on the back fondly. Laurent walked with a limp, Alex noticed, slight but discernible, and a faint fan of lines had begun to form around his eyes, as darkly intense as ever. But other than that, he, too, looked largely unchanged, with no grey or receding hair to show for having entered into middle age. Indeed, the biggest difference was that he seemed to be happier and palpably more relaxed; a little more like his brother Thierry used to be, and less like his old, tense, edgy self.

Married life must suit him, thought Alex. Or perhaps it was simply that peacetime suited them all?

'This is my wife,' Alex said proudly, switching to English and putting an arm around Ruth as Sarah, Tyler and Willow tumbled chaotically out of the car. 'And our horrible children. Ruth, this is my cousin Laurent.'

'Thank you so much for having us all,' said Ruth, shaking Laurent's hand while simultaneously trying to remove a half-chewed toffee from Tyler's hair. 'Alex thinks I'm being shamefully American about it, but I simply cannot get over your house.'

'It's ridiculous, isn't it?' A blond, bosomy girl in a headscarf, with a tiny bundle of a baby strapped to her chest, emerged from the house and stood leaning against Laurent. 'When I first met Laurent, he was practically a communist. Didn't let on *at all* that he was part of the ruling classes. I thought he was pulling my leg when he first brought me here. I mean, how does one grow up in Burgundy's equivalent of Blenheim Palace and fail to mention it, even in passing? I'm Anne, by the way.'

Her accent was BBC English, like the wartime wireless announcers on the World Service, but with more warmth to it. Alex and Ruth introduced themselves, and cooed over the baby, a little boy named Edouard. Soon the whole group had decamped inside, with Alex's children scattering off like excited mice in search of their bedrooms, and Anne helping Ruth to unpack, while Laurent and Alex decamped to Roger's old study for a much-needed drink.

'She was right about you being a communist, back in the day,' Alex teased, admiring a photograph of Anne in her wedding dress. 'How the mighty have fallen, eh?' He gestured to the opulence around them.

'I was a socialist, not a communist,' Laurent insisted. 'I think I probably still am one, for that matter. Remember, I never expected to inherit Brancion.'

'I know that,' Alex said seriously. 'I was so sorry to hear about Thierry. Just awful.'

Laurent nodded sadly. 'Thank you. It was hardest on Maman, of course.'

'Of course.'

Both men sipped their wine contemplatively. There was so much to say, so many questions to ask and gaps to fill after so long an absence, it was hard to know where to begin.

'Did you ever think you'd come back?' Laurent asked eventually. 'To Sainte Madeleine? I'll be honest and say I was surprised when I first heard the news.'

'I told myself I wouldn't,' said Alex. 'I think I even believed it for a good long while. But in my heart I always knew I'd return. In an awful way, I think Papa's death made it easier.'

'Were you happy in America?'

'Very.' Alex looked surprised by the question. 'Tricycle, our vineyard, was going gangbusters, even through the war. Where we lived was idyllic. And Ruth's family were . . . are . . . lovely. We were very happy.'

'But?'

Alex shrugged. 'But life's not only about being happy, is it? The war, all the loss. It changed things. Changed me. It forced me to remember the importance of things like roots. Heritage. *Duty*. That was something my father never understood. Yours did, though.'

'Yes.' Laurent smiled nostalgically. 'Papa was a good man.'

'The best,' Alex nodded. 'Without him, I doubt there would have been a Sainte Madeleine to return to. And by the way, I'm well aware that we still have a large loan outstanding to Uncle Roger's estate.'

Laurent waved a hand dismissively. 'Papa never expected to see that money again. It was a gift, dressed up as a loan to spare your father's blushes. Forget it.'

'Absolutely not,' Alex said firmly. 'I've no idea *when* we'll be able to make good on it. We're still just barely getting back on our feet. But one day, I'll pay you back every penny. You have my word as a Salignac.'

After that, the conversation turned to family in general, both memories from their shared childhoods, when Roger and Louis were alive and in their prime, and more recent news. Alex told Laurent the latest about Didier.

'They say he's unlikely ever to be fully well, as in the way he was before. I visited him once at the convent, when we first moved back.'

'How was that?'

A small muscle at the side of Alex's jaw twitched. 'Sad. For me, anyway. He wasn't the brother I knew.'

Laurent nodded understandingly. Thierry was dead, but in a way, what had happened to Didier was worse. He'd seen these 'living deaths' before, in Africa and in Italy, men broken beyond repair by trauma and shock. For Didier it hadn't happened on the battlefield but in Vézelay town square. But the Nazis were still very much to blame.

'He seemed happy enough to see me at the time,' Alex went on. 'But afterwards the nuns wrote to me to say he'd been upset by my visit. That it had brought up too many old and painful emotions. So I don't go any more. My mother still does, though. Twice a year.'

'And what about Elise?' Laurent steeled himself to ask the one question that had been at the forefront of his mind ever since Alex arrived. He'd had no direct contact with Elise himself since their very kind, very forgiving exchange of letters in 1945, the year he married Anne. And though he thought of her often, there was a peace to knowing that that chapter in his life had been concluded with love.

'She's still in London. Last I heard.' Alex seemed to writhe on each word, like a captured butterfly being stuck with a pin. The subject of his sister was clearly a source of pain for him. But Laurent couldn't leave it there. He had to know more.

'You're not in touch?' he probed gently.

'Not . . . actively.' Alex winced.

'Do you mind my asking why not?' said Laurent. 'You used to be so close.'

'Oh, God, I know. I know, I know.' Alex sighed heavily, running a hand through his blond hair. 'Part of it's my fault. When I left for America, I didn't look back. I was angry. And ambitious, I suppose, if I'm honest. Selfish.'

'You were young,' Laurent reminded him kindly.

Alex shrugged. 'In any event, I met Ruth and we had Will and . . .' He pinched the bridge of his nose, struggling to find the right words. 'My life moved on, that's all. I think Elise felt abandoned. I didn't realize how bad things were for her, with Papa's drinking and everything. It was an awful time.'

'But since you came back?' Laurent pressed. God knew he was the last person on earth with the right to judge anybody for leaving home and not looking back. 'Was that not an opportunity to reach out? Rebuild some bridges?'

'It was, and I *tried*,' Alex said desperately. 'I wrote to her, several times. I sent telegrams, inviting her back to Sainte Madeleine. I even offered to come to London myself, saying I'd love to meet her boys, my nephews. She didn't want to know.'

Laurent frowned. That didn't sound at all like the Elise

he knew. He could imagine her angry, and stubborn. But not vengeful. 'Did she say why?'

'Yes and no,' said Alex. 'She implied that legally, she has to stay in London and can't travel to France. Reading between the lines, the Greek husband seems to be a very bad egg. I think he might have threatened her in some way, about taking their boys away from her.'

Laurent looked horrified. 'But that's appalling! Can't you do something?'

Alex gave him a reproachful look. 'How?'

'Well, I don't know exactly,' Laurent stammered. 'But if you're saying she's trapped, shouldn't someone do something to help her?'

'I completely agree, but it's difficult without knowing the full story, I only get radio silence,' Alex said with a sigh. 'Even Chantelle Delorme, who's remained close to Elise over the years, can barely get a word out of her. My sister's a proud and stubborn person, as you know. She gets that from both our parents. I also suspect she resents the fact that Ruth and I are living back at Sainte Madeleine, and trying to rebuild things at the vineyard. Almost as if we've usurped her or something. Which is ridiculous, obviously.'

Privately, Laurent wasn't sure that that was so ridiculous. He suspected that Alex had never fully understood quite how much Sainte Madeleine meant to his little sister. In the world they'd all grown up in, it had been accepted and expected that Elise would marry while her brothers took over the family chateau and estate. But Elise had always resented that idea, and kicked back against it, even as a child. And now, in these modern, post-war times, those old notions of male entitlement probably felt more unjust and anachronistic than ever. Women had run businesses and estates all over Europe during the war, while their menfolk fought at the front, and proved themselves every bit as capable as their husbands or brothers. Laurent could quite see how it might sting for Elise to be 'invited' to her own childhood home by the brother who, in her eyes, had abandoned all of them long ago.

But he kept these thoughts to himself. Instead, sensing Alex's frustration building, he said something conciliatory about how much work it must be, attempting to relaunch the Sainte Madeleine Grand Cru brand.

'You don't know the half of it,' said Alex with feeling. 'It's been hard work for all of us, but I actually think poor Ruth's borne the brunt of it, what with the children to take care of as well.' He paused for a moment, thinking. 'To be perfectly frank with you, that's another reason I've been hesitant to push things any further with Elise.'

Laurent frowned. 'I don't follow.'

Alex sighed heavily. 'Elise is so like our father. She always has been. Charming, but volatile, and a totally different person when she drinks. I love her. I do. But between the two of us, Laurent, I'm not sure I need that sort of chaos back in my life. Not now I have Ruth and the children to think about. If it were just me, it might be different.'

'Is Elise drinking?' Laurent stiffened. All these years, he'd comforted himself with a mental picture of Elise, happy and healthy in London with her sons. With the husband living in Athens, he assumed they'd come to some sort of 'arrangement' and that Elise had been left free to forge her own life. But this picture Alex was painting, of his sister lonely, trapped, resentful and even, God forbid, turning to drink, shattered the rosy fiction of his imagination.

'I don't know for sure,' said Alex, 'but that's the impression I get from Chantelle.'

'Knock, knock?' Ruth appeared at the door, looking lovely as ever but slightly frazzled, with her cheeks flushed and strands of red hair escaping from her hastily tied topknot. 'Could I possibly borrow Alex for a second? Willow and

Tyler got into it over who was getting the top bunk, and now Tyler's nose is bleeding like a firehose. I could use your help.'

'Go.' Laurent smiled, relieved suddenly for the chance to be alone with his thoughts. 'We'll talk more later.'

'You're lucky you only have one baby,' Ruth told him. 'Enjoy the peace while it lasts. Once Edouard gets older and has siblings, you'll spend half your life refereeing.'

The next few days at Chateau Brancion raced by. As the time drew nearer for them to return home, all the Salignac children were sad to go, even Willow.

'You'll miss the dogs the most, won't you?' she asked Tyler, watching her brother rolling around on the lawn with two of the Senards' six dogs. Willow herself was sprawled out under the shade of the big sycamore tree, reading a book about fairies that Great-Aunt Camille had given her, along with a beautiful string of pearls for when she was older.

'The dogs and the lake swing,' said Tyler. 'I wish we had a lake.'

'So do I,' admitted Willow, jumping guiltily when Sarah appeared at the front door and shouted at them to come in for lunch.

'Race you!' announced Tyler, jumping up and setting off for the house at a sprint.

Tucking her book under one arm, Willow tore after him. Bursting, breathless, into the hall, she stopped when she saw her mother talking on the telephone, with a serious look on her face.

'All right,' said Ruth. 'Thank you for letting me know. We were planning on driving home on Friday, but we could always come sooner if you think . . . ? Right. OK then. Well we'll leave it as it is in that case. But if he gets worse, you will call us?'

'If what gets worse?' Willow asked anxiously, once Ruth had hung up.

'Oh, hello darling. I didn't see you there.' Ruth hugged her. 'It's nothing to worry about. Poor old Arnaud's not been very well, that's all. He developed a nasty cough a few days ago, and Dr Grandsire thought he might be better off spending a night or two in hospital.'

'Hospital?' Willow blinked back tears.

'Honestly darling, it's all right. Isabelle said there was no reason for us to race back. He'll be home in a few days right as rain, you'll see.'

Willow tried to feel comforted as she followed her mother into lunch. But all of a sudden, she wanted to go home too. Swings and lakes and pearl necklaces were all very well. But nothing meant as much to her as walking through the vines at Sainte Madeleine with Arnaud, hand in hand.

Gaston, the new lurcher puppy, arrived at Sainte Madeleine in the last week of September, to a rapturous reception from both Tyler and Willow.

'We couldn't get you a lake,' Alex told Tyler. 'But we thought this little chap would be better than nothing.'

'Better than nothing?' Willow exclaimed. 'Oh Daddy, he's perfect! Just perfect.'

A week later, however, her joy turned to devastation. Arnaud Berger returned home from hospital as promised. But a few days after his discharge, he died in his sleep, at the age of eighty-one.

'She's barely stopped crying,' a worried Ruth told Alex, who was muttering under his breath as he cleared up yet more dog poop, this time from behind the sofa in the study. 'Nothing I say or do seems to help.'

'Do you want me to talk to her?'

'It couldn't hurt,' said Ruth.

She felt bad bothering Alex, when she knew his own

stress levels were sky-high. Having decided to telephone Elise, to try to break the news about Arnaud's death in person, he'd been unable to reach her and ended up leaving two messages with her British housekeeper, Mrs Dalton. This polite-sounding woman had rung back a few days later, clearly embarrassed that Elise had refused to telephone herself, and informed Alex that 'family circumstances' meant that her mistress could not return to France for Arnaud's funeral. Alex had put a brave face on it, but Ruth could tell he was hurt. If ever there was a moment for Elise to relent and try to bury the hatchet between them, Arnaud Berger's death was that moment. Elise and Alex had both grown up with him and loved him like family. But it wasn't to be.

And then there was all the worry over the estate. Before Arnaud died, he and Alex had been brainstorming about how best to relaunch the new Sainte Madeleine Pinots, while ensuring they retained both their quality and precious Grand Cru appellation. Alex was torn. On the one hand, Sainte Madeleine was an old and venerable name, a brand-advantage he was loath to walk away from, quite apart from his emotional attachment to it. But on the other, they needed to reach new customers, new markets, many of whom either didn't know the name or, worse, associated it with a label in terminal decline, a sort of faded throwback to pre-war days. Arnaud Berger had argued vehemently for keeping the traditional labels and branding, which had afforded Alex the luxury of playing devil's advocate and pushing for change. But since the old man's death, all the responsibility for the decision fell on Alex's shoulders, and suddenly he wasn't so sure.

To make matters worse, on the day of Arnaud's funeral, at the big family lunch that Ruth had organized in his honour, Thérèse had risen unexpectedly to her feet, tapping her wine glass.

'Quiet please, children,' said Alex, 'your grandmother's going to say a few words about Arnaud.'

'Oh!' Thérèse looked embarrassed. 'Well, of course, I'd be happy to talk about dear Arnaud. And perhaps . . . later. But I was actually going to tell you all some news of my own.'

An uncomfortable silence fell. Every face at the table turned expectantly in Thérèse's direction.

Clearing her throat, she blurted, 'I've decided to formally become a lay sister at the convent where I've been staying.'

'What does that mean?' asked Willow.

'Well, darling,' Thérèse went on, 'among other things it means that I must give up all my worldly possessions. Including this house.' She smiled nervously at Alex. 'I'm legally relinquishing my ownership of Sainte Madeleine in favour of my children.'

'All of them?' asked Willow. 'Aunt Elise and Uncle Didier too?'

'That's right,' said Thérèse.

Alex and Ruth looked at one another. It wasn't bad news, exactly. Rather it was just completely unexpected, and a lot to take in in such a tumultuous moment.

'Originally your father had intended to leave a third of his estate in cash to Elise, and the house and vineyard to you boys,' Thérèse explained to Alex in private after the meal. 'But of course, at this point there *is* no cash.'

'No,' Alex agreed ruefully.

'And I can't leave your sister nothing. As for Didier, obviously he's not capable of handling his share in Sainte Madeleine. So I've given you full power of attorney over his third . . .'

'OK,' Alex nodded, still somewhat in shock. 'Good. That's good.'

'Just make sure he's taken care of financially,' said Thérèse. 'I'll still be able to visit him, once I take up my lay sistership. But I don't want him worrying about money or legal things.'

'Of course not,' said Alex. 'I'll take care of everything. Have you spoken to Elise, Maman?' he asked awkwardly.

Thérèse sighed. 'I've written to her, explaining my decision and what's happening. I know you and Ruth run the place, darling, and you both work so hard. Please don't think I'm not grateful.'

'I don't think that,' Alex smiled thinly. To be honest, he wasn't sure what he thought, about any of this. Everything was moving far too fast.

'Sainte Madeleine is your home,' Thérèse went on, 'and Didier and Elise are both far away. But it wouldn't feel right leaving the entire estate to just one of you. Not when your father left no other cash or assets, to make things fair. You understand, don't you?'

Alex reassured her that he did. Although deep down it was hard not to feel a small amount of resentment. By all accounts Elise's estranged husband was as rich as Croesus and she lived in his vast mansion in London worth God knows what, presumably with a generous allowance. Meanwhile, Alex had worked tirelessly for every penny he had. More than that, ever since they left Napa, Alex and Ruth had broken their backs to get Sainte Madeleine back to a point where the vineyard was finally breaking even again. If by some miracle they eventually reached a point where they were actually turning a profit, was he supposed to hand over a third of that to Elise? Elise, who continued to shut down his every overture of reconciliation or friendship? Who never asked after him, or his family, or anything?

That conversation had been two weeks ago, and Alex had been too preoccupied with work since then to give it much further thought. And now on top of everything else, he had Willow's inconsolable grief to deal with.

He found his daughter in the dining room, sitting on the window seat, alone, with the curtains drawn, gazing mournfully at the wall. In other circumstances, the melodrama of the pose would have made him laugh. But Alex could see that the child's suffering was real. Her pale, freckled face was splotchy and red from prolonged crying, and her tangled red hair stuck out at all sorts of unusual angles, poor mite.

'Can we talk about it, Willow?'

Pulling a chair up beside her, he placed a loving hand over hers. 'I know you miss Arnaud terribly.'

'He was my best friend.' Willow's lower lip wobbled and her eyes filled up with tears. 'My *best*.'

'I know he was,' said Alex, his own heart bursting with love for her. 'And I'm sure he would have said the same thing about you.'

'Do you really think so?' For a moment, hope flickered in her eyes.

'There's no doubt in my mind,' Alex said firmly. 'But I'm also sure he'd hate to see you sitting like this, so sad, just staring at the wall.'

'No, he wouldn't,' Willow said fiercely. 'He'd understand.'

Clearing his throat, Alex tried again. 'What would he understand, sweetie?' he asked gently. 'What are Mommy and I missing?'

'That I'm not "staring at the wall",' sighed Willow. 'I'm staring at *them*. They're helping me. Arnaud would have known that.'

'Them?'

'The butterflies, of course.' Willow looked at her father pityingly, wiping her eyes on the back of her sleeve and pointing to the carved *papillons* lining the wood-panelled room. 'The Salignac butterflies. Daddy, you do know they're magic, don't you? That they can heal a broken heart?'

'Ah,' said Alex, nodding. Willow was so totally, painfully,

like Elise. 'Of course they can. How silly of me. I forgot all about the magic. So are the *papillons* healing your heart, my Willow?'

She nodded solemnly. 'They are. Not quickly. But they are. They always do, if you're a true child of Sainte Madeleine.'

'That's right,' Alex nodded sagely.

'And I am a true child,' said Willow. 'I believe.'

'I know you do, my love.'

He kissed the top of her head, breathing in the sweet, clean, childhood smell that he loved so much, and that always reminded him of her long-dead brother, William. 'How about this,' he proposed. 'I'll have Lysette bring you a plate of supper in here, so you can stay with the butter-flies. As long as you promise to go to your bath and bed on time afterwards, and not to squabble too badly with Tyler. He misses you, you know.'

'I promise,' said Willow, reaching up and hugging him. 'Thank you, Daddy. Thank you for understanding.'

A few hours later, Ruth found her youngest daughter fast asleep, still curled up on the window seat and with Gaston snoring contentedly in her lap. Stepping over the half-eaten plate of bread and cheese on the floor, Ruth gently lifted the puppy down and scooped Willow into her arms, carrying her upstairs and tucking her into bed.

'She was out like a light,' Ruth told Alex later, climbing into their bed. 'She didn't even stir.'

'I think she was exhausted, after all that crying,' Alex muttered into his pillow. He sounded exhausted himself.

'I don't think that's it,' Ruth said, kissing him on the neck. 'I think she felt better, after you spoke to her. You could see the change instantly. She looked so peaceful and content there, snuggled up with Gaston. Daddy worked his magic.'

'Not my magic,' Alex corrected her, rolling over so that

they were face to face. 'It was the butterflies. You'd under-stand if you were a true child of Sainte Madeleine,' he added, smiling.

'Oooooh.' Ruth smiled back. 'I see. Pulling rank, are we? You Salignacs are all the same.'

Alex was almost asleep when she spoke again.

'The butterflies!' Ruth sat bolt upright, like Archimedes in the bath.

'Hmmm?'

'The magic butterflies.' Ruth shook him by the shoulder excitedly. 'That's what we should do. For the rebranding. The new labels, the new name. It's so obvious, I can't believe we never thought of it before.'

'Is it?' Alex rubbed his eyes blearily.

'Of course it is,' said Ruth, sounding just like Willow. 'The butterfly is the spirit of Sainte Madeleine, right? It's who we *are*, Alex. It's our magic.'

Closing her eyes, she spread her hands wide, visualizing the new wine label, a simple, iconic image of two spread wings.

'*Papillon*,' she whispered, as much to herself to him. 'That's our new name, Alex. Papillon.'

CHAPTER TWENTY-FOUR

One fine spring afternoon, an unexpected guest arrived at the house at Eaton Terrace.

'Good afternoon. I wonder, is Mrs Goulandris at home?'

Swaddled from head to toe in a luxurious fox-fur coat, and with diamonds the size of grapes at her wrists and throat, the woman standing on the doorstep was easily the most glamorous creature Mrs Dalton had ever seen. Older, in her early sixties perhaps, she spoke with a soft French accent, deeper and more mellifluous than Elise's, and smelled of some exotic, no doubt wildly expensive perfume. On the floor at her feet was what looked like a real crocodile-skin suitcase.

'I'm afraid she's out at present,' the awestruck housekeeper answered. 'May I let her know who called?'

'Chantelle Delorme,' the vision replied. 'I'm Elise's godmother.'

'Oh! I see. I'm sorry, I didn't realize.'

'Don't be silly. Why would you? And you must be Mrs Dalton.' Extending a slender, jewel-encrusted hand, Chantelle shook the housekeeper's pudgy, bare-fingered one, smiling broadly. 'I've heard *so* much about you over the years.'

'Really?' Mrs Dalton blushed. 'Well, I . . .'

'Is it all right if I come in and wait?' Sweeping past her into the hall, without waiting for an answer, Chantelle left her suitcase just inside the door. Shimmying out of her fur, she hung it on the coat rack.

'Well!' she sighed happily, looking around and peering up the grand staircase. 'What a divine house. I must say I hadn't expected something quite so spectacular. Although I suppose, knowing Costas, he was never going to go for the understated option.' Her eyes narrowed, leaving the housekeeper in no doubt as to where her loyalties lay. 'Are the children here?'

She wandered regally into the drawing room, leaving Mrs Dalton little choice but to follow. 'I'm longing to meet them. Last time I was in London they were both away in Greece.' Sitting down in an overstuffed, Liberty-print armchair, she pulled a skinny, dark Gitane out of a silver case and lit it, taking a long, satisfying inhale.

'They're both at rugby practice this afternoon,' said Mrs D. 'But I'm expecting them back any minute. Can I get you a cup of tea while you wait?'

'I don't suppose there's any chance of a coffee?' Chantelle asked, leaning forward conspiratorially. 'I realize that's sacrilege here in London, but we French never quite took to watered-down-leaves the way that you English did.'

'Of course,' Mrs Dalton laughed, taking the joke.

There was something so warm about her, the housekeeper decided, that made it impossible not to like her. The mistress could certainly use some cheering up, not to mention a little taking in hand. Perhaps this Delorme woman would be the person to do it?

It was almost midnight by the time Elise got home.

Chantelle had spent an enjoyable evening getting to know Andreas and Giorgios and settling into her palatial guest room. The boys were both sweet, but quite different from one another. Andreas, the older one, looked a lot like a handsome, youthful, blonder version of his father, and was clearly both bright and self-confident. Giorgios, smaller, darker and round-cheeked, like an adorable little teddy bear, was less articulate and forthcoming than his brother, but much more affectionate, attaching himself to Chantelle instantly and kissing and hugging her at the very slightest opportunity.

The children had gone to bed hours ago, neither of them appearing in the least bit anxious or surprised by their mother's absence. 'I put myself to bed,' Andreas informed Chantelle maturely, 'but if Mummy's not here then Mrs D usually tucks Giorgios in. He likes it.'

'I can see that,' Chantelle said, kissing Andreas goodnight on both cheeks in the French fashion. 'Out of interest, darling, is Mummy often not here at bedtime?'

Andreas looked at her suspiciously. 'You're Mummy's friend, aren't you? Not Papa's?'

Chantelle took his face in her hands. 'Andreas: I am your mother's friend, only and always,' she said solemnly. 'Nothing you say to me will *ever* get back to your father, I promise you that.'

'OK,' he said with a sniff. 'I just wanted to . . . check.'

'So *is* Mummy out a lot in the evenings?'

He shrugged. 'I wouldn't say "a lot". Sometimes.' Yawning, he kissed her again. 'Goodnight, Chantelle.'

That telling little exchange had been more than three hours ago. And now, after the loud slamming of a taxi door and much futile jangling of keys and cursing, Elise finally staggered through the door.

It took her a moment to recognize Chantelle. Or rather, to place her, in such an unexpected context. It didn't help that both her godmother and the hallway were spinning at about a hundred miles an hour, and in opposite directions.

'Chantelle!' she squealed excitedly, lurching forwards.

'What . . . whadda you *doing* here? I dinnknow . . . I didn't know you'rrrre in, you're gonna be in London?'

'My God. Elise,' Chantelle gasped, a distressed hand flying to cover her mouth. 'What *happened*?'

It wasn't simply that she was drunk. Blind drunk, drunk the way that Louis used to be. That was bad enough. But it was the physical changes that really knocked the breath from Chantelle. The once-lithe figure now doughy and running to fat. The sallow skin, greasy, thinning hair, and puffy complexion. All had turned the stunning girl Chantelle knew and remembered into a ghastly parody of her young, pre-married self.

Unable to stop herself, Chantelle started to cry. Confused, Elise stumbled towards her, reaching out an arm to offer comfort. But she lost her footing on the edge of the rug and fell face first onto the floor.

The thud brought Mrs Dalton running. 'Oh Lord!' she sighed, seeing her mistress's prone, motionless form. 'Not again.'

In her old-fashioned, woollen dressing gown and slippers and with her hair tied up in curlers, the poor woman looked exhausted. And no wonder, thought Chantelle, if this is what Elise's life had become.

'I should have come sooner,' she said guiltily, squatting down and rolling Elise onto her side. Loud, rhythmic breathing that was almost a snore, reassured her that her goddaughter was alive. Alive but out cold. 'Have the boys seen her like this?'

'No,' Mrs Dalton said firmly, and with a touch of pride. 'Never. I always get her into bed in the end, and out of sight.'

'By yourself?' Chantelle's eyes widened.

'Mr Evans usually helps me. The butler. Tonight's his night off though, unfortunately.'

'Lucky I'm here, then,' said Chantelle, rolling up the

sleeves of her nightgown. 'Come on. You take one side and I'll take the other.'

When Elise awoke the next morning, she was in the back seat of a Daimler. A rough tartan travel blanket covered her lower body, and she was wearing an old cotton nightgown that she hadn't put on in years, with her hair pulled back in simple black elastic.

'Where am I?' she croaked. Dear God, her throat was on *fire*. Her head throbbed as if someone had removed her heart from her chest and transplanted it into her skull. *Boom, boom, boom.*

'Don't talk.' Chantelle's voice floated back from the driver's seat. 'Sip some water if you can, Elise. I left a bottle back there for you.'

So I wasn't dreaming. Chantelle really did come!

Elise mentally reached for the happiness that ought to have accompanied this realization, but it refused to come. Something was wrong.

'Where am I?' she asked again. 'Where are the boys?'

Chantelle's only answer was to put her foot down even harder on the accelerator pedal, sending the car lurching forwards.

'I'm going to be sick,' groaned Elise. 'Stop the car.'

'I'm not stopping,' Chantelle said harshly. 'Use the bucket if you need to.'

Elise's nausea receded, replaced with a stiller, more visceral fear. Why was Chantelle talking to her like this? So meanly. And where was she taking her?

Light streamed through the car windows, and once her eyes adjusted, Elise could see that she was being driven through the countryside, hurtling along a narrow, deserted wooded lane.

'Please tell me where we're going,' Elise asked again, more meekly.

'I'm taking you to a clinic in the New Forest,' said Chantelle. 'We're almost there. They're going to help you.'

'A clinic? You mean, a drying-out place?' Elise gripped the car door as fear turned to panic.

'Yes.' Even from behind, Elise could see the rigid set of her godmother's jaw, the ruthless determination. 'You'll be staying there for twelve weeks.'

'Twelve *weeks?*'

'That's how long it takes. It's a gruelling regimen, but it works. There's a suitcase of your things in the boot.'

'No.' Elise's voice was quiet, but deathly serious. 'I won't go. I know you mean well and I'll . . . I'll get treatment, in London, I promise. But I can't leave my boys for three *months.*'

'You can and you must,' Chantelle said bluntly. 'If you don't, I will contact their father and let him know that their welfare is in danger if left in your care. I'll fly them to Greece myself if I have to.'

'You wouldn't!' Elise gasped.

'Try me.' Chantelle drove on, turning right through a set of wrought-iron gates into a long, private driveway.

'You bitch!' Elise exploded, terror and desperation getting the better of her. 'You turn up out of the blue, acting like you care, and then you try to, to lock me away? To take my boys away from me? Costas has got to you, hasn't he, hm? How much is he paying you? Because I'll pay you more. I will, I swear it! Somehow, I'll find the money. Please, Chantelle. *Please!*'

Chantelle's eyes welled with tears, but she blinked them away, keeping her eyes on the road ahead. It broke her heart to see Elise like this: frightened, threatening, pleading. But there was no way around it, none at all. She must stay strong, for Elise's sake.

Like everyone else who loved him, Chantelle had spent years watching Louis Salignac let alcoholism defeat him, trying shortcut after shortcut but never finding the courage to get serious help. She couldn't let Elise meet the same fate. Not while she had the power to change it, or at least to try.

At last they stopped in front of a charming, red-brick building in the William and Mary style, square and symmetrical like a doll's house, with elegant sash windows and its facade part-covered with thick-stemmed wisteria.

It could have been mistaken for a country house hotel, were it not for the two male orderlies in white coats who emerged and approached the car. After a few words with Chantelle, they opened the rear passenger door.

'Welcome to Greenwood, Mrs Goulandris. If you'd like to come with us, we can check you in now.'

'Chantelle, I'm begging you!' Elise sobbed, cringing away from the men to the far side of the back seat. 'Don't do this. You don't have to do this.'

'I do, my darling,' Chantelle replied, her voice breaking.

Just then the other rear door opened, and a third, strong man physically grabbed Elise under the arms and dragged her out of the car.

'No!' she kicked out wildly, spit flying from her bruised lips. 'I'll never forgive you for this,' she shouted at Chantelle. 'Never. I hope you rot in hell!'

Only once Chantelle had driven back along the drive and through the iron gates did she pull over, bury her head in her hands and cry.

'I can't do this.'

Elise looked at the nurse with horror. She was an older woman, with pinched features and a red, flaky face that looked like it had been scrubbed raw with lye soap and a boot brush. Elise hated her on sight, even before she insisted on handing her a toothbrush, a flannel and an enormous pitcher full of neat brandy.

'You can and you will,' the nurse replied matter-of-factly, setting the pitcher down next to the porcelain bowl on Elise's dresser and pressing the toothbrush into her shaking hand. 'Immersion therapy is a vital part of the programme here at Greenwood, mandatory for all our patients. I'll see you in the morning, Mrs Goulandris.'

Stunned, Elise watched her bedroom door close, then heard it lock. There was no water in the room. No soap. No lavatory. No facilities of any kind except a bed, a chamber pot, and the brandy. Elise was expected to brush her teeth in it. To wash her face with it. To bathe in it. The idea was that at some point a revulsion instinct would kick in that was stronger than the instinct to drink. In a week or two, supposedly, patients could no longer stand the sight or smell of whatever had been their drink of choice and were 'cured'. The ones who didn't die first, that is. Or go mad.

Staring at her reflection in the mirror, Elise wondered if she were already mad.

How had she been reduced to this? The horror. The humiliation. How was this her life? Tossing the toothbrush aside in disgust, she lay down, trembling, on the bed.

She wouldn't do it. She wouldn't touch that pitcher. Wouldn't look at the brandy, wouldn't smell it. Nothing.

I am not an animal. I am a human being. I am Elise Salignac and I won't be broken.

That first night was the worst, although there were many terrible, indescribable nights. Once the worst of the physical symptoms of withdrawal began to wear off, the hardest part for Elise was having so much time alone. There was nowhere to go, not just physically but mentally. No escape from one's thoughts. One's regrets. One's weaknesses.

One by one, Elise's mistakes stalked her. There was nowhere to hide.

Her failures as a mother. As a daughter. As a sister.

Her unkindness to Alex since he'd come back home.

Had anyone asked, Elise would have told them that her annoyance with Alex was a simple one. He'd abandoned the family completely, for years, and then swanned back in like the prodigal son to claim Sainte Madeleine as his birthright, without so much as an apology, to her or anybody else. Beneath the righteous anger, however, a deeper, infinitely more complicated torrent of sadness burbled and rushed through Elise's veins. Sadness and, if she were honest, resentment. Alex had everything she wanted. A happy marriage. Freedom. The chateau and the vineyard. On a primal, childish level, whenever Elise thought about Sainte Madeleine, one emotion superseded all others, trumping even Elise's lasting love for her brother: it wasn't fair.

She'd been so angry with him, and with Maman for taking his side, that she hadn't even sent flowers for Arnaud Berger's funeral. *Dear, lovely Arnaud! How could she?*

One by one, Elise's small acts of bitterness, of selfishness, came back to haunt her. Yes, she had been hurt and wronged, and shamefully so. But she had also chosen to be a victim. In the long, lonely, tortured hours at Greenwood, that truth was unavoidable.

It wasn't just the drinking she must leave behind. It was the lesser, diminished version of herself that drinking had turned her into.

If I get through this . . . when I get through this . . . life will be different.

I must find a way to bring the old Elise back.

It was mid-June when the call came through to Eaton Terrace that Elise's treatment was completed and it was time for her to come home.

Chantelle had had no contact of any kind with her since that awful day in March when she'd dropped her off at Greenwood. Nobody had. There was a strict policy of isolation and, as harsh as that sounded, the clinic's results spoke for themselves. The boys had been told that their mother was 'resting' somewhere peaceful, under doctor's orders, and that she would return to them as soon as she was well. Both seemed to have accepted this explanation unquestioningly, and though Giorgios in particular missed his mother, they had the routine of school and their sports and Mrs D to occupy them, not to mention the unexpected bonus of Chantelle's presence in the house, taking them out for treats at the zoo or the cinema and regularly letting them stay up *far* later than Mummy or Mrs D would have allowed.

Costas, helpfully, had spent the last six months on his yacht in the Caribbean with his latest paramour, and was easily fobbed off by Mrs Dalton on the rare occasions when he did call to make perfunctory enquiries after his children. And so, for everybody else, the period of Elise's treatment had passed in relative tranquillity. But as she drove once again up the winding, Hampshire drive, Chantelle couldn't help but wonder how hard things had been for Elise herself, and what version of her goddaughter might emerge from the idyllic Greenwood House.

She needn't have worried. The Elise who stood in the foyer, waiting for her, was quite unrecognizable as the dishevelled, puffy, wreck of a woman Chantelle had left here three months earlier. Slender and girlish in a buttermilk cotton shirtwaister dress and sandals, and with her longer hair tied back with a simple yellow ribbon, Elise's skin was clear and her eyes bright. Walking calmly over to her godmother, she immediately enveloped her in a hug. Delighted, Chantelle breathed in the scent of her; she smelt of shampoo and Pears soap, of health and youth and *hope*.

'I hesitate to talk about miracles,' Chantelle said once they were both in the car, side by side this time in the front. 'And heaven knows I don't want to sound like your mother.

But I can't help feeling God might have had a hand in this. I can't believe how well you look.'

'No,' Elise said robustly. 'You saved me, Chantelle. You did this.'

Reaching over the gearstick, Chantelle clasped her hand tightly. 'No, Elise. You did this. Never forget it. You can do anything you put your mind to. Anything.'

They drove on, through some of the loveliest woodland Elise had ever seen. Huge, ancient oaks and sycamores towered over a carpet of ferns and mosses, while dappled sunlight filtered through the canopy and danced off the watery surface of the myriad streams rushing below. Elise took it in this time. She took everything in, every colour, sound and scent, every breath of fresh breeze. After so long a confinement, it was like being reborn. But her principal joy was the prospect of seeing Andreas and Giorgios again, and for the first hour straight she bombarded Chantelle with questions about them. How had school been, what was new with their friends, had they both started cricket yet, and *surely* Chantelle hadn't come without a photograph of the two of them looking dazzling in their whites?

'That's the one part I feel most ashamed about,' Elise said finally, once the questions had dried up. 'Letting them down as a mother.'

To her surprise, Chantelle immediately pulled over. Turning off the engine, she looked at her sternly.

'You are a wonderful, loving mother,' she insisted fiercely. 'You've sacrificed so much for those boys. You adore them and they adore you.'

'Yes, but . . .'

'But nothing, Elise. You are a human being. Did you make a mistake, turning to drink? Of course you did. But you have rectified that mistake. Now it's time to rectify some of the others.'

'You mean put things right with Alex?' asked Elise. 'I've been thinking about him and Sainte Madeleine a lot.'

'Actually, that wasn't what I meant,' said Chantelle. 'Although I certainly think reaching out to your brother would be a good thing. But I'm talking about something more fundamental.'

Elise looked confused.

'All right,' said Chantelle. 'Let me ask you this. Why did you start drinking again?'

'Because I was unhappy,' Elise answered, matter-of-factly and without self-pity.

'Exactly,' said Chantelle. 'And why were you unhappy?'

Elise exhaled. 'That's more complicated. I was unhappy for all sorts of reasons. It's a long story.'

'I disagree,' said Chantelle. 'I think it's a short story. So short, in fact, you can sum it up in one word: Costas.'

Elise smiled wryly. 'He's certainly been a big part of it,' she admitted. 'When I first came to London, I told myself it was enough, just being here with the boys. Away from Athens. Away from him. But over time, I don't know. It got harder. Not having any freedom, or any life of my own outside of the children and the house. Not being able to go home to France.'

'Of course it did,' said Chantelle miserably. 'I should never have let you marry him. I should have done something in St Tropez.'

'Oh darling, like what?' Elise said kindly. 'You didn't know. No one knew what we were planning. But it all just . . . spiralled away from me, I suppose.' She looked away. 'And then in London, when he started again with the spies and the threats, I just sort of crumpled. I don't really know . . .'

'Divorce him,' Chantelle interrupted.

Elise laughed. 'I can't just divorce him. I'll lose the boys. I'll lose everything.'

'Rubbish,' said Chantelle. 'That's what he wants you to

think, but it's not true. It's never been true. He's been using fear to control you all these years, Elise. But the time has come to call his bluff. Do you think Costas wants a messy, public divorce case, dragged through the courts in Greece and London? Do you think he gives a damn about those boys?'

'No, I don't,' Elise agreed. 'But he *does* care about winning. Especially when it comes to me.'

'I'm sure he does,' said Chantelle. 'And don't misunderstand me, I'm not saying he won't behave spitefully in a divorce. There's every chance you'll be left with very little financially.'

'I don't care about the money,' Elise blurted, and in that instant she realized that it was true.

'Then all the more reason to do it!' Chantelle implored her. 'Divorce him, my darling. Take back your freedom! You won't lose your boys, and honestly, what's the alternative? If you return to your life the way it was before, you'll return to drinking. It's that simple. And then you'll have lost your boys *and* yourself.'

Elise opened her mouth to speak, then closed it again.

What Chantelle had just said was true. It was all true. And just like that, somewhere deep inside her, a gate that had been rusted shut for almost twenty years began, creakily, to open. Closing her eyes, Elise envisaged her spirit flying through it, like one of Sainte Madeleine's carved *papillons* coming to life.

I'm a Salignac. I'm Elise Salignac.

I'm strong and I'm brave and I can do anything.

Snapping open her eyes, she looked at Chantelle.

'You're right,' she told her. 'I'm going to do it. I'm going to divorce my husband.'

It took just over a year for the divorce to be finalized. A year in which Elise not only remained sober but began the slow and awkward process of rebuilding her relationship with Alex. Until everything was legally settled with Costas, she didn't feel comfortable leaving London. But after a warm exchange of letters, Alex came to visit her in London and met Andreas and Giorgios for the first time.

'The younger one looks just like you,' he told Elise that evening, once the boys had gone to bed. It was so strange seeing him sitting there, in her drawing room, sprawled on her Liberty-print armchair. As if the distance of the last decade and more had never happened. As if it could be wished away. Alex looked older, of course, simultaneously filled out in the middle and hollowed out in the face compared to the boy Elise remembered. But he was still handsome, and still had that same impish confidence and easy charm that made him so magnetic and likeable.

'I think Giorgios looks like Papa,' Elise reflected, the mere mention of Louis introducing a palpable awkwardness into the room that hadn't been there before.

'Yes. Perhaps,' said Alex.

And that had been the problem. Despite the love between them, and the sincere wish on both sides to leave the past behind and regain their old, easy bond as brother and sister, after everything that had happened, it wasn't quite that easy. Even the 'common ground' of Sainte Madeleine, their mutual home, full of shared and cherished memories, had become a subject fraught with emotion and complexity. On the one hand Elise was hugely looking forward to her return, once her divorce was finalized. But when Alex spoke about Sainte Madeleine, he did so unconsciously as *his* house, *his* family's home. Every discussion about the chateau was peppered with references to Ruth and his children. Understandably, of course. But the fact remained that these people were still strangers to Elise, no more than names or ideas that had no place in her own memories of her childhood home. It was hard not to feel usurped. Not to feel jealous of these mysterious people who had laid claim not just to Elise's beloved brother, whom she'd missed so terribly for so long; but in some unexplainable way to her own past as well. Sainte Madeleine was *her* identity, *her* birthright. But faced here – finally – with Alex, the more Elise felt those ties fraying, and that sense of belonging that she needed so badly slipping away.

The day that Alex left London, he'd hugged her tightly on the doorstep.

'I don't always know what to say,' he admitted, his warm breath tickling her ear through her curtain of blond hair. It was easier to talk honestly, somehow, when one didn't have to make eye contact. 'But I have missed you, Elise. I'm glad I came.'

'So am I,' Elise choked, the conflicting emotions too much for her.

I love you, Alex. In her head the words rang out, loud and clear. But what actually came out of her mouth as she let him go was a muted, 'Safe journey. Take care of yourself.'

These things take time, she told herself afterwards. The important thing was that the work of reconciliation had begun.

Elise's divorce papers came through on the same day that she dropped Andreas off for a new term at Eton.

'Do stop blubbing, Mummy,' Andreas begged her, mortified by Elise's red-eyed howling as he heaved his trunk out of the back of the car. 'It's boarding school, not prison. I'll be home again in a few weeks.'

By the time he returned for the Christmas holidays, Elise had moved out of Eaton Terrace and into a small but cosy mews cottage in Chelsea, tucked away behind the Physick Gardens. As Chantelle predicted, Costas had played hardball with the financial settlement in exchange for leaving the boys solely in their mother's care. He'd never had the slightest interest in raising Andreas and Giorgios himself and was far more concerned with preserving his fortune and financial control. But Elise could not have been happier. She had successfully bought her freedom.

Next summer, when Andreas was home for the long vacation, she would finally take him and Georgios home to Sainte Madeleine. It was all agreed with Alex, who sounded almost as excited about it on the phone as Elise was, albeit for different reasons.

'I can't wait for you to meet Ruth,' he gushed, 'and for our children to get to know one another at last. Willow, my youngest, is longing to meet you. You won't believe how alike the two of you are, Elise. It'll be like looking in a mirror.'

'I'm sure it will be magical,' said Elise, stifling her own misgivings. *You must be positive*, she told herself. *His family will probably be lovely. And Sainte Madeleine will fix whatever awkwardness there is in the beginning. Sainte Madeleine always fixes everything.*

All in all, life was as good as Elise could remember it being in a very, very long time. Having both her boys home, helping her to decorate their first Christmas tree at Holborn Mews, was the icing on the cake.

'Get that, would you, darling?' Elise asked Giorgios, as a ringing phone distracted her from positioning the angel on the top of the tree.

'It's for you,' her younger son announced a few moments later, while Elise descended the stepladder. 'Someone called Laurent.'

Elise gripped the sides of the ladder tightly.

'Are you all right, Mummy?' asked Andreas. 'You've gone white as a sheet.'

'I'm fine,' said Elise, unconvincingly. 'Just give me a moment, would you boys?'

Walking unsteadily into the hallway, she closed the door

behind her. Giorgios had left the receiver on the side table next to the telephone. Elise took three calming breaths before picking it up.

'Laurent?'

'Elise.'

His voice! Oh God. It had been so long since she'd heard his voice. But hearing him say her name, it felt like yesterday. That one word was all it took for a torrent of feelings to come flooding back to her.

'My dear, dear Elise.'

Reaching out a hand, Elise steadied herself against the wall.

'I'm so sorry to be calling you with such painful news.'

Painful? What was painful? She tried to speak, to respond to him, but her voice seemed stuck in her throat.

'Elise, are you there?'

'Yes. Yes, I'm here,' she finally whispered. 'I'm sorry, it's just . . . such a surprise to hear from you.'

A heavy sigh floated across the line.

'I know, and as I say, I'm truly sorry that the first time we speak in so long should be under these dreadful circumstances. Ruth wanted to call you herself, but I felt you should hear it from me.'

'Hear what?' Elise asked him, a feeling of dread settling in her chest. 'I'm sorry Laurent, but I've no idea what you're talking about.'

'It's Alex.' A tremor crept into Laurent's voice that sent shivers rippling over Elise's skin.

'What about him?' Elise swallowed.

'I'm so sorry, Elise. I wish there were an easier way to say it. But Alex suffered a massive stroke this morning, completely out of the blue. He was taken to Vézelay hospital but there was nothing anyone could do. He died a few hours ago.'

383

CHAPTER TWENTY-FIVE

Willow Salignac sat in the window seat in her father's study, peering out at the falling snow. A taxi had just spluttered its way up the gritted drive at Sainte Madeleine, depositing its lone, black-clad passenger in front of the house, with her suitcase beside her. Willow waited for the figure to walk up to the front door and ring the bell. But instead the woman just stood there, in the bitter cold, staring up at the house as if she'd seen a ghost.

'*Qu'est-ce que tu fais, chipie?*' Willow's grandmother Thérèse hovered behind her in the doorway. 'You mustn't skulk in here all alone.'

Tyler and Sarah both found Granny T to be distant and austere, but Willow had always felt a close bond with her paternal grandmother and loved the fact that they spoke in French together. Granny T had come to stay the day after Daddy died, ostensibly to support Ruth, although in reality her own brittle grief didn't really lend itself to the comfort of others. Alex's stroke had been so sudden and so utterly unexpected, none of them had had time to process it properly. But while Ruth focused on the children and keeping busy with 'arrangements' and practical things, Granny T preferred the comfort of her rosary beads, retreating into a Catholic stoicism that, again, left little room for others.

'I'm fine, Granny,' said Willow. 'I'm not skulking. I'm just watching.'

'Watching what? The snow?'

Willow shook her head. 'The lady. She still hasn't moved.'

Thérèse followed the little girl's line of vision towards the black-coated figure and let out a little cry. 'Good God. Elise!'

Willow looked on, bemused, as her grandmother rushed outside without so much as a shawl and proceeded to fling her rail-thin arms around the stranger, picking up her suit-case and coaxing her inside. *So that's my aunt Elise.* As a little girl, Willow had been entranced by the idea of her aunt, this mysterious woman to whom she was apparently so similar. In recent years, that had shifted somewhat. Willow understood that Elise and Daddy had fallen out years ago, and that his efforts to heal the rift between them had yielded mixed results. So the jury was out. Presumably Elise had come for Daddy's funeral tomorrow, although it was rather strange that Mummy hadn't mentioned anything about it.

A few minutes later, Tyler burst in. 'There you are.'

At eight, Willow's brother was a year older than her and a full head taller. The spitting image of Alex, he'd dissolved into hysterical tears on the day his father died, continued crying for two days straight, and then bounced back to something close to his normal self in a way that Willow couldn't understand and instinctively resented, despite her older sister Sarah's assurances that 'we all grieve in different ways, Will'.

'Our aunt's here, Daddy's sister!' Tyler announced breath-lessly. 'Come and meet her. She looks so like Daddy, you won't believe it.'

'No thank you,' Willow said haughtily, turning back to the window and the softly falling snow.

'What?' Tyler frowned. 'Don't be silly. Come and meet her. She's here for the funeral but I heard her tell Granny T she planned to stay for a week or more. Mummy's going to be so surprised when she gets back from Vézelay.'

'I *said*, no thank you,' snapped Willow. 'You go and meet her if you want.'

Willow wasn't ready to share Alex's memory yet with anyone. It felt like a betrayal.

'Well, you'll have to meet her at supper,' Tyler replied crossly. He couldn't understand why Willow was being so mean to him all of a sudden. As if she were the only one who felt sad about Daddy or was worried about Mom.

'I'll meet her at supper then,' said Willow. 'And please close the door on your way out.'

Ruth was her usual warm and polite self at supper. But it was obvious to everyone, even seven-year-old Willow, that Elise's unannounced arrival had both surprised and upset her.

'Laurent Senard told me he wasn't sure whether you'd make it back for the funeral,' she explained, passing a basket of freshly baked bread in Elise's direction. 'I just wish you'd called, so I could have made your room up properly and organized a decent welcome.'

'You must have misunderstood,' Elise replied brusquely. 'Laurent knows perfectly well I would never miss my own brother's funeral.'

You missed everything else, thought Willow, watching Elise distrustfully through narrowed eyes. *You never bothered to visit Daddy here when he was alive. Or to meet any of us.*

'Well, it's lovely that you're here and that the children and I can all meet you at last,' said Ruth, choosing to ignore Elise's abrupt manner. 'It's a shame you weren't able to bring your boys.'

'It is,' agreed Thérèse sadly. 'Why didn't you bring them, Elise?'

'I wanted to. But they had to go back to boarding school,' Elise mumbled. 'They're very strict about these things in England.'

It was an excuse, of course. Andreas and Giorgios's school would have allowed them to travel for a family funeral. And Elise had considered bringing them. But she decided in the end that she would be better able to cope alone. They'd already been through so much, what with her drying out and the divorce. They didn't need any more trauma. Plus she wanted their first experience of Sainte Madeleine to be a happy one, not one of grief and loss.

'Maybe next time you visit,' Ruth said kindly.

'Yes. Maybe.'

Elise forced a smile. She tried to like Ruth. Wanted to like her, for Alex's sake. But the traumatized, hurt child in her couldn't bring herself to do it. Sainte Madeleine was *her* home. Alex was *her* brother. Rationally Elise understood she was being unfair and unreasonable. But emotionally she couldn't help feeling that Ruth had stolen something from her, something precious and irreplaceable.

'I've put you in the blue room for tonight,' Ruth told her brightly. 'Lysette's made everything up in there and it's easily the most comfortable bed, with a bathroom right next to it, so you should be . . .'

'Actually, I'd prefer to sleep in my own room, if you don't mind,' Elise interrupted.

'Your room?' Ruth looked confused.

'Yes,' said Elise. 'After so long away it will be nice to see something familiar. You and Alex have made so many changes to the house, it's almost unrecognizable inside.'

Her tone made it plain that this was not a compliment.

'*Elise!*' Thérèse admonished her, shocked by her insensitivity and bad manners. 'Don't talk such nonsense. Of course it's recognizable. It's been updated, that's all, and thank heavens it has. You should have seen the state this house was in after the war, when Alex and Ruth first took it on. Ruth has worked absolute wonders with the redecorating.'

'Thank you, Thérèse.' Ruth looked at her mother-in-law with grateful astonishment. When Alex was alive, Thérèse had done her fair share of grumbling about Ruth's 'new-fangled' introductions at Sainte Madeleine. When Ruth's parents, Jean and Bob, had sent their daughter a state-of-the-art Kenmore electric toaster for Christmas last year, Thérèse had jumped back in alarm as if Ruth were unwrapping a bomb. So it was a surprise to hear herself being defended in front of Elise.

'I didn't mean to offend,' Elise said, slightly chastened. 'I'm simply saying that I would prefer to sleep in my own room on my first night back home. I'm sure you understand.'

Ruth shot Thérèse a panicked look. 'The thing is—'

'Oh for heaven's sake, Elise,' Thérèse jumped in, riding to her rescue. 'Your old bedroom is Willow's room now.'

'Willow's room?' Elise looked genuinely stricken.

'You haven't lived here for over twenty years, darling,' Thérèse reminded her, softening her tone slightly and reaching for her daughter's hand. 'You can hardly have expected nothing to have changed.'

'Of course not,' said Elise. But the simple truth was, that was exactly what she'd expected. The image of Sainte Madeleine, precisely as it had been in her childhood, had sustained her through her long and painful absence. Foolishly, she realized now. But so it was. Now with Alex, Papa and Arnaud all gone, Elise had been clinging to that mirage more tightly than ever.

'Less than a decade ago we had SS officers sleeping in that room,' Thérèse reminded them all with a shiver. 'We must never forget how lucky we are to have Sainte Madeleine back.'

'Never,' said Willow, with unexpected passion. She caught Elise's eye, and the two of them looked at one another appraisingly.

'You'll be very comfortable in the blue room,' Thérèse told Elise with crisp finality.

Elise nodded curtly, too emotional to say anything further. An awkward silence fell.

After a few moments, Tyler broke it.

'You know, you really look like our father,' he told Elise.

'Do I?' Elise smiled.

How strange it felt to be talking to Alex's son, and for the boy to be an American! Then again, her own boys came across as British to the bone, and though they both understood French, neither spoke it at home. Nothing had turned out as it was supposed to.

'Well, I take that as a compliment. You look a lot like him too.'

She tried to shake off the terrible feeling of sadness, but it was no use. Tonight had been hard; much harder than she'd expected. The return to Sainte Madeleine that she'd dreamed of for so long hadn't played out at all in line with her fantasy. On top of everything else, that was more grief than Elise could bear.

'I'm sorry,' she told Ruth. 'I'm afraid I'm dreadfully tired and I don't seem to be able to muster much of an appetite. I trust you won't mind if I turn in now?'

'Of course not,' said Ruth. 'I hope you sleep well.'

Tyler and Sarah were both out for the count by the time Ruth poked her head around their bedroom doors. But Willow, always a light sleeper, was still awake and wide-eyed.

'You must try to rest, my darling,' said Ruth, kissing her forehead. 'Tomorrow will be a big day for all of us.'

'I don't like her,' Willow responded bitterly.

'Who?' asked Ruth, although she knew the answer.

'Aunt Elise. She's rude.'

Ruth chuckled. 'I'm sure she's not always rude. She was probably just overwhelmed this evening. Overwhelmed, and sad about Daddy.'

'Hmmm.' Willow grunted disdainfully. 'How long is she staying?'

'I'm not sure,' said Ruth, privately hoping that it would be no more than a few days. As sorry as she felt for Alex's sister, the truth was that Elise was a stranger, and Ruth had more than enough to cope with right now with her own family's grief. Not to mention the daunting task of taking over the reins completely at the vineyard. With no Alex, and no Arnaud, Ruth would be managing the nascent Papillon label all by herself from now on.

'I want her to leave.' Willow was uncompromising. 'I feel like her being here makes things worse.'

'Well, let's just get through tomorrow, shall we?' Ruth replied diplomatically. 'And then we'll see. Goodnight, my Willow.'

'Goodnight, Mommy. I'll say a prayer to the butterflies for you.'

'Thank you, my angel.' Ruth kissed her again, touched by her childhood faith in Sainte Madeleine's magic. Willow was her father's daughter, all right. As long as she was here, Alex would never be completely gone.

'I am the resurrection and the life. He who believes in me . . .'

The priest's droning, somnolent voice echoed through the tiny stone church, but Elise wasn't listening. For the first half hour of the service, she'd been unable to tear her eyes away from Alex's coffin. A simple, dark lacquered affair, it looked too small to hold a grown man, let alone the huge personality her brother had been. The thought of him inside it was awful, terrifying. Alex had always hated the feeling of being shut in, and Elise felt an irrational, at times overwhelming urge to run over and open it, to 'let him out'.

But it passed, and as the Mass wore on she calmed herself by taking in all the tiny details of this ancient building, in which she'd spent so much of her childhood. The pattern of cracks in the wall above the altar. The faded gilt stars behind the blessed sacrament that she and Alex used to count to try to combat their boredom every Sunday, while Didier hung on the priest's every word, enraptured. How desperately long ago those days felt now! Happy days mostly, despite the tension between Maman and Papa, and the anxiety so ever present in poor Didier, even then. Papa had been embarrassed by him, and his shame had made him cruel at times. Exacerbated by his alcoholism, of course, the Salignac curse that Louis and Elise both shared. Why was it that every time she tried to remember her father fondly, some painful recollection would leap, unbidden, into her mind? *Is that how it will be with Andreas and Giorgios?* she thought sadly. *Will every happy memory be overshadowed by one of me passed out drunk on the floor, or forgetting their cricket matches or school plays?*

As if reading Elise's mind, Chantelle reached over and squeezed her hand. In a painfully chic black Stanley Sherman shift dress, topped off with a netted, Rose Descart pillbox hat, Elise's godmother was the epitome of modern elegance, and easily the best-dressed woman in the church. Chantelle had always kept up with modern designers, and the 1950s were the most exciting time in Parisian high fashion since the founding of Chanel in 1910. Just because this was a funeral, she saw no reason whatsoever to let her standards drop.

She and Elise were seated next to one another in the second row of pews, behind Ruth, the children and Thérèse.

That had stung Elise. To be second row, no longer considered Alex's most immediate family. It was particularly hard in the light of the fact that they'd really only just started the work of rebuilding their relationship as brother and sister. Naively, Elise assumed that she and Alex had plenty of time left to fix things. But she was wrong. What was done was done and could never be undone. She had never made it back to that front pew.

Laurent and his family still hadn't arrived by the time the service started. They must have been delayed on the icy roads from Chateau Brancion. Elise had resisted the urge to look behind her during the Mass and see if she could spot him, but as the congregation filed out for the burial, she couldn't help but scan the pews.

He's not here, she thought, not sure whether to be disappointed or relieved as the bitter outside air sliced into her cheeks, so cold it brought tears to her eyes. Outside in the little churchyard, she watched, shivering with the others as Alex's coffin was lowered into the frozen earth. Sarah and Tyler, both sobbing, threw the first handfuls of earth, followed by an ashen but composed Ruth. Little Willow, the youngest, refused, shaking her head 'no', her lips set in a thin, bitter line.

She's angry, thought Elise. *I don't blame her.*

Just then, to Elise's amazement, she saw Thérèse walk over and take the little girl's hand, the two of them leaning into one another for support like two saplings in the wind. A painful knot of resentment formed in Elise's chest like a tumour, making it suddenly hard to breathe. It wasn't the child she resented, but her mother. Maman had never, *ever*, behaved with that sort of compassion towards her.

'Are you all right?' Chantelle asked, her beautiful dress now enveloped in a divine, full-length couture mink. The service was over and the mourners had begun to dissipate. 'You look dreadful. Where's your coat?'

392

'I'm fine,' Elise said stiffly. 'I'm not cold.'

Chantelle opened her mouth to protest but Elise waved her away.

'I need a little time on my own, that's all. I won't be long. I'll see you back at the house.'

She wasn't conscious of time passing, or even of the cold seeping through her skin and into her bones. People were there, and then they were gone. Light began to fade. Two gravediggers came, old men from the village, and began silently shovelling loose earth back into the pit until it formed a softly curved mound at the surface. Elise stood and watched as they worked, ghostly still, her grief too deep for tears or thoughts or words. A grief not only for her brother, but for herself and for all that was lost.

At some point she became dimly aware of a hand being pressed on the small of her back, and a heavy overcoat being draped around her frozen shoulders. She heard her name spoken in a familiar voice, a lovely voice that felt at once far away and very close. She sensed Laurent before she saw him. His strength, his solidity. A smell of cologne and wool and leather. A feeling of being cocooned and cherished, of safety and warmth. And then she was in a car, and he was stroking her hair, and perhaps it was all a dream but it was beautiful, so beautiful, until at last sleep overtook her as the engine rumbled on.

CHAPTER TWENTY-SIX

In the days after the funeral, Elise's behaviour at Sainte Madeleine deteriorated from bad to worse to disgraceful.

'You're behaving like a spoiled teenager,' Thérèse told her in no uncertain terms, after another mortifying tantrum in which Elise had been unconscionably rude to Ruth, criticizing the 'ugly' and 'cheap' new Papillon wine labels.

'The butterflies look like Walt Disney cartoons,' Elise had observed caustically. 'Mass market, trite and just horribly vulgar. Nothing like Sainte Madeleine's butterflies at all.'

'I disagree,' Ruth defended herself. 'They're simple line drawings like we had at Tricycle.'

'*Tricycle?* Please,' Elise scoffed. 'Your little hobby vineyard in Napa? Sainte Madeleine has produced Grand Cru Burgundy of the very highest quality for centuries. It's hardly the same thing.'

'That's true, but I still think a modern label is vital for effective branding. Alex loved the new butterflies.'

'He was obviously humouring you,' Elise announced haughtily. 'My brother had plenty of faults, but he always had good taste.'

'Oh really? And I don't?' Ruth bridled.

'You're American,' Elise shrugged. 'It's not your fault.'

Ruth had just about managed to keep her temper on that occasion. But Thérèse had taken Elise to task afterwards.

'I really don't know what's got into you,' she berated her daughter. 'First there was all that attention-seeking nonsense at the funeral, when Laurent had to drive down to the churchyard and save you from freezing to death. As if it were all about you.'

'Leave Laurent out of it,' muttered Elise. 'He has nothing to do with this.'

Being reprimanded by her mother was bad enough. But she simply couldn't face having to explain her feelings about Laurent. About seeing him again, here, at Alex's funeral with his English wife and their baby, the picture of domestic bliss. Concerned for her, but not hers. Loving, but not in love. Or at least, not with Elise. No one could understand the pain of that, least of all Thérèse. It was the worst single moment of Elise's life and she did *not* want to talk about it.

'And then being so poisonous to poor Ruth ever since?' Thérèse went on. 'I simply don't understand it, Elise. Sainte Madeleine is Ruth's home. You're here as her guest.'

'I don't agree,' Elise protested furiously. 'I'm not a guest, Maman. It's my home too. It's our family home. Ruth's not even a real Salignac.'

'Of course she is,' Thérèse said brusquely. 'She's Alex's wife.'

'Widow,' Elise snapped.

'Sainte Madeleine may be your home emotionally, Elise,' said Thérèse, draining the last reserves of her patience, 'but you are nonetheless Ruth's guest. I hesitate to point out the obvious darling, but you don't live here. She does.'

'Only because Alex swanned in and stole it!' Elise seethed. 'He took everything for himself and you let him.'

'If you keep this up, Ruth is going to turf you out,' Thérèse warned her starkly.

395

'I'd like to see her try,' Elise scoffed.

'And I have to say, I wouldn't blame her.'

'Of course you wouldn't, Maman,' Elise said bitterly, her eyes narrowing. 'You never blame her for anything.'

Why couldn't her mother see how much she was suffering? Why didn't she care? Elise had lost Alex, lost Laurent, lost her beloved Sainte Madeleine. She needed someone to blame, and Ruth with her American accent and confidence and entitlement was an easy target. Or she would be, if only Thérèse would step out of the way.

Less than two days later, Thérèse's prediction came to pass. Elise had made a snide comment to Willow about her father that had left the little girl in tears, and Ruth had finally snapped, tearing into her sister-in-law with a venom and ferocity that Elise had had no idea she was capable of.

'How dare you disparage my husband in my house? *Our* house?' Ruth's usually soft, kind features contorted into a twisted mask of outrage. 'Alex always made excuses for you, Elise, right to the end. He always tried to see the good, because he *was* good. But you? You're the opposite. You're not good. Not decent. You're selfish and spiteful, and I won't have you around my children, do you understand? Either you pack a bag right now and leave or I swear to God I will call the gendarmes and have you dragged out of here by force. And you'd better believe I mean it!'

Elise did believe it. And with Thérèse firmly on Ruth's side, there was nothing she could do, at least not for now. A few hours later, she was gone.

That night at Sainte Madeleine, Willow rejoiced unashamedly at her aunt's banishment.

'Let's not ever have her back, Mommy. Never ever *ever*.'

Ruth chuckled. As much as she shared the little girl's sentiments, she was shocked by the ferocity of her own reaction earlier. 'Oh, I'm sure we'll have your aunt to stay again one day. And your cousins too, under happier circumstances. But I'm glad it's just us for now.'

After Ruth had gone and turned out the lights, Willow lay awake, worrying. The uncomfortable thought occurred to her that perhaps, in certain ways, she and her aunt Elise actually *were* alike, just like Daddy always used to tell her. That would explain the fact that Willow, alone amongst her family, seemed to be the one person who recognized Elise's true intentions; and what a serious threat they were.

She wants Sainte Madeleine back, thought Willow. *She wants the magic and the butterflies. She wants it all for herself.*

Well she couldn't have it.

Sainte Madeleine was Willow's kingdom now. It was her home, her birthright, her magical land. No one, not Aunt Elise nor anyone else, was going to take it from her. Not now. Not ever.

Laurent buttoned his overcoat up to the neck and thrust his gloved hands in his pockets, but still the wind sliced through him as he left his lawyer's offices and turned onto Rue Saint-Germain-des-Prés.

It was a strange time to be in Paris. Despite the lingering post-war optimism, that intangible, exciting feeling that a new, modern era was being ushered in in every aspect of cultural life – fashion, the arts, literature, theatre – an uneasy tension still hung in the air. At dinner parties and soirees, all the talk was of politics, specifically the war in Indochina and the Algerian question. Laurent had strong views on both, and was a firm believer in national independence and the end of the old order of colonialism in all its forms. But the tone of the discourse, even among his own side, worried him. There seemed to him to be a growing tide of anger and self-righteousness. A 'dangerous illiberalism of thought,' as he put it to Anne. Back home in Burgundy, and especially within the rarefied environs of Chateau Brancion, it was easy to put one's head in the sand and ignore the tumult. There, all the talk was of farming, and the revival of great old vineyards, and whose daughter was engaged to be married to whose son. But here in Paris, the shifting zeitgeist was ever present and unavoidable. It made Laurent anxious. Although, to be honest, he was anxious anyway, a feeling that had been building uncomfortably ever since his cousin Alex's funeral.

Seeing Elise again, after all these years, had been . . . What? What had it been? He still didn't know. Watching her standing, alone and frozen at the graveside, as beautiful as a marble Aphrodite; wrapping his coat around her and leading her away, almost as one would a child; he'd felt a surge of love so unexpectedly powerful it had knocked him for six. He told himself that it was the old love between them, the unconditional, cousinly bond of their childhood, resurrected now by the awful tragedy of Alex's death. But if that were really all it was, why had he felt so panicked and flustered going back inside to Anne? Why had he sat in the car beside Elise and said nothing, not a single word, but just held her frozen hand in his until she felt ready to come into the house, willing the moment never to end, sad as it was?

He'd felt better as soon as he and Anne left Sainte Madeleine and returned home to Chateau Brancion and normality. Seeing one another after so long was always going to be emotional for both him and Elise, and how much more so in the wake of Alex's death? As the days passed Laurent convinced himself that both his feelings and behaviour had been normal under the circumstances and were to be expected. That the happy life he had with Anne and Edouard, and that he cherished so deeply, was not under any threat. Even so, it had been a wrench to have to leave his family again and come to Paris, the last thing he wanted. But unfortunately urgent estate business dictated that he must.

Laurent's father Roger Senard had been a diligent steward of Brancion in many ways, but tax planning had never been his forte. Laurent's *avocat* had assured him and Anne that without urgent action, a 'significant' retrospective settlement was likely to be demanded by the Département des Finances sooner rather than later. Especially with the socialist Monsieur Mendès-France elected as premier.

'Come with me,' Laurent had begged Anne, once it was clear a meeting was needed. 'Edouard's never been to Paris. We could make a mini vacation of it, take him to see all the sights.'

But Anne had laughed off the suggestion, pointing out sensibly that Edouard was far too young to get anything out of sightseeing and was only just settling back into his routine after the trip away for Alex's funeral.

'If it were just the two of us, it would be lovely,' Anne reassured Laurent, who had been noticeably more clingy and needy towards her for some reason since their return from Sainte Madeleine. 'But you know I can't leave Edouard with your mother or the nanny, not overnight.'

Laurent did know it. That was another thing that worried him, feeding into the anxiety that was starting to become his constant companion. He strongly suspected that Edouard's 'challenging' behaviour worried Anne as much as it did him. The unexplained tantrums; the delayed speech and other milestones; the pronounced unwillingness to make eye contact or connect in any way with anyone other than his parents. But neither he nor Anne wanted to be the first one to raise these things out loud. As if saying words would make the boy's problems real, or *not* saying them might have the power to change things.

And so Laurent had come to Paris alone, for two full days of tedious legal meetings, to be broken only by lonely dinners at his hotel. He'd contemplated dropping into the Louvre after today's appointment. It was very rare that he got to spend any time in the city, and he hadn't been back to the museum since his fateful trip to the Rubens exhibition with Elise, the day before he left for Spain. But by the time he emerged from the lawyer's office he was exhausted. It was already pitch black and sleeting heavily, and the urge to return to his room for a hot bath and a cognac was suddenly overwhelming.

Hurrying along in a world of his own, Laurent turned briefly to look into the windows of the Hotel des Balcons, whose grand *salle à manger* faced directly onto the street, a warm, dazzlingly lit room of chandeliers and crystalware and elaborately laid tables. There was no 1950s modernity here, no Eames chairs with their pared-back, Scandinavian lines. The Hotel des Balcons was frozen in an earlier, unashamedly decadent time, and by God it looked appealing. Colder and hungrier than ever, Laurent brought his face closer to the glass, then suddenly stopped dead in his tracks.

It couldn't be.

But it was! Sitting at a table right there in the window, her pale, hauntingly lovely face buried deep in the menu, was Elise. She had her hair tied up in a loose chignon, and wore a simple woollen dress in light grey, that clung to her body like morning mist. Suddenly aware of the figure stopped outside, she looked up and let out a startled yelp when she saw Laurent peering in at her.

Moments later he walked in, peeling off his dripping coat and greeting her with a mixture of warmth and astonishment.

'Elise.'

Somehow it was easy to find the words here. It seemed ridiculous now, the way they'd both been struck dumb at Sainte Madeleine. He couldn't fathom what had got into them.

'What on earth are you doing here?'

She stood and kissed him on both freezing cheeks.

'I might ask you the same thing,' she smiled. 'Shouldn't you be in Burgundy?'

He explained his business, briefly, but was far more interested in hers. 'I assumed you'd go straight back to London after the funeral. I know you must be longing to see your boys.'

'I am,' she admitted, gesturing for him to sit. 'But these blasted English boarding schools have terribly strict rules, and I'm not allowed to see either of them until half-term now. And you know, it's been so long since I've been in France – before my divorce, it wasn't really possible – I decided I might as well make the most of it.'

'Are you staying with Chantelle?' Laurent asked, trying to flag down a waiter. Pleased with himself for managing to keep things friendly and normal, he nonetheless found himself craving a fortifying glass of wine.

Elise's expression clouded over. 'Actually no. I was going to stay with her but . . . no. I'm not.'

Laurent looked puzzled, but the waiter arrived before he could probe any further. 'What would you like?' he asked Elise. 'A glass of Bourgogne? Or what's your poison these days?'

'Actually, I don't drink,' she replied, blushing. 'Any more.'

Laurent hid his surprise. Putting two and two together, he looked at her with admiration. '*Deux verres d'eau, s'il vous plaît*,' he asked the waiter.

'Oh, no, please! You must have a glass of wine, I insist,' said Elise, her blush deepening. 'And you will join me for supper, won't you? I mean, you don't have plans?'

The vulnerability in her voice, the loneliness, broke his heart.

'I don't have plans,' he assured her. Although he was

starting to wonder whether some unseen force in the universe might.

The evening began well. Laurent did order some wine, the food was excellent, and the unexpected company a genuine joy. Having effectively missed the chance to reconnect at Sainte Madeleine, they both had lifetimes to catch up on, with family gossip alone enough to last them through several hundred dinners.

Only when Laurent brought the conversation back to Chantelle and why Elise wasn't staying with her, did things take a turn for the worse.

'Oh, it was nothing really,' Elise said tersely. 'I wasn't in the mood for a lecture and I told her so. That's all.'

'A lecture about what?' Laurent asked innocently.

'Ruth.' Elise pulled a face that clearly indicated it was a source of pain to her even to utter her sister-in-law's name. 'Can you believe she had the nerve to throw me out of my own house? All for making a harmless comment about my own brother, who you and I both know wasn't a saint, no matter what she might like to pretend.'

'Oh, Elise.' Laurent shook his head. 'What happened? What did you do?'

'I just told you what happened,' Elise bridled. 'And it wasn't what *I* did. It was what *she* did. Did you not hear a word I just said? She threw me out of Sainte Madeleine, Laurent. With Maman's blessing, if you can believe that. And Chantelle's.'

Unfortunately, Laurent could believe it all too easily. Through the distorted lens of her own pain, her own loss, Elise couldn't see how unreasonably she'd behaved towards Alex's grieving widow. Clearly her own mother and godmother had both pointed out the truth to her. Equally clearly, Elise didn't like it one bit. Nor did she like the pained look on Laurent's face.

'I need you to be on my side,' she told him passionately, but with the same vulnerability as before, her eyes pleading even through her defiance. 'Truly, Laurent. I do. I honestly don't think I could stand another lecture.'

He held up his hands. 'No lectures.'

'Or another speech about how bloody marvellous Ruth is, and how perfect Alex was, and how I have no rights to . . . how I . . . how Sainte Madeleine isn't . . .'

Elise's hands flew to her face. All at once, the tears she'd been holding back burst out of her.

'Oh, Elise! Don't cry, *chérie*.' Filled with compassion, and with something more than compassion that he dared not name, Laurent leaned forwards across the table and took both her hands in his, prying them away from her face, which was twisted into an expression of stark despair. 'It's all right, my Elise. I understand.'

'It's not all right!' she sobbed, entwining her fingers tightly with his.

Then, gazing at him from beneath long, wet lashes, she said it.

'I love you.'

Laurent swallowed hard. Those three words were at once wonderful, magical and awful. Part of him needed to hear them, needed to know that they were still true. But another part dreaded them. Dreaded the response they demanded, a response that was also true, but was no longer his to give.

'Please.' He held her hands tighter, his fingers caressing hers with a life of their own. 'Don't.'

'Don't what? Say it?'

'Yes,' he groaned.

'I have to,' Elise went on, still crying. 'I have to say it. I've loved you all my life, Laurent. All my life. And I know you love me, just the same.'

He shook his head hopelessly. 'Please . . .'

'It's all right,' said Elise. 'You don't have to say it back. I already know it. We both do.'

'Then why—'

'Because we must be together, Laurent. We must!'

Her voice began to rise as the desperation crept into it. Other diners were turning to look, sneaking glances at the drama unfolding between the two people by the window.

With a supreme effort, Laurent kept his own voice steady and low. 'Elise, we can't,' he whispered. 'I do love you. I do. I won't deny it.'

Elise exhaled, loosening the desperate grip of her fingers. 'Thank God.'

'But I can't leave Anne.'

Elise slumped back in her chair, deflated.

'You mean you won't,' she sighed, her voice hollow.

'I mean both,' said Laurent, truthfully. 'It's not like you leaving Costas, Elise. By all accounts your husband was a bully whom you needed to escape, and I'm glad you did. But my Anne's the opposite of that. She's been the kindest, most loving, most loyal wife I could have asked for. If I left, it would destroy her.'

'And if you don't leave, it will destroy me!' Elise sobbed. 'Again. Don't I matter? Doesn't my happiness count for anything? My heart?'

Laurent twisted his napkin miserably between his fingers. What could he say? What could he possibly say, when every word he uttered, true or otherwise, was a betrayal of somebody?

'Do you love her?' Elise forced herself to ask the question. She didn't doubt that everything Laurent had said about his wife was true. But it was this she needed to know.

'Yes.'

He looked at Elise directly when he said this, even though he knew he might as well have tossed acid into her eyes. But it was the truth, and he owed her the truth, if nothing else. 'I do love her. Not in the same way that I love you. But I do love Anne. If I could hurt her in the way that you're asking me to, I wouldn't be the man that you love.'

'Stop it.' Elise shook her head, her voice trembling. 'Stop saying these things.'

But Laurent couldn't stop, any more than she could. He needed her to know, to understand. 'I wouldn't be worthy of your love, or anyone's, if I just walked away from my family. Please, Elise. Please say you can see that.'

Pushing back her chair, shaking her head wildly, Elise turned and ran, stumbling through the restaurant and out into the lobby, desperate to be anywhere but with him. Shaking, Laurent put his head in his hands.

What was he doing? What had he done? How many times could he push her away before he lost her forever?

Upstairs in her suite, Elise locked the door, then moved like a magnet to the small icebox filled with miniature bottles of liquor. Carefully removing each of them, two cheap brandies, a single malt Scotch and a half bottle of Chablis, she lined them up along the coffee table like tiny glass soldiers and sat back on the couch, looking at them. It was two years since she'd last had a drink. Two years in which she'd pulled herself back from the brink, broken free from Costas, and more importantly from her own fears, her own demons. But right now, in the midst of her pain, her anguish, none of that mattered. The urge to reach forward and open the bottles was so strong it made her hands shake.

In the space of a few weeks Elise had lost her brother, and with him all her hopes of reconciliation. The return to her family, to France and Sainte Madeleine, that she had longed for for decades had proved to be an empty fantasy. Ashes and dust. Sainte Madeleine was no longer her home. Seized and altered, usurped by Alex's 'family' – strangers to Elise – she was no longer welcome there.

Worse, her own mother, and even Chantelle, had colluded in her banishment.

And now, to top it all off, Laurent had rejected her. *Her* Laurent, Laurent who by his own admission still loved her just as she loved him. But love, it seemed, was not enough. Another woman's heart was to be spared. While she, Elise, was to have her own hopes and dreams shattered, her own heart shredded like old paper. Unimportant. Unwanted.

Why not open the brandy? Why not numb the pain? What was there left to ruin?

Picking up one of the miniatures, she turned it over in her hand, pressing the smooth glass against her palm. How easy it would be to open it and drink. To step back into that warm cocoon of oblivion that had numbed her through the misery of her marriage and the loneliness of her exile in London.

Closing her eyes, she pictured her sons. Handsome, athletic Andreas, almost on the verge of manhood now, and dear, devoted Giorgios, as affectionate and sweet as a little bear cub. She should resist for them, she knew she should. They should be enough. But the simple, inescapable truth was that they weren't. Yes, she loved them. By God she loved them, more than life. But this battle, this awful choice to drink or not to drink; this was a part of *her*. Of Elise. It was a battle for her own soul, her own life and worth. A battle that many Salignacs had fought before her. That Papa had fought, and lost.

Time passed. How much time, she couldn't say. But eventually, as her tears ran dry, she picked up each of the bottles and placed them back into the icebox. She didn't empty them dramatically into the sink, as she had seen Louis do so many times, with doomed theatrical finality, only to restock his cellar a few months later. No. If she was going to drink, she was going to drink. And perhaps she was. But not tonight. Not right now.

The knock on her door startled her. It was late for turn-down service, and she hadn't ordered anything, but she answered it anyway, too tired to think about it any further.

Laurent stood in the doorway, as still and silent as a tree. Elise was silent too. Looking up at his face, the most beautiful face in the world, her eyes were drawn to his uncontrollably, pulled by some invisible current. Reaching up, she pressed a hand to his cheek. And for Laurent, that was the end. The unlocking of a door that he'd exhausted himself trying to keep closed his whole life. Thirty years of love and longing poured out of him like water from a burst main. Sliding both arms around Elise's back he pulled her in and up, kicking the door closed behind him as he pressed his lips hard against hers.

Staggering backwards, entwined like vines, they spun towards the bed, falling onto it in a frenzy of hands and lips and discarded clothes. Pinned beneath him, Elise tried to slow things down, pushing up against his shoulders so she could see his face, see the love in his eyes at last. She wanted to drink in every moment of this magic, this submission, to savour images and sensations, every sound and touch and smell so she could replay them afterwards, make them last forever. But Laurent was like a man possessed. Falling on her body like a starving prisoner on fresh baked bread, his hands and tongue devoured every inch of her. Neck, shoulders, breasts, belly, thighs. His fingers coiled themselves into her hair, and as his knees roughly pushed apart her legs and he powered inside of her, Elise's own hands clung to his back and shoulders, pressing deeper and deeper into the soft warmth of his skin.

He said her name, twice, its sound on his lips, his breath bringing her close to her own climax. When it came finally, as Laurent shuddered into her, panting and clawing at the headboard behind them like a lion unleashed, Elise felt as if her soul had left her body. This was more than pleasure, more than the salty, sweat-soaked ecstasy of lovemaking. It was an awakening, a prayer, a rebirth.

The day she stopped drinking she had stopped dying. But tonight, for the first time in many, many years, she had begun to live.

For the next few hours, they spoke very little. They made love a second time, a less desperate affair than the first, but equally intense. But for much of the night they simply lay and looked at one another in the darkness, running searching fingers over the other's eyes and cheeks and lips, drinking in the wonder of their love. Of feelings long acknowledged but now finally realized, consummated, blessed. They both knew it couldn't last. Everything Laurent had said downstairs earlier was true, and would always be true. If he left Anne, he would not be himself. Such an act would destroy all three of them. Tonight's miracle must stand alone. It must be enough, forever.

And yet, despite that knowledge, or perhaps because of it, there was no sadness in the air, no cloud of fear casting shadows over them. Instead, in their different ways, Laurent and Elise both felt light.

'You don't regret it, do you?' Elise asked, half asleep as the sun threatened to creep up over the horizon. Coiled tight against him, the small of her back pressed to his belly, she breathed to the rhythm of his heart as if they were one body, one spirit.

'No,' he sighed. 'Not at all.'

It was true. He had no regrets. No doubt he ought to feel guilty, but when he searched his heart for the expected doubt or remorse, there was none to be found. Anne would never know what had happened tonight. She would never be hurt by it. And Laurent didn't think he could have gone on living if he'd let Elise walk away again. If he'd let his love for her, the truest, most profound constant of his life, wither and die.

'Can I ask you something?' His breath warmed the back of Elise's ear and she felt happier than she'd ever believed possible.

'Of course. Anything.'

'Why did you marry Goulandris?'

It was the very last question Elise had been expecting. Turning around to face him, she gave him a curious look.

'I mean, was he different when you married him?' Laurent tried to clarify. 'Was he kinder, or . . .' he shook his head, aware he was probably expressing himself badly. 'I just feel sad that *you* were sad, Elise, for so many years.'

Arching her neck up towards him, Elise kissed him softly on the lips.

'Don't feel sad. It's in the past now. And I have my boys, so I can't regret it.'

'Of course,' said Laurent. 'I didn't mean that.'

'It's OK,' she shushed him. 'It's a fair question. Was Costas kinder in the beginning?' she thought about it. 'To me, perhaps, for a time. But not to others. I saw the bullying side to him even then, but I chose to ignore it. He offered me . . . other things, besides kindness. And you know, when I married him I was young and impetuous. And heart-broken,' she added, tenderly stroking Laurent's chest. 'I thought you were married.'

Laurent pulled back, horrified. 'What do you mean, you thought I was married?'

'Oh my goodness,' Elise sighed, half to herself. 'You never knew? But then how could you?'

She told him the story of what had happened in St Tropez. How the Spanish girl had come aboard Costas's yacht and told her and Chantelle that Laurent had married a fellow revolutionary from Seville. 'It was all Chinese whispers, of

409

course, but at the time I had no reason to disbelieve it,' she explained.

'Because of the way I left things between us?' Laurent asked, stricken. 'In Paris?'

Elise nodded. 'I thought I'd lost you. And Costas was there.'

She didn't go on. Poor Laurent looked as if he'd seen a ghost, or as if he might burst into tears at any moment. Overwhelmed with compassion, Elise pulled him into her arms.

'It's all right, my darling,' she whispered, rocking him gently like a mother. 'Everything's all right.'

'But . . . the *waste*!' he gasped. 'All those years!'

'It wasn't your fault. It wasn't anybody's fault,' said Elise. 'We did the best we could.'

A few hours later, after kind and tender goodbyes, a calmer, thoughtful Laurent walked along the banks of the Seine. As the sun rose, blood-red, over the city, he thought about Anne and Edouard and Chateau Brancion, the home he would return to tomorrow. His family. His life.

Then he thought about Elise. About the love he'd never stopped feeling, and of the lie, the stupid mistake, that had changed the course of their lives. Elise had married Costas Goulandris because she believed he was married. Laurent had married Anne because Elise was with Costas, and he believed he had lost her forever.

Laurent Senard: He did the best he could.

Is that what they would write on his gravestone?

The thought made him shiver.

Back in her suite at the Hotel des Balcons, Elise too was thoughtful as she carefully folded her sweaters and skirts, pressing them between sheets of tissue paper before placing them into her valise. But her emotions were quite different to Laurent's.

It was time to go back to London. To her dear little cottage in Chelsea. To her boys. To reality.

Once there, she would begin to regroup. She accepted that Laurent would never leave his family. They had had last night, and Elise knew now for certain that he loved her, every bit as fiercely and deeply as she loved him. For the moment at least, it was enough, and Elise had learned the hard way that 'the moment' was all she could control.

But there were other things – other needs, other, even older loves – that she was not yet ready to walk away from. She knew now who her enemies were, and she could see clearly all the myriad obstacles in her path. But she also knew her own strength.

I am Elise Salignac, she told herself. *I can do anything I put my mind to.*

Anything.

The next chapter of her life was hers to write, hers for the taking.

Snapping shut her suitcase with a determined smile, epitaphs were the very last thing on Elise's mind.

CHAPTER TWENTY-SEVEN

'Happy birthday to you, happy birthday to you. Happy birthday dear Will-oooooow . . .'

'You belong in a zoo!'

Tyler finished the song, ignoring his grandparents' eye-rolls and his mother's half-hearted frown. It was so great having Nana Jean and Grandpa Bob at Sainte Madeleine for the summer, nothing could dampen his spirits, especially now that he and Willow were buddies again.

'How does it feel to be ten, Willamina?' Bob Ballard asked, stooping over to kiss his youngest granddaughter on the top of her fiery red head. They were celebrating Willow's big day in the new tasting room up at Papillon, as the Sainte Madeleine winery was now officially known, and the birthday girl sat in pride of place at the head of a long trestle table, surrounded by balloons and presents. 'Double figures.'

'It feels aces!' Willow beamed back at him, blowing out her candles and helping herself to a large slice of frosted cake, which she shared with a slavering Gaston, before turning her attention to her parcels. '*Formidable! Super! Vraiment génial!*'

'Willow,' Ruth chided gently. 'You know Pops doesn't speak French.'

'He can learn,' Willow shot back cheekily, knowing that today was probably the one day she could get away with it. 'Can I have some wine?'

'No!' Jean Ballard looked suitably shocked.

'Just a tiny dribble,' Ruth answered simultaneously, earning herself a look of astonished disapproval from her mother. 'Things are different here.' She shrugged apologetically. 'It's normal on their birthdays. Just as long as it's watered down.'

Joyously tearing open gift after gift, many of them wine-related – Willow was as obsessed with the wonder and alchemy of winemaking as her father had been at the same age, and already quite the expert on grape varieties and the latest pressing techniques. Willow didn't think she'd ever felt happier. Her birthday was part of it, of course, but there was more to it than that.

Mom was happy, properly, deeply happy in a way that she hadn't been since before Dad died. Grandpa Bob and Nana Jean coming to stay for the first time had meant so much to her. And Willow could tell that Ruth felt proud to be able to show them not just the chateau, but the thriving business she'd built at Sainte Madeleine, pretty much single-handedly. The new Papillon Grand Cru label had been a runaway success, and all of a sudden there was money coming in like Willow had never known before. Money for new dresses and shoes, money to redecorate Willow and Tyler's rooms and to buy Sarah an entire, immaculate new wardrobe for Berkeley, when she started in the fall.

That had been a huge thing too: Sarah going away to college. And not just college, but college back in the States, back in California which had always been her home, and Ruth's, emotionally, in the same way that Burgundy and Sainte Madeleine would always be home to Willow. California had changed a lot since Mom's day, of course.

The whole world was changing, but nowhere more than America, home of Willow's idol, Elvis Presley, and the new movement for civil rights that was so dramatically sweeping the South. Sarah going back had made Ruth feel reconnected, and that had been a good thing for all of them.

What else was Willow happy about? She and Tyler were best friends again. And though they would always miss Daddy, and Willow would always miss Arnaud and all the lost faces of her childhood, there was a definite feeling of closure. Of a new chapter opening for the entire Salignac family that was full of success and happiness and opportunity, full of wine and love and hope.

After the party, and the consumption of much cake and watered-down wine, Willow took Grandpa Bob for a walk up to the top vineyard.

'I'm so happy you're here!' she told him, leading him by his gnarled, veiny hand to the bench that her French grandfather had built, the one she'd never met. 'Arnaud and I used to sit here all the time, watching the sun set. Isn't Burgundy amazing?'

'It certainly is,' Bob Ballard wheezed, catching his breath. He'd never left the United States before, never imagined that his Ruthie would end up making a life for herself in another country, so very far from Winsome. But he couldn't deny she'd made a great success of it. And he couldn't deny that Sainte Madeleine was a gem, idyllic beyond words. Rows of serried vines tumbled down the hillside towards the softly burbling river, and the ancient tiled rooftops of the hamlet beyond. And to the right of where he and Willow sat was the chateau itself, rose-covered and lovely, with its sloping lawns and yew hedges and immaculately manicured gardens full of hollyhocks and lupins and foxgloves and all manner of blossoming fruit trees.

'You know, California's beautiful too, Willow,' Bob sighed. 'It's different, but beautiful.'

'Oh, I know,' Willow said kindly, indulging him. When one lived at Sainte Madeleine, one could afford to be generous to others less fortunate. 'Mom's showed us lots of pictures. She says we'll definitely come out to visit, now that Sarah's going to be studying there.'

'I sure hope you will.'

'She wanted to come before, you know,' Willow assured him. 'But it's awfully tricky when you manage a vineyard, Pops. It's like Dad used to say, "nature doesn't take vacations".'

Bob Ballard chuckled. 'Is that so?'

Willow *looked* like a carbon copy of Ruth, but there was Salignac blood in her veins, that was for sure. Ruth had done a terrific job raising her, raising all of them, all on her own. Bob worried sometimes that his only daughter might be lonely, or homesick, stuck in a foreign land with no family or husband to support her. Alex had been born into this life, as had Willow. But Ruth was a transplant. If she was unhappy, though, she certainly did a good job of hiding it.

'Well, my Willow, your grandmother and I still have another four weeks left of our stay. So right now, we don't want to think about anything but right here.'

'Good,' Willow sighed contentedly, squeezing his hand.

'And it just so happens,' he reached into his jacket pocket, 'we have one last birthday surprise for you. Something you'll be able to remember us by when we do go home.'

'Ooo, I love surprises!' Willow's eyes lit up, then narrowed when he handed her a small cutting, wrapped in brown paper and lined with damp tissue at the base. It was basically a twig.

'What is it?'

'Well now, it may not look like much. But that there is a vine by the name of Scuppernong.'

Willow giggled.

'Funny old name, I know. But it's a Muscadine grape variety,' her grandfather explained. 'Only found in North America, and between you and me it's a pain in the ass to grow. You need to harvest each grape individually. But the wines are sensational.' Leaning over, he whispered conspiratorially in her ear. 'No one in France is growing these babies, Willow. Your grandmother had to smuggle this little guy in in her suitcase.'

'Nana Jean broke the law?' Willow's eyes widened. 'But she doesn't even like us having wine.'

Bob grinned. 'Well, I guess she thought this was different. If you and your mom can find a spot to grow this, and if it takes, well, who knows? You might just end up taking Papillon wines to the next level.'

Reaching up, Willow flung her arms around his neck and kissed him. That he would trust *her* with such a gift meant everything.

'Thank you, Pops,' she sighed. 'I love it.'

'Really?' Bob smiled.

'Really. It's the best present ever.'

Elise yawned, lit a cigarette and poured herself a second cup of tea, before idly picking up the copy of today's *Times* that her charwoman, Brenda, had left for her on the table. It felt sinfully decadent, still to be in one's dressing gown at almost ten in the morning, and on a weekday too. But Andreas and Giorgios's annual summer trip to see their father in Greece did afford *some* compensations, despite the worry and loneliness it always caused her. These days, Elise's fears had shifted. She no longer panicked about Costas 'kidnapping' their sons. But she did worry about his harmful, immoral, money-obsessed influence over them. Especially with Andreas, who had reached an age where fast cars, yachts and beautiful young women were all things that impressed him. It would break Elise's heart if either of her darling boys were to grow up aspiring to Costas's life-style, and she prayed fervently that Andreas's current hero-worship phase with his father passed quickly and without any serious damage to his character.

On the other hand, with both children gone, and so few vices now left to her, what with being both sober and effectively celibate, Elise reasoned that the occasional lazy morning at home being utterly unproductive really ought to be allowed.

As it turned out, the morning's news was unusually depressing. An underground explosion in a mine in Barnburgh had buried six poor souls alive. The so-called 'Asian flu' which had already killed thousands of people across the world was now said to have reached Britain. And some blasted killjoy from the Medical Research Council was trying to suggest that tobacco smoking could be linked to lung cancer.

Ridiculous, thought Elise, inhaling ever more deeply on her Gitane for good measure. What would they ban next? Sunshine?

'Post for you, Mrs G.' Brenda shuffled in from the hallway, where she was making a half-hearted attempt at dusting the furniture, with a small sheaf of envelopes. 'Most of 'em brown, I'm afraid.'

'Oh, that's all right, Brenda,' Elise replied cheerfully. A brown envelope usually meant a bill, but Elise wasn't concerned. Although her life now was a far cry from the grandeur of her marital home at Eaton Terrace, and the fag-smoking, slipper-wearing Brenda was certainly no Mrs Dalton, she was in no danger of being unable to pay for her gas or water, and the brown envelopes were a chore rather than a worry.

Tucked in amongst the boring demands, one crisp, white envelope caught Elise's eye. Even before she saw the post-mark, she recognized the elaborately cursive handwriting as distinctively French, although the formal formatting of her address suggested that this, too, was a business communication and not a personal one.

Slicing it open with a clean butter knife, she removed the folded letter and read it. Then she read it again. Although it pained her to admit it, her French was a little rusty. Perhaps she'd misunderstood? But no. Despite the legalese, it seemed clear.

Well, well, well. Pushing the letter to one side, she leaned back in her chair, lit another cigarette, and began to think. Was this fate? It felt like fate. Like the gods reaching out to offer her, what? Another chance? A shot at redemption? Or even, though she hardly dare think it, happiness?

'Everything all right, Mrs G?'

'Hm?' Elise looked up. At some point Brenda must have reappeared. She wasn't sure how long she'd been sitting there, but her cigarette had burnt away to ashes and the tea had long since gone cold.

'I'm fine, thank you,' she said briskly, belting her dressing gown tightly around her waist as she got to her feet.

Nothing would happen quickly, that much she knew. She would have to write to the nuns first, make a plan. The tone of her letter would be all-important, so Elise must take her time composing it, carefully weighing every word. But already the cogs of her mind were beginning to turn.

It was the autumn of 1957 by the time Elise arrived at the Cistercian abbey deep in the Morvan mountains where her brother Didier had spent most of his adult life. Elise hadn't set eyes on him for twenty-three years.

The day was cold and clear. There was frost on the ground, and the thin, pine-scented air and dazzling blue sky seemed to Elise to presage the coming winter. She'd been warned by the nuns who cared for Didier what to expect, and had felt quite prepared for their encounter when she left London. But now that she was actually here in Burgundy, crunching her way towards the studded oak front doors of this ancient, peaceful place, she felt horribly nervous.

'I'm afraid your brother never fully recovered from the shock of Father Bercault's death during the war,' Sister Bernadette had explained to Elise in her second letter.

> *That is to say, spiritually we believe he has found peace. But in terms of his psychosis and mental functioning, and in particular his anxiety, things continue to ebb and flow. Your brother Alexandre's death certainly seemed to set him back in that regard, and for a while we were rather worried. There was a period when even your mother's visits became too much for him. But the Lord has answered our prayers since then, and Didier has expressed a clear wish to see you.*
>
> *As long as he remains well enough to do so, we would be happy to welcome you here at the abbey . . .*

It was too late to turn back now, Elise reminded herself, smoothing down the front of her coat and taking a deep breath as she rang the brass bell. Moments later the door swung open, Sister Bernadette greeted her with a warm smile and a *'Bienvenue, ma fille'*, and before she knew what had happened, Elise found herself drawn into the belly of the beast.

Didier's room was on one of the upper floors, at the end of a long, flagstone corridor. The set-up reminded Elise a little of the old servants' quarters in the attic at Sainte Madeleine: reams of tiny box bedrooms, effectively cells, with a single, basic bathroom at the end to serve them all. But at home there had at least been an old runner on the floor and a few paintings hung to brighten up the walls. Here all was bare. There was a cleanness to it, a simplicity

419

that Elise supposed might be considered calming by some, although to her eyes it felt cold and austere. It struck her that Thérèse would love it and, on that basis, Dids probably loved it too. For some reason that thought brought a smile to her face as she walked into her brother's room and saw him, face to face.

'Hello, Dids.'

'Elise.'

To her credit, Elise hid her shock. Walking towards her, enfolding her in his frail embrace, was an old man. And not just any old man. It was Louis. It was quite astonishing, now that his hair had receded and turned fully grey, how much Didier resembled their father. God knew they'd had little enough in common when Louis was alive, physically or in any other way. But underneath it all, evidently, Louis's Salignac genes had been there all along.

'How are you, Dids?'

He smiled and nodded shyly, fiddling with the button on his shirt cuff. *Old man meets little boy*, thought Elise, suddenly finding herself overwhelmed with emotion and with the pathos of it all. Didier's lost, wasted life. A private world shattered, like so many after the horrors of the war, but there was no comfort in numbers. She had so much to ask him, to tell him, so much to say. Twenty-three years! And yet now that she was here, she couldn't seem to summon a single word.

'I have some papers. For you.' He shuffled over to the wooden desk under the window, his bony shoulders rounded into a stoop that brought tears to Elise's eyes. He was only forty-six, for heaven's sake. Was being locked away in this place really the best that could have been done for him? With Papa gone, and she and Alex both far from Sainte Madeleine, living their own lives, Didier's fate had been left entirely in Maman's hands. Elise didn't doubt that Thérèse loved him, nor that the nuns were kind and had done their best. But they weren't doctors. Watching her brother now, it was painfully obvious that he had desperately needed some clinical attention, but had been cut off from things that might have helped him.

Then again, she thought guiltily, who was she to judge? *Especially given the reason for today's visit, and what she was about to do.*

'How did you find him?' Sister Bernadette asked, walking Elise back down the stone stairs after an hour with Dids, one of the longest, saddest hours of Elise's life.

Elise struggled to come up with an answer that was true, but that wouldn't offend. 'Changed,' she said eventually. 'I found him . . . much changed.'

'Forgive me, my dear,' the elderly nun placed a gnarled hand on Elise's shoulder. 'But I sense your sorrow. And perhaps something else? If you would like to unburden yourself, Father Troudeau is here this afternoon. I'm sure he would be happy to hear your confession.'

'Thank you, Sister,' said Elise, hastily belting her coat. 'But there's no need. I'm fine.'

Driving away, with Didier's papers on the passenger seat beside her, Elise felt a bewildering tumult of emotions, and somewhere among them: relief. It was done.

Would confession have made her feel better? Perhaps. The problem was that one was really supposed to have stopped the sinning first. For better or worse, Elise was only just getting started.

It was two years before Elise next returned to Burgundy and Sainte Madeleine, this time with Giorgios in tow.

'I still don't see *why* we had to invite her,' Willow grumbled, walking with Ruth through the small field of white Muscadine grapes now known as 'Grandpa's vineyard'.

'Oh yes you do,' said Ruth, slipping an arm around her waist. 'You just don't like it, that's all.'

At twelve Willow was already inches taller than her mother, and living up to her name with her slender limbs and long, flowing strawberry-blond hair. She'd also matured enormously, to the point where she was genuinely a huge help to Ruth up at Papillon. With Sarah away at Berkeley, and Tyler, bless him, utterly uninterested in winemaking, or anything other than planes and flying, his current obsession, Willow had almost become like a junior partner in the business.

In other ways, however, she was very much still a child. Particularly when it came to her aunt Elise.

'She's my nemesis,' she announced to Ruth dramatically, her eyes narrowing.

'Oh, baloney!' Ruth scoffed. 'She's your aunt, honey. What happened all those years ago is water under the bridge.'

'I'd like to throw Aunt Elise under a bridge,' Willow muttered.

'And Giorgios is your cousin,' said Ruth, ignoring her, 'who's never been to Sainte Madeleine before and who you've never even met. Aren't you even a tiny bit curious?'

'Nope,' Willow insisted, tossing back her glossy mane imperiously, like a deeply unimpressed racehorse. 'Not even a smidgen.'

It was therefore a great source of amusement to both Ruth and Tyler when Elise and Giorgios arrived a few hours later, and Willow spent the entire first night at supper staring at her shy but devilishly handsome eighteen-year-old cousin Giorgios with open-mouthed adoration.

'So how do you like France so far, Giorgios?' Ruth asked, making the polite conversation Willow seemed temporarily incapable of. 'Is it what you expected?'

'I'm not sure what I expected, to be honest.' The accent was cut-glass English, notwithstanding the boy's dark, Franco-Greek features. 'Mummy's told Andreas and me so much about Sainte Madeleine over the years, but the rest of the country's a bit of a blank.'

'According to Willow, that's because the rest of the country pales by comparison,' said Tyler, who already liked Giorgios and felt sure they would become friends.

'It does,' Willow and Elise said in unison.

To Willow's surprise, her aunt promptly broke into a grin.

'That's one thing you and I can agree on, at least,' Elise said warmly. 'I did also want to say that I know I behaved badly the last time I was here.' Clearing her throat, she addressed the table at large. 'But I very much hope we can all put that behind us and start again.'

'Of course we can,' said Ruth, catching Elise's eye across the table and feeling quite emotional suddenly. 'It's what Alex would have wanted.'

Inside Elise's heart, a tiny, guilt-sharpened dagger twisted painfully. *Why did she have to mention Alex?*

'Sainte Madeleine runs in the blood of *every* Salignac,' she continued. 'It means so much to me to be bringing Giorgios back home, for the first time.'

It struck Willow that you could hardly call it coming *back home* if it was the first time you'd been somewhere, but she allowed herself to be mollified. Aunt Elise had at least said sorry, a first as far as Willow knew. And she did seem to be trying to be nice. As for Cousin Giorgios, he was already an extremely welcome addition to Sainte Madeleine, and to Willow's life in general. Things were looking up.

'It's a shame Andreas couldn't come with you,' said Ruth. 'How old is he now?'

'He's twenty,' Giorgios answered for his mother, sensing Elise's tension at the mention of his brother's name and not wanting to ruin things. It would be fair to say that relations were not at an all-time high between Elise and her eldest son, in large part thanks to Costas's increasingly destabilizing influence on the boy.

'My brother's in Greece with our father at the moment though,' explained Giorgios, 'so I'm afraid you'll have to make do with just me and Mummy.'

'Not "making do" at all. Is it Willow?' said Tyler archly, still greatly enjoying himself. It wasn't often one got to see Willow tongue-tied and he intended to enjoy it. 'We can't wait to show you around.'

Giorgios knew nothing about wine, and even less about light aircraft, Tyler's current passion. But he was a good listener, and more than happy to spend hours having his ears bent on both topics by his two American cousins. Wine lessons from Willow included multiple 'practical' sessions up at the vineyard, which Giorgios enjoyed as they meant both getting outside and exploring more of the fabled Sainte Madeleine – a fantasy kingdom now gloriously and tangibly real. These sessions often included Elise as well, as Ruth and Willow walked mother and son through both the rows of vines, both the old and new varieties, and the new and improved Papillon winery, a far more sophisticated operation than the version Elise had grown up with.

'I simply can't get my head around all this technology,' Elise announced, wide-eyed, as they moved from one state-of-the-art building to the next. 'It looks more like a NASA space station than an ancient Burgundy domaine.'

Luckily, she made the observation in a tone of awed admiration for the changes Ruth had introduced, rather than with the resentment she'd exhibited after Alex's funeral.

'It is a bit overwhelming when you first see it,' Ruth agreed. 'And definitely not as pretty as it used to be, I'll grant you. But so much has changed in the industry over the last decade. It's hard to believe it's almost 1960 now, and things are *still* changing.'

'It is hard to believe,' Elise agreed.

1960. It still felt strange to say it. Unreal.

'Not just the technology, but all the regulations,' Ruth went on. 'There's such a visceral dread of phylloxera returning, after what happened in Napa, with growers planting ungrafted vines. I'm sure you read about it.'

'Mmmm,' nodded Elise, who hadn't. Ever since her fateful visit to see Didier, she'd been much too busy to keep up to speed on the latest global winemaking gossip. There'd be time enough for that in the future, if everything went according to plan.

'I thought California was bad with all the red tape,' said Ruth, unaware of her sister-in-law's tortured thoughts. 'But the French are really starting to clamp down now.'

'I can imagine,' said Elise, taking it all in. She wondered idly about the plump, white, Scuppernong grapes that young Willow was so proud of, and that she harvested and pressed by hand, the old-fashioned way.

I'll bet they haven't shown those to the ministry of agriculture inspectors. Or told anyone the 'funny' story about the American grandparents smuggling a cutting into the country.

Giorgios noticed that his mother had taken to bringing a small notebook with her on these mini-tours, jotting things down.

'What's that for, Mummy?' he asked her one evening, watching her slip the book into her bedside drawer as she got ready for dinner. He wasn't suspicious by nature, and he adored his mother unconditionally, but he couldn't help but wonder what all the secretive scribbling was for.

'Oh, just, keeping up. You know. With all the changes,' Elise said vaguely.

'Yes, but why?' Giorgios pressed, walking over to her dressing table and helping to pull up the top of her zip at the back.

They only had a few more days left of their holiday at Sainte Madeleine, and he was so enjoying himself roaming the estate with Tyler and Willow, listening to their stories about Arnaud and Brolio and the old days. He couldn't bear it if Mummy were up to something, and the precious détente were to be ruined.

'I'm interested, darling, that's all,' Elise replied breezily. Standing up, she turned and kissed him on the cheek, marvelling again at how tall and grown-up and stunningly handsome he seemed to have become.

'I – we – have a stake in Papillon, don't forget, and in any income Sainte Madeleine produces.'

'Do we?' asked Giorgios. It was the first he'd heard of it.

'Of course we do!' Elise looked shocked. 'Not to reopen old wounds or anything. But this is a family estate. Which is why it's important to stay informed. As your aunt Ruth rightly says, a lot has changed since the war.'

'Hmm,' said Giorgios, still a little suspicious.

'Besides,' Elise said briskly. 'I might notice something that could be changed, or improved upon. Sales do seem to be booming at Papillon. But as far as I can tell Ruth has rather lost interest in our old, bread and butter varieties. Branching into whites is all very well, but our traditional Sainte Madeleine Grand Cru Burgundies must remain a priority in the long term.'

'Oh, Mummy.' Giorgios smiled indulgently, kissing Elise on top of her head like a child. 'Come off it!'

'Come off what?' Elise frowned.

'You know nothing about wine,' he informed her, with all the brutal, unconscious tactlessness of youth. 'Ruth and Willow are the experts. So let's just leave it to them and go down and enjoy a nice dinner, shall we? We've only got a few nights left.'

Biting back her anger – *know nothing about wine,*

indeed! – Elise studied her younger son's features intently. She loved both her boys equally. But there was no doubt that she was closest to Giorgios at the moment. In a world without Laurent, or any other man to love her romantically, her younger son's affection and endless support meant everything to Elise. Somehow she must make sure to keep him with her, and on her side, no matter how things played out.

'Will you miss it here?' she asked him wistfully. 'When we go back to London?'

He looked at her as if she were mad.

'Miss it? Of course I'll miss it. Sainte Madeleine's amazing, Mummy. Just like you always told us it would be.'

Mollified, Elise snaked her arm around his waist. 'Right then. No more shop talk. Let's go down and eat with your cousins, shall we? Enjoy our last few days.'

Sarah Salignac graduated Berkeley in the summer of 1960 and returned to Sainte Madeleine just in time for her sister Willow's thirteenth birthday.

'Look at you. You're a teenager!' Sarah exclaimed, watching Willow twirling around in the bright orange corduroy minidress she'd brought her back as a present from San Francisco. 'You look sensational, Will.'

'Oh, Sarah, I *love* it.' Willow beamed, looking from her grown-up sister to her mother for approval. '*Qu'est-ce que tu penses, Maman?*'

'I think that we speak English at home, and that the dress is *at least* four inches too short,' Ruth said primly.

But not even she could completely keep the smile off her face, or the admiration out of her expression when she looked at Willow. At thirteen going on twenty-three, there was no doubt Ruth and Alex's youngest child was a raving beauty.

Ruth thanked God that, so far at least, barring a harmless long-distance crush on her cousin Giorgios, Willow showed precious little interest in boys. Instead she lived, breathed and slept the wine business, to a degree that her mother sometimes worried was obsessive. But as it was such a useful obsession, and Willow's schoolwork and friendships didn't seem to be suffering, Ruth had taken the path of least resistance and accepted Willow's passion as an innate and unchangeable part of her character.

A knock on the salon door made Ruth turn around. Sandrinee, a useless pudding of a girl from Vézelay whom Ruth had employed in a rash fit of pity last year to be Sainte Madeleine's new housemaid, stuck her moon face around the door.

'There's a man here to see you,' she announced.

Ruth sighed. 'What sort of a man?'

This was typical Sandrine. No relevant information was ever provided about visitors to the chateau, such as whether they were tradesmen or friends, still less an actual name.

The girl looked confused. 'A normal one?' Sensing something else was wanted, she added helpfully, 'He has very clean shoes. I asked him to wait in the hall.'

Ruth found the clean-shoed man exactly where Sandrine said he would be, and quickly learned that his name was Michel Chaumet and that he was a lawyer, from Paris.

'I'm so sorry to intrude, madame,' he said, and looked as if he meant it, shuffling from foot to foot before reaching reluctantly into his leather briefcase for a sheaf of documents. 'Unfortunately, the law dictates that I must hand these to you in person.'

'Well, what are they?' Ruth frowned, taking the various envelopes with her name on the front and reaching into the pocket of her housecoat for her reading glasses. 'Who are they from?'

'My client is a Mrs Elise Goulandris, from London.'

'Elise?' Even more confused, Ruth tore open the first letter. She skim-read, skipping over the unwieldy formal language, and soon the full import of what Elise was actually doing began to sink in.

'This isn't possible,' Ruth whispered aloud. 'She can't.'

'You have twenty-eight days to respond,' the lawyer blurted, turning his clean shoes in the direction of the front door and starting to make his escape. 'You're entitled to legal representation of course.'

'Damn right I'm getting legal representation!' Ruth shot back, without looking up. She was furious, inadvertently scrunching up the letter in a tight fist, her knuckles turning white.

'Some of the other documents m-might make things clearer,' Monsieur Chaumet stammered.

'Oh, I'd say things are pretty clear.' Ruth was shaking, moving on to the second letter.

'Again, madame, I'm very sorry.'

It was almost six in the evening when Sarah finally found her mother again, closeted away in her office up at the winery.

'There you are! What happened? You totally disappeared on us. I told Willow to go ahead and open the rest of her gifts without you.'

Ruth looked up from her desk, exhausted. 'Oh, poor Will. I'm so sorry, I forgot all about her. Is she OK?'

'She's completely fine,' said Sarah. 'She's thirteen, it's her birthday, she got so many presents. Sorry to say it, but she barely noticed you were gone. Last time I saw her she was taunting Tyler about how much richer than him she is now and all the fancy Mamas and the Papas records she's going to buy with her— *Mom!*'

To her horror, Sarah saw that Ruth was crying. Apart from when Dad died, Sarah had never seen her mother shed a tear. Never. Ruth was a rock.

'Mom, what is it, what's happened?' Sarah pulled up a

chair. Brown-haired and freckled, with a kind, intelligent face and gentle manner, she had grown into a lovely young woman, but physically was like the cuckoo in the nest, retaining none of Alex's features as she got older, nor Ruth's. 'Is it Nana?' she asked, her voice full of concern. 'Did something happen?'

Ruth shook her head.

'Pops, then? Please, Mom, tell me.'

'It's your aunt Elise,' Ruth muttered grimly.

Sarah waited for her to go on.

'As you know, your Grandmère Thérèse passed on the ownership of Sainte Madeleine to all three of her children equally when she joined the community at Cerveaux,' said Ruth.

Sarah nodded. 'Right. But you and Dad took over the estate and ran it.'

'Exactly. Your aunt Elise was living in London at that time and hadn't been back to Burgundy in donkey's years. And your uncle Didier was in no fit state to manage anything. So Alex – your dad – was given legal control over Didier's third.'

'What's happened, Mom?' said Sarah, her anxiety rising. It was obvious from Ruth's expression that this wasn't a story with a happy ending, and she wanted to cut to the chase.

Sighing deeply, Ruth passed her two documents from the sheaf the lawyer had left her.

'In a nutshell, your aunt Elise has played us. Played me, anyway. Evidently an estate lawyer from Paris, one of your grandfather Louis's trustees, contacted her in London shortly after Dad died, to discuss the issue of power of attorney over Didier's affairs.'

'Okaaaay,' said Sarah, who was listening and girding herself at the same time.

'The way your grandmother set things up, Elise legally

became her brother's next of kin once Dad was gone,' Ruth went on. 'Obviously it never occurred for a moment to Thérèse that Dad would die so young. Anyway, that doesn't matter. The point is, it seems that your aunt Elise went to visit your uncle Didier behind everyone's backs and got him to sign some papers, formally passing his share in Sainte Madeleine over to her. That makes her the majority owner of the estate.'

'But that's ridiculous,' Sarah said angrily. 'Uncle Didier's in no mental state to be able to make those kinds of decisions. Any court worth its salt would see she manipulated him and throw that out. Right?'

Ruth shrugged. 'They might. But from what I can see here Elise has covered her back pretty effectively. She has the nuns on her side, and two doctors have signed affidavits. Plus French law already favours her claim, as the closest blood relative. I believe it's what's known as a fait accompli.'

'So, what?' Sarah threw down the papers indignantly. 'She takes two thirds of our profits at Papillon now? Is that it?'

'I'm afraid it's worse than that.' Ruth looked at her eldest daughter bleakly. 'She's giving us notice of her intention to take possession of Sainte Madeleine. The house, the farms, the winery. All of it.'

'She's *evicting* us?' Sarah's eyes widened. 'Mom, she *can't.*'

'She's not technically evicting us,' said Ruth. 'If you can believe it, the woman had the brass balls to offer me the opportunity to stay on at Papillon as a "manager". Reporting to her, of course. And to work out some "accommodation" about living at the chateau. Basically, Elise is graciously allowing me to continue to live in my own house as her lodger.'

'Bitch!' said Sarah.

Ruth didn't think she had ever seen her calm, level-headed daughter so impassioned. It was rather a welcome change.

'I hope you told her where she could stick her offer?' said Sarah.

'I haven't yet. But I will,' said Ruth. 'We have twenty-eight days to respond.'

'What are you going to do?'

Ruth shook her head miserably. 'What can I do? Legally, she has us over a barrel. I guess I don't have any choice but to pack up thirteen years of my life – our lives – and go home.'

'You're going to leave Sainte Madeleine?' Sarah looked at her, incredulous. 'Leave France? Go back to the States?'

'Yes,' said Ruth matter-of-factly. 'I am. I mean, what's the alternative? I can't sit back and watch while your aunt invades our home. While she takes over the business that Dad and I broke our backs building. I just don't know how on earth I'm going to tell Willow.'

'You don't need to tell me. I heard everything.'

Ruth and Sarah both turned around to see Willow standing in the doorway. Her back was ramrod straight and her jaw thrust forward in a familiar pose of defiance.

'I won't leave Sainte Madeleine,' she announced bluntly. 'You run away if you want to. But I'm staying.'

'Willow, sweetheart,' Ruth sighed. 'I wish that were possible. But you *can't* stay. Not if your aunt Elise really goes through with this.'

'Watch me!' Willow spat, hissing like a cornered snake. 'I'll chain myself to the walls if I need to. I mean it! I won't let that devil woman steal our home. I'll kill her if I have to! I'll stab her in the heart.'

'You mustn't say things like that, Will,' said Sarah, walking over to try and comfort her. But Willow pushed her angrily away.

'Why not, if I mean them?'

'You don't mean them, darling,' said Sarah.

'I do!' Willow shouted. 'I hate Aunt Elise! I hate her. She

lied to us, she tricked us. I wish she were *dead!* And I am NOT leaving Sainte Madeleine. Not now, not ever, do you hear me? Never!'

Sobbing, she turned and fled.

Ruth got up to go after her, but Sarah put a gentle hand on her shoulder.

'Leave her,' she said. 'Nothing you say will get through right now. Let her cry it out and we'll all talk in the morning. There has to be a way round this, Mom. There just has to be.'

Running back down the hill towards the house, with the wind in her hair and tears streaming down her face, Willow howled like an animal. It was a cry of grief, of anguish, of desperation. But it was also a cry of battle.

Later, looking back, she would remember this as the moment her childhood ended. She was thirteen years old, and the fight for her life, her future, had just begun.

May the spirit of the butterflies be with me, she prayed. *May Aunt Elise be defeated, and may my home be returned to me.*

The butterflies would decide who was the true child of Sainte Madeleine, and the estate's rightful heir. All Willow had to do was keep believing in them. No matter what.

Vive toujours les papillons.

CHAPTER TWENTY-EIGHT

'You're very good with him,' Anne Senard told Elise grate-fully, watching her smiling son leave the room. Elise had just allowed herself to be beaten by Edouard at battleships for at least the fourth time that day, and her de facto godson could not have been more delighted by his latest triumph. 'Very patient. He gets so dreadfully obsessive with these games.'

'Ha!' Elise laughed. 'Patient? That's not usually a word people associate with me.'

'Only because it's not a word that usually applies to you,' Laurent observed laconically, wandering in and plonking himself down on the sofa next to Anne. 'But I have to agree, you've been an absolute saint with Ed. He adores you for it, you know.'

'And I him,' said Elise truthfully.

She reflected, not for the first time, on the miracle of her friendship with Laurent and his family. How much it meant to her. And how little she deserved it.

Of course, she was well aware of those who believed Elise was undeserving of any friendship, from anyone, after the way she'd treated Alex's family. Perhaps, deep down, a part of her believed that too. It was five years now since Elise had 'reclaimed' Sainte Madeleine in a scandal that

434

had rocked not just the Salignac family, but all of Burgundy high society. And while she'd known it was wrong at the time, betraying Ruth and her children in the way that she did, Elise also knew that, for her, returning to her childhood home had become a matter of life and death. Of survival. It wasn't something she could control any more than breathing.

'It's not good enough, Elise!' Laurent had told her furiously at the time. 'It's not an excuse.'

'I never said it was an excuse,' Elise tried to make him understand. 'I'm not looking to be excused, and I accept I don't deserve to be. All I'm trying to do is explain. Ruth has her parents. She has her home in California, a whole other life. She has her children and plenty of money.'

'What's that got to do with anything?' Laurent demanded.

'All I'm trying to say is, Ruth will be OK. She'll survive without Sainte Madeleine. She'll thrive, eventually. I won't. I can't. Oh please, Laurent, don't look at me like that!'

For more than a year, things had been very strained between the two of them. But over time, Laurent had softened. He still disapproved vehemently of what Elise had done, and from time to time he continued to encourage her to try to make amends, although any reconciliation was hard to envisage. But little by little, he also came to view Elise's wrongdoing in a wider context, one that allowed for more compassion. She'd survived an abusive marriage, alcoholism and decades of painful exile. She had lost the father and brother she adored, and was alienated from the rest of her family. In a romantic sense, she'd 'lost' him too, something for which Laurent carried his own burden of guilt. Added up, it was a lot of pain for one person to bear. And although she had her boys, and loved them fiercely, Sainte Madeleine was a part of Elise in a way that it had never, fully, been a part of Ruth. It was Elise's beating heart, the breath in her body. When she said that she simply could not go on living without it, Laurent suspected that she meant it literally. And so slowly, he'd reached out to her.

At first Elise had resisted his offers of friendship and hospitality. Not because she was bitter or ungrateful, but rather because she was convinced it would prove too painful for both of them to spend time in one another's company. Nothing had changed regarding her feelings for him, besides the inevitable dulling of the pain of their separation, after so many years. But as the months turned into years, and it became clear that no one else in Burgundy was willing to extend a similar olive branch towards her – not after what she'd done to poor Ruth – loneliness began to trump both fear and pride, and eventually Elise accepted an invitation to supper at Brancion.

Bizarrely, despite Elise's raging nerves, it had turned out to be a wonderful, relaxed evening, the first of many with Laurent, Anne and Edouard. To her own surprise, and Laurent's relief, Elise found as soon as they got talking that she liked Anne enormously, and the two women quickly became firm friends. Of course, some emotional 'compartmentalizing' was required on Elise's part. Anne, obviously, knew nothing about the night Elise had spent with Laurent in Paris the year that Alex died, a betrayal that Elise imagined would break not just Anne's heart, but their friendship, into a million tiny pieces.

But the point was, she *didn't* know. Would never know. And although there were moments when the lie on which their friendship was based pricked at Elise's conscience, she consoled herself with the fact that it was Anne who had 'won', even if she didn't know there had ever been a war between the two of them. Anne got to live with Laurent, and love him, and have him love her, for the rest of her life, while Elise would spend the rest of her days alone; even if she did now have her beloved Sainte Madeleine.

Surely this entitled her to the consolation prize of both Anne and Laurent's friendship? As long as nobody was getting hurt?

As for Laurent himself, he never alluded to that fateful night, or to the love that still burned, albeit quietly, between them. That had been one chapter, and this was another. He seemed content, happy even, with the new arrangement. And as the alternative would have meant banishing Elise from his life completely, there really wasn't much to think about.

'How did your meeting go with your accountants?' Anne asked Elise idly, pouring herself a second mug of tea from the china pot in front of her. 'Did you ask them about that second mortgage?'

Laurent's ears pricked up. 'What second mortgage?'

Elise shot Anne a horrified look and she realized at once she'd put her foot in it.

'Sorry,' she said sheepishly. 'I didn't know it was supposed to be a secret.'

'It's not a *secret*,' Elise clarified, not daring to meet Laurent's eye. 'I just wasn't going to bring it up until I knew what I was going to do.'

'Elise Salignac,' Laurent chided her sternly, sounding like a disappointed father. 'I can't believe you set up a finance meeting behind my back.'

'I know, I know.' Elise bit her lower lip guiltily.

Laurent had been a rock over the last few years, helping her to navigate crisis after crisis. Unfortunately, Giorgios's assessment of his mother's suitability to manage a modern, 1960s wine business had proved to be sadly prophetic. Elise was a disaster.

Within a year of her taking over the thriving Papillon label that Ruth and Alex had built up, the estate had begun to haemorrhage money at an alarming rate. Thanks to her well-intentioned but disastrous interventions at the winery, largely stemming from her nostalgic insistence on returning to both the old grape varieties and the old ways of doing things – her beloved Arnaud's ways – not only had sales collapsed, but the quality of Sainte Madeleine's wines had deteriorated dramatically. Not since the bad old days under Louis at the height of his drinking had the estate been in such a sorry state financially.

If it hadn't been for Laurent's calm, consistent advice – and Giorgios's insistence that they continue producing at least a small amount of Muscadet from Willow's trans-planted American vines – Sainte Madeleine would already be bankrupt. And despite tightening her belt, the thought of a nice, fat loan, just to tide her over, was so very tempting.

'How many times do I have to tell you that more debt is *not* the answer to Sainte Madeleine's problems?' he sighed, looking at her crossly now.

'No more times, please.' Elise groaned. 'In any case, you needn't worry. The accountants said no.'

'Well thank God for that,' Laurent grumbled. 'At least somebody's got some sense.'

'Oh, do stop being such a curmudgeon, darling,' said Anne, rallying to Elise's defence. 'It's all very well banging on about what Elise shouldn't do. But what she needs is some constructive suggestions.'

'Thank you.' Elise smiled at her gratefully.

'I've given her constructive suggestions!' Laurent defended himself. 'Either hire someone who knows what they're doing to run the vineyard—'

'And how am I supposed to pay them?' Elise protested. 'I can barely afford to keep the heat on at Sainte Madeleine in winter, never mind another full-time salary.'

'Offer a profit-share, then,' said Laurent. 'Find a partner.'

'A partner? Outside of the family, you mean?' Elise looked horrified. 'Don't be ridiculous.'

Both Laurent and Anne refrained from saying what they

were thinking: that Elise had *had* a partner, and a brilliant one, within the family. But she had treated Ruth so shoddily, those bridges had long since been burned.

'Your options are finite, my dear,' Laurent said bluntly. 'You either find a partner, rent out the vineyards to a third party, or—'

'Rent them out?' The way Elise said it, Laurent might as well have proposed exhuming her father's body and desecrating his grave. 'You do realize that Salignacs have been producing Burgundy at Sainte Madeleine since before the revolution? Long before.'

'Or sell,' Laurent continued, finishing his point despite Elise's outbursts. 'Not the whole estate, necessarily. But you could sell off the vineyards to save the house.'

Elise went white. 'I'd rather rip out my eyeballs with my bare hands.'

Laurent sighed. 'Must you always be so melodramatic?'

'Have you forgotten what happened when Papa sold off the farms?' Elise reminded him with a shudder. 'That was the beginning of the end for my family.'

'I remember,' Laurent said, more gently. He knew how painful and loaded these memories were for Elise. 'But those were different times. The majority of noble families have had to downsize since the war. Once you get Sainte Madeleine back on a sounder economic footing, you can rebuild.'

Appalled by the nonchalant way in which Laurent was making such drastic suggestions, Elise turned away pointedly and addressed herself to Anne. 'Please tell your husband that if he's simply going to be *ridiculous* and say deliberately provocative things, then I'd rather spend my time with Edouard.'

'Elise,' Laurent pleaded with her, but to no avail. She was already moving towards the door.

Anne chuckled. She'd seen this movie countless times.

Laurent and Elise, squabbling like children, before Elise eventually gave in and took Laurent's advice, whatever it was.

'I'll tell him,' she told Elise solemnly. 'And when you see Edouard, please let him know that he still needs to finish his maths homework, and that if he wants to go out hunting with his favourite godmother tomorrow, it had better get done tonight.'

Elise gave Anne a wide-eyed look. 'I'll remind him about the homework. But you can't seriously expect me to tell my godson that *maths* is more important than *hunting*? He's not a fool, you know Anne.'

Sometimes, Anne reflected, it was hard to know who was the bigger child: Edouard or Elise.

Andreas Goulandris turned the steering wheel of his new, midnight blue Aston Martin DB5 sharply to the left, sighing contentedly as a gratifying arc of gravel sprayed, rainbow-like, into the air, landing with a clatter in front of the chateau. It was mid-July, and Andreas had grudgingly agreed to spend part of the summer in France, helping Elise and Giorgios up at the Papillon winery and 'getting to know' his French relatives. *Snore.*

Still, he thought, heaving his Louis Vuitton case out of the back seat, it wasn't all bad. His mother's ancestral home was, he had to admit, a pretty house. Although too small and too feminine for his taste – Sainte Madeleine was romantic rather than grand, idyllic rather than awe-inspiring – he nevertheless acknowledged its charms. There was pedigree here, and history, both of which appealed to the snob in Andreas. But the estate, like Burgundy in general, lacked the pizazz of Athens, and the wow factor of his father's various, palatial homes. Salignac money might be older, but they had a lot less of it than the Goulandrises. And where wealth was concerned, as with so many other things,

Andreas was very firmly a believer in the 'more is more' philosophy.

'What time do you call this?' Giorgios, shirtless, tanned and lean after a summer spent in the vineyards, greeted his brother warmly. With his unkempt curls, threadbare Bermuda shorts, and roughly calloused hands, he looked more like Andreas's slave boy than his brother.

Andreas, meanwhile, looked every inch the wealthy playboy in a Saint Laurent jacket, bespoke slacks from Jermyn Street, and with his perfectly coiffed blond hair slicked back in the latest mode du jour.

'I call it lunchtime,' he announced cheerfully, glancing at the heavy gold Rolex gleaming at his wrist. 'Who does one have to sleep with around here to get a Mimosa?'

'*Mimosa* indeed!' Giorgios scoffed, hugging him. 'You won't get a drink here till supper, and then it'll be Burgundy or nothing. Come on. There's work to be done.'

Despite all the tension surrounding Andreas's visit, and despite how different they were, Giorgios was still pleased to see him. He loved Sainte Madeleine, but it got lonely sometimes, being the only one here with Mummy. He really hoped that this time things went well between Andreas and Elise, and that the mutual sniping might be kept to a minimum. But it wasn't to be. Within a day Andreas had begun complaining about his 'bloody awful' guest suite ('Papa's dogs have more comfortable beds than this!') and the 'stingy' provision of alcohol.

'Don't we have any d'Yquem?' he grumbled, after a common-or-garden port was produced at the end of his welcome home meal. 'Just because you can't drink, Mummy, there's no need to condemn the rest of us to this pigswill.'

'It doesn't make you sound impressive, you know, Andreas,' Elise replied coolly, shooting her eldest son a look that would have melted a lesser man as she helped Giorgios to more queen of puddings, a favourite from the boys' London days. 'Dropping the names of all these expensive labels. It makes you sound spoiled and foolish.'

'Yawn,' Andreas snapped back, leaning back in his chair and rocking back and forth in an affectation of boredom.

'And *nouveau*,' Elise added, unable to restrain herself. 'Just like your father.'

'Mummy!' Giorgios scolded her, but it was too late. Once Costas's name was uttered in a conversation, it was all downhill from there.

'That's all right, G,' Andreas drawled, his eyes flashing with anger. 'Mummy's trying to insult me, but it all falls rather flat, I'm afraid. Because the truth is I'd far rather be *nouveau riche* than *vieux pauvre*. Or in Mummy's case, *dépourvu*.'

Giorgios had to look the word up later. Infuriatingly, Andreas's French was still better than his, even though Giorgios had lived at Sainte Madeleine full-time for five years now. Apparently it meant 'destitute' or 'bankrupt'. Which might have gone some way to explaining the thin-lipped, white-hot rage it inspired in Elise, and the spectacular row that followed.

'Must you always provoke her?' Giorgios challenged Andreas afterwards.

'Me? Provoke her?' Andreas spluttered. 'Didn't you hear her earlier?'

'She works so hard,' Giorgios pressed on. 'And she misses you, deep down. We both do.'

'*You* might,' Andreas said bitterly, tapping a hand-rolled cigarette out of an exquisite, engraved sterling silver case, a present from Costas's latest concubine. 'But Mummy's never given a damn about anything except her precious Sainte Madeleine. It's like a *cult* with her.'

'That's not true,' said Giorgios, upset both because there was some truth to what his brother said, and because the 'cult' line had been lifted from Costas word for word. 'Mummy loves us. You know she does.'

Giorgios simply couldn't understand how Andreas could have defected to their father's camp. It had happened slowly, insidiously, but by this point it was starting to feel distressingly permanent. Didn't he remember how appallingly Costas had treated their mother, not to mention his utter abandonment of the two of them as children? As far as Giorgios was concerned, Costas Goulandris was a stranger, no more, no less, and he intended to keep it that way. As for Andreas, it was hard to draw any other conclusion but that his older brother had been bought; bribed with money and cars and cigarette cases to turn to the dark side. It was no good blaming Elise for that.

A few weeks after Andreas returned to Athens, to everyone's unspoken relief, the Senards came to stay at Sainte Madeleine. Sensing that Elise needed someone to talk to, Anne persuaded her to join her for an early morning ride in the woods above the vineyard.

'It's years since I've done this,' Elise admitted, weaving her way slowly through the silver birch, being careful to duck for low branches. It was a damp, misty September morning, almost cold enough to see one's breath. Everything was quiet and smelled of woodsmoke and rich, fertile earth.

'Done what?' asked Anne, trotting along more confidently on her borrowed bay mare. An experienced horsewoman since her earliest childhood in England, being in the saddle was like breathing for her. 'Ridden before breakfast?'

'Ridden for pleasure at all,' said Elise, nudging her roan into a small clearing. 'Thank you for suggesting it.'

It didn't take long for the conversation to move on to Andreas's disastrous visit, and from there to motherhood in general.

'You try so hard to set them a good example. To be there for them, to make sacrifices,' said Elise, leaning forward to pat her horse's neck. 'But what's it all for in the end?'

'I'm not sure it's "for" anything,' said Anne. 'It's an end in itself, isn't it? Loving one's children? Loving at all, for that matter.'

Elise sighed. 'That's true, I suppose.'

'And let's face it, it's not as if we have a choice,' Anne went on. 'We love who we love.'

Was it Elise's imagination, or was Anne looking at her curiously? Her words were a statement, yet Elise got the distinct impression there was a question in them somewhere. A question that she dreaded being asked, and couldn't answer.

'Look at me and Edouard,' Anne continued after a few moments, breaking the spell. 'I love and adore him more than life. Despite all the times I'm exhausted and want to strangle him. Which, as you well know, are many.'

Elise chuckled.

'And I know he loves me. But does he show it?' asked Anne. 'Not always. Not often, even, if I'm honest, if "showing it" means hugs or affection or thanks or any of those normal things. The other day, in the kitchen, I scalded my hand horribly being cack-handed with the kettle,' she told Elise. 'I cried out – I mean, really *shrieked*. Ed didn't so much as glance up from his jigsaw puzzle.'

'Yes, but that's different,' said Elise. 'Edouard can't help that. It's part of his condition. Part of who he is. Andreas is perfectly capable of showing affection. Did Giorgios tell you I caught him on his last night with *two* village girls in his room, both of them half naked? You should have seen how much affection he was showing them!'

Anne roared with laughter, throwing her head back and guffawing in the raucous, unladylike way that Elise had grown to love her for.

'Oh my goodness, that's priceless. Did he really? Naughty boy.'

'It's not *naughty*,' Elise said crossly. 'It's entitled, its narcissistic, it's . . .' she threw up her hands in despair. 'He's so spoiled, Anne. So materialistic and lazy. It breaks my heart.'

'He's young,' said Anne. 'What were you doing at his age?'

Elise rolled her eyes. 'Marrying his father.'

'Exactly,' said Anne. 'Marrying Costas. A rich, spoiled, flashy Greek playboy twice your age, who whisked you away on his yacht. Admit it, you were hardly saving orphans, Elise, or bent double over your books.'

'That was different,' Elise said defensively. 'I was broken-h—'

She stopped herself just in time.

'You were what?' Anne asked.

'Nothing,' said Elise. Gathering up her reins, she nudged her horse sharply in the ribs. 'It was a different time, that's all. But I take your point. I suppose I was hardly a moral exemplar, then or now. Anyway, enough moping. I'd best get back to the office and the son who does love me before he decides to sail off into the sunset as well. Those grapes aren't going to harvest themselves.'

'Here. Let me help you with that.'

Jason Danson grabbed the heavy case of Syrah from out of Willow's arms and stacked it on top of the others behind the desk. Shy and bookish, despite his handsome features and lean athletic physique, Jason had been in love with Willow since she first started working at his family's Napa vineyard. Even in the cut-off overalls and Bob Dylan T-shirt she was wearing now, and with her hair pulled back in a wonky ponytail, Jason believed she was the most divine-looking woman on earth. Unfortunately the feeling wasn't mutual. Not because Willow didn't like him, or consider him attractive. But because, at eighteen, she was so utterly obsessed with the wine business, there was no time left for romance. No time for anything else at all, for that matter.

'Thanks. How many have we moved now? Six?'

Wiping her brow, Willow leaned back against the desk for a moment to catch her breath. Today was a Saturday, always the busiest day in the tasting room at Danson's, with the first party of tourists from San Francisco expected to show up around ten. The 1964 Syrah was one of their biggest sellers, so she and Jason were stacking it front and centre before the tastings began.

Willow loved working at Danson's. She loved that this was the place where her father had got his start when he first came to Napa. The place where he'd been working when he met her mom, and Tyler, his legendary buddy who'd died in the war and after whom her brother had been named. Nothing would ever make up for the loss of Sainte Madeleine. But these little pieces of family history, these connections with the past, and particularly with Alex, helped to sustain Willow while she waited. Because that's what she was doing: waiting. Plotting and scheming day and night, year in, year out, until she could find a way to get back to France.

'Are you busy tonight?' Jason asked bravely, trying his best to sound casual as he lifted the bottles one by one from each case. 'Me and some buddies were gonna go to the drive-in at Winsome. They're showing *The Sound of Music*. It's supposed to be outta sight.'

'Oh thanks, but I can't tonight,' said Willow. 'My sister Sarah's visiting from the city and my mom invited my grandparents over for a big family dinner. Next time, though,' she added kindly, registering Jason's crestfallen expression.

They finished setting up for the tastings, and both were

wolfing down a late breakfast of Skippy peanut butter sandwiches and Coca-Cola when the mailman arrived with the day's post.

'I'll take that,' said Willow, lunging for the latest copy of *Fine Wine* magazine as enthusiastically as a teenage boy grabbing a new *Playboy*. 'There's supposed to be a big feature on Inglenook this month, and John Daniel Jr.'

Jason sighed, knowing he'd lost her. Napa's most visionary winemaker, John Daniel, was something akin to Mick Jagger or Paul McCartney in Willow's eyes, and she devoured every word about him like a groupie. But a few moments later, she amazed him by grabbing his hand.

'Oh my God,' she gasped, stricken.

'Oh my God, what?' asked Jason.

'There's a bit in here about our domaine. About Sainte Madeleine. Look.'

He glanced at the half-page article on Burgundy wines, skimming it for the two words that would always be magic in Willow's heart.

'Papillon's been downgraded,' whispered Willow, squeezing his hand tighter. She sounded close to tears. 'They're certifying our wines as *Appellation Régionale*.'

'Is that so bad?' Jason asked.

Willow looked at him as if he were mad. For someone born and raised in a winemaking family, just like her, it never failed to astonish her how little Jason knew about the business. Then again, he probably knew more than Tyler, not that that was hard.

'It's extremely bad,' she explained. 'When my aunt stole the estate, our wines were certified Grand Crus. That's as high as you can go in Burgundy, higher than Premier Crus. *Appellation Régionale* is as low as you can go.'

'I see,' said Jason, trying to sound understanding.

'I don't think you do,' said Willow. She threw down the magazine in disgust. 'She's ruined us, basically. That's what

447

happened. She's destroyed our estate and the Salignac reputation. Ugh, I can't bear it.'

'Well, chin up,' said Jason, hastily clearing away their snacks and putting on his best smile as the door opened and the first of the day's customers wandered in. 'We'll talk about it later, OK? Journalists always exaggerate. I'm sure things aren't as bad as you think.'

He was wrong. Willow got through the day, professional as ever. But those awful, shaming two words – *Appellation Régionale* – rang in her head constantly, like a death knell.

'She's ruined our lives,' Willow complained bitterly to her family at dinner, unable to enjoy anyone's company, not even her grandparents'.

'Oh, now, darling, that's not true,' Ruth admonished her. 'Look around you. We have a beautiful home and a wonderful life. Aunt Elise hasn't ruined those things.'

'And we have each other,' Nana Jean added, tiny and frail now at the other end of the table, but her mind still as sharp as ever.

'I don't care,' Willow insisted stubbornly. 'She ruined my life. She stole Sainte Madeleine and now she's using it to grow grapes so crappy they're selling our wines as paint stripper.'

'Jesus Christ, who cares, Will?' Tyler snapped. He loved his little sister, but there were times when her obsession with Sainte Madeleine, and with the past, brought everyone down. 'It's not our problem anymore. It hasn't been for years.'

'*I* care!' Willow shot back, hurt.

'I thought you wanted Aunt Elise to fail?' Tyler pointed out, reasonably.

'I did,' Willow admitted. 'I do.'

'So, now she is. This is what failure looks like, right? I'd say it's a case of being careful what you wish for.'

Later, in bed, Willow thought about what her brother

had said at dinner. As usual he'd been insensitive. Tyler had never fully understood her unbreakable attachment to Sainte Madeleine, and certainly didn't share her view that they owed it to their father to get it back. Because, Willow realized now with crystal clarity, her love for Sainte Madeleine was greater than anything else. Greater, even, than her hatred for her aunt. And that was saying something.

She must save Sainte Madeleine from ruin.

She could only pray that, in the process, she might also save herself.

CHAPTER TWENTY-NINE

'Oh Andreas! *Min stamatas!*'

The curvaceous brunette threw back her head so that the tips of her long hair skimmed the top of her backside, rocking her hips back and forth enthusiastically as she hastened towards climax. Andreas had been desperate to bed her last night at the casino. He'd lost heavily, not for the first time, and the buxom barmaid in her tight sequined dress with her huge breasts spilling out had seemed like the perfect consolation prize. But when he'd woken up this morning to find her not only still in his bed, but clambering on top of him, demanding round two, all her earlier allure had faded. In the cold light of day her streaked make-up could no longer conceal the first creeping signs of middle age. Lines around the eyes, a certain slackness in the skin around the mouth. It was all Andreas could do to keep his erection long enough to finish the job.

But he did, jumping out of bed afterwards and into the shower, hustling her out of the door.

'Will I see you tonight, at the tables?' she asked plaintively, pulling on the dress that had looked so enticing last night. 'Perhaps you'll have better luck?'

'No. Not tonight,' he said curtly, making a mental note to indulge his blackjack habit at another of Athens' high-end gambling establishments for at least the next month. 'And please make sure you use the back door when you leave. My father prefers not to have to run into my overnight guests.'

'I see,' the girl pouted. 'You have many of them then, do you?'

Andreas's only answer was a scowl and a firmly closed door. He was in a bad mood, and not only because of the girl, or the eye-watering amounts of money he'd lost last night. Although it pained him to admit it, he was starting to get bored in Athens, drifting around aimlessly spending Costas's money. Little by little he'd learned that accepting his father's largesse came at a price – namely his self-esteem. He had no job, no purpose, no successes he could claim as his own. And while Costas never openly disparaged him, he equally made it very clear that he expected his son to toe the line and do as he was told, should their whims or wishes ever differ. If Costas expressed a dislike for a jacket Andreas was wearing, for example, the unspoken understanding was that it would be discarded and replaced. At first, it hadn't occurred to Andreas to mind about such trifling things. But as the years wore on, and he grew older, they added up, and a creeping feeling of something that might have been shame was becoming harder and harder to ignore.

Then, last week, something had happened that brought things to a head. His mother had rung from Burgundy to inform him that his uncle Didier had died. In his sleep, apparently, and from a massive heart attack.

'He didn't suffer,' Elise explained. 'According to Sister Bernadette he went to bed perfectly happily, just as normal, and simply didn't wake up.'

'I'm sorry, Mummy,' Andreas mumbled guiltily. 'I know he meant a lot to you.'

'Thank you, darling,' said Elise, touched and surprised

by his concern. 'He requested a private funeral service, with only the nuns, and to be buried up at the abbey, so there's nothing to fly in for. But it would be nice to see you, Andreas. It's been almost three years since your last visit.'

Ever since that phone call, Andreas had been waiting with a growing sense of dread for everything to unravel. Once his mother found out what he'd done, he strongly suspected that any wish she might have to see him would evaporate faster than a puddle in the Greek sun. And he wouldn't blame her. He regretted his actions, he really did.

After his last painful visit to Sainte Madeleine, when he felt Elise had put him down and belittled him on purpose, Andreas had done something genuinely terrible in a fit of rage, wanting to spite his mother. Something that involved his uncle Didier. But of course, since then, he'd put it to the back of his mind, assuming that he had decades left to fix things. How was he supposed to know his uncle was going to shuffle off this mortal coil in his fifties?

Having showered, dressed, and made a pretence of dealing with the day's 'business' in his office, a charming suite of rooms in one of the converted coach houses at Costas's mansion, Andreas was heading back into the house for lunch when the hammer blow finally fell.

'There's a phone call for you, sir. Long distance.' A liveried footman approached him. 'I believe your brother is on the line.'

Bracing himself, Andreas took the call in Costas's private study.

'Giorgios. So nice to hear from you. What's new?'

He hated himself for the forced cheeriness, but didn't know what else to do, how else to behave.

'You bastard.' Giorgios spoke quietly, but his voice quivered with anger and hurt. 'You utter, utter, bastard. How could you do it? How could you live with yourself?'

Andreas cleared his throat. 'I assume you're referring to Uncle Didier's will?'

'Of course I'm referring to the bloody will!' Giorgios erupted. 'Didier left his share to Mummy. It was all agreed, all done and dusted. But you had to go and stir the shit, didn't you? And with the Catholic bloody Church of all people.'

'I'm sorry,' Andreas began wretchedly. But Giorgios was in no mood to hear it.

'You're *sorry*?' he scoffed. 'You convinced the Church to challenge the will and get the old one reinstated! Now they're claiming Didier's share in Sainte Madeleine belongs to them, and if we don't buy them out they have the right to force a sale. Do you even know what you've done, Andreas? You've finished us!'

'Like I said, I'm sorry,' Andreas pleaded. 'It was years ago and I was just so lost and angry with Mummy. I didn't expect Uncle Didier to die.'

'Well he did, didn't he?' seethed Giorgios. 'And now we stand to lose the estate. Thanks to you. How *could* you?'

'I told you, I was angry,' Andreas repeated, defensive but only because he knew he was in the wrong. 'Besides, you know as well as I do Mummy coerced Didier into giving her his share in the first place. She's been no saint in this herself.'

'Who cares how she got him to give it to her?' said Giorgios. 'He didn't need it, did he?'

'Maybe not. But Aunt Ruth did,' Andreas pointed out.

'I don't disagree, but that isn't our battle. And she's our mother, for God's sake. *Your* mother. Why can't you ever be on her side?'

'Why can't she ever be on mine?' Andreas shot back, doing his level best to smother his guilt with anger. 'You talk about her like she was some kind of perfect mother. Some kind of saint. Don't you remember the drinking?'

'Of course I do,' said Giorgios quietly. 'She was ill.'

'Was she ill when she turned her own brother's children out of their home?' Andreas's voice was rising.

'That's not fair,' said Giorgios. 'There was more to it than that and you know it.'

'Or when she duped her mentally ill brother into handing over his inheritance?' Andreas continued, on a roll now.

'You make me sick,' Giorgios spat contemptuously. 'Trying to make this about Mummy, to deflect from your own behaviour. How dare you judge her, after what you've done? And not just to her, but to me. Did you ever stop to think about that? I've given the last six years of my life to Sainte Madeleine. Six *years*.'

'Yes, well. I am sorry about that,' muttered Andreas. 'I'll admit I didn't totally think it through.'

It was so overwhelmingly an understatement that Giorgios was momentarily lost for words. 'Couldn't Mummy find a way to buy the Church out of their share?' Andreas suggested, prompting bitter laughter from his brother.

'Mummy can't afford to buy bread most weeks.'

'Take them to court, then?' offered Andreas.

'Take the Catholic Church to court? In France? Quite apart from all the judges they have in their pocket, don't you realize how rich the Vatican is? We wouldn't stand a chance.'

'I don't know what to say,' admitted a chastened Andreas, after a long pause. 'I genuinely never thought that it would come to this.'

'That's the problem. You never thought at all,' said Giorgios, his voice breaking with emotion. 'Mummy might forgive you for this one day, Andreas, but I won't. Not ever.'

'Giorg—'

But it was too late. The line had gone dead.

* * *

Elise sat in the *avocat*'s office, pen in hand.

In an exquisite, couture suit, a hand-me-down from Chantelle that still fit her perfectly and made her look two things that she certainly wasn't – rich and powerful – Elise did her best to project an air of confidence.

'I sign just here?' she asked nonchalantly. 'And do I need to initial anywhere?'

'Er, yes, madame. Pages two and four.' The *avocat* pointed out the relevant dotted lines on the contract.

Elise stared at the paper, her eyes swimming. The misery she felt at that moment was indescribable. Not just because of what she was about to do, but because of the reason she was about to do it. Because she'd been stabbed in the back by her own son.

'Madame Goulandris, are you quite sure about this?' the *avocat* asked, sensing her distress. 'I must stress that, once this is signed, the terms are binding.'

'Quite sure, thank you.' Elise signed with a flourish.

As it happened, she was quite sure. Quite sure that, thanks to Andreas's betrayal, she had no other choice.

Laurent was in Edouard's bedroom in Chateau Brancion, trying and failing to explain the rules of backgammon, when a worried-looking Anne came in.

'Giorgios Goulandris is here,' she told Laurent. 'He's waiting for you downstairs.'

'Giorgios?' Laurent smiled, happy both to see Elise's son and to have an excuse to abandon the frustrating business of trying to teach anything to Edouard. 'What a nice surprise. We weren't expecting him, were we?'

'No,' said Anne, 'And by the look on his face, I rather suspect that whatever's brought him here isn't good news.'

'Oh God,' Laurent sighed.

A few minutes later, he ushered an ashen-looking Giorgios into his study. He was carrying an old briefcase of Louis's with the Salignac coat of arms on it, and he looked almost as worn down and battered as it was.

'What is it?' Laurent asked him bluntly. 'What's happened?'

Pulling some legal documents out of the case, Giorgios handed them over.

'See for yourself,' he said bleakly. 'First Andreas, now Mummy. No one ever tells me anything. Or at least, not until it's too late for me to do anything about it.'

Sitting down, Laurent read the documents carefully and in silence, taking his time over every word.

'Stupid girl,' he muttered under his breath. 'Stupid, stupid girl.' Looking up, he asked Giorgios, 'Where is your mother now?'

'At home. Climbing the walls, I expect,' said Giorgios. 'I'm afraid we had a bit of a row.'

'Not as big of a row as we're going to have,' Laurent announced, grabbing his jacket. 'Did you drive here?'

Giorgios nodded. 'My car's outside. I'm sorry to turn up out of the blue like this and I'm sorry to dump this on you. I honestly didn't know who else to call.'

'No, no,' said Laurent. 'You did the right thing. But you'd better go and start the car.'

'Now?'

'Right now. Don't worry, I'll handle things with your mother.'

'It's some sort of consortium,' Elise wailed, frantically running her hands through her hair. 'That's what they called themselves. The name's on the top of the contract.'

'Yes, I can see that,' said Laurent gently. 'I'm just wondering who they *are*, really.'

Now that he was actually here and could see for himself how distressed Elise was, he didn't have the heart to yell at her, despite what he'd promised Giorgios.

They were walking together in the lower gardens at Sainte

Madeleine, beside the tennis court where, years ago, Louis Salignac had so publicly and unfairly bullied poor Didier after he and Alex lost at doubles to Laurent and Thierry. The court was overgrown now, weed-infested and neglected like so much of the estate grounds. Elise had had to let the gardener go two years ago, and since then all her and Giorgios's efforts and energy had been focused exclusively on the vineyards. Abortively, as it turned out.

It made Laurent sad to see the neglected court. Sad also to reflect that of the four players in that match, incredibly he was now the only one left alive. But nothing was as bad as seeing Elise, beautiful as ever despite her exhaustion, tormenting herself over her latest, catastrophic error of judgement.

'How did you first get in contact with these people?' he asked, quietly taking her hand as they walked.

'I didn't. They contacted me,' Elise said miserably. 'Or at least, they contacted my lawyer. They knew about the changes to Didier's will. About the Church now having majority ownership of Sainte Madeleine, and the Diocese's intention to force a sale. Oh, Laurent, I know I should have come to you about it! But I thought you'd disapprove, and the loan these people were offering was so enormous and at such an unbelievably good rate of interest. It felt—'

'Too good to be true?'

'I was going to say it felt like a lifeline, but of course you're right.' Elise bit her lower lip, willing herself not to cry. 'It *was* too good to be true. It wasn't a rope they were throwing me, it was a noose. I've been a fool, haven't I?'

Laurent squeezed her hand supportively, determined for once not to sound judgemental. It had always been the one thing Elise complained about in him – the holier-than-thou side to his nature – even though deep down, he suspected that his moral certainty might be one of the things that drew her to him. Perhaps because she struggled so painfully at times with her own conscience.

'This isn't all your fault, you know,' he told her now. 'Didn't your lawyer smell a rat? I can't believe he didn't warn you, didn't say anything. I mean it's here in black and white that these charlatans can demand repayment and interest *in full* at any time, and under the most draconian terms. Five days!'

'He might have said something,' Elise looked away guiltily. 'Implied it anyway. I wasn't really listening, to be frank with you.'

'Elise!' Laurent couldn't help himself.

'I know, I know. But I was still reeling from what Andreas did . . . from being in this awful situation in the first place. About to lose my home, after fighting so long to win it back.' She blinked back tears. Then Elise said something that Laurent had been waiting years to hear her say, and had long since given up believing she ever would.

'It's made me realize how hard it must have been for Ruth and the children. When I . . . came back.'

'Did it?' Laurent asked quietly.

'Oh Lord.' She ran a hand through her hair. 'I've been feeling so hurt by Andreas, going behind my back with Didier and the will. But it's poetic justice, isn't it? After what I did to Alex's family? All of this is no more than I deserve.'

'I'm not sure it's any sort of justice,' Laurent said kindly, wrapping an arm around Elise's despondent shoulders. 'I do believe that the way you treated Ruth and the children was wrong. But in your defence, you were still reeling with grief over Alex at the time. And you weren't *trying* to hurt them. Your motivation was a profound need to have Sainte Madeleine back in your life, a lifelong yearning to come home.'

'That's true,' said Elise. 'I'm just not sure that makes it any better.'

'Perhaps not,' said Laurent. 'But I think it makes what Andreas has done far worse. As far as I can see, he got the Church to act against you and Giorgios out of sheer spite.'

'I still can't believe he'd do such a thing. Like father like son . . .' she said, her voice cracking, as she leaned into Laurent gratefully.

'Well,' he said briskly, clearing his throat and removing his arm, before the emotion of the moment got the better of him. 'Let's not waste time crying over spilled milk. What's done is done. What we need now is a practical plan of action to get you out of this mess.'

'Agreed.' Elise nodded bravely. 'Any suggestions?'

'As a matter of fact, I do have one suggestion,' said Laurent. 'Although I strongly suspect you aren't going to like it.'

Giorgios looked from his mother to Laurent and back again in disbelief.

'*My* name?'

'That's right,' said Elise.

'You're signing over your share in Sainte Madeleine to me?'

'With immediate effect,' Laurent announced firmly. Only very reluctantly had Elise agreed to his rescue plan. He wanted to get this over with before she changed her mind. 'You simply need to sign here, and I'll act as witness.'

'It would have been yours one day anyway,' Elise said bravely, unable entirely to keep the tremor out of her voice.

'The reality is, this is our only choice,' Laurent explained. 'The con men behind this so-called "consortium", whoever they are, signed a contract with your mother. If Sainte Madeleine no longer belongs to Elise, we can argue that the agreement is invalid. That they have no right to force a sale.'

'Surely they'll contest that?' argued Giorgios. 'I mean,

won't it be obvious that Mummy transferred the title to me simply so that she could wriggle out of this five-day deadline?'

'It will be obvious, and they may contest it,' admitted Laurent. 'But that doesn't mean they'll win. If nothing else, it buys you some time. Which you badly need, now that you're potentially facing legal challenges on two fronts, from these bastards *and* the Catholic Church.' Turning to Elise, he asked, 'I assume you've already approached Aunt Thérèse for help on the latter front? She must have some influence with the bishop.'

Elise shook her head. 'Maman wouldn't help me, even if she could. She's never forgiven me for "stealing" Sainte Madeleine from Ruth.'

'I wouldn't be so sure about that,' said Giorgios. 'Especially if the alternative would be the family losing the estate altogether. There's no way Granny wants that.'

'I agree,' said Laurent.

Elise let out a groan. 'I can't face talking to her about this. I just . . . I can't.'

'All right,' said Laurent. 'In that case, I will go and see Thérèse. She may be more amenable if the approach comes from me. It has to be worth a try.'

Elise opened her mouth to protest but then closed it again. He was right, as usual. No stone could be left unturned.

'Giorgios, your job is to put the fear of God into your mother's lawyer first thing tomorrow morning,' Laurent went on. 'Tell him you're thinking of suing for negligence and unprofessional advice. At a minimum it might get you some free representation, if this consortium end up getting nasty. Which I fear they may.'

'OK,' Giorgios nodded solemnly, deeply grateful that Laurent was taking charge. Not for the first time he wondered how different life might have been if Laurent Senard had been his father.

'And see if you can do some digging and find out who the hell they really are, and why they approached Elise in the first place.'

'What about me?' Elise asked meekly. 'What should I do?'

'Nothing,' snapped Giorgios, more angrily than he'd meant to.

It was really Andreas he should be angry with. Andreas who'd started all of this. But his mother's 'secret' interventions certainly hadn't helped, and it still stung that she hadn't confided in him.

'Try to keep the winery going,' Laurent told Elise, more kindly. 'Go to work as usual. However things turn out, you're still going to have a business to save.'

Giorgios followed Laurent's advice to the letter. Amazingly, Elise's lawyer caved instantly, terrified of reprisals, and proclaimed himself happy to provide pro bono services until 'this current confusion' was resolved.

Unearthing information about the 'WTS Consortium,' a shadowy group based in the Cayman Islands, proved considerably more challenging. Giorgios telephoned and wrote to banks, lawyers, accountancy firms, and even other wineries who may have been targeted, trying to find out anything he could. But on each occasion he ended up banging his head against a brick wall. So much so that when he finally got a break, from a provincial state registrar in Delaware, of all places, he almost didn't believe it.

But what he found out next, he did believe. And it changed everything.

WTS. Of course.

His first call was to Laurent.

'I'm sorry to ask,' he said, once he'd explained the situation. 'Especially after everything you've already done for Maman and me. But do you think you might be able to lend me the money for a plane ticket to America? I need to jump on this right away.'

'Absolutely not,' said Laurent.

For a moment, a crestfallen Giorgios didn't know what to say. But Laurent quickly put him out of his misery.

'I'll give you the money. The last thing you and your mother need is more loans.'

'Oh my God, thank you, Laurent. Thank you so much.'

'Just don't get your hopes up too high,' Laurent cautioned.

'I won't,' said Giorgios.

'And don't say anything to your mother either. Not until you're sure.'

'No chance,' said Giorgios. 'Mummy can't know about this.'

CHAPTER THIRTY

Willow walked into Chez Antoine, St Helena's newest and fanciest French restaurant, buzzing with confidence. Not only were all her big life plans finally starting to come to fruition – nothing was in the bag yet, but she felt sure at this point that it was only a matter of time – but she'd been asked out to lunch by a feature writer from *Fine Wine Today*, as one of the up-and-coming 'new faces' of the Napa Valley. Quite an accolade at twenty-one, in anybody's book.

She'd chosen her outfit carefully: a fashionable Mary Quant dress in cobalt blue, short but not too short, paired with knee-high boots and a smart fitted jacket from the City of Paris department store in San Francisco's Union Square. 'Young but businesslike' was the look she was going for. 'Pretty but no pushover.' She didn't know if photographs were going to be taken, but had swept up her wild Titian tresses into a chic chignon just in case, and taken the rare step of applying some make-up: winged eyeliner, mascara and a shimmery eyeshadow in a paler blue, to go with her dress.

Willow wasn't vain by nature, but she couldn't help but feel pleased by her reflection in the restaurant window, and by the admiring glances she received from pretty much everyone when she walked in.

'I'm joining someone,' she told the maître d', scanning the tables for anyone who looked like a journalist. 'A Mr George.'

She pictured a serious-looking man in a trilby and glasses, with a notepad and fancy silver pen, or maybe even a tape-recorder.

'Mr George? Ah yes, here we are. He's already been seated, miss, if you'd like to follow me?'

It wasn't until Willow was almost at the table, and he looked up from behind the menu, that the penny dropped. 'You!'

It was getting on for a decade now since she'd last seen Giorgios Goulandris in person, but her cousin had changed remarkably little. Standing up to greet her, he was still tall, still dark, and still disarmingly handsome.

'Hello, Willow.'

Willow spun around, looking for the maître d' to demand an explanation, but he'd already gone.

'Don't you "hello, Willow" me,' she scowled, sitting down but only because it was easier to talk that way, and to give him a piece of her mind without being thrown out of the restaurant. 'You ambushed me. You lied to get me here under false pretences.'

Giorgios sat back, his eyes wide. The brass neck of the girl!

'You'll forgive me if I don't take a lecture from you on ambushes. Or lies. Or false pretences. *WTS*.'

'Ah.' Willow smiled smugly. 'You finally figured it out.'

'I assumed the WS must be Willow Salignac. And the T is your middle name . . . Thérèse?'

'Actually my middle name is Jean,' Willow informed him curtly, 'after my other grandmother. WTS stands for Willow, Tyler, Sarah. After all, it was all three of us Aunt Elise betrayed, when she lied and cheated her way back into Sainte Madeleine. All three of us who deserve to see her suffer.'

Giorgios recoiled, shocked by the depth of Willow's vitriol. Clearly, persuading her to work with him was going to be an uphill struggle. Still, he had to try.

'Look,' he said, spreading his hands wide in a gesture of openness and submission. 'I know that the way Mummy went about things after your father's death was wrong. I can imagine how hurtful that was to you and your siblings.'

'Hurtful?' Willow scoffed. 'It was devastating. It was also fraudulent, illegal and morally repugnant.'

'OK, well hold on just a minute,' said Giorgios, instinctively moving to Elise's defence, despite promising himself he wouldn't.

But Willow was in no mood to 'hold on'.

'In fact, those are the nicest adjectives I can think of to describe it,' she informed him bitterly. 'I can think of plenty worse. Can you believe that *your* mother actually had the audacity to write to *my* mother, eight years after she ruined our lives, and say sorry? As if one lousy apology letter could fix things, after all this time?'

'I . . . didn't know that,' stammered Giorgios, starting to feel more and more on the back foot. He was astonished to learn that Elise had written to Ruth, and secretly delighted that she had finally begun to take some responsibility for her part in what had happened, although it was plain his cousin Willow did not see matters in the same light.

'I'm not here to defend my mother,' he told her, hoping to take the edge off her rage. 'I agree that what she did back then was wrong. But she suffered too, Willow.'

'She suffered? Really? How?' Willow challenged him.

'Well, for one thing, she didn't *take* Aunt Ruth's share in Sainte Madeleine. She bought it, and at the very top of the market. She had to sell our house in London and what little else she owned after the divorce from my father. She practically bankrupted herself to do it.'

Willow shrugged. 'More fool her.'

465

Giorgios cleared his throat nervously. 'You know, it's not something Mum talks about. But my parents' marriage was seriously abusive. My father used to hit her all the time when we were little.'

'I didn't know that,' said Willow, chastened. 'I'm sorry.'

'Even afterwards, once we moved to London, he was verbally abusive and belittling,' Giorgios went on. 'Mum lived in fear of him for years. So when you ask how she suffered? Well, that was one of the ways. My father cut her off from her home, her family, from everything she loved.'

'OK,' said Willow, becoming defensive again. 'Well like I say, I'm sorry to hear that. I am. But it doesn't change what she did *to us*.'

'No,' Giorgios agreed.

'It doesn't make that OK. And it doesn't change the fact that she was arrogant enough to think she could swan in with no experience and run a serious wine label without cash reserves,' said Willow.

'Yes, well, it was certainly a mistake,' Giorgios frowned, pinching the bridge of his nose. Christ, Willow was a tough customer! The last time he'd seen his cousin, she was more or less a child. He wasn't sure what he'd been expecting exactly, but definitely not the well-informed, hard-nosed businesswoman sitting opposite him now.

'When we left Sainte Madeleine – when my mom was forced to move us all back to Napa – Papillon wines were thriving,' Willow continued, twisting the knife. 'Now? They're an embarrassment. A stain on the Salignac name. I mean, come on. *Appellation Régionale?*' She let the two shameful words hang in the air between them. 'So I decided to do something about it. Somebody had to.'

'I'm curious,' he asked her. 'Where did you come up with the money? To be able to offer Mummy such a huge loan?'

'I came into a small trust fund from my grandparents when I turned eighteen. I used that as seed money,' she said proudly. 'And then I set about finding backers.'

'What sort of backers?'

'People who could see the potential in the Papillon label,' Willow replied archly. 'And in me. Because, unlike Aunt Elise, I do know how to run a successful vineyard. Removing your mother is just step one. Step two will be to buy the Church out of their share, so that I can take over and rebuild.'

Georgios sat back and looked at her. 'Wow,' he shook his head. 'And you think Elise is arrogant.'

Despite herself, Willow blushed. Grovelling from Giorgios was one thing, but she hadn't expected him to go on the offensive.

'It isn't arrogance,' she retorted, more defensively than she'd intended. 'I've paid my dues.'

'And I haven't?' Giorgios challenged her, leaning forward across the table. 'I've broken my back for the last six years, learning the business, trying to help my mother stop the ship from sinking,' he insisted furiously. 'I've been doing the work of ten men. Literally, I mean it.'

'OK,' said Willow, shocked by this sudden loss of temper, and not quite sure how to handle it.

'No, it's not OK!' Giorgios ranted. 'I've been field hand, sales manager and accountant all in one. I've worked sixteen-hour days for as long as I can remember, when I could have been lounging around on a yacht in the Aegean like my useless brother. Who, by the way, is the one that got us all into this mess in the first place, if you want to swap notes on feeling betrayed by your family. And yes, Willow, you're right, it *is* impossible to run a wine business with no cash, never mind keeping a chateau the size of Sainte Madeleine from crumbling into the earth,' Giorgios went on. 'But I kept trying. Because Sainte Madeleine's my home and I love it. You of all people should understand that.'

'I do understand it.' Willow's eyes narrowed. Somehow, he seemed to have snatched the moral high ground from under her feet. 'What do you want?' she asked him bluntly. 'Why did you come here, Giorgios?'

Clearing his throat, he looked her right in the eye.

'I want you to tear up the contract you tricked my mother into signing. Because it's not just Elise you're hurting.'

'I'm sorry. I can't do that.'

'I get that Sainte Madeleine's your home,' said Giorgios. 'But it's my home too.'

'Not in the same way,' said Willow, her voice breaking.

'I want to work out some agreement where we share the estate,' Giorgios ploughed on regardless. 'Where our two branches of the family rebuild Papillon together.'

Willow shook her head vigorously.

'But why not?' Giorgios pleaded. 'Sainte Madeleine belongs to all of us. To the family, not to some gaggle of outside investors you've managed to cobble together. If what my mother did to your family was wrong, then surely you throwing us out is just as bad? Two wrongs don't make a right.'

'NO!'

Pushing her chair back angrily, Willow threw her napkin on the table. She'd felt so sure of herself when she walked in, so confident and happy. But now her handsome, manip-ulative cousin was making her second-guess herself. Well she wouldn't have it.

'Your mother lost her claim to be considered "family" the day she betrayed us. I always swore I would get Sainte Madeleine back and avenge my father's memory. And now I have, or at least I'm about to. So if you think you can shame me into "sharing" with that woman, or you, you are sorely mistaken.'

'And if you think I'm going to cave in to your bullying and let this fraud stand without a fight, *you're* mistaken!' Giorgios shouted back, oblivious to the open-mouthed stares of fellow diners as Willow blushed vermilion, turned on her heel and stalked out. 'See you in court, Cousin!'

Outside, Willow practically ran down the street, her heart beating nineteen to the dozen and her hands shaking. Until now, she'd felt nothing but pride for the way she'd taken her revenge on her hated aunt. Not even her mother or Tyler knew about 'WTS'. She hadn't planned to tell a soul until the deal was done, and she finally had the deeds to her beloved Sainte Madeleine in her hands, a transition she'd expected to occur seamlessly, sealing her triumph.

But she hadn't counted on Giorgios's reaction. Hadn't thought about him at all, if she were honest. Hearing him describe Sainte Madeleine as his home, and in such emotive language, made Willow feel simultaneously sick, furious, and deeply, deeply afraid.

He'd flown all the way out here just to confront her.

Clearly, he wasn't about to give up.

Giorgios was still in a black mood from the meeting with Willow when he landed. He retrieved his casc from the baggage hall at Paris Aeroport, too tired and depressed to appreciate any of the glamour or excitement of having taken his first transatlantic flight. Now he had to catch a train from Paris to Dijon, where Laurent Senard had kindly agreed to meet him and drive him out to Sainte Madeleine. He wouldn't get home for several hours yet, but that was all right. The longer he got to put off breaking the news to Elise – that Willow Salignac was the puppet-master pulling WTS's strings, and that she was hell-bent on ruining them – the better.

'Giorgios?'

Emerging from the customs hall, he did a double-take. It took him a moment to place the rail-thin, glamorous elderly woman waiting for him.

'Chantelle?'

For the first time in forty-eight hours, Giorgios smiled. He hadn't seen his mother's godmother since London days, or spoken to her since she and Elise fell out over Elise's 'reclaiming' of the family estate. Dropping his case, he hugged her tightly.

'What a lovely surprise. But what on earth are you doing here?'

Chantelle returned the hug, but when she pulled away he could see from her expression that something was wrong.

'Darling boy. My driver's outside,' she told him. 'He's going to take us both straight to Vézelay. It'll be faster than the Dijon train.'

'I don't understand,' said Giorgios. 'I mean, thank you. But why the rush?'

Chantelle clasped both his hands tightly in her own. 'I'm afraid there's been an accident, sweetheart,' she told him. 'A very serious accident.'

CHAPTER THIRTY-ONE

'May I help you?' The young nurse approached the handsome, haggard young man who'd just walked in on the arm of an older lady. 'If you're here to see a patient I'm afraid visiting hours are over until tomorrow morning.'

'Now, look here, Mademoiselle,' Chantelle began pugnaciously, inserting herself between Giorgios and the nurse. 'We've just driven all the way from Paris, and this young man has flown in from America. I demand . . .'

'Chantelle?'

Elise, her eyes red-raw from crying, stepped out of an elevator and into the reception area. All the years spent apart meant nothing in that moment. She fell into her godmother's arms, a vulnerable girl again.

'Thank God you're here!' she whispered.

'I'll leave you,' the nurse said tactfully, backing away. She recognized Elise as the woman who'd signed the forms for the car crash victims this morning. The poor thing had been shaking head to foot, her whole face a crumpled study in anguish. If this other, older woman was her family, then the nurse was willing to overlook her rudeness and bend the rules a little, for Elise's sake.

'Giorgios is here too,' Chantelle pointed behind her. 'We came straight from the airport.'

'Giorgios! Oh darling.' Elise lit up. Despite the awful circumstances, it was wonderful to see him. She needed him now more than ever.

'What happened, Mummy?' he asked. 'Laurent's always been such a careful driver.'

'Anne was driving,' Elise said bleakly.

'Anne? But Laurent always drives when they're together.'

'I know, and don't ask me why he wasn't this time, I've no idea. Maybe he'd had a glass of wine or wasn't feeling well? I just don't know. I don't know what caused the accident either, other than that they were on their way to Sainte Madeleine to see me, and they somehow skidded clean off the road at that sharp bend before the Duponts' farm.'

Giorgios winced. He knew that bend well. It was lethal, especially at speed. He'd lost count of the times he'd warned his mother to slow down there.

'They found the car at the bottom of the gorge, on its roof. Laurent was unconscious. Anne . . .' Elise teared up, biting down hard on her lower lip to try to hold her emotions in check. 'The doctors said it would have been instant. A broken neck.'

Giorgios gulped, looked down at his feet. 'And what about Laurent?' Giorgios asked. 'How is he now?'

'He broke some ribs and ruptured his spleen,' said Elise, her voice trembling. 'They operated on that a few hours ago. Apparently it went well, but he hasn't woken up yet.'

'Was he conscious before the op?' Chantelle asked.

'On and off,' said Elise, the tears flowing freely now despite her efforts.

'Does he . . . does he know Anne is dead?'

Elise shook her head. 'No. Not yet,' she whispered. 'Oh Chantelle, how on earth am I going to tell him? Anne was everything to him.'

'What about Edouard?' Giorgios cut in.

472

'He's at home with the housekeeper at Brancion,' said Elise. 'The poor boy doesn't know either. But I didn't want to say anything until . . . I wanted Laurent to wake up first.'

'Of course,' Chantelle said gently. 'And he will, my darling. If the doctors say the procedure went well, I'm sure it did.'

'You should get some sleep, Mummy,' said Giorgios, hugging her tightly. 'Let Chantelle drive you home to Sainte Madeleine.'

'No, no. I'm fine here,' said Elise.

'When did you last have any food?' Chantelle asked her.

'I don't know,' Elise mumbled. 'I can't remember.'

'You must eat, Mummy,' Giorgios said firmly. 'And sleep. You need your strength. Laurent's going to need you when he wakes up.'

'Which is why I have to stay here,' Elise protested.

'I'll stay here tonight. All night,' Giorgios promised. 'And as soon as he wakes up, I'll call you.'

'I'm not sure . . .' Elise hesitated. She couldn't stand the thought of abandoning Laurent. But she was, suddenly, ravenously hungry, and as exhausted as she could ever remember being.

Anne. Poor, lovely, loving Anne. How was this even possible?

'Giorgios is right,' said Chantelle. 'You need a meal and some rest. And I don't mean this unkindly, Elise, but when Laurent does wake up, the news about Anne will be better coming from the doctors. I don't think he should hear that from you.'

'I loved her too, you know,' Elise sobbed. It was true, as strange as it might seem. She *had* loved Anne, for her own sake as well as for Laurent's.

'She brought him a peace that I never could. We were good friends.'

'I'm sure you were,' said Chantelle gently. 'And I know

473

you'd undo all this if you could. Come on, darling. Let me drive you home.'

Elise nodded, too tired to argue any more.

'I forgot to ask,' she said, turning to Giorgios as she wearily slipped on her coat. 'How was America?'

Giorgios kissed her on the cheek.

'It doesn't matter now. I'll see you tomorrow, Mummy.'

Laurent looked out of the window beside his bed at the fat white blossoms of a magnolia tree. Anne had loved magnolias. She'd once described their petals as being like 'puppies' ears', soft and furry on one side, smooth and pliable on the other, like skin. He'd always remembered that. Now those memories, that patchwork of shared moments, thoughts and laughs, would be all that was left to him. Anne's way with words. Her smile. Her kindness. Her practicality. He would carry them all in his heart, of course. But *she* was gone. She was gone and it was his fault.

'It should have been me.' He was still staring out of the window, but the words were addressed to Elise, sitting in the chair at his side. 'I should have been driving.'

'Don't do that to yourself,' said Elise.

'Well I shouldn't have, should I?' he snapped, wincing at the pain in his ribs as he turned back to face her. 'Why did I drink that day? Why? I almost never drink at lunch.'

'I don't know,' Elise ignored his anger, returning his gaze calmly. 'Why did you?'

He closed his eyes.

'Because I was happy,' he admitted, with a brief half-flicker of a smile. 'Edouard had just won a place at the college we wanted for him, this wonderful school that Anne had found. I opened a bottle of 1915 Beaune Les Aigrots to celebrate.'

'Of course you did,' Elise reassured him. 'There's nothing wrong in that.'

'Tell that to Edouard, now his mother's dead,' Laurent replied bleakly.

It was three days since the accident. Two since Laurent had regained consciousness, and learned of Anne's death. One since he'd broken the awful news to their son. Today was the first day that he'd been able to bring himself to talk to Elise about it.

It wasn't that he was angry with Elise. Quite the opposite, in fact. She'd been wonderful with Edouard, holding him for hours and hours while he cried his eyes out, poor boy, and even offering to move in at Chateau Brancion and take care of him while Laurent recuperated in hospital, which was likely to be for a few more weeks at least. She'd been incredibly patient with *him* too, sitting there through his rages and silences, knowing instinctively not to try and comfort him, to allow him his space.

No, it wasn't Elise Laurent was angry with. It was himself. Angry and confused and *guilty*, hideously, unbearably guilty, that he could grieve Anne as much as he did, miss her as deeply as he did, and yet still feel comforted whenever he saw Elise's face.

It's like a spell, he thought miserably. *A curse*. Or perhaps addiction was a better analogy. All he knew was that his feelings for Elise were wrong, more wrong now than ever, and that he owed it to Anne to shut them out, shut them down.

And yet he couldn't. In his behaviour, perhaps, but not in his heart. Even in death, it seemed, he was destined to let Anne down. To be less than she deserved.

'Speaking of Edouard, I'd better get back,' Elise said, getting creakily to her feet. 'I've promised to take him out riding tomorrow all day. I think it'll be good for him. But we'll both come in to see you together on Saturday.'

'Thank you,' Laurent said weakly. 'Anne always used to

say how wonderful you were with Edouard, and you really are. I appreciate it.'

'I love him,' Elise said simply.

Laurent looked away.

'I understand, you know,' she told him. 'About the guilt. More than you think.'

'Do you?' Laurent sounded disbelieving.

'Yes. I think so,' said Elise. 'I feel it too, all the time. Anne's death changes everything.'

Laurent let out a long sigh.

'It does. I'm so sorry, Elise, but it just does.'

'You've nothing to be sorry for,' she assured him. 'I came to terms with *this*,' she gestured between the two of them. 'With us, and the way things have to be, a long time ago. I'm not asking for anything, Laurent. Not expecting anything. I loved her too, you know.'

The next few months were difficult for Giorgios. With Elise spending more and more time at Chateau Brancion, helping care for Edouard while Laurent continued to recuperate, and all the domestic staff laid off, he often found himself completely alone at Sainte Madeleine. He generally rose early and ate breakfast in the kitchen, keeping mess to a minimum, before walking up to the winery to spend the rest of the day in either the office, strategizing with lawyers, or out in the vineyards, helping the domaine's skeleton staff tend to this year's crop. Although still much reduced in terms of output, due to all the cost-cutting, ironically it looked as if some of this year's vintage might actually be half decent. Willow's Scuppernong vines, in particular, had produced a huge bounty of unusually fat and flavourful grapes. For many years now, these whites had been the one shining light amid the unremitting gloom of Sainte Madeleine's decline, a bittersweet success for Giorgios, who had overruled his mother and insisted that they continue putting out a Muscadet, in addition to their more traditional reds.

Being outside was always the best part of his day: feeling the fruit in his hands, gazing out over Sainte Madeleine's overgrown but still lovely grounds to the idyllic village beyond. But at the same time it was the end of an era. The end of a dream that had once been solely his mother's, but which at some point, without him even realizing it, had become Giorgios's dream too.

The worst part of his days were the evenings, leaving the winery to return to the cold and lonely chateau and a scratched supper, more often than not consisting of cheap sausages, left-over bread, and tinned ratatouille. Rattling around such a vast house by himself would have been depressing enough anyway. But it was the waiting that made it unbearable. Knowing that at any time an eviction notice or final demand for payment might arrive from Willow's consortium, or from the Catholic Church, left Giorgios under a permanent cloud of dread.

So when the house telephone rang, one gloomy night in November, he picked up the receiver with a heavy heart.

'*Bonsoir*, Monsieur Goulandris.'

The voice of Elise's lawyer did nothing to lift Giorgios's spirits. 'I'm sorry to call so late, but I have some significant news.'

'Significant good, or significant bad?' asked Giorgios, taking a fortifying sip from his delicious glass of 1947 Clos de Vougeot. By the time his cousin managed to turf him out, he fully intended to have drunk all the best wines in their grandfather's cellar, so Willow could put that in her self-righteous American pipe and smoke it.

'Hopefully the former,' the lawyer purred. 'You mentioned some months ago that your grandmother had been attempting to liaise with the Diocese on your mother's behalf. This was regarding your uncle Didier's share in . . .'

'Yes, yes, I know what it was regarding,' Giorgios interrupted impatiently, his hopes rising despite himself. What with the accident and the cloud of grief that had descended with Anne's death, he'd totally forgotten that Laurent Senard had offered to try and convince Thérèse to use her influence with the local bishop.

'So what's happened?' he asked breathlessly. 'Did my grandmother persuade the Church to relinquish their claim?'

'Ah, well, no. Not to relinquish it, as such,' the lawyer said awkwardly. 'I don't think they were ever very likely to do that.'

Giorgios's hopes plummeted.

'But it may be the next best thing. I can report that they've sold off their interest in Sainte Madeleine to a third party.' He said it triumphantly, as if it were great news. But Giorgios's head was spinning.

'Who?'

'I beg your pardon?'

'Who did they sell their stake to?'

'Ah, yes, well, I'm afraid I'm not privy to that information,' the lawyer blustered.

'You mean you don't *know*?' Giorgios took another slug of wine.

'The buyer wished to remain anonymous,' the lawyer replied defensively. 'As is their right. But at a minimum this means you won't be dragged into a lawsuit with the Vatican. That alone is good news, Monsieur Goulandris. And who knows, perhaps there won't be a lawsuit at all? The new majority owner may be amenable to some sort of arrangement with you and your mother.'

'Oh my God. How stupid are you?' Giorgios muttered miserably. He hadn't intended to be so rude. The words just slipped out. 'It's Willow. The new owner. It's my cousin, Willow Salignac. It has to be. She convinced her backers to pony up and buy the Church out of their stake. God damn her. God damn both of you.'

'Really, Mr Goulandris,' the lawyer bristled. 'There's no need for—'

But Giorgios had already hung up.

That was it. It was over. Willow had won. While he'd been frantically trying to hold her at bay, she'd attacked from behind, wheedling her way in with God knows who at the Diocese in Vézelay. Outmanoeuvring him once again.

Returning to the kitchen with his wine, Giorgios drained what was left of the bottle and opened another. He felt reckless and bitter. The more he drank, the more his anger and suspicions veered off at tangents, with one family member after another each taking turns as the focus.

Perhaps his grandmother Thérèse had secretly been helping Willow all along? She could have *arranged* for the Church to sell to her favourite grandchild, bypassing Giorgios, whom she'd never been close to, and Elise, who she'd always disapproved of? Now that was a theory.

Then again, why blame a harmless old woman when it was Andreas, his own brother, who'd sold them out to the Church in the first place? Andreas was to blame, surely, the selfish, money-obsessed spider at the centre of the tangled family web.

But then again, who had corrupted Andreas if not their father, Costas? The man whose abandonment and abuse had so blighted their mother's life, and their own? Could he be behind this?

Like images in a kaleidoscope, Giorgios's enemies swam dreamlike before his eyes. With each swallow of wine, each glass, each bottle, he sank deeper and deeper into a swamp of 'if only's. If only Elise hadn't taken that loan. If only Uncle Didier hadn't changed his stupid will. If only Willow Salignac weren't such a blinkered, vengeful bitch.

But underlying all the self-pity, ran a deeper, more painful vein of self-loathing.

I should have done something. *I* should have saved us.

Not that it mattered now. It was all over. All ruined. All gone.

'Giorgios? Giorgios!'

A voice, dimly familiar, echoed somewhere in the back of Giorgios's skull. Right behind the hundreds of little men with pickaxes who seemed to be hammering mercilessly into his brain, compounding a headache that already felt like a brain tumour.

Giorgios contemplated opening his eyes, but discovered he was too drunk to remember how his eyelids worked. The next best option seemed to be to remain *very still indeed* and hope that both the voice, and the little men, went away.

Just as he was settling back into sleep, oblivion, a large jug-full of iced water was emptied over his head.

'What the blazes?!' Sitting up like a jack-in-the-box, he pushed his wet hair out of his eyes and glared up into the faces of his attacker. Three at first, then two, then one, as the hated features slowly came into focus.

'Hello, little brother.' Andreas's handsome, bronzed face broke into a grin. 'Had a few too many last night, did you?'

'What the hell are you doing here?' Giorgios attempted a scowl, but his throbbing head made any sort of facial movement impossible. The inside of his mouth felt like it was stuffed with cotton rolled in sand, and tasted of something unspeakable. But the worst thing, he realized slowly, was the nausea, rising up from the pit of his stomach like lava in a volcano about to blow.

'Bucket?' Andreas offered, handing him one. Giorgios would have liked to decline, but beggars couldn't be choosers. A few minutes later, having vomited profusely, cleaned up and mustered enough strength to take a seat at the kitchen table, a green-faced Giorgios winced while his older brother threw back the shutters, opened the windows, and allowed the afternoon sunlight to stream into the room.

'Must you?' he groaned.

'I fear so,' Andreas replied glibly, 'if we're ever going to get rid of this smell. Coffee?'

'No,' Giorgios snarled. 'What time is it?'

Andreas glanced at his gleaming, gold Omega Constellation watch. 'Two fifteen. So may I ask what precipitated your world-record solo Burgundy drinking attempt last night? Or is this a regular occurrence now? Please tell me you haven't strayed into Mummy territory.'

'Don't you dare insult her,' Giorgios shot back furiously.

'It was a joke.' Andreas held his arms out wide in a 'no harm, no foul' gesture. But Giorgios wasn't interested.

'Was it? Well, no one's laughing,' he said bitterly. 'Why are you even here, Andreas?'

'I'm here to help.' Filling up the pewter coffee pot and setting it on the ancient Sainte Madeleine range, despite his brother's objections, Andreas sat down opposite him. 'And by the looks of things, not a moment too soon. I'd like to try to put things right.'

Giorgios let out a clipped, mirthless laugh. 'I'm afraid it's a bit too late for that.'

'Meaning?'

'Meaning we lost the estate last night. That's why I was drinking, if you must know. Mummy doesn't even know yet,' he groaned. 'As soon as I'm sober enough I'm going to have to drive over to Chateau Brancion and . . . why the hell are you *smiling*? You think this is funny?'

'Yes and no,' Andreas drawled. In his designer suit and gold cufflinks, smelling of some wildly expensive cologne, he looked every inch the carefree playboy. In that instant, Giorgios thought, he hated his brother more than anyone alive. 'The thing is, you haven't lost the estate.'

'Yes we *have*,' Giorgios seethed. 'Mummy's lawyer called last night. The Church have sold off Didier's share.'

'I know.'

'Clearly Willow managed to— Wait, what do you mean, you know?'

'I mean I *know*,' said Andreas, getting up to remove the boiling coffee from the hot plate. 'I know the Church sold Didier's share. Because I bought it.'

Giorgios's mouth opened, then closed again. The cogs of his Burgundy-addled brain were turning rustily.

'You?' he said eventually.

Andreas nodded. 'Believe it or not, I do have a conscience. I always felt bad about getting Didier to change the will, my little vendetta against Mummy. And then when he died and everything snowballed, I knew I had to do something.'

Giorgios's eyes narrowed distrustfully. 'Why didn't you say anything to Mummy? Or me?'

For the first time, Andreas looked a little shamefaced. 'I couldn't face her,' he admitted. 'And with you, I wanted to be sure I could pull it off before I said anything. The bishop was asking a king's ransom. I didn't have that sort of money just lying around.'

'So how did you raise it?' Giorgios asked. Then suddenly, the penny dropped. 'Not from *Costas*?' his eyes widened.

Andreas smiled cryptically.

'But he hates Mummy.'

'Well, quite,' said Andreas. 'And he hates Sainte Madeleine even more, although for the life of me I've never understood why. So I did have to get fairly . . . creative . . . with the truth to squeeze a cheque out of him.'

'I'll bet!' said Giorgios, genuinely impressed.

'I had a pretty tense time of it, waiting for the funds to

clear and praying for the deal to go through before he figured out what I was up to.'

'And did he? Figure it out?'

'Yesterday.' Andreas grinned. 'Hence my unexpected visit. Let's just say he didn't take it well.'

'He's cut you off?'

'Without a penny,' Andreas confirmed cheerfully. 'So I'm rather hoping that you and your new partner will be able to turn this shambles around sharpish and start producing some drinkable wines again. Because as of now, you're the only hope of an income I've got.'

'New partner?' Giorgios cocked his throbbing head to one side. 'What new partner?'

'Ah. Yes,' said Andreas, his aura of confidence fading just a little. 'About that . . .'

CHAPTER THIRTY-TWO

'*C'est un coup!*'

Elise looked accusingly around the table, her lips set in a tight, quivering line of unhappiness. She rarely spoke French at home with her children, but in moments of extreme stress it came naturally.

'It's not a coup, Mummy,' Giorgios replied wearily.

'No? What would you call it then? Going behind my back like this? All of you?'

'It's a compromise,' said Andreas firmly. 'A fair deal for both sides of the family, and more importantly, the best option for Sainte Madeleine.'

'What do you know about Sainte Madeleine, you snake?' Elise turned on her eldest son, a vision of righteous indignation in her elegant black Chanel suit and her great grandmother's pearl choker. 'If it hadn't been for *you* . . .'

'Mummy, please,' said Giorgios, laying a hand over hers. 'I know this isn't easy. But in this case, Andreas is right. This is the right thing, and deep down I think you know it.'

They were all sitting around the ancient oak table in Sainte Madeleine's dining room: Elise and Giorgios at one end, Willow and Tyler at the other, and Andreas, the unlikely broker of today's peace summit, in the middle.

Laurent had driven Elise back over to Sainte Madeleine this morning for what Giorgios had billed as an 'important meeting', but had flat out refused to attend the discussions himself.

'This is your family business, Elise, not mine,' he reasoned, taking her hand.

'But I need you!' Elise had begged him. 'The Americans are going to be there, Laurent. I need your support.'

'*The Americans*, as you call them, are Alex's children,' Laurent reminded her. 'Remember how bad you felt about the way you'd treated them? When you thought you were going to lose Sainte Madeleine yourself?'

Elise did remember. Not that it made her feel any better. But no amount of begging could convince Laurent to change his mind.

'You're perfectly capable of handling a business meeting by yourself, without dragging me into it,' he told her firmly. 'I'll be walking the dogs outside.'

'Coward,' Elise hissed, although she knew perfectly well that she was the one being cowardly. Something was up, something significant. She'd known that for weeks, ever since she learned about Andreas buying back Didier's share of the estate. But now she was going to find out what that something was, she was frankly terrified.

It transpired that, not content with 'putting right' his meddling in the will, Andreas had secretly reached out to his American cousins; not just Willow, but crucially Tyler too, who'd been extremely helpful in talking his sister around; and succeeded in persuading them to ditch the money men and outside investors behind WTS, and to form a partnership with him and Giorgios instead.

'All this infighting is only going to make the lawyers rich,' Andreas argued passionately. 'Sainte Madeleine is a family estate. Let's come together as a family to make it great again.'

485

The plan was for Willow and Giorgios to run the domaine together. Both of them were expert winemakers with a passion for the business, and while Willow had broader experience, Giorgios knew the strengths and weaknesses of Sainte Madeleine's vineyards better than anyone. Tyler, a born salesman, would take charge of international promotion and advertising, pushing their wines in the lucrative US market. And Andreas would manage the rest of the estate, including the farms and the much-needed restoration of the chateau and grounds.

Elise would still receive her share of Papillon's profits, once they managed to climb their way out of the red. But her role in the winery was to be that of a silent partner. Willow had insisted on it, but privately both Giorgios and Andreas agreed. Their mother had many extraordinary talents, and no one was more devoted to Sainte Madeleine than Elise. But she was a horrible businesswoman. It was time for the next generation to take over.

'You can continue living here, of course, for as long as you like,' said Giorgios, inadvertently pouring petrol on Elise's fire.

'Oh, can I? Well how generous of you Giorgios. And am I to be allowed my own bedroom? Or perhaps one of you already has your eye on it?'

'Come on, Mummy.'

'I dare say Brolio's old room off the nursery will be quite good enough for me, will it? Or the blue room?'

'Aunt Elise, may I say something?' Willow tossed her thick mane of pre-Raphaelite curls behind her as she leaned forward over the table.

'Yes,' Elise said, chastened. 'Of course.'

Losing her temper with her own sons was one thing. But she was learning to be more patient, more understanding, with Alex's children. It was the least they deserved.

'I understand how you feel.'

It was the last thing Elise had been expecting her to say, and it completely pulled the rug out from under her. 'Do you?' she asked, almost timidly.

'I do,' Willow insisted. 'I really think I do. I'll be honest with you. I didn't want this either, not at the beginning. I wanted Sainte Madeleine back. I felt that I'd been . . . banished. Unfairly, wrongly banished. And I wanted Sainte Madeleine for myself and just myself. I wanted her selfishly. Jealously. Like a lover.'

Elise startled. Meeting her niece's gaze was like looking in a mirror. The eyes, ablaze with passion, willing Elise to understand. And her words, so perfectly describing Elise's own love for Sainte Madeleine, for this magical place, that was such an intrinsic part of her. Jealous. Possessive. Obsessive. Destructive, ultimately, on so many levels.

'But Andreas made me see things differently,' said Willow. 'He made me see that if you truly love someone, or something, you put them first.'

'*Andreas* made you see that?' Giorgios interjected, struggling to think of a single time in his brother's life, his adult life at least, when he had put someone else first.

'He did,' said Willow, smiling across the table at Andreas. 'I realized I was thinking about what I wanted, and not about what was best for Sainte Madeleine.'

'But you *did* do what was best, Willow, in the end,' Andreas replied graciously. 'Best for all of us. You've been wonderful.'

'Thank you, Andreas.'

Giorgios and Tyler exchanged amused glances at this rare display of diplomacy from their respective siblings.

Not best for me! The voice in Elise's head refused to be silenced. *None of this is best for me!* But she could see that the deal was done. And deep down, she understood that the children were right. That it was for the best. Looking from Willow, back to her sons, and then to Tyler, who looked so like a young Alex it was shocking, like seeing a ghost, she suddenly felt overwhelmed with emotion. Covering her face in her hands, she fled the room.

Giorgios stood up to go after her, but Andreas put a hand on his arm. 'Don't. It won't help. Laurent's out there. Let him talk to her.'

'She'll come around eventually,' said Willow. 'She just needs time.'

I hope so, thought Giorgios. Because honestly, without his mother's blessing, he didn't know if he could do this. It was all right for Andreas, swanning in like the prodigal son and saving the day, charming his cousins and everyone else. Andreas was used to Elise's disapproval. But for Giorgios, none of this was easy. His mother relied on him. She always had done, ever since he was a tiny boy, when she would try to drink away her sorrows. She trusted him.

Why did family politics always have to be so complicated?

Laurent saw Elise run out of the house, obviously distressed. He was a good hundred yards away, pacing the crest of the hill above the vineyards with Edouard's two-year-old lurcher, Amie. But he knew Elise's body language as well as he knew his own. The agitated hands that fluttered like butterfly wings whenever she was really unhappy, or felt trapped. The pacing around in circles, first in one direction, then the other, to ward off anxiety, or fear. *Poor Elise.* His first urge was to go to her directly, to comfort her as only he could. But when she set off purposefully down the hilly gardens towards the estate gates and the village beyond, he decided to wait for a while. Whatever had happened, it looked as if she needed some time alone first, to sort through her feelings.

Or perhaps not quite alone.

Laurent had a good idea where Elise was headed.

* * *

The tiny churchyard in the village was picture-postcard pretty in the summer, but had a desolate feel to it at this time of year. The bare branches of the plane trees waved their twig fingers forlornly over the lichened graves, and almost no sunlight filtered down through the slate-grey clouds. Everything was cold, shadowy and spare, and even the cast-iron railings surrounding the church took on the look of prison bars.

It wasn't as cold as it had been the day they buried Alex, when Elise had stood at this same spot, staring down at Alex's grave until hypothermia and exhaustion overtook her. Laurent had rescued her that day. Come to find her and take her home, tortured with longing and torn with guilt.

Now, again, he crept up beside her, draping an arm around her shoulder.

'I thought I'd find you here,' he said, letting Amie off the leash to explore the churchyard's sights and smells at his leisure. 'His headstone could do with a bit of a clean. You can hardly read it for the moss.'

'That's my fault. I never come down here,' Elise admitted. 'Hardly ever anyway.'

'Why not?' asked Laurent, although he suspected he knew the answer.

'I couldn't face him, I suppose.' Elise swallowed hard. 'Couldn't face myself after what I did, throwing out his family. I justified it at the time. Told myself I *needed* Sainte Madeleine more than they did. And perhaps I did. But at what cost?'

'Giorgios told me you wrote to Ruth, apologizing,' said Laurent. 'Did she ever reply?'

'She did.' Elise tried to smile, but it wouldn't come. 'She was very kind. Very gracious. She said it was all a long time ago and . . . Oh, Laurent!'

Bursting into tears suddenly, Elise buried her face in his chest.

'It's all right, my love.' He pulled her in close, breathing in the scent of her hair as she pressed her wet cheeks against his woollen overcoat.

'It's not all right! Nothing's all right!'

'What happened up at the house just now?' he asked her quietly. 'Tell me everything.'

Slowly, agonizingly, Elise explained the new 'arrangement'. How Andreas had returned from Greece and somehow managed to build bridges with his Salignac cousins, so that now the younger generation would be running Sainte Madeleine together.

'Sarah won't be involved,' she sniffed. 'Her life's in America now. And Ruth has given her blessing apparently, but has no wish to come back here herself. So Giorgios and Willow will be running the show together. And meanwhile I'm to be a "silent partner"!'

She looked so stricken when she said it, Laurent couldn't help but chuckle.

'What?' Elise looked aghast. 'What's funny?'

'Oh, I don't know. Just the idea of you being a "silent" anything, I suppose.'

Elise hit him playfully on the arm, and for a moment the mood lightened. But her anxious expression soon returned.

'Do you think Alex is looking down?' she asked. 'Do you think he can see us?'

'I do,' said Laurent. 'I don't know how, exactly, but in some fashion, yes, I believe that.'

'Do you think he forgives me?' Elise's lower lip wobbled like a child's.

'Oh Elise. Of course he does,' said Laurent, placing a firm hand on each of her shoulders. 'Alex loved you.'

'And I him.' She welled up again. 'Seeing Tyler today, after all these years,' she shook her head. 'My heart nearly stopped. He could be Alex's twin.'

'So isn't there a part of you that thinks this new plan for

Sainte Madeleine might be the best one?' asked Laurent. 'Your children and Alex's children, taking it on together? There's something right about that, surely?'

'There is,' Elise nodded, but then looked away.

Something was clearly still bothering her.

'Do you know what I think?' said Laurent. 'I think the question isn't whether Alex would forgive you. But whether you can learn to forgive yourself.'

She nodded again, but still with her back to him.

'It's a concept I've been wrestling with myself recently,' Laurent continued. 'Forgiveness. Ever since Anne died. Knowing how I felt about her. And how I felt . . . feel . . . about you.'

He cleared his throat. Elise's shoulders stiffened. She neither spoke, nor moved, but Laurent sensed the change in her at once. She was listening, alert, frozen in place like a hunted deer. But there was no peace in her stillness, no quiet in her silence. The former represented a lifetime of hope, barely suppressed. And the latter the silent, anguished scream of a love too long denied. But it was a love that had survived, despite everything.

'Anne knew,' Laurent told her. 'About us. About Paris and that night.'

That broke the spell. Elise spun around, astonished.

'She knew? I don't understand. When? How?'

'I told her,' he admitted. 'Not right away. Only a few years ago, in fact. You were staying at the house, and Anne and I were watching you and Edouard throw paper aeroplanes on the lawn. And she suddenly said, "You're in love with her, aren't you?"'

'Oh God!' Elise gasped.

'It wasn't an accusation,' Laurent clarified. 'That was the incredible thing, she wasn't angry, not at all. I think she just sensed that I needed to tell her, and I couldn't find the strength on my own. So she asked me.'

'And what did you tell her?' Elise croaked, her mouth suddenly bone-dry.

Laurent shrugged. 'The truth. That I was in love with you, and with her too. That I kept waiting for one love to kill off the other, to change the other, but it never did. I told her about Paris. That it had only happened once and that it would never happen again. I've never felt guilt like it, Elise. It was awful.'

'And what did she say?'

'She said "OK".'

Elise frowned. '"OK"? That was it?'

'That was it.' Laurent smiled. 'She said "OK" and that she was glad I told her and that she understood completely. Then she asked me if I'd like a cup of tea, and I said I would, and so we had one.'

Elise exhaled slowly. 'I can't believe it. All those years. She must have hated me.'

'But that's just the thing,' said Laurent earnestly. 'She didn't hate you at all. I don't think she was capable of hate, honestly. She loved you, Elise. She did. She loved us both enough to understand that the love between us began in innocence, long before she and I ever met. And she found a way to let it continue in innocence. She accepted it as a part of me that I was powerless to change. Anne forgave me long ago.' Reaching out, Laurent took both of Elise's hands and pressed them between his own. 'I'm afraid it's taken me rather longer to forgive myself.'

'And have you?' Elise asked, staring up into the soulful brown eyes that she had loved completely for as long as she could remember.

'I have.' Leaning down, he kissed her. And Elise kissed him back. For a long, long time.

Clasping each other's hands tightly, they began to walk back up towards the chateau with Amie trotting obediently behind them.

Walking up through the gardens to the house she had loved since she drew her first breath – the magical house whose butterflies had always protected her – Elise realized that it no longer mattered whether she spent the rest of her life living within its four walls. Because wherever she was, Sainte Madeleine would always live inside *her*.

And as long as Laurent's hand was in hers, she was already home.

EPILOGUE

Christmas, 1971

'By the power invested in me by the Département de Yonne, I now pronounce you man and wife. *Vous pouvext embrasser la mariee!*'

The round, ruddy-cheeked figure of Vézelay's mayor stepped back, smiling, as Laurent tenderly leaned in to kiss Elise. They were standing in front of Sainte Madeleine's vast Christmas tree, decked out spectacularly as always with its gold porcelain butterflies peeking out from amidst the other baubles, and a ripple of applause and approval echoed round the salon from the seven guests present.

Having decided on a quiet, private winter wedding at Sainte Madeleine, the bride and groom had both agreed that, apart from their respective sons and mothers, the only people who needed to be at the ceremony were Willow, who Elise had already grown deeply fond of (and who'd sweetly offered to host). And Chantelle, who'd basically insisted.

'After you rudely left me out of your first wedding, I'll be damned if I'm going to miss this one,' she told her goddaughter firmly, the day she learned that Laurent had proposed. 'What's more, I expect to be consulted on the

494

dress. We can go shopping in Paris together. It'll be like old times.'

She'd been crushed when Elise announced that there would be no new dress – *'I'm far too old for all that nonsense'* – and that she would marry Laurent in her favourite cream wool Hardy Amies suit, with a butterfly brooch of Brolio's as her 'something old' and the sapphire ring Louis had given her on her twenty-first birthday as her 'something new'. Chantelle had insisted on adding a fabulous fox-fur stole as the 'something borrowed'.

'You must have *some* glamour, Elise, or you can't call it a wedding.'

The bride did indeed look dazzling, gazing up into her new husband's eyes. Although in truth it was her smile that shone the brightest.

'I don't think I've ever seen her so happy,' Giorgios whispered to Andreas, as the two brothers followed the happy couple down the flagstone corridor into Sainte Madeleine's grand *salle à manger*. 'Have you?'

Andreas shook his head. 'Nope. They're quite sickening, the pair of them. Laurent grins like the cat that got the cream every time Mummy so much as glances at him.'

'Shut up, you.' Willow nudged her cousin playfully in the ribs. 'It's not *sickening*. It's romantic! You're just jealous because they've found true love and you haven't.'

'Yet,' Andreas winked at her. 'You mustn't give up on me, you know. I'm a late starter, that's all.'

Willow rolled her eyes. Andreas was incorrigible, but she'd always liked him. Ever since she and Giorgios had started working together at Sainte Madeleine – touch wood it had been a seamless partnership so far – Willow had gone out of her way to try to help smooth the remaining rough edges in the brothers' relationship. They would always be very different people. But largely thanks to Willow's efforts, they were closer now than they had been in years, which gave Elise another reason to love her, beyond the fact that she and Giorgios between them had worked day and night to bring Sainte Madeleine's vineyards back from the dead.

'I'd like to propose a toast,' said Laurent. 'To Willow, for laying on today's beautiful spread . . .'

A rumble of 'hear hear's arose from around the table.

'To Mayor Polignac, for officiating . . .'

The little fat man bowed his head graciously, raising his glass of delicious Papillon 1956 Burgundy.

'And to my wife—'

A roar of shouts and whoops cut him off, with Edouard and Giorgios both banging their cutlery noisily and joyously on the table.

'My Elise.' Laurent choked back tears. '*Enfin.*'

Standing up slowly, Elise wrapped her arms around him. It was a tender moment, and an oddly private one, despite the circumstances. A hush fell over the table as the two of them embraced. When they finally released one another, Elise indicated that she would like to speak.

Looking around the room as Laurent sat down, and the rest of her family waited for her to begin, Elise paused for a moment. Outside, a light shower of snow was falling, adding a fresh layer of sparkle to Sainte Madeleine's already frosted gardens.

Watching the flakes fall, Elise's mind flew back to all the Christmases she'd spent here. To Papa in the nursery on Christmas Eve night, telling her and Didier and Alex the story of the young man from Noyers and the butterflies, for the thousandth time. To festive roast goose lunches, right here in this room, at this table, with Maman saying grace. To snowball fights out on the lawn. When she closed her eyes, she could see them – her darling brothers, Papa; all gone now. She could hear their voices, along with the other ghosts of her childhood. Brolio, calling her in for supper. Arnaud, laughing as she skipped towards him, laden with presents.

Happy days. Magical days, truly.

But this was also a magical day. Turning back to the table, to her sons, and Alex's daughter, and dearest Edouard; to the next generation, here with her and Laurent, and with Thérèse and Camille and Chantelle – three generations – Elise realized that life had come full circle. Everything had happened as it was meant to happen. Sainte Madeleine's butterflies had worked their magic, bringing her to Laurent, and her children home.

She raised her glass.

'No speeches,' she said, smiling. 'Just a final toast. To Sainte Madeleine.'

'Sainte Madeleine!' echoed the reply.

Elise sat down. Beneath the table, she slipped her cold hand into Laurent's warm one.

The best was yet to come.

ACKNOWLEDGEMENTS

It's a long time since I've had quite so many people to thank on a book. But *Sainte Madeleine* has been a total team effort from the very beginning, and I am sincerely grateful for everyone who helped make it happen.

Firstly, thanks to Luke Janklow, my agent and friend, for idly suggesting one day that 'a big saga, set in the wine business' might be something I would want to write. From that small seed, everything else (eventually) grew. Also to Allison Hunter in New York and Hellie Ogden in London, for patiently reading chunks of the manuscript as I went along and providing much needed advice and encouragement. At times, this story proved to be a labour of love, for all of us. But I am so very proud of the finished book, which would not have happened without you both. Thanks also to Claire Dippel, for twenty years of kindness, humour and good advice, on this book and all the others.

To everyone at HarperCollins in London, especially my editor Charlotte Brabbin, and Kim Young, I can't thank you enough. It is such a pleasure to be working with you both again, my old A-team! Also to Ellie Game for the stunning cover, Isabel Coburn, Sarah Munro and Alice Gomer in sales, Jaime Witcomb in publicity, as well as Zoe Shine, Grace Dent, and the entire team. And not forgetting my brilliant copyeditor, Anne O'Brien, and proofreader, Rhian McKay, for weeding out my many mistakes. I am profoundly grateful for everyone's hard work and talent.

Finally, thanks as always to my beautiful family: Robin, Sefi, Zac, Theo and Summer. And especially to my sister Alice, my absolute best friend in times of trouble. So very grateful for you, Al.

I wrote *Sainte Madeleine* during the Covid-19 pandemic, a difficult and strange time for the entire world, but also in our small way, for me and my family. There were some beautiful moments, and some very hard ones. But this novel, these characters and their stories, became a constant light for me during these bizarre and sometimes lonely months. I hope more than anything that this book brings my readers as much joy and hope as writing it brought to me.

TB, 2021